THE
BELLS

CROSSE GLOCKE IM HOHEN THURM ZU ST. STEPHAN IN WIEN.

RICHARD HARVELL

THE BELLS

A NOVEL

RANDOM HOUSE CANADA

Library and Archives Canada Cataloguing in Publication

Harvell, Richard
The bells / Richard Harvell.

Issued also in electronic format.

ISBN 978-0-307-35823-3

I. Title.

PS3608.A7885B44 2010   813'.6   C2010-901392-1

Design by Lynne Amft

Printed in the United States of America

10 9 8 7 6 5 4 3 2 1

To Dominique

A Note to the Reader

I grew up as the son of a man who could not possibly have been my father. Though there was never any doubt that my seed had come from another man, Moses Froben, *Lo Svizzero*, called me "son." And I called him "father." On the rare occasions when someone dared to ask for clarification, he simply laughed as though the questioner were being obtuse. "Of course he's not my son!" he would say. "Don't be ridiculous."

But whenever I myself gained the courage to ask him further of our past, he just looked at me sadly. "Please, Nicolai," he would say after a moment, as though we had made a pact I had forgotten. With time, I came to understand I would never know the secrets of my birth, for my father was the only one who knew these secrets, and he would take them to his grave.

This aside, no child could have wished for more. I accompanied him from Venice to Naples and, finally, here, to London. Indeed, I rarely left his side until I entered Oxford. Even after that, as I began my own, unrelated, career, at no time were we ever more than two months absent from each other's company. I heard him sing in Europe's greatest opera houses. I sat beside him in his carriage as mobs of admirers ran alongside and begged him to grace them with a smile. Through all of this, I never knew anything of the poor Moses Froben, but only of the renowned *Lo Svizzero*, who could make ladies swoon with a mere wave of his hand, who could bring an audience to tears with his voice.

And so you can imagine my surprise, a week after my father's death last spring, to find among his things this stack of papers. And more, to find within them all I had sought to know: of my father's birth and mine; of the origin of my name; of my mother; and of the crime that had kept my father silent.

Though he appears to have had me in mind as his reader, I cannot believe he did not wish these words for other eyes as well. This was a singer, remember, who practiced with an open window, so any man or woman passing on the street would have the chance to hear an angel sing.

Nicolai Froben
London, October 6, 1806

ACT I

I.

First, there were the bells. Three of them, cast from warped shovels, rakes, and hoes, cracked cauldrons, dulled ploughshares, one rusted stove, and, melted into each, a single golden coin. They were rough and black except along their silvery lips, where my mother's mallets had struck a million strokes. She was small enough to dance beneath them in the belfry. When she swung, her feet leapt from the polished wooden planks, so that when the mallet met the bell, it rang from the bell's crown to the tips of my mother's pointed toes.

They were the Loudest Bells on Earth, all the Urners said, and though now I know a louder one, their place high above the Uri Valley made them very loud indeed. The peal could be heard from the waters of Lake Lucerne to the snows of the Gotthard Pass. The ringing greeted traders come from Italy. Columns of Swiss soldiers pressed their palms against their ears as they marched the Uri Road. When the bells began to sound, teams of oxen refused to move. Even the fattest men lost the urge to eat, from the quivering of their bowels. The cows that grazed the nearby pastures were all long since deaf. Even the youngest herders had the dull ears of old men, though they hid in their huts morning, noon, and night when my mother rang her bells.

I was born in that belfry, above the tiny church. There I was nursed. When it was warm enough, there we slept. Whenever my mother did not swing her mallets, we huddled beneath the bells, the four walls of the belfry open to the world. She sheltered me from the wind and stroked my brow. Though she never spoke a word to me, nor I to her, she watched my mouth as I babbled infant sounds. She tickled me so I would laugh. When I learned to crawl, she held my foot so I did not creep off the edge and fall to my death on the jutting rocks below. She helped me stand. I held a finger in each fist, and she led me round and round, past each edge a hundred times a day. In terms of space, our belfry was a tiny world—most would have thought it a prison for a child. But in terms of sound, it was the most massive home on earth. For every sound ever made was trapped in the metal of those bells, and the instant my mother struck them, she released their beauty to the world. So many ears heard the thunderous pealing echo through the mountains. They hated it; or were inspired by its might; or were entranced until they stared blindly into space; or cried as the vibrations shook their sadness out. But they did not find it beautiful. They could not. The beauty of the pealing was reserved for my mother, and for me, alone.

I wish that were the beginning: my mother and those bells, the Eve and Adam of my voice, my joys, and my sorrows. But of course that is not true. I have a father; my mother had one as well. And the bells, too; they had a father. Theirs was Richard Kilchmar, who, one night in 1725, tottered on a table, so drunk he saw two moons instead of one.

He shut one eye and squished the other so the two moons resolved into a single fuzzy orb. He looked about: Two hundred men filled Altdorf's square, in a town that was, and was proud to be, at the very center of the Swiss Confederation. These men were celebrating the harvest, and the coronation of the new pope, and the warm summer night. Two hundred men ankle-deep in piss-soaked mud. Two hundred men with mugs of acrid Schnapps burned from Uri pears. Two hundred men as drunk as Richard Kilchmar.

"Quiet!" he yelled into the night, which seemed as warm and clear to him as the thoughts within his head. "I will speak!"

"Speak!" they yelled.

They were quiet. High above, the Alps shone in the moonlight like teeth in black, rotting gums.

"Protestants are dogs!" he yelled, raised his mug, and nearly stumbled off the table. They cheered and cursed the dogs in Zurich, who were rich. They cursed the dogs in Bern, who had guns and an army that could climb the mountains and conquer Uri if they wished. They cursed the dogs in German lands farther north, who had never

heard of Uri. They cursed the dogs for hating music, for defaming
Mary, for wishing to rewrite the Holy Book.

These curses, two hundred years dull in the capitals of Europe,
pierced Kilchmar's heart. They brought tears to his eyes—these men
before him were his brothers! But what could he reply? What could
he promise them? So little. He could not build them a fort with cannons. He was one of Uri's richest men, but still, he could not afford
an army. He could not soothe them with his wisdom, for he was not a
man of words.

Then they all heard it, the answer to his silent plea. A ringing
that made them raise their bleary eyes toward heaven. Someone had
climbed the church's belfry and tolled the church's bell. It was the
most beautiful, heartaching sound Richard Kilchmar had ever heard.
It resounded off the houses. It echoed off the mountains. The peal
tickled his swollen belly. When the ringing ceased, the silence was as
warm and wet as the tears Kilchmar rubbed from out his eyes.

He nodded at the crowd. Two hundred heads nodded back at him.

"I will give you bells," he whispered. He sloshed his drink at the
midnight sky. His voice rose to a shout. "I will build a church to house
them, high up in the mountains, so the ringing echoes to every inch
of Uri soil! They will be the Loudest and Most Beautiful Bells Ever!"

They cheered even more loudly now than they had before. He
raised his arms in triumph. Schnapps washed his brow. Then he and
every man plunged their eyes into the bottom of their mugs and
drank them empty, sealing Kilchmar's pledge.

As he drank the final drop, Kilchmar stumbled back, tripped,
and fell. He spent the rest of the night lying in the mud, dreaming of
his bells.

He awoke to a circle of blue sky ringed by twenty reverent faces.

"Lead us!" they implored him.

Their veneration seemed to lift him to his feet, and after six or
eight swigs from their flasks, he felt more weightless still. Soon he
found himself on his horse leading a procession: fifty horses; several

carts filled with women; children and dogs darting through the grasses. Where to lead them he did not know, for until that day he'd found the mountains menacing and hostile. But now he led them up the Uri Road toward Italy, toward the pope, toward snowfields glittering in the sun, and then, when inspiration took him, turned off and began to climb.

Up and up they went, almost to the cliffs and snow. Kilchmar now led five hundred Urners, and they followed him until they reached a rocky promontory and beheld the valley stretched before them, the river Reuss a thin white thread stitching it together.

"Here," he whispered. "Here."

"Here," they echoed. "Here."

They turned then to regard the tiny village just below them, a mere jumble of squalid houses. The villagers and their scrawny cows stared back in awe at the assemblage on the rocky hill.

This tiny, starved village I write of is Nebelmatt. In this village I was born (may it burn to the ground and be covered by an avalanche).

Kilchmar's church was completed in 1727, built of only Uri sweat and Uri stone, so that, in the winter months, no matter how much wood was wasted in the stove, the church remained as cold as the mountain upon which it was built. It was a stocky church, shaped something like a boot. The bishop was petitioned for a priest well suited to the frigid and lonesome aspects of the post. His reply came a few days later in the form of a young priest scowling at Kilchmar's door—a learned father Karl Victor Vonderach. "Just the man," read the bishop's letter, "for a posting on a cold, distant mountain. Do not send him back."

Now the church had a master, twelve rustic pews, and a roof that kept out a good deal of the rain, but it still did not have what Kilchmar had promised them. It did not have its bells. And so Kilchmar packed his cart, kissed his wife, and said he would undertake an expedition to St. Gall to find the greatest bell maker in the Catholic world. He rumbled off northward to patriotic cries, and was never seen in Uri again.

The building of the church had ruined him.

And so, one year after the last slate had been laid on its roof, the church built to house the Loudest and Most Beautiful Bells Ever did not even have a cowbell hanging in its belfry.

Urners are a proud and resourceful folk. *How hard can it be to make a bell?* they thought. Clay molds, some molten metal, some beams on which to hang the finished bells—nothing more. Perhaps God had sent them Kilchmar only to set them on their way.

God needs your iron, went the call. *Bring Him your copper and your tin.*

Rusted shovels, broken hoes, corroded knives, cracked cauldrons—all of these were thrown into a pile that soon towered over Altdorf's square on the very spot where Kilchmar had sealed his pledge three years before. Crowds cheered every new donation. One man lugged the stove that should have kept him warm that winter. *God bless her*, was the murmur when an old widow tossed in her jewelry. Tears flowed when the three best families gathered to contribute three golden coins. Ten oxcarts were needed to transport the metal to the village.

The villagers, though they had little metal of their own to offer, would not be outdone. As they minded the makeshift smelter for nine days and nights, they contributed whatever Schnapps remained in their flasks at daybreak, plus a full set of wolf's teeth, a carved ibex horn, and a dusty chunk of quartz.

Twelve men were scarred for life with burns the day they poured the glowing soup into the molds. The first bell was as round as a fat turkey, the second, large enough to hide a small goat beneath it, and the third, the extraordinary third bell, was as high as a man and took sixteen horses to hoist into the belfry.

All of Uri gathered on the hill below the church to hear the bells ring for the first time. When all was set, the crowd turned their reverent eyes to Father Karl Victor Vonderach. He stared back at them as if they were merely a flock of sheep.

"A blessing, Father?" one woman whispered. "Would you bless our bells?"

He rubbed his temples and then stepped before the crowd. He bowed his head, and everyone else did the same. "Heavenly Father," he croaked through the spittle gathered in his throat. "Bless these bells that You have—" He sniffed and looked around him, and then glanced down at his shoe, which rested in a moist cake of dung. "Damn them all," he muttered. He stalked back through the crowd. They watched his form until it vanished into his house, which had glass in its windows, but no slates yet on its roof.

Then the silent crowd turned to watch seven of Kilchmar's cousins march resolutely into the church—one to ring the smallest, two the middle, and four the largest bell. Many in the crowd held their breath as, in the belfry, the three great bells began to rock.

And then the Loudest and Most Beautiful Bells Ever began to ring.

The mountain air shuddered. The pealing flooded the valley. It was as shrill as a rusty hinge and as rumbling as an avalanche and as piercing as a scream and as soothing as a mother's whisper. Every person cried out and flinched and threw his hands over his ears. They stumbled back. Father Karl Victor's windows cracked. Teeth were clenched so hard they chipped. Eardrums burst. A cow, two goats, and one woman felt the sudden pangs of labor.

When the echoes from the distant peaks finally faded, there was silence. Every person stared at the church as if it might collapse. Then the door burst open and the Kilchmar cousins poured out, their palms held to their ruined ears. They faced the crowd like thieves caught with treasure in their stockings.

Then the cheering began. Hands rose toward heaven. Fists shook. Tears flowed. They had done it! The Loudest Bells Ever had been rung!

God's kingdom on earth was safe!

The crowd retreated slowly down the hill. When someone yelled, "Ring them again!" there was a collective cringe, and soon began a stampede—men, women, children, dogs, and cows ran, slid, rolled down the muddy hill and hid behind the decrepit houses as if trying to outrun an avalanche. Then there was silence. Several heads peered around the houses and toward the church. The Kilchmar cousins were nowhere to be found. Indeed, soon there was no one within two hundred paces of that church. There was no one brave enough to ring the bells again.

Or was there? Whispers filled the air. Children pointed at a brown smudge moving lightly up the hill, like a knot of hay, blown by a gentle wind. A person? No, not a person. A child—a little girl—in dirty rags.

It so happened that this village possessed, among its treasures, a deaf idiot girl. She was wont to stare down the villagers with a haunting glare, as though she knew the sins they fought to hide, and so they drove her off with buckets of dirty wash water whenever she came near. This deaf child was staring at the belfry as she climbed the hill, for she, too, had heard the bells, not in her vacant ears, but as we hear holiness: a vibration in the gut.

They all watched her climb, knowing that God had sent this idiot girl to them, just as God had sent them Kilchmar, had sent them the stone to build this church, and the metal to cast the bells.

She looked upward at the belfry as though she wished that she could fly.

"Go," they whispered. "Go."

She does not hear them urge her on. But the memory of the bells' peal pulls her to the doors and into the church, where she has never been before. There are shards of glass on the floor—the shattered windows—and so she leaves bloody footprints as she climbs the narrow stairs at the back of the church. On the first level of the bell tower, the three ropes hang through the ceiling. But she knows of ropes, and knows this magic is not from them, that they direct her farther up, and so she climbs the ladder and lifts the trap with her head. The sides of the belfry are open—there is no railing to stop a fall—and she sees four different scenes: to the left, blank cliffs; in front, the valley winding upward toward Italy; to her right, the snow-covered Susten Pass; and when she climbs through the trapdoor, behind her, her audience gathered around the homes like maggots swarming rotting meat.

She walks beneath the largest bell and looks up into its shadows. Its body is black and rough. She reaches up and slaps it with her hand. It does not move. She does not feel a sound. There are two copper mallets leaning in the corner. She lifts one of them and swings it at the largest bell.

She feels it first in her belly, like the touch of a warm hand. It has been years since anyone has touched her. She closes her eyes and feels that touch radiate down into her thighs. It travels along the tracks of her ribs. She sighs. She hits the bell again with the mallet, as hard as she can, and the touch goes farther. It snakes around her back and up her shoulders. It seems to hold her up; she is floating in the sound. Again and again she strikes the bell, and that sound grows warmer.

She rings the middle bell. She hears it in her neck, in her arms, in the hollows behind her knees. The sound pulls at her, like warm hands are spreading her apart, and she is taller and broader in that little body than she has ever been before.

The small bell she hears in her jaw, in the flesh of her ears, in the arches of her feet. She swings the mallet again and again. She lifts the second mallet so she can use both arms to pound against the bells.

In the village, at first, they cheered and cried at the miracle. The echoes of pealing returned from across the valley. They closed their eyes and listened to their glory.

She rang the bells. A half hour passed. They could not hear each other speak. Some yelled to be heard; most just sat on logs or leaned against the houses and pressed their hands against their ears. The pigs had already been roasted. The casks of wine had been tapped, but how could they begin the feast of victory without a blessing?

"Stop it!" someone shouted.

"Quiet!"

"Enough!"

They shook their fists at the church.

"Someone has to stop her!"

At this demand, everyone looked shyly at his neighbor. No one stepped forward.

"Get her father!" they yelled. "This is a father's job!"

Old Iso Froben, the shepherd whose wife had given him this one, malformed child after twenty years of marriage, was pushed forward. He was not more than fifty, but his eyes were sunk, and his forearms, the fleshless stalks of a great-grandfather. He rubbed the back of his hand across his dripping nose and gazed up at the church as if he were being sent to slay a dragon. A woman came forward, stopped his ears with wool, and then wrapped dirty trousers around his head, tying them at the back like a turban.   •

He shouted something at the man next to him, who disappeared into the crowd and then, moments later, returned with a mule whip.

So many times I would overhear the story: Brave Iso Froben struggled up the hill, one hand keeping the trousers from slipping over his eyes, the other on the whip. The steep path had been so muddied by thousands of eager feet that he slipped often, skidded two steps backward on his knees, clawed himself to his feet again. When he reached the church at last, he was covered from head to toe in mud. The whip sprinkled specks as it swung in his hand. Even with the wool in his ears and the trousers around his brow, the bells clenched and shook his head with each new ring.

The sound only grew louder as he entered the church and climbed the stairs, which seemed to shake beneath him. He held his palms over his stopped ears, but it did no good. He cursed God for the thousandth time for sending him this child.

At the first level of the belfry, he saw that the ropes were still, and yet the bells rang. He saw black spots before his eyes. As the world began to spin, he suddenly understood: These were not God's bells at all! They had been tricked. These were the devil's bells! They were all the devil's fools. They had built his church. They had cast his bells!

He turned to run down the stairs, but then he glimpsed above him, in the cracks between the ceiling planks, the dancing of tiny, devilish feet.

There was courage left in that meager, withered frame. He clutched that whip as his sword. He climbed the ladder to the belfry and pushed open the trapdoor just far enough to peek.

She leapt. She twirled. She swayed and stretched. She swung the mallet and hung in the air as it impacted. The bells seemed to toll from within her, as if the bells she struck were her own black heart. She pranced along the edge, an invisible hand guiding her back to safety. She rang the largest bell: a sound like nails driven in his ears.

The pleasure glowing in her eyes was the last proof Iso Froben needed: his daughter was possessed by the devil. He threw open the trapdoor and clambered through. The aged man was a warrior. He whipped the devil-child until she lay on the floor of the belfry without moving. Soon the bells' tolling was but a gentle ringing in the air. Cheers erupted from the village far below him. His daughter whimpered.

He dropped his whip beside her and then descended. He passed through the celebrating town without pausing, and was never seen in Uri again, and so, after Kilchmar, he was the second, but not the final, victim of the bells.

Back in the church, only after dark did that child move. She lifted her head to make sure that her father was gone, and then sat up. Her clothes were bloody. The gashes in her back burned. Her dead ears were blank to the revelry in the village below. She took her mallets and opened the trapdoor.

Tomorrow, she thought as she looked up at the bells. *Tomorrow I will ring you again.*

The next day she did ring them, as she did the day after that, and every morning, noon, and night until her death.

This child was named Adelheid Froben, and I, Moses Froben, am her son.

II.

My mother had a filthy nest of hair, knots of iron muscle in her arms, and, for me alone, a smile as warm as August's sun. By the time of my birth she had been living for some years in a small alpine hut adjacent to the church. No, that is inaccurate. My mother lived in the belfry. She came to the hut only when the belfry, exposed to the mountains' bitter weather, became too cold, or too full of snow, or when she had hunger for the cheese rinds and cold gruel the villagers left for her, or when the summer lightning storms swept down the valley and struck our belfry—they often did, the bells ringing as if tolled by ghosts. Though she was filthy, and never washed herself her entire life, every week she scrubbed me from head to toe in the frigid water of the stream. She fed me from a wooden spoon until I was full to bursting. I did not then know of how other children played and laughed, how they pretended to be kings and soldiers, how they danced and sang songs together. I wanted nothing more for my life. I wanted only to sit there, my four-year-old legs dangling over the edge of the belfry. To look at the mountains. To listen to the beauty of the bells.

And so the villagers' oversight does not surprise me. A boy seemingly oblivious to bells that burst eardrums at fifty paces? A boy who never speaks, whose feet do not even seem to rustle in the grass, who never makes any noise at all? A child who ignores even the furious yells of Father Karl Victor Vonderach? There is no other explanation. That child is deaf. He is as stupid as his mother.

And yet, approach this boy who sits on the edge of his world, who stares blankly at a scene that only God could have created. It is early summer, and the Alps are so verdant that one envies the cows their grasses, and would like to stoop beside them and feast until green drool dribbles down one's chin. High above, patches of snow remain in hollows and underneath cliffs. The distant, greener peaks to the north are infested with dots of grazing sheep like lice upon a beggar's head.

This boy listens. All three bells are ringing behind him, and he hears the strident strike tones, the myriad part tones. A bell is a tower of tiny bands, stacked thinly one upon the other, and each of these bands rings a different pitch, just as a thousand shades of paint shine slightly different hues. In his mind, he lays out these notes like other children their collection of toys. He fits part tones together so they make him smile or grit his teeth. He finds the tones that the hawk uses in his cry. He finds those that compose thunder's rumble and those of the marmot's whistle. He hears the notes that he himself uses when he laughs. The bells are loud, very loud, but they do not hurt his ears. His ears were formed around these sounds, and each massive ring just makes his ears that much more resilient.

There is the sound of his mother's inhalation as she draws her mallet back; the sound of her exhalation as she brings it forward; the rustle of her tattered robe against her bare leg; the creak of the bells' rusty bearings; the whistle of the warm wind through the chinks in the roof above his head; the lowing of the cows in the field below the church; the tearing of the grass as the cows graze; the cry of the buzzard above the field; the rush of the snowmelt that pours down the cliffs.

He also hears that the water on the cliff is many waters: it is stones being dragged and rolled; it is drips exploding into drops; it is the giggle of a bubbling pool; it is the laughter of the cascades. Each of these he can pry from the next: the part of his mother's lips, the rush of breath in her nose, the air that whistles past her tongue. In her throat, she groans. Her lungs croak open. Like a baby exploring an object with its fumbling hands and mouth, he grasps at each sound until he sighs, *Yes!*

This is not magic—I promise you as your faithful witness. He cannot hear through mountains or to the other side of the earth. This is merely selection. And if this boy, at four years of age, can do so little—neither speak, nor write, nor read—the selection of sounds, the *dissection* of sounds, is something he can do like no other. This his mother and her bells have gifted him.

And so the boy sits on his perch and dissects the world. He selects the bells, hears them as a whole, dissects their pealing, and then places them aside. He grasps the sound of the wind. He hears in wind what we see in waves of water: a multitude of currents, chaotic and yet ordered by some law of God. He loves to listen to the wind cut through the holes in the roof above him, or whip around the corner of the tower, or flutter through the long grasses in the meadows.

And though he delights in any new sound, he soon learns that sounds are not only something for him to love. He learns that the whistle of the wind through the chinks is duller if rain is coming. He dreads the dragging feet of the first worshippers on Sunday morning, because it means that soon his mother will flee to hide in the caves above the church until, hours later, she reappears only as Father Karl Victor's silhouette disappears back into the village. He hates the sound of her cough, because it means that she will grow sick, as she does every winter, and her eyes will fog, and she will walk as if asleep.

When he is five he begins to wander, less skittish than his mother. He dissects the village: The winds that creak among the wooden houses. The tinkling of wash water and animal urine out of the stalls and down the slope. The creak and grind of wagon wheels on the stony tracks. The dog's bark, the rooster's cackle, and, in the winter, the cow's lowing and the sheep's moan, as if a madman is caged in every stall.

He is overwhelmed by the sounds of men; breath, sigh, groan, curse. They scold and cry and laugh, and each of these has a million forms. But the shelves of his memory have no limit. Now there are words to speak—and he carries these back to the belfry. As his mother rings her bells, he jabbers, yells insults at the sky, spits prayers into his fist so he sounds like the village farmer who bit off half his tongue.

Of the sounds he hates, chief among them are those of Father Karl Victor Vonderach: his limping step; his wheezing breath; the swishing and mashing of his lips, like a calf at a teat; the slam when he opens the great Bible on the pulpit; the clunky turn of the key in the empty offertory box; the groan when he leans over and clutches at his back; the exhalation when he looks at my—

How your sounds gave you away, Karl Victor! With my ears, I knew enough at six years to condemn you to the eternal fire! I knew the pop of your eyes when you squeezed them shut, the bubbling of phlegm in your throat when you preached on Sunday in our church. I heard your hateful mumbles when you looked down at your flock. And when you hiked up on other days—when I heard in your eager wheeze that you were not on an errand of God, when you called for my mother, banged on the door of our hut at night, or even, when you could not hold back, in the light of day—even though she did not hear you, I did. The cries that poured from her unlearned mouth, which to you sounded like the babbling of an idiot—those cries were the clearest of all pleas to me.

III.

The villagers said my mother was not of sound mind. She was skittish, had a wild look; she was dirty, and cried or laughed at nothing. She hid from them in caves; she sometimes went without clothes; she raised her son in a belfry; she ate with her hands; she cared for nothing but her child and the ringing of her bells.

Several times I watched my mother climb onto the rafters of the belfry so she could creep along the headstock of that middle bell, then hang down and wrap her legs around its waist, hugging the crown with one arm while she beat the dampened bell with her mallet. One day, she stacked a tower of logs beneath the largest bell and stood inside it, so the crisscrossing waves of sound tickled every fiber. She stole a braided horsehair bridle, tied one end to a headstock and the other to her waist. She swung amid the bells, closed her eyes, and, I believe, fantasized that she was one of them.

Another time, she coated the bells with mud and struck them. She held a flaming torch to their lips and struck them. She struck them with her hand. With her skull. With a cow's femur bone. With a crystal she found in her cave. With the Bible she took from Karl Victor's pulpit (and then threw it in the mud when the dampened ring did not suit her). Sometimes she sat serenely in the corner and rang a bell by pulling the bell rope rhythmically with one hand. But always, in the end, she returned to her dance: she leapt and swung the mallets and closed her eyes as the waves passed through her.

As my mother rang her bells, she tuned the fibers of her body as a violinist tunes his strings. There in her neck, she rings faintly with a part tone of the middle bell. There in her thighs, with another. In the bottom of her feet, I heard the strike tone of the smallest bell. Each tone, ringing in her flesh, was itself the faintest echo of the vast concert. I cannot remember my mother's face, but I remember this landscape of her sounds. And though I have no likeness with which I might recall her, when I close my eyes and hear her body ringing with those bells, it is as though I have a portrait in my hands.

They would have stolen a normal child and put him to work under the guise of charity. But I was allowed to stay with my mother because they thought I was as deaf and mad as she. Sometimes I watched the village children playing and wished I could join, but they threw stones at me whenever I came too close. We lived for eight years in the belfry and the hut, never working (except for the bell ringing, which for both of us was a reward, not a task), never so much as cooking, though the villagers' meager meals of charity we soon dispensed with.

As a master of sounds, it was little trouble for me to slip into a house in the village, listen until I was sure the pantry was empty, snatch a choice sausage, slide past a door (behind which a husband and his wife were deep in a conversation about the neighbor's cows), steal a fresh loaf of bread cooling by the hearth, and be gone without making a sound. Though I remained a tiny thing, I developed a taste for legs of lamb, for half-cooked bacon, for eggs sucked from out their shells. By my eighth birthday, I had stolen eggs from under hens, pots of stew from hearths, and whole wheels of cheese from cellars. Sometimes I listened to other mothers telling stories to their children before the hearth, or watched a playful son climb into his father's arms. Once, in the evening, sneaking into a house, I came upon a mother soothing her son who could not sleep, for his friends had told him that Iso Froben's ghost haunted the town. The father sat exhausted at a table. "It's him that stole the ham," the boy told his mother. "And the Eggerses' cheese, and the cauldron from—"

"Shhhh," his mother whispered, "there is no ghost." And then she sang softly in his ear. I stood mesmerized by her singing, and by the warmth of their hearth, forgetting for a moment that these people could even see me. She paced back and forth and held her son's drooping head at her neck. Then, suddenly, she glimpsed my shining eyes. "Aagg!" she bleated as if she had seen a rat. The gallant father leapt from his bench. One shoe flew past my head; the next hit my back as I scurried out the door. I stumbled and fell into the mud. As the father came after me swinging a bridle like a whip, I scurried off into the shadows. For several minutes, I cried behind a stall, but hunger soon overwhelmed me. I slipped inside the stall, and, on my knees, squirted warm goat's milk into my mouth. I stole an earthen jar, filled it with milk, and carried it to my mother.

We always feasted in the belfry, and threw the bones and pots and spits to the ravine below, where they gathered like the refuse of a bloody battle. We ate with our hands and tore the meat with our teeth, wiping our palms on the rags we wore. We had the luxurious freedom of the wretched.

But this ended the day Father Karl Victor Vonderach realized I was not as helpless as I seemed.

It was late spring, and an evening sun had just broken through after days of rain. The cows' hooves squelched into the muddy fields. Water carved trenches in the soft earth, and then seeped into the ground, like sand pouring through loosely held fingers. Torrents rumbled in the ravines. Far off I heard the low hush of the river Reuss flowing through the valley.

Then I heard an odd sound. It was like thunder, only smoother, and I had never heard such a noise before. At the same time, I heard a scream. I looked up at my mother, who was swinging her mallets. I pushed aside the bells, the running water, the cows, my mother, and for a few seconds I heard nothing.

Then again—a scream.

This sound was human, but not the weave of sound I knew from the town—a mess of hunger, anger, joy, and want. This was the sound of pain.

I shut my eyes and held its memory. Four or five times it rose, vibrated at its highest note, and then was choked off as the screamer ran out of air. It terrified me, but still I climbed down the ladder from the belfry, freezing with every new scream, then hurrying on when it ended, chasing the echo. I ran out the side door of the church, climbed over a fence, and slid down the muddy field into the woods below the church.

There is nothing above Nebelmatt but pasture and rock and snow. Below the village, the mountains drop away into forests and ravines, and there is only the occasional clearing until the pine forest meets the valley. I ran as fast as I could along a footpath into this steep forest, jumping off the larger rocks, letting the incline propel me. In a clearing that a fire had ravaged the summer before the path suddenly ended.

I can still picture her face. Muscle and tendon bulged in her cheeks, in her neck, in her arms and in her hands, which clawed at the ground in front of her. Her skin was flushed the color of blood.

The earth was trying to eat her. Its jaws grasped at her gut and tendrils of blood ran up the seams of her dress. All around her lay loose stones and dirt. A basket of wild garlic was strewn on the ground before her, like rose petals at a wedding.

The screaming had stopped. I took several steps toward her on the loose ground and my feet were swallowed in streams of dirt and stones.

There was a gargle of bile and blood in her throat. I heard the hum of taut muscles, the ferocious beating of her heart. She turned toward me with those blank eyes, and I wanted to stop her pain. I wanted to hold her like my mother had held me. I took another step, setting loose a rock the size of my torso. I jumped back to solid ground. This monster wanted me as well.

Then I ran. It was late by then. The bells were silent and no one was in the fields. I could still feel her breath, and the subtle, hopeful change in the beating of her heart when she had seen me, so I ran faster, past the first quiet houses, past children playing on the rocky track, past Karl Victor's house, whose high oaken door was closed. A few steps farther on, a dozen men sat at a wooden table of rough-hewn planks. The men were ruddy with drink, their strong backs a wall high above my head.

"Ivo says she has eyes like jewels," one man said.

"Please," I whispered. The wall of backs did not break.

"Even if they're diamonds, he'll still have to break her in," said another. The others laughed. "Women from town are soft."

"Come," I said louder. "She dies."

"There's nothing wrong with soft." The man above me had spoken now, and as I laid my hand on his back I felt the rumble of his laughter.

I heard her scream again, this time from within my head, from that library of sounds I never can discard. I heard the bubbling in her throat, heard her claw at the dirt in front of her. Was she buried yet? I grabbed his shirt. A hand slapped mine away.

"Please!" I yelled.

The line of backs was as high as a cliff.

I screamed.

This was a sound even I did not hear coming. It was like a door thrown open in a space where only a wall had been before. It was as though so many spirits—of my mother, of that woman buried, of Father Karl Victor—flew out of my mouth.

The scream lasted only the time it takes a stone to fall from the belfry and plop into the mud of the field. But in that time, the wall of backs had turned. Sober faces, startled eyes stared down at me. The children who had been playing were frozen in place. Women with babies in their arms hunched at the thresholds of their houses.

Father Karl Victor Vonderach stood at his open door.

"A woman is dying," I said to the faces. "You must come."

At my command, the men stood up, knocking over the benches.

I ran down the path through the woods, an army of feet behind me.

"Landslide!" I heard one of them yell, and then they overtook me.

They trod the loose ground, slipped, sent boulders rolling, fought through the landslide like swimming for a drowning woman in a river's rapids. They were soon wiping blood and dirt and tears from their eyes, as they pulled her from the landslide, so gently, like a midwife with a newborn babe. They laid her on the path just downhill from where I hid behind a sapling.

"Is she dead?"

"She is warm."

"That does not mean anything."

The blood and dirt blotted her dress. Her face was slack and white, with brown streaks where the men's fingers had held her neck and head.

An older man limped down the path.

"Keep him back. No father should see this."

Two men tried to hold him back, but he pushed past. He collapsed onto her, grasping her face in both his hands.

"Please, God!"

The men were pale, and I heard that pity was a clamp, quieting their steps, their heaving breaths, their racing hearts.

I stepped from behind the tree and stood next to the man as he clasped his daughter and cried.

I whispered in his ear: "She is alive."

He looked up at me. He swallowed. "How do you know?"

"Listen." I pointed to her lips. Her breath was a gentle but steady wave.

For a moment he looked at me, and then I was pushed aside by a group of women. I climbed back up to the sapling and hid myself once more.

As they prodded her and slapped and pinched her, as her eyes fluttered open and she smiled weakly at her father, their sounds grew louder. They laughed because tears were in their eyes. Women shouted orders. Behind the tree, I was invisible to all, save one.

Father Karl Victor stood but three paces up the path. He didn't seem to notice the injured woman. He ignored their pleas for a prayer. He stared as though he would burn me with his gaze. He growled each time he exhaled.

"You can hear," he whispered under his breath.

I backed away, fleeing up the hill.

"You can speak."

IV.

In the belfry my mother saw the terror in my eyes, but when she tried to soothe me in her arms, I pushed her away. I shook my head. I took her hand and tried to pull her down the ladder. I pointed at a distant mountain—somewhere there would be a place where we could hide.

In the sadness of her eyes, I saw she understood something of what I meant, my wish to flee him and this village. But she shook her head.

I cannot leave, she seemed to say.

And so we slept that night in the belfry, huddled under blankets as the falling night swept warm gusts up from the valley. My mother clutched her mallets to her chest. I could not sleep—only my ears would protect us in the night. I listened for an approaching step, for a hand on the ladder below us. But after midnight a wind came up, and lightning flickered up the valley. Rain began to fall. It soaked us through the open walls. My mother held me, and when the lightning flashed, I glimpsed terror in her eyes. At least twice a summer the church was struck, and I know she was thinking we should be huddled in our hut. As the storm moved over us, the bells sung a soft warning. My mother looked up, for she heard it in her gut. *Run*, they said.

She took me in her arms and fled down the ladder. Lightning crashed, the echoes rumbled in the valley. I listened for the sounds of feet trudging in the mud, but in the torrent I heard the splotch of a thousand boots, the mashing of a thousand lips. In the thunder's rumble I heard a million Karl Victors curse. She carried me across the field to our hut and barred the door. In the occasional flashes through the cracks I saw she held a mallet in her hand.

Karl Victor came at the height of the storm, beating at our door. My mother shoved me into a corner, and though I tried to pull her down beside me, she slipped away and stood between the flimsy door and me. It lasted but three kicks. Timber snapped, and a white hand struggled through the gap and fumbled with the bar.

"Goddamn you!" the priest yelled. He limped, for he had hurt his toes kicking in the door. His boots and cassock shone with mud when the lightning flashed.

My mother leapt at him. But in the next flash of lightning he saw her coming—and without her bells she could not fight him. She swung her mallet with one hand while she clawed his face with the other. I pressed my hands against my ears as his one backhand slap dropped her to our muddy floor. I cringed and cried each time he kicked her with his boot. Then lightning struck our church with a crash and the bells rang out. Karl Victor covered his ears in pain, but the ringing only fed his fury. He kicked her again and again until she ceased to jerk in pain, and only then did he stop. She did not move.

As the storm passed, the rain slowed. The bells still faintly hummed. My mother breathed in gasps. Karl Victor stood still, listening, waiting for the next lightning strike so he could see me. I huddled in the corner, pressing myself into the wood, but then a sob fought up my throat and burst in the darkness. Karl Victor stepped toward me and kicked the wall until he found me—then he kicked harder and faster, so hard into my gut I was sure I would never breathe again. He grabbed me by the neck and lifted me close.

"You deceiving brat," he said. He stank of uncooked onions. "I will see that you will never say a word."

Father Karl Victor Vonderach dragged me out of our hut. I screamed and reached for my mother, who lay unmoving on the ground, moaning as she exhaled. In a flash of distant lightning I saw her bloodied face. Karl Victor dragged me by my shirt until it tore, removed his belt, and looped it around my neck like a leash. "Try and run," he hissed into my ear as if he would bite it off. "Go ahead and try." As gray dawn rose, we descended into the forest. He tore off a pine branch and whipped me when I swayed too far to the side, when I walked too fast or too slow, or simply when his anger bubbled over. Tears fogged my eyes. I slipped and tripped and choked on my leash.

He conducted me to the Uri Road, which was scarred with hoof-prints, and my bare feet sank in mud almost to my knees. Karl Victor cursed. He looked up and down the road, but in the early morning he saw no horses or cart of which to beg a ride. He yanked at the scraps of my shirt, but that only tore it off. He took my thin arm and tugged until I felt that I might split, but the mud would not release me. Then suddenly there was a pop, and a sucking, and we tumbled, me before him. My face pressed into the cold mud, and then was lifted up by the belt around my neck. He dragged me down the road like a sack of oats, with a hand under each of my arms. When he slipped, he heaved me under him, and for a moment the world was black with mud. When he lifted me I gasped for air and clawed at my noose.

We struggled like this for what seemed hours, before we reached the hard ground of a wooden bridge across the Reuss, and he dropped me on the mud-spattered boards. I lay panting, leaning up against the bridge railing, and he wheezed and coughed and spat globs of mud in my face. The flooded Reuss flowed beneath the bridge with the anger of spring rains and melting snow, and I tried to escape into its sounds: I pried current from current, heard the thunder of churning water, heard rocks rolled downstream by the flood. But my ears forced me to return. Karl Victor ground his hands together like a tightening rope about to break. His feet beat against the ground. His teeth chewed at his lip. He growled.

I looked up through mud and tears. I perceived his face, which was crossed by scars from my mother's nails. Blood flowed from his bitten lip. His cassock was soaked so much it clung about his legs. He grasped his hair with his hands as if he would pull it out, and he growled once more into the wind.

I have often wished I could have heard inside Karl Victor's head at this moment. What exactly had he planned? I am generous enough to believe that he had something in mind: perhaps to take me to Lucerne and deposit me at an orphanage; to sell me to a farmer in Canton Schwyz. But this mud—this knee-deep sludge that burped and sucked and splattered—made an island of that bridge. To bring me back to Nebelmatt was impossible, for there I would spread his shameful secrets. To continue dragging me for even another hundred steps might kill us both.

His growl turned to a yell, and he kicked the bridge's railing as he had my mother, again and again, but it was sturdy and would not break under his boot. He looked at me with red eyes, and when he spoke he spat blood into my face.

"You were supposed to be deaf!"

At that moment, I would have promised never to speak again. I would have offered to bite off my own tongue, if only he would let me go back to my mother. I would never leave our belfry again, even when the lightning threatened.

He bent over me, his face so close that his sucking, mashing lips were as loud as the river. He heaved me up by the belt, pressing me against the rail with his hip. Then he clutched my head with both hands.

"If God will not make you deaf, then I will have to do it."

Two fingers pressed into my ears like spikes. I howled and thrashed, but they pressed harder, tunneling so far they seemed to meet inside my head. I finally knew the pain that others felt when they heard my mother's bells. His face was all I saw. His grimace turned from white to red. He pressed his fingers harder, and I screamed.

My tiny hands pulled at his, but I could not move them.

"Father!" I yelled.

He dropped me as if I were a burning coal.

I lay on the ground and held my head, awaiting the next attack, but it did not come. He stood frozen over me, his eyes wide and startled.

I had not meant it as an accusation. In Nebelmatt they called him "Father." I meant no more than that.

"I am not your father," he whispered. But I did not hear the words. I heard the trembling of his voice, the clamp upon his lungs, the shaking in his hands and jaw. And I heard how that single word, which had burnt him like fire, was true.

Father? This word I knew: Fathers held their sons when they were hurt, whipped them when they were bad. They let them walk beside them as they drove cows up to pasture. I knew it well, but I had never thought it was a word for me.

"I am not your father," he said again.

My father lifted me up. He held me up above him as if offering me to heaven. "You shall be silent," he said.

And then with a grunt, he threw me off the bridge and into the roaring Reuss.

V.

Had he watched the currents swallow me? Or turned to shield his eyes from his sin? All I know is that he did not venture to confirm that his son was actually dead. He did not follow the river long enough to see me washed clean of my rags and noose, as I flailed and gasped, as one current pulled me under and the next pushed me up. He did not watch as my strength gave out, as the white of the waves turned to black, and I began to drown. He did not watch my corpse sink as my lungs filled with water. He did not repent and try to save me.

But his were not the only eyes on the Uri Road that morning. When I awoke, I heard their voices before I opened my eyes.

"No, stay back. I would not touch him anymore."

The first voice was thin and tight, as though spoken through taut lips, but the second was deep and warm: "No need to worry. He is freshly bathed."

"Such a scrawny thing," said the first. "Mere bones. He must have some disease. Listen to him cough."

"He drank half the river. And skin and bones, that's normal here—nothing to eat in the mountains. Just grass and dirt."

Sharp stones jutted into my naked back. The sun was warm, but the wet bank was icy. I coughed again, bringing up water and a good deal else, then opened my eyes and saw two men looming above me. I looked from one to the other, and then back again, and my first thought was that God had never made two men more dissimilar.

One was a handsome giant, with a halo of fair hair, a thick gray beard, a smile fixed upon his face. The other was smaller, pale. He chewed his lip. He wrung his greasy hands. They both wore black tunics, drawn with leathern belts. The giant's tunic was sopping, for he had saved me from the river and then thumped my chest until I revived.

"It is Moses swimming in the Nile," said the giant, his grin as warm as the sun. He offered me a massive hand. "Come and be our king."

I cowered from the hand, dreading any touch but my mother's. In any case, the smaller man quickly batted the larger's hand away. "I said you should not touch him," he muttered.

"He's just a boy," the giant said, and he bent down and clutched both hands around my ribs, his thumbs pressing into my heart. His hands were warm and soft, yet every muscle in my body tightened. He held me up like a goatherd might inspect a kid. I was entirely naked, washed clean by the river. "What's your name?"

I did not answer. In fact, I could not answer—the villagers had only ever called me "that Froben boy" or "the idiot child." I kept rigid and hoped that he would put me down so I could run away and find my mother. He shrugged. "Well, Moses is a fine enough name for boys swimming in rivers. Mine is Nicolai. The wolf here is Remus. We are monks."

I looked from the one man to the next, trying to extract a meaning from this term. *Monks?* I found nothing in common between the two except their tunics.

"All right," this Remus said, impatiently, his face screwed up as if against a noxious smell. "He is alive. Send him on his way."

"No!" the giant cried. "Are you so heartless?" He swung me down so I sat in the crux of his elbow and forced my cheek against the wet wool of his tunic until I itched from ear to hip. His heart thumped into my ear.

"You've done your duty. You saved his life," Remus said.

Nicolai's body recoiled in shock. "Remus, someone threw him in that river!"

"You don't know that. He could have fallen."

"Did you fall into the water?" the giant asked me. I did not answer—in fact, I did not even hear, for I was mesmerized by the beating of his heart, so much slower and deeper than my mother's. The heart of a bull.

"Come on," Nicolai urged. "You can tell me. Who threw you in?"

I closed my eyes. My heart was slowing, matching itself to the measured rhythm of the giant's. My muscles loosened and, without willing it, I melted into his arms.

"It doesn't matter," Remus said. "He'll probably lie to us in any case. Watch your purse."

"Remus!"

"You must leave him here." Remus pointed at the grassy bank.

"Here? Naked in the grass? How can you say that? What if those monks who found me on their doorstep had left me there? Where would you be now?"

"I would be reading in my cell. In peace."

"Exactly. And instead you are seeing the world."

"I don't want to see the world. I have told you that before. I want to go home. We are two months late."

"Another day won't matter."

"Put him down."

Nicolai turned his back to Remus. He carried me several steps along the bank. I opened my eyes and looked up into his face. He peered down with the friendliest gaze I had ever seen. His breath was like a warm draft flitting up a cliff. "Remus is right," he whispered to me. "He always is, and that's why no one likes him. But I won't just leave you here. Point me toward your home, and I'll help you find your father."

I started so violently that Nicolai nearly dropped me. I looked around in a panic, worried I might see Karl Victor crouching in the grass.

"My God," Nicolai said. "That's it! Isn't it? It was your father! Remus," Nicolai shouted, rushing back to the scowling, smaller monk. "His father threw him in!"

"You don't know that."

"He tried to kill his own son. That means this boy is an orphan. Just like me."

Remus covered his face with his hands. "Nicolai, you are not an orphan anymore—have not been for forty years. You are a monk. And monks cannot take in children."

Nicolai considered this. His beard bristled as he smiled. "He can become a novice."

"Staudach will not have him."

"I will speak with him." Nicolai nodded confidently. "Make him understand what is at stake. His father tried to kill him."

"Nicolai," Remus said calmly, as if explaining a simple formula, "you cannot take this child."

"Remus, he was floating down the river. Sinking. He would have drowned."

"And you saved him. But taking him with us is a responsibility you cannot bear."

Nicolai shifted me so I was cradled in his arms, looking up at his halo of curly hair, the sky beyond. He stroked my cheek with a finger as thick as a bell rope. "Do you want to come with us?" he said.

How was I to know what he offered? For all I knew, the world terminated at those distant peaks, and every village had a Karl Victor. If someone had told me that there were but a thousand men in the wide world, I would have thought, *My God! So many!* But I saw in this face above me such a look of hope. *Say yes*, his eyes said. *Tell me you need me. I will not fail.*

I wanted to go home to my mother.

"Nicolai, listen to me, you have made a vow—"

"I can make another."

"That is not how it works. Such vows are perpet—"

"I vow—"

"Nicolai, don't. You can take him until we find a safe place to leave him, but don't—"

Nicolai looked into my eyes. Such kindness. But where was my mother? Still lying on the floor of our hut?

"I vow," he said, "that whatever happens, I will protect you."

Remus groaned. He began to say more, but Nicolai could not hear him, because suddenly, as though my mother had felt my yearning, the bells of Nebelmatt began to ring. Nicolai and Remus both cringed as the pealing shook them to their cores. Remus hunched his shoulders and stuck a dirty finger in each of his ears. Nicolai covered one side of my head with a huge palm and pressed my other ear against his chest, but I struggled until he put me down. I stepped down to the bank of the Reuss and looked up at the mountains. My mother was alive!

I ignored the kind man who had saved me from the river. Remus tried to pull him away, but Nicolai just stood and covered his ears and watched me—the little boy who was clearly not harmed by this sound that shook the ground beneath our feet.

My mother was well enough to have pulled herself off the muddy floor and climb to her bells! She played them now so fiercely it was as though she played the mountains themselves with her mallets.

A quarter hour passed, and then the same again. Remus stuffed his ears with scraps of wool and took out a book. Nicolai just watched me—fingers plugging his ears—as if I were a wild beast he had never glimpsed before. My mother rang her bells far longer than she was allowed. It had been many years since she was beaten for such excess. Now, I knew, the Nebelmatters crouched behind their doors, switches in their hands, ready to climb to the church as soon as it was safe.

And still she played the bells. She stroked them more ferociously than I had ever heard. There was almost no pause between the strikes. Then I heard a sudden change: she had cracked the soundbow of the smallest bell. Still she did not stop.

I heard that she was calling *him*. As my father struggled back up the rocky path, drenched in mud and sweat and shame, he would have heard the pealing as a judgment resounding throughout the world. And he would have hated her for every ring, just as he hated her for tempting him, for exposing his sin with a child, and for making him a murderer. With each ring, he must have sworn that he would silence her.

She taunted him up the muddy track with the promise she would sound his guilt until he stopped her. I am sure she watched him coming, but she did not slow or soften the ringing. Tears ran down my face and I screamed for my mother. "I am here!" I yelled. "I am alive!" But even Nicolai could not hear me. She beat those bells louder still, daring my father to climb to her tower and make her stop. In this tempest, the ground rumbled and the river crashed its waves around our feet, and I closed my eyes and imagined at the center of it all, my mother pounding her bells, summoning my father.

Twenty years later, when I would first return to that valley, the legend of the priest who had saved the ears of Nebelmatt was still recounted in every tavern. They took me for a foreigner and told me of the gentle priest and the evil witch who laid siege to the town from her belfry, who rang the bells day and night until the villagers began to lose their minds. They told me how the holy priest climbed the track to that church and disappeared inside—God had given him unearthly courage. From the village, they saw his silhouette leap through the trapdoor into the belfry. She danced around him, striking her bells until his ears were blown useless by the noise. And then, in his silent world, he lunged at her, the nimble demon, as she darted among the devil's bells. He grabbed her gown, nearly fell, tottered on the edge of the belfry, hanging on the merest scrap of fabric in his fist. He yelled for her help. She leapt at him, as if she would embrace him. Then every eye in the village watched them fall.

No new priest was ever sent for. The bells were melted back into hoes.

But on that day, standing by that river, as I screamed up to my mother that I lived, what I imagined was very different. She struck her bells so hard that there, at the center of that noise, I was sure the world began to lose its firmness, the waves of sound rent apart my parents' every fiber. I alone, above the pealing, heard my father's scream echo off the mountains. Perhaps this was the moment his eardrums burst. But that child was certain his father screamed because his body was torn apart by the waves.

The bells did not ring again. Was she gone? Somehow I knew she was. The echoes around me hummed for several minutes. Just as every drop of ocean water was once a drop of rain, I heard then that every sound in the world had once been in my mother's bells: the tinkling river, the whoosh of swallows darting after flies, the warm breath of the kind monk standing behind me. She was gone and she was everywhere.

Nicolai gently coughed. He lifted me as I crumpled into his arms. With each cry and sob, he held me tighter. When Remus opened his mouth to protest, Nicolai simply showed him a giant palm. The ugly monk closed his mouth and shook his head. Nicolai carried me to the road, where stood the three largest horses I had ever seen. Remus slunk after us. Nicolai swung both of us onto the lead horse, and placed me between his massive thighs.

"Hold tight," he said. I could not see anything to hold, and as the horse took his first rocking step, I yelled in fright and tried to leap to the safety of the ground. Nicolai pulled me back. I closed my eyes, sloshing tears down my cheeks, and tried to picture my mother's face, but I could not hold it in my mind. Instead, for comfort, I listened to the hollow thump of Nicolai's gentle kicks into the horse's ribs, the slurp of the monstrous hooves in the mud, the swish of the horse's mane. And I looked ahead, down the bleary road, and wondered how far my mother's bells had reached.

We turned off the road at Gurtnellen, and in that town of three hundred souls, I thought we had reached the center of the universe. Men wore clothes that were gray or white instead of brown. One of them withdrew a watch, and I took its tick-tick-tick as the beating heart of some tiny pocket beast. A lady, leaving a house made of stone, opened a parasol—*whoop*—that made me clasp Nicolai's thick arm in fright.

Remus muttered to Nicolai that a naked boy on a monk's lap was a sight that could cause us trouble, and so, from a tailor, Nicolai bought me linen underclothes and woolen breeches. The linen was as soft as a feather, but the breeches were as uncomfortable as Karl Victor's belt around my neck. Later, we went into a tavern and ate plates of steaming stew and drank wine. After eight or ten glasses of the sour stuff, Nicolai stood with one foot on his chair. "Gentlemen," he said to the traders and farmers in the room, "let me teach you what I learned in Rome." He clapped his huge hands together, dropped his chin, and, in a booming bass, sang such a silly song in a language I took for gibberish that I smiled for the first time in many days. The other men in the room cheered and clapped, but Remus turned red and, after a second song, pulled us on our way.

We slept in inns along the road. I wrapped myself in blankets on the floor, and Nicolai and Remus slept in beds. When I sniffled in the night, Nicolai always woke and curled beside me on the floor, whose planks creaked beneath him. "Little Moses," he'd whisper in my ear, "this is a massive world, full of joys, each one just waiting for you to claim. Don't worry, there's nothing more to fear. Nicolai is with you now."

On the third day, we passed out of Canton Uri into Canton Schwyz, and walked along Lake Lucerne, which I knew must be full of fearsome beasts. But even the imagined monsters of those depths were more familiar to me than the civilization we encountered. The world was so much vaster than I had ever envisioned. I stored every sound away with the frantic urgency of the miser who finds a money box spilled in the street: the lap of waves, the oarlock's whine, the soldiers' measured march, the boom of their musket practice, the wheezing of a plough through mud, the wind through a field of spring oats. Traders passed us speaking a thousand different tongues, and Nicolai told me how they had crossed the Alps to Italy.

Along the road, beggars swarmed around our horses and strained toward Nicolai and Remus with bony fingers, moaning like goats. Nicolai threw them coppers. Remus made as if he did not hear them cry. I feared they would pull me off the saddle and cook me in a stew. I began to understand that in this world there were a million people with a million fates, most of them unlucky. And here was I—no father, no mother, no home I could return to.

VI.

In the mornings, Nicolai woke us with his chanting of Matins. He was fastidious in his observance of the Holy Offices, steadfast in his completion of the weekly Psalm cycle. He carried no other book on his journey than a thin, leather-bound *Rule of St. Benedict*, which he did not need, for he had committed it to heart through daily readings over almost forty years. Remus and I stayed in bed until he had finished his prayers. Then we breakfasted on porridge, great hunks of cheese, and ale.

Each day, as we mounted our horses, we observed a moment of silence, our hearts heavy with our future, but Nicolai always relieved us quickly of this burden. He began to talk, and did not cease until the candle was blown out at night and we were asleep.

"Have you ever been to Rome?" he asked me on one of our first days together. Remus snorted at the question. I shook my head.

"What a place! One day we will go together, Moses—you, me, and the wolf. Despite his heart aching for his own bed, Remus surely wants to return. You see, in Rome they have whole libraries full of books no one reads—that's why the abbot let us go. Remus has taken it upon himself to read every book in the entire world, no matter how boring or useless the material."

"This from a man who believes that libraries should offer their patrons wine," Remus muttered without looking up.

"And well they should," Nicolai said. "Then I would gladly stop by to read a page or two." He spread his arms wide and leaned gently back so he could bask for a moment in the sun. His laughter shook the horse. "But just for a few minutes! There are enough books in Saint Gall for me—more than enough. Rome, Moses! *Rome!* The dust of gods lingering in every corner! Such music! Opera! How could I waste a moment with a book!"

He told me that we were on our way back to their home, this

St. Gall, which was so named because a man called Gallus from a place called Ireland had gotten a fever and stumbled into a forest there more than a thousand years before. The place was an abbey—a word repeated often between Nicolai and Remus, and so I was eager to learn its meaning. Other facts I gleaned about this place: its cellars were stocked with the world's finest wines; the beds were softer than any in Rome; it had the greatest library in the land, and Remus had read every book in it (Nicolai had read three); it had a distasteful thing called an abbot, which was a man named either Coelestin von Staudach or Choleric von Stuckduck—which, I could not be sure. Mostly Nicolai referred to him only as Stuckduck.

Nicolai told me that most people called Remus Dominikus, but that his friends (of which there was only one at present, but I could be the second if I wished) knew that his real name was Remus and that he had been raised by wolves. I did not doubt it: Remus continued to scowl at me at regular intervals, though as we rode, his face was mostly hidden by his book; his horse seemed well trained to follow Nicolai's. On several occasions Nicolai instructed Remus to read aloud to us, and the sounds he spoke were like magic spells in some wizard's language. I was always thankful, when, after a minute or two, Nicolai would interrupt him and say, "Remus, that is enough. Moses and I are bored."

Though Nicolai spoke so fondly of the abbey, he lamented the end of their travels. The day we left Lake Lucerne behind and began to ascend into the hills, Nicolai suddenly stopped the horses. "Remus," he said, "I have changed my mind."

"Do not stop so abruptly," Remus said, not looking up from his book. "It makes me sick."

Nicolai stared back into the southern horizon, as if he saw something troubling there. "We must turn back," he said. "I do indeed wish to visit Venice."

Remus looked up sharply. The name of that city clearly alarmed him. "Nicolai, it is too late for that. Months too late. We decided for the abbey."

"I gave in too easily. I should have *made* you go."

"Nicolai, continue on." Remus spoke as if to a child.

"Remus, I must visit Venice before I die." Nicolai banged his fist into his thigh.

"Another time." Remus looked cautiously back down at his book.

Nicolai pulled our horse so close to Remus's that his knee rubbed that of the other monk. The reading monk did not look up, though he twitched his leg away. At the same moment, Nicolai reached over and snatched the book.

The two monks looked into each other's eyes. "And what if we never leave the abbey for the rest of our lives?" Nicolai asked.

Remus did not reply. He held out his empty hand until Nicolai passed back the book. He opened it again. "I hope it will be so," he said, and began to read again. He kicked his horse and it ambled past us.

Nicolai called after him. "You are so dull. I am talking about *Venice*, Remus. The most beautiful city in the entire world. And we just let it pass us by."

Remus spoke into his book. "It will be dark soon."

"I think I could find peace there," Nicolai whispered, almost to himself. When I looked up, I almost believed the giant was about to cry. He looked down at me, and we smiled at each other. In my face I hoped he saw, *But Nicolai, I will go!* It seemed I gave the big man courage, for he kicked our horse and we drew even with Remus again.

"In Venice it will all be different."

"Don't be such a fool." With a snap, Remus turned a page. "Forty years a monk and still such idolatry. Just another excuse."

"Then take me there; then I won't have any more excuses left. I will stop bothering you."

"You will find another reason for your discontent. Everyone always does."

Nicolai stopped our horse again. He shook his head. "You, at least," he muttered, "don't need excuses to be unhappy."

Remus closed his book and looked over his shoulder at Nicolai. I thought I saw a smile—a flash of affection—break that scowl, but then it was gone. "Nicolai, do not stall in what we long ago agreed upon."

Nicolai looked back for a moment more, as if he could see the fork toward Venice, which was in fact hundreds of miles behind us on the other side of the Alps, and then he turned toward his home and spurred on his horse.

"My dear Moses," Nicolai said to me one particularly beautiful morning, soon after we had mounted. "There are monks and there are monks. I am a monk. Remus here is a monk, and Abbot Choleric von Stuckduck is a monk. We chant the same chants, pray the same prayers, and drink the same wine. We are of the same flesh, one could say." We were passing from forest to pasture and back again, slowly climbing away from the vast lake glittering behind us. Nicolai reached out his hand and brushed the saplings alongside the track. "Our souls, too, Moses, should be the same, right? But no, Abbot Stuckduck's is a shriveled dried-out thing, and mine is fattened like a pig." He thumped his round gut. "And so one of us must be *on the wrong path*, as the little man so likes to say. But what we'd all like to know is who is right and who is wrong?"

He poked a huge finger into my knee. "It's my heart against his head, Moses. He'd say as much if you asked him, though I wouldn't if I were you."

For several minutes none of us spoke and Nicolai hummed some Italian march. He reached down and snatched a dead branch. He swung it at the brambles growing along the track. "You see, Moses," he continued suddenly, "I've got a lot to lose. I love so many things. *Too many*, the abbot would say. *Too much. Shed a little love*, he'd suggest. *Cure yourself of that sin*. But that's exactly what I'm afraid of, don't you see? That's exactly my biggest fear, what keeps me awake every night. What I fear is this: I'll wake up the next morning and everything is just the same, the world is the world, but all the love I feel for it has vanished, and I realize that all along my love was only a disease—like smallpox of the soul." Nicolai looked at his friend riding beside us. "Could that happen, Remus?" Remus did not answer, so Nicolai prodded him in the ribs with the branch.

"Yes, it could," Remus grumbled. "It probably will tomorrow."

Nicolai raised the branch, hesitated for a moment, and then swung it at the other horse's thigh. The horse darted forward, Remus grabbed his pommel and just barely managed both to stay in his saddle and to keep his book from falling into the mud. I put my hand in front of my mouth to mask my laughter. When Remus was stable again, he turned angrily to Nicolai, but Nicolai held up a hand. "You're just trying to hurt me, Remus. You don't even believe what you say." He swished the branch through the air like a sword. Remus cringed.

Remus seemed very ugly to me then, and I wished he'd ride farther on. I did not understand what Nicolai meant, but I liked listening to him talk. Nicolai must have seen me cross my arms in displeasure, because he put a hand on my shoulder. "Don't let his grumbling trick you," he said, "he's not half as mean as he wants you to believe." And then he leaned closer still, and spoke low so the reading monk could not hear. "That wolf believes in love as much as any man in the world. As much as I do. I've heard him whisper that he does, just as I, too, have whispered it, just as you will one day whisper to someone, when you feel that flash, as two halves become one."

Suddenly Remus's book was closed. He stared angrily at Nicolai. "Careful whom you tell your secrets to," he said.

Nicolai reddened, but then he shrugged and splintered his branch on a passing tree. "Don't worry, Remus," he said. "We can trust Moses with our secrets."

VII.

Abbot Coelestin Gugger von Staudach turned out to be a small man whose most distinctive feature was his giant forehead, which took up over half the canvas of his face, and behind which must have pulsed a massive brain. "A peasant novice in this abbey?" he asked when Nicolai explained why he had brought this child to his office. "An orphan novice?"

Nicolai nodded eagerly. Remus looked at the polished oaken floor.

The abbot stood up from his long desk. Like Nicolai and Remus, he, too, wore a black tunic, though over it hung a black, hooded robe. A golden cross shone at his chest, and as he approached me, I stared at the red stone glimmering on his finger. I would have backed away, but I was already cowering up against a wall. He peered at my bare feet, at my dusty clothes, at the smudges Nicolai had not washed off my face. He sniffed.

"Surely not," he said.

"He's quiet," said Nicolai. "He's . . . he's small." Nicolai spread his hands as if to show the size of a modest fish.

The abbot stared down at me. His breath was shallow, and rushed mechanically like bellows at a forge. In, out. In, out. Until now, every sound I had heard in the enormous world—from the blast of soldiers' muskets to a woman singing at her window—I was sure I could trace back to the endless depths of my mother's bells. But I was also sure that somewhere in this world, the sounds of my father, torn apart and scattered in the flood, also were preserved. The moment I heard this breath, I knew from whence this man's sounds had come.

We had traveled through the abbey's lands for the final four days of our journey, for the Abbey of St. Gall was the vastest and richest in the Swiss Confederation. Its abbot answers to no man, Nicolai had explained to me as he swept his hand to indicate the rolling hills, neither king above nor republic below. When we entered the gates of the Protestant city, which surrounded the abbey like a shell around a nut, I gasped. The streets were wide and paved with even cobbles, the high half-timbered houses blazing white. The men and women of the city were tall, beautiful, and proud, with woolen and linen costumes, frills of airy muslin. The sounds of industry filtered from every cellar, every lane: the creak and slide of the loom, the clang of silver and golden coins, the rumble of carts laden with bolts of sun-bleached linen. As we penetrated the city, the houses grew only higher, more majestic: white stone buildings like the cliffs above my mother's church.

Finally the three of us had reached a gate guarded by two soldiers, who stepped aside at the sight of the two returning monks, and we passed into the vast Abbey Square. Nicolai reached out his hand to touch Remus lightly at his elbow, just two fingers and his thumb on the fabric of his tunic. The touch remained an instant, as the men regarded their home for the first time in two years, and then Remus turned to see me watching them.

He jerked his arm away.

The square had space enough for ten thousand souls. It was bordered by three vast wings of cream-colored stone, each as grand as a palace, with so many windows, every one as high as the door on Karl Victor's house. And in the middle of the space was an enormous pit in which two dozen men were raising walls of massive blocks of stone. Nicolai touched my shoulder and pointed toward the pit.

"Look, Moses," he said. "They've begun—in a few years that will be Europe's most beautiful church."

I nodded, though the enormous hole looked nothing like the church I had known. Nicolai took my hand and led me into the vast square. *Some perfect beings must inhabit this palace*, I thought, and I hoped they would let me sleep here on the grass.

But in the abbot's chamber, as he glared down at me, I finally understood my position. He was, indeed, the perfect being, and I was merely a stain that must be wiped away.

"The orphanage in Rorschach," he said, and nodded with a grunt.

"No!" said Nicolai, surely louder than he intended. Remus cringed. The big monk stepped forward and the wooden floor creaked under his massive feet. Remus tugged a warning at his sleeve, but Nicolai shook him off.

"He can stay with me," Nicolai continued.

The abbot's displeased gaze rose from my face to Nicolai's.

"In my cell. He can be my servant."

I pictured myself carrying Nicolai's wine, putting on his shoes, rubbing his shoulders when he was tired. For a home in this magnificent place, I would do all that and more.

"Monks do not have servants."

"Father Abbot," said Nicolai, and smiled as if the abbot had made a jest. "Where is your heart?"

The abbot cast one more reproving look my way. *This is all your fault,* I understood his eyes to say, *all of it—your dead mother, your evil father, the dirt your calloused feet leave on my pristine floors.* And I did feel sorry—had I had the courage to speak, I would have asked for his forgiveness for everything, and then I would have begged him not to send me away, because Nicolai was now the one person left in the world whom I trusted, and I did not want to be taken from him just as I had been taken from my mother.

But of course I said none of this. I was too terrified even to stand upright.

And then the abbot approached Nicolai. He was not old, but he moved as if every step he took on our behalf were a burden. Nicolai slouched to meet his glare.

"I will have you back at this monastery, Brother Nicolai, because I must, though I know you do not share our path. It is a difficult path. Some are destined to wander. I hoped that you would wander farther. I hoped, these two years, that you would not return. But return you have. You will see, that in the time you have been gone, here at this abbey we have *progressed.*" He gestured through the window to the workers in the pit, then moved even closer to Nicolai, glaring up at him.

Nicolai cocked his head as if to hear a secret. "I advise you to look for this progress, Brother Nicolai," the abbot said. "Look for it in your brothers' faces, in their works, in the sermons that we preach, in the songs we sing. Look for it in the new church we are building. And do not simply look, Brother Nicolai, but consider. Do you have anything to contribute to this beauty? To the culmination of God's will? Or do you impede it? Are you standing in the way of what God has destined for this abbey?"

Nicolai opened his mouth to speak, closed it, and then looked at Remus as if to gain a hint as to which of the several questions he was meant to answer. The abbot shook his head and grunted. He turned away and waved a hand as he went back to his desk. "You may stay here, if you wish," he said. "You may leave—choose that, and I will give you gold to take with you." Then the abbot turned back again. He raised a finger at Nicolai. "But if you wish to stay, do not obstruct us. And know that I am watching, am waiting until I have reason enough to bar you from this abbey, and to send letters to every abbot within five hundred miles so you will never again receive a drop of abbey wine."

The room seemed to spin a bit. I realized I had forgotten to breathe. I took several careful breaths as the abbot's eyes stayed fixed on Nicolai's. Nicolai looked from the cold eyes to the abbot's pointed finger and back again. The giant monk looked so meek and kind. For a moment, I almost believed that he would take the small abbot in his arms and embrace him. Could he melt that frigid stare? Nicolai glanced briefly at Remus, as if offering the bookish monk a chance to resolve this slight misunderstanding between brothers. But Remus said nothing. So Nicolai cleared his throat, and a look of uncertainty flashed across his face.

"F-father Abbot," he began.

But the abbot held up a hand and said slowly, softly, "Take this boy to the orphanage in Rorschach, or depart."

.   .   .

Remus led us in single file back out to the Abbey Square.

"It could have been worse," Nicolai said when the porter had closed the great door behind us. I made sure to stay as close as possible to Nicolai's giant legs so no one would snatch me away. "He did not mention that we were late returning, or that we spent all his money and borrowed more in his name, or that you angered every monk in Rome with your wisdom of the Scots, or that I lost—"

"I have told you before," Remus said, "'Father Abbot' is redundant. It means 'father father.'"

"He likes it."

"He likes you to sound the fool."

Nicolai snorted. "He will see to that one way or another."

For a moment the two monks gazed at the pit out of which the new, perfect church was rising, as if it were the source of all our troubles. "Well, then, Socrates, what shall we do?" Nicolai asked. I turned toward the wolfish monk, realizing that this unattractive man was my second best friend in the world.

"What shall we do?" Remus repeated.

"You must have an idea."

"Nicolai, an orphanage."

"The orphanage," corrected Nicolai, "was Stuckduck's idea. I will not send Moses to a workhouse." He smiled and winked down at me, but I could not bring myself to smile back.

"Nicolai, it's the only solution."

"We'll just have to wait, then," said Nicolai. He shrugged and patted me on the head. "Give God a chance to find another."

Nicolai's cell, on the second story of the monks' dormitory, was paneled in oak. A desk, two chairs, a divan upholstered in brown velvet, and several low tables were placed around the edge of a woolen carpet, which, when I stepped on it, warmed my bare feet like stones placed around a fire. At one end of the room was a massive bed and wardrobe, and at the other, a fireplace. Nicolai held me up so I could see myself in the mirror above the marble fireplace—clearer than the clearest puddle. When he caught me admiring the two silver candlesticks on the mantel, he took one down and gave it to me. "It's yours," he said. "One is enough for me." I thanked him, but then, when he turned around, shyly placed it on a table.

Nicolai slowly unpacked, laying out for my inspection each of the treasures he had acquired during his travels: a pearly shell, a leather wallet stuffed with tickets from the many operas he had seen, a wooden flute he told me he would one day learn to play, a lock of yellow hair that made Nicolai's neck flush red when the golden ends glinted in the sun.

He unrolled a watercolor and asked me if it was not the most beautiful picture I had ever seen. I gasped at the image of Venice's Grand Canal. I hadn't known any place on earth could be so colorful. Nicolai propped it on his table. We stared at it for several seconds, and then he turned toward me, his face suddenly very grave. "Moses," he said. "It is very important that you not be seen by anyone but Remus. This is not forever, but we must give God time to tell us what to do. If you hear a knock, you must hide in there." He pointed at the wardrobe and then had me practice lying very still inside it.

That night, I slept on the divan. Nicolai snored in his bed. In the morning, a knock at our door came at a quarter to four, and Nicolai roared himself awake as if to scare away the devil sleep that pinned him to his bed. At four he was in the provisional wooden church for Matins and Lauds. I heard his voice rise up above the rest. So it went for several days. I heard that he alone was never late for these early morning chants, that his sonorous voice never wavered. As I lay on my divan listening to the sleeping city outside our window, I heard Nicolai's brimming voice as if the chants were always fresh creations of his mind, not recitations of works centuries old.

Prime, then Low Mass, then Terce, then High Mass, then Sext—it all lasted until half past ten in the morning. Then came the midday meal, from which Nicolai brought me what he called scraps, but to me they were the greatest feasts ever imagined: thick slabs of succulent lamb or beef, smoked pork, blood sausage, cheese, grapes, apricots, apples, almonds. He hid these treasures in his pockets and placed them on my lap for me to devour. As I fed, we sipped from a jug of wine, of which each monk was allowed two mass per day, but Nicolai took somewhat more. "My girth," he said, banging his stomach, "requires it. The two-mass rule is for people of Stuckduck's stature." At three, Nicolai left for Vespers, and again his chanting rose up above the city. He would appear once more at the door just before seven, rosy from supper and wine, and leave me another feast to dispose of alone while he chanted Compline, which, under the influence of his satiation, reached the highest elation of any of the Offices.

At eight the monks retired, which meant that Nicolai returned, often with Remus, or, if not, with a loquacious tongue that spoke or sang until the night grew dark. Sometimes another monk knocked on the door, curious to see with whom Nicolai was speaking. If he had drunk only his allowance, he would call out that he was a lonely monk who liked to speak to the walls sometimes, but if he had drunk more, he would roar at the door, "Go away! The prophet Moses speaks with me alone! Be gone, you fool!"

I thought every day of my mother, and wept so much I stained Nicolai's divan with my salty tears, but I did not regret my confinement, since it was not unlike my former life in the belfry. I did not grasp my new peril as I listened to the distant city, to the monks chatting in their cloister below, or to the stonemasons chiseling at the blocks of stone in the walls of the new church. There was a new sound as well, that was a mystery to my ears. I went to the open window, like a dog following the scent of meat. When the air was still, I blocked out every other sound and tried to grasp it, but this new sound was too fragile to be held like other sounds. My hold on one part slipped away, and its other parts vanished, too. The strands of this new sound were built upon each other, like a gathering of poppies on a hillside viewed from a distance; the single blossoms are invisible, but in combination, they light the hillside red.

Each afternoon I heard it. Perhaps this was the God of whom Nicolai had spoken? Not Karl Victor's frightful God, but a God of beauty and of joy. The God who would find a way for me to stay in this beautiful and perfect place.

And then, on Sunday morning, my sixth day in Nicolai's room, the sound was suddenly louder, and instead of coming from the sky, it seemed to come from every direction: through the walls, down the passage, through the keyhole. God was coming closer, and I could not miss Him. And so, six days after we arrived in the abbey, I broke Nicolai's interdiction. I left his cell.

VIII.

I held my ear to the keyhole until I was sure the passage was empty. Then I opened the door. I closed my eyes and listened for a footfall or the abbot's sawing breath. My legs trembled as I took a step onto the smooth wooden floor of the vast passage.

The sound was louder here. It was composed of human voices; now I was sure of that. They were singing. I tried to count them. One moment there were two, then eight, and then I heard at least . . . twelve? Then again only two. And for a moment, only a single voice remained, and I doubted I had ever heard any others.

I descended the wide stairwell. Compared to Nicolai's room, these new spaces were huge. I did not make a noise, and there were no other human sounds in the abbey, except for these voices. The workmen had ceased their work. No monks paced the cloister. I heard only the wind. It was as if all the humans of the world had vanished.

I crept into the cloister. The damp grass was cold on my bare feet. Across the pit of the new church stood the vacant Abbey Square. I stopped. One voice began anew, alone, and then, moments later, another voice uttered the same phrase, and then another voice and another, all nearly the same, yet not quite: faster, or more slowly, or sung with different notes. I grew dizzy trying to sort it out. Surely these must be angels singing.

I squeezed my eyes shut so tightly they began to ache. Swirls of pinkish light danced with the magic voices. And suddenly it all made sense. A realization stirred inside me. In the clanging of my mother's bells, I had already heard this beauty—in flashes of random harmony. And these men and boys who sang, they had learned what was surely a magic feat. They could work that ocean of sound, infinite and overwhelming, and mold it into something beautiful. And I realized that I, too, could know this magic. Perhaps I did already.

I passed the edge of the new church's pit and walked through a tunnel made of planks that led across the Abbey Square to the provisional wooden church. I followed the sounds to a high oaken door. I heaved it open with all my might.

I should have seen the simple church packed with monks and laity, the two groups separated by a wooden fence. I should have seen the Choir of St. Gall singing before the altar. I should have been alarmed enough to run. But the opening of the door released a flood of sound, and for a moment I knew nothing but this music. I belonged to my ears.

The moments of discordance made me ache. When the voices lined up in thirds, they warmed my neck and back. I closed my eyes and heard the music. I felt the slight resonance of their song in my jaw and in my temples. I felt it in my tiny chest, and when I exhaled, I sighed, and so the slight ringing of my voice mingled with the music. My sigh was a spark. My voice sprang to life. I moaned, trying to find the notes to match my tiny body's ringing with this beauty.

I did not know the words, or even that what they sang were words, so I spat whatever sounds came upon my lips. One moment I felt the ecstasy of harmony, then the next, a cold tingle in my spine, as my noise clashed with their song. I sang as a puppy runs with hounds—frantically, ecstatically, foolishly—until suddenly I realized that the singing had stopped. I was moaning into shocked silence.

A hand slapped my head so hard that stars flashed across my eyes. I fell to my knees. The great door opened, the hand lifted me by the neck, and I was thrown out of the church and into the dirt.

I ran. I scrambled up the stairs. Each doorway I rushed past looked identical to the ones before it, and I tried five before I found the one that I had sought. I hid in the wardrobe and pulled one of Nicolai's black woolen tunics over me. It was terribly hot, and soon I was sweating and gasping for air. But I remained there until two pairs of footsteps entered the room. One I recognized as Nicolai's heavy tread. The other—I heard that breathing. The bellows at a forge.

The door slammed shut.

"Father Abbot—" Nicolai began.

"I should expel you from the abbey," Abbot Coelestin roared. "Hiding a child in your cell!"

"He has no place to go," Nicolai pleaded. He whispered as if he did not wish to be overheard. "If you would only accept him as a—"

"Do you hear me?" the abbot shouted. "Expulsion! What would you do then? Sing for your food?"

"Father Abbot, please."

"Where is he?"

There was silence in the room. Very, very slowly I leaned so I could peer out through the crack between the wardrobe doors. Glaring up at giant Nicolai, the abbot looked almost like an angry child.

Nicolai shrugged his massive shoulders. "Perhaps he ran away."

The abbot's glare held fast.

"Abbot, please. Do not punish this boy for what I have done." Nicolai laid a hand on the abbot's shoulder.

Without unfixing his eyes, the abbot grasped Nicolai's wrist. He lifted it from off his shoulder. Nicolai grimaced as the abbot's claws dug into his flesh. The abbot spoke slowly, carefully forming every word. "You seem to think that charity is as plentiful as air." He flung Nicolai's arm away.

Nicolai rubbed his wrist. "One boy cannot hurt."

The abbot seemed not to hear him.

Nicolai put his palms together. "Abbot," he said. "Please, I beg you."

That face! Was there ever one so large that was so innocent? So kind? It seemed to say to the abbot, *But we are brothers, you and I!*

"Beg me?" the abbot said, surprised by the suggestion. He looked about the room. "Beg me for what? Nicolai, I have already given you everything there is to give. I have given you a room princes would be happy to live in. I have given you food. I have given you more wine than any man should drink. I am building you the greatest church in the Confederation. And you? What have you given me? What have you given this abbey? You pray. You eat. You chant. You drink. You sleep. Nothing more."

Nicolai spoke weakly, "Saint Benedict said—"

"Saint Benedict?" The abbot snorted. He drove a thumb into his own chest. "You quote Saint Benedict to me? Go be a hermit like Saint Benedict, Nicolai. There are caves enough for you and your Dominikus. And while you, far away, live like the saints of the past, we will continue to strive to be the saints of the future."

There was silence in the room as the abbot drew a long, calming breath and lowered his voice. "Here, Nicolai, we have mouths to feed. We have souls to save. The peasants in my lands would like one day to know what beauty is, for once in their lives to see and hear and taste God's glory here on earth as you have every day of your wasted life in this abbey. You see, I can tolerate useless monks, Nicolai, if I must. If Dominikus wants to read and translate books that no one else cares about, all very well. If you were only a useless monk then I would simply leave you here in this cell until you died, and then I would fill it with a monk who could be of use to God."

"Abbot, you do not mean wha—"

"I do." The abbot nodded coldly as he advanced another step. "And if you ever cross me again, Nicolai, if you ever show me the faintest sign that you are anything other than the useless, archaic monk I have come to tolerate, I will make sure that every monastery in Europe knows never to let you through their gate."

Nicolai's jaw hung open. He gave a tiny nod. "Yes, Abbot," he whispered.

The abbot wiped his brow with a handkerchief drawn from a pocket. He took several breaths and then he tipped his giant forehead as if to say he was satisfied with the culmination of the discussion. He looked around the room. His eyes fell on the watercolor of Venice propped on the table. Without examining it closely, he lifted it, creased a fold through the middle with his fingernails, and tore it in two. Nicolai merely cringed at the rip. The abbot placed the scraps back on the table and looked at Nicolai. "Now get me that boy," he said.

There was silence. Then Nicolai spoke in a low whisper: "I cannot."

I wished I could dissolve into sound.

"Then I will get him myself."

Footsteps crossed to the wardrobe. The door opened, and I felt the cloth lifted off of me. I kept my eyes shut, but I heard his breath above me. Fingers grabbed me by the hair and I cried against the pain, but he just pulled harder until I was on my feet and next to Nicolai's bed.

Nicolai stood in the middle of the room. He slouched as if he carried a sack of potatoes on his shoulders. "I am so sorry," he said to me.

"You are forgiven," said the abbot. "For now."

"Abbot," said Nicolai. He stepped forward and reached out a hand as if to grasp me. "Let me find a place for him, I will find a farmer. I will—"

The abbot stuck a finger into Nicolai's face to stop him. "You will visit your Offices." He jabbed his finger again. "You will consider the wrong you have done this abbey. You will forget this boy. And I, I will take him to one of my orphanages and care for him just as I care for the other hundred thousand souls that are my charge. He shall have neither penalty nor advantage for the damage he has done today."

The abbot clamped my neck with two sharp fingers and pulled me out of the room. I began to cry.

He dragged me down the stairs, lifting me enough with his pincers that my feet only just skimmed each stair. "If you ever interrupt my Mass again," he whispered in my ear, "I will cut out your tongue and feed it to—"

"Stop!"

We turned. Nicolai stood at the top of the stairs. The potato sack had disappeared. There were tears in his eyes.

"You cannot do this," he said.

"Do you know what you are saying?" asked the abbot.

"Abbot, I vowed to protect that child."

For a moment, the abbot was speechless. I heard the breath catch in his throat. I felt his clamped hand shake with anger, as did his voice when he finally spoke. "You have a single vow, Brother Nicolai, and that is to *this* abbey. And so, let me make myself clear: You have a choice. You can return to your first and perpetual vow, and I will take this child where I please. Or you may sever that vow, and you and this child can leave the monastery together, immediately. I prefer the second option."

Nicolai's face was red, like when he was drunk. "Father, I beg forgiveness, I choose—"

His choice was never revealed, because at that moment we heard a fourth person stumbling up the stairs. "Praise God," this new voice said. "Abbot, you have found him."

IX.

"Ulrich von Güttigen," the yellow-skinned man gasped and held out a sweaty hand to me. "I am Regens Chori at the abbey." I shrank from the hand as though it too meant to pull me down the stairs. I recognized this man from the church. It was he who had stood before the singers I had tried to join.

"Yes, I have found him," said the abbot. He pushed me down another step so I stood between the two men. "And now he is off to Rorschach. He will not disturb us again."

"No!" the choirmaster said. He grabbed my arm.

The abbot tightened his fingers on my neck. "What do you mean?" he asked.

Ulrich looked from the abbot to Nicolai and back to the abbot. I tried to pry away my arm, but the choirmaster's hold was firm.

"For the choir, of course."

"The choir?"

"Yes."

In the silence that followed, I gave up my squirming and looked closely at this Ulrich von Güttigen. His yellow skin was taut and translucent, like the skin of a chicken plunged briefly in boiling water. His white hair, too, seemed to have been boiled off like feathers, and clung only behind his ears and on the top of his head in wisps.

Yet his looks did not strike me so much as his sounds. Though he heaved for air, his breath was a mere whisper, like a breeze under a door. His heart beat too quietly for me to hear, and though I strained for more clues by which to know him—rubbing hands or twisting feet or a click in his knees—I heard nothing.

"We need to hear him sing," Ulrich said. He pulled me toward him and chewed his lip in eagerness.

"We have heard him sing. Most disturbingly."

"A few notes, Abbot. Merely a glimpse, perhaps, of something extraordinary."

"Hear him," Nicolai interrupted.

The abbot and Ulrich turned to the large monk, who still stood at the top of the stairs.

"This does not concern you," the abbot said. But he turned back to the choirmaster and muttered, "Fine, we will hear the boy."

The four of us descended the stairs and wound through a series of unfamiliar corridors. Ulrich did not release my arm until we entered a large room with mirrors along one wall. A small stage ran across the other end of the room. In the room's center stood a device that appeared to me a coffin with three rows of keys at one end. I was afraid they meant to bury me alive in it. Ulrich placed a stool next to this casket and lifted me up onto it. He saw my frightened eyes staring down at the wooden box and said as kindly as his nervous voice could manage, "But have you never seen a harpsichord before?" He pressed one of the keys, and a beautiful, clear ringing filled the room. "You can sing that note, can't you, my boy?"

As the three men watched me eagerly, the stool felt like it might topple beneath me. Ulrich licked his lips and hit the key again. "That note." My mouth was dry, my tongue thick with dread.

"Sing," the abbot said. He slapped the back of his hand. "I do not have time for games." The key was hit again. Ulrich sang the note, his voice clear and cold.

"Go ahead, Moses," Nicolai said. He nodded, smiled, and raised his thick eyebrows as far as they would go. "They just want to hear you sing."

The abbot looked in disgust at Nicolai's smile and said coldly, "Boy, sing or you will never see Nicolai again."

Ulrich hit the key again, bowing with the gentle effort.

"Just that note," Nicolai urged me, as if the abbot had not spoken. "Just once."

I doubt that even an angel could have coaxed me into song. The twang of the harpsichord's string could have been a dog's bark for all I cared to mimic it. I would stand there until they took me down.

"He has had his chance," the abbot said. He grabbed me by the arm and would have pulled me from my perch, but Ulrich interrupted him.

"Alone," he said. He laid his pale hand on the abbot's. "Leave us alone. Then he will sing."

"Why would he do it alone with you if he will not sing when his future is at stake?"

"I need to speak with him."

The abbot threw up his arms. "Then speak!"

"Alone."

"Aagg!" the abbot bleated. "I do not have time for this. You have ten minutes. Then he will be on a wagon to Rorschach."

He left. Nicolai just watched him go, but did not move to follow.

"Please, Brother Nicolai." Ulrich gestured toward the door.

The large monk looked stricken at the thought of leaving me. "He is not afraid of me."

I nodded in agreement. I prayed my protector would not leave me alone with this man.

But Ulrich stepped to Nicolai and began to push him out. "I need to speak with him alone," he whispered gravely. "Please."

Nicolai shook his arm from the man's touch. "I vowed to protect him."

Ulrich spoke softly, firmly. "Leaving us alone is the best thing you can do for him. Stand outside the door, if you like."

Nicolai looked at me. He must have seen my wide eyes, my open mouth. I clenched my hands into fists. "Moses," he said. "He will not hurt you. I promise. Do what he says." But he looked pale and worried as he turned and stepped outside the door.

Then I was alone with this yellow man of so few sounds. He stood so close that I should have heard more—a squishing when he turned his neck, his tongue behind his teeth, his feet sliding on the wooden floor, a wetness in his throat as he exhaled. But all I heard was that gentle draft of air from his mouth. He studied my face, then bent closer.

"I heard you," he whispered, as if he were afraid Nicolai might overhear. "The others might have heard your voice. It's imperfect. It's not yet trained. But they are fools. I heard *you*. I heard your lungs. I heard you here." He reached up and, with a cold finger, gently traced the line of my throat. "You could not help it, could you? You would have burst if you had stayed silent another second?"

The choirmaster smelled like rotted hay. His nose was level with mine. I almost wished the abbot would come back and take me far away.

"I think you have heard me, too. I cannot sing like you, Moses. We have different gifts. But we fit together." Ulrich intertwined his fingers in front of my face.

I closed my eyes, terrified to look at him so close, willing him to disappear.

"The abbot cannot take you from me, Moses. I have heard you and you have heard me. God meant for us to meet."

He touched my throat again, this time with his full hand, as if he meant to choke me. But his cold touch was gentle. I swallowed hard.

"I can open your voice, Moses. I will. We can leave this abbey if you wish. We can go back from whence you came. But Moses, listen to me: the abbot, who is ready to send you to a filthy workhouse, will, the moment I say, give you the greatest luxury any boy like you could dream of. They need people like you and me, Moses."

As he whispered into my ear, I felt the warmth of his face against my skin. "They need us like they need their gold and their beautiful churches and their libraries. Do you want to see Nicolai again? Do you want to stay here? Or do you want to leave? It is no matter to me. I will share a horse's stall with you, if that is your choice. But if you want to stay, then sing."

Then Ulrich von Güttigen began to whisper a melody I had heard in the church that morning. His voice was not warm like the voices I had tried to accompany, but it moved lightly and precisely from one note to the next. When Nicolai sang, his whole body reverberated with the sound. In contrast, Ulrich von Güttigen was like a poorly constructed violin, whose strings vibrate perfectly but whose body resonates as weakly as a cask of wine.

Was this what Nicolai meant? Was this God's design? I had dreamed of something else, less repulsive than this soundless man and his entreaties. But perhaps God, it occurred to me, was not so good and perfect as the abbot claimed, and perhaps this man was all He could offer me.

And so I sang.

I chose one voice that I remembered from the church. At first my notes were soft and unsure, but I felt the sound spread outward from my throat, just as a bell's ring spreads quickly throughout the metal. The sound moved along my jaw, to the hollows below my ears. I felt it in my back, and downward to my navel. I sang no words, just sounds.

Ulrich's weak voice ceased as mine grew louder. He still held my neck, and then his hand probed downward. It stroked from my chin to my chest, like a doctor's cold instrument, and in that moment I felt that he was right; his hand seemed to open me. Its touch made my sounds fuller, like my mother's ringing bells. His other hand joined the first. He caressed my face, my chest. The hands reached around my back and held me tight, as if he wanted the sound to flow from me down to his yellowed, bony arms, into his empty chest. A sob escaped from his mouth, though there were no tears in those eyes. And then he stepped back and, for a moment, rose up on his toes, closed his eyes, and skewed his head violently, as if jolted by a sudden pain.

I stopped.

He stumbled backward and leaned against the harpsichord as if his legs would not hold him. His eyes were fixed on my face. I saw fear in his eyes. "My God," he said. "I am damned."

X.

And so my singing life began. I lay one last night on Nicolai's divan, and he spoke long into the morning of the splendor of my fortune. "You won't have to share a room anymore with an old, snoring monk," he said, and his smile was so sad one would have thought I was moving farther away than down the two flights of stairs. "You'll have friends your own age to play with. You'll laugh and run about. At night you'll whisper secrets to each other."

Even after Nicolai began to snore, I lay awake. His hope had infected me. I had never wanted for more when I lived with my mother, but now I realized I would have friends. Would we have fun? Would we play together as the children in the village had? Would I start to speak?

The next morning, Nicolai packed a parcel with two apples, some nuts, and a rosary, and put it in my hand. He opened his door and motioned for me to precede him out. I hesitated for a moment, and then reached up for the giant palm. I looked into his face. "Thank you, Nicolai," I said.

Tears leapt into his eyes and he took me in his arms.

He carried me down the stairs and along a hallway to where Ulrich waited outside the practice room. When Ulrich bade him leave us, Nicolai hugged me even tighter, then took a deep breath and set me down. He bit his lip, nodded, and tried to smile, and then turned and hurried away, never glancing back.

There had not yet been time to get me new clothes, and so I still wore the simple ones that Nicolai had bought for me several weeks before in Uri. I still had no shoes. When Ulrich opened the door, twelve pairs of prepubescent eyes had turned on me.

Ulrich told these boys what little he knew of me: that I was from a wild mountain village; that I had an extraordinary, untrained voice that one day might be the finest their choir had ever known. He said all this as if I were a bottle of fine wine about to be stored in the abbey's cellar.

"He is your brother now," Ulrich said to them, "and for as long as you and he remain in this choir. Help him to understand this world, which is so unfamiliar to him."

The boys nodded at their master. I watched this man who had repulsed me so, and now I felt such gratitude. I hadn't been so happy since before I lost my mother.

Next, Ulrich instructed a boy named Feder to lead us in warm-up exercises. He pushed me lightly toward the boys, and then left the room. The boys gathered about this Feder. "Hello," he said to me. He looked about my age, but taller. He smiled.

I nodded and smiled back—the warmest, most genuine smile the world had ever known. I thought to say something, but my mouth would not comply. I was too frightened that I might sound foolish in front of my new friends.

Feder walked toward me, still smiling, until he towered over me. I only reached his shoulders. Then the smile vanished from his face so suddenly I cringed in surprise. The boys behind him laughed.

"You may sing with us—if you can," he said. His eyes were as cold as his voice. "But you are not one of us." He peered down into my eyes as if looking for the signal that I understood, and I did not disappoint him. Tears began to pool. I struggled not to blink, but then I did, and two drops rolled down my cheeks. The boys snickered and shouted for him to knock me down, but he did not. As my tears flowed freely, he sniffed the air and said, "Does everyone in your family smell like a goat?"

And so my brief dream of friends my own age was abandoned almost as soon as I had conceived it. But I did not complain to Nicolai or to anyone else, for, as an orphan, what more could I expect? At noon I followed the pack of boys to the refectory. I took a plate of food, and in the other hand the largest, reddest apple I had ever seen. But then Feder appeared behind me, pinched my arm, and led me to a chair that faced the wall. "This is your seat," he whispered in my ear. "And that food is a gift from me. *A gift from me.* That peasant who does the spooning out—his cousin works on our estate." Feder pointed at the blank wall. "You'll look at that wall. If you dare turn around to look at us, I'll take my gift away. You say a word to my friends, I'll take my gift away. Understand?" He pinched my arm so hard I almost dropped my plate. "And this," he said, taking the apple from my other hand, "is not meant for those like you."

My bed was as soft and warm as my mother's embrace, and I would have slept the deepest sleep on it if only I had been allowed. Five other boys shared my room, and though Feder was not one of them, his orders were communicated. "What are you doing?" fat Thomas asked when he found me lying on my bed that first night. "Dogs sleep on the floor." He kicked me in the shin and again in my behind as I scrambled off the bed. No one complained when I sneaked up a hand to grab a blanket. I curled up underneath my bed, and fell asleep to the boys telling jokes about foul-smelling hounds.

The very next day Nicolai rushed into the practice room bearing new clothes and shoes for me. I turned red and the boys sniggered as he stripped me naked in the corner. But at least, it seemed to me, I looked just like them now. However, I soon learned that there were other signals of their supremacy too faint for me to read. These sons of officials, master weavers, or heirs to landed farmers had fathers, uncles, cousins with names that made the others lick their lips. Their parents merely stored them here in the choir for some years, hoping frequent contact with God and so much gold would prepare them for their destinies as landed gentry. And so it was their constant struggle to climb a ladder, which I anchored from the very bottom. Balthasar beat Thomas's term *dog* with *swine.* Proud Gerhard pretended not to see me, but ground his heel into my foot as he passed. Johannes, blond and angel-faced, saw me admiring the rosary Nicolai had gifted me. He made sure that the others were gathered around when he tore it from my hands, snapped the string, and scattered the beads down the passage. Hubert, a gaunt, yellow child with sunken eyes, who could not sing but was said to be the richest of the lot, had a devil's ear for

taunts. "Look, it's the giant monk's plaything," he said one night as I
entered the crowded room. And then to me: "I am sure you preferred
sleeping in *his* room." I turned red even though at the time I did not
understand the implication. I came to dread passing Nicolai when I
was with the boys. "Why does he always smile at you?" Feder would ask,
so innocently. "Perhaps tonight, *late at night*, you should visit him in his
room."

And when I began to sing with relish, Feder whispered to the
boys, "Look, he so wants to be *a singer*! Of course he does! But what
else lies open to those like him?" He turned to me. "Who did you say
your parents were? Did they keep swine?" For the first time in my life
I was ashamed of my mother. I knew a swineherd would have looked
down upon her. I feared that somehow Feder knew more than he said;
that cruel smile told me as much. He walked toward me, and though
I backed away, he wrapped an arm around my neck and drew me
tighter with each word. "Don't worry, boy," he growled. "In five years,
when that fine voice of yours is rough, and that vile monk doesn't
want you as his toy, there will still be pigs enough for you to tend."

We rose at six, long after the monks. After breakfast we rehearsed
until Mass, then studied pronunciation of the Latin texts, practiced
letters, and performed exercises until lunch. After a midday break,
Ulrich sat us on the floor around the harpsichord and supplied us with
sheets of paper and stubs of pencils. He pounded the keys, and the boys
stared blankly up at him. He explained the difference between the hy-
pophrygian and Ionian modes, or paced back and forth berating the
Council of Trent. Almost every day he'd poke a single finger into the
keys. "That's the monks," he'd say. "A thousand years the same: chro-
matic, mostly monophonic, with dashes of bravado slipped in by the
geniuses." And then he'd pound some chords. "It is all different now.
What you must learn to sing—polyphony. Heavy sonorities, contrasts.
Even if you cannot learn to hear it here," he tapped his head, "and most
of us never do, you must understand it, or you will remain brainless
tools, as stupid as this harpsichord." Then he'd play some Vivaldi and
tell us to write it down, which I could soon do as easily as other children could sketch a house with two windows and a door. The other boys

would peer over my shoulder and copy exactly what I wrote. When Ulrich's patience waned, he set us free until our rehearsal with the adult
singers and instrumental accompaniment, which continued until supper. In all those years, we learned neither mathematics nor French,
and what I know of the Bible and of God I learned only from the daily
sermons.

For the first six months after I joined his choir, though Ulrich
owned my days, he left me alone from supper until breakfast. But as I
learned to control my voice, he grew more frantic in his attention.
When we were lined up in front of our practice mirrors, it was always
I who saw him in my glass, just behind me, his eyes closed, as if he
were trying to catch the scent of my hair. Soon, rarely an evening
passed in which he did not linger outside the refectory door. He'd lay
a firm hand on my shoulder. "Moses," he'd say, "there was one last
thing I wished to show you," and then he'd lead me to the practice
room, his hand never straying from my shoulder. I loathed being
alone with him—his stink, his cold voice, his lack of human sounds.
Sometimes I thought I would have preferred to spend the time with a
corpse, for at least it could not have reached out to touch me.

Yet, just as I had learned to hear in the belfry, it was there, alone
with Ulrich in the studio, that I learned to master my voice. A goat
could have learned to sing if it had had the attention of that man! To
those who say I am a genius who appeared from nothing, my talent
needing no time to ripen—to them I say, *Practice! Practice!* There is no
other path to greatness.

In those many hours with Ulrich, I learned my fluid poise, exact
phrasing, precise pronunciation of the Latin. He would touch me.
His icy hands ran down my back or caressed my chest, sometimes
reaching down as far as the backs of my knees or up to my temples. It
was the kind of touch one might use to stroke a flower's petals. Ulrich's hand found those parts of me that were still quiet—he reached
the stubborn limits to my ringing. And so it seemed to me his touch
was magic, for the voice that first came only from my throat spread in
just seconds to my jaw, and with his yellowed hands on my chest and
back, soon song rang through me as though I were a bell. The hands

sought deeper. They found more song hidden in tightened thighs, in clenched fists, in the slumping arches of my feet. Mine was a tiny body, but he made it huge with song.

The first time he came at night, he stumbled into our room, tripped over a bed, and drove knees and elbows into the guts of sleeping boys. I crawled from beneath my bed and peeked across the room—a mole from out his hole. Ulrich shook Thomas. "Where is Moses?" he asked the boy, whose wide eyes perceived a murderer. "There's something . . . I must . . ." Thomas raised a shaking finger and pointed at my gleaming eyes.

Ulrich yanked me onto his shoulder and carried me from the room. The halls were dark; the abbey slept. He held me against the wall, his warm breath of rotting hay wafting across my face. His nose brushed mine. "I have forgotten it," he whispered, and I would have thought him drunk, but everyone knew wine never touched his lips. "It is gone again!"

He put me on the floor, took my wrist, and dragged me through the halls, both our steps as quiet as ghosts'.

The practice room was dark, but he lifted me again and I found the stool below my feet. I listened for him, and did not hear a sound. I just prayed that he was gone. When he spoke again I felt a chill.

"There are deaf composers," he whispered from the darkness, "who hear the music in their heads. As beautiful in deafness as in life, they claim!"

I reached a hand out to locate the voice. Before my elbow was straight, my hand brushed his face. He gasped at my touch, and I withdrew in terror. But then he grabbed my arm and clenched my wrist so hard I whimpered. "I would give my ears for that!" he shouted. "Cut them off and never hear you sing again, if only I could hear it there!" He tapped my head firmly with his finger, and I almost fell, but he pulled me toward him by the wrist until I was pressed up against him. Again, I felt his breath along my cheek. He whispered in my ear. "I lie awake, Moses. Every night since you came. It is as though you were outside my window, but there is a wind blowing, and though I strain to hear you, I cannot."

He pressed his forehead to mine, his cold cheek against my warmth. "You shouldn't have come," he whispered.

He let go of my arm and pushed me back so I could stand. His footsteps retreated. His fingers fumbled at the harpsichord. He played a note.

"Sing," he said. I sang the single note. Terror made it small.

"No!" he cried. "Sing!" He slammed his finger into the key.

I took a breath, and as I exhaled again I heard my breath in my chest. I did not force it open, but as Ulrich had taught me, I felt my next inhalation flow to those closed places, so that they, too, were open. My fear receded. With my next exhalation came the note—this time not loud, but clear. I sang, filling the room with my voice, until my breath ended. There was a silence.

"The Credo from today," he said and played the soprano melody from the third movement. I sang.

Suddenly his hands were on me again—the hand petting the flower. On my chest, under my arms, the small of my back, until all these parts were vibrating with the song. Then his hands pushed against my back and pressed my chest against his ear.

"Sing!" he ordered. I felt the song spread through me. It shook my knees.

"Yes!" he gasped. I felt that he was right, that my voice had never rung so brilliantly. As I stood and sang for many minutes, he kept his head against my chest, like a child against his mother's bosom.

XI.

We should blame St. Paul for the choirboy. Without his interdiction *Mulier taceat in ecclesia*, the world would have no need for these brats. For St. Paul, in ordering women silent in his churches, could not silence the female voice. From months before our birth, our ears are tuned to our mother's sounds (as mine were to my mother's bells), and thus, in the quest for perfect beauty, the church needed a substitution. In the choir of St. Gall, I was the best substitute they had ever known.

Suddenly the abbot prized me as he prized the jewel in his ring, or the pure white stone of the twin towers of his new church, which began to rise like two unfinished staircases to heaven. When he heard me sing, or took a moment to observe our practice, he smiled greedily as if a feast were being prepared for him to eat. My reticence was an asset. I spoke only to Nicolai, in whose room I hid whenever I could evade Ulrich and the choir, but even then I offered little more than mumbles. When Nicolai asked me who my father was, I shrugged. When he asked me my real name, I said, "Moses."

For the Holy Offices, and most of the Masses, the chanting of the choir monks such as Nicolai was adequate to raise Staudach's flock toward heaven. But on Holy Days, or for the celebration of the arrival of holy relics, or for Masses in memory of a generous bequest, the abbot called on Ulrich's choir and we assumed our liturgical reason for existing. In all, we sang some twenty Masses each year as a united choir, and portions of our group were sent out on many more occasions to honor the smaller parishes in the abbey's vast lands. Ulrich's sublime taste selected our repertoire, which included ethereal masses from Cavalli, Charpentier, Monteverdi, Vivaldi, and Dufay. At our furtive midnight rehearsals, the repulsive man withdrew cantatas smuggled in from Leipzig, and in secret, I polluted the abbey with Bach's Protestant song.

Just as the richest St. Gall Catholics desired cotton from America, books from Paris, tea from India, and coffee from Turkey, neither funeral nor parish procession nor parish feast day could be complete without some musical accompaniment from the Choir of St. Gall. In my memory, these many venues are just a blur of frilly muslin in dank chapels, a hush of snores and wheezes.

All of them, that is, except for one.

We typically traveled in oxcarts to our concerts, for the majority of the St. Gall Catholics lived outside the city walls. On one particular evening, however, we marched single file out the abbey's western gate and into the Protestant city. Ulrich led the way, followed by two gray-faced, gray-haired violinists; fat-necked Harpsichord Heinrich; the bass Andreas; two fully grown tenors and two prepubescent contraltos; the soprano Feder; Ueli, a former choirboy whom cruel puberty had reduced to a gangly luggage carrier and page turner; and lastly, stalling more often than not to capture every sound that leaked out of the city's open windows, me.

I lost sight of Ueli's rear several times as we crossed the city, but it was no trouble to catch up. I closed my eyes and tuned my ears to his heels dragging on the street. After ten minutes of walking, I found the others waiting at a palatial house of gray stone. This was Haus Duft, Ulrich told us, the home of the Duft und Söhne textile family. "A Catholic house," he said, "though we are inside the city's walls." Feder whispered a little too loudly that *his family* would never live among the rats. "Be this a lesson to you," Ulrich replied severely. "Those who put industry before religion benefit from their tolerance. Indeed, the Dufts are by far the wealthiest in our canton, Catholic or Reformer. Tonight you must perform at your best."

We entered through a side door, like contracted pastry chefs. The cellar passage to the chapel was murky and damp. I followed Ueli's coattails for several steps, but then I stopped. I heard the clanging of metal pots distinctly to my left, but when I turned to look, I saw only the gray stone of the wall. I took a step forward; the clanging faded, but now a woman spoke. Two more steps forward and I heard chatter: a group of men, at least a dozen.

I paused. The sound flowed as though I had passed three open windows, to three different rooms, but the wall was merely blank stone. I studied it minutely. I could find no holes, so I shuddered, concluding that ghosts must inhabit this passage. However, today I can see that it was not a miracle or devilry at all, just a *phénomène*. I have read that limestone is composed of ancient shells, and the Duft shells must have been particularly cavernous, because, like the seashell of our cochlea, they trapped all the sounds emitted in that giant house, and transmitted them farther. Just as the buzz of a trumpetist's lips is conveyed from the mouthpiece to the bell along the twists and turns of brass, so too the sounds in the Duft house were swallowed up, conveyed from shell to shell, and spat out through the walls of an entirely different room.

As I continued down that gloomy corridor after my companions, I heard a glass shattering on a floor, a hand pounding a desk, a man singing a silly song, a child weeping, and a woman relieving herself. (If you wonder how I ascertained gender from the hiss you should be banned from concert halls. God gave you ears to listen.) Behind these identifiable sounds, flitting in and out, I heard a great number of clangs and bangs, as if a mute army were mining silver within the walls.

It took me several minutes to descend that short passage. I stopped at every sound and tried in vain to spy a hole in the stone. When I finally reached the end, where the passage split left and right, I was alone. I listened for Ueli's heels, determined their direction, walked two steps left, realized I had been mistaken, returned to the fork, heard the scuffing heels both to the left and to the right, then heard them above my head.

I was lost.

I am useless without my ears. My other senses were stunted from disuse. With each step in any direction, the walls of Haus Duft spat out new sounds that I tried to fit into a map—but to no avail. Though to others the long halls and right angles of Haus Duft might have been as plain as an open field, to me they were a labyrinth.

Finally, I chose one direction and walked to the end of the passage. To my left was a door, and to my right the passage continued into darkness. I was about to choose the door when I heard a friendly voice call from the shadows.

"Come on," the voice said. "Come on now. I'm your friend. Don't be shy."

I crept down the dark passage and toward the voice. A door opened into some sort of dimly lit pantry in which hundreds of glass jars filled rows of wooden shelves.

"It's all right," the kind voice said. "I'm not going to hurt you. I want to help you."

Reassured, I stepped into the room.

I was so focused on the sounds that it took me several steps into the room before I glimpsed an eye peering at me. I froze. Then I saw another, then two more, and then a thousand severed heads glared down at me. I saw the heads of chickens, of dozens of wild birds, the head of a pig, of a goat with tiny horns. In green glass vats along the top shelf floated the heads of wild beasts: deer, a wolf, the giant head of a bear, three huge cats, and the smaller heads of several marmots. Gaping, clouded eyes stared through the clear liquid. *Run!* they seemed to say. *They will get your head as well.*

But just as I turned to flee, the soothing voice spoke again. "It's all right," it said. "Don't be afraid."

But then I realized the comfort in this voice was not meant for me at all, for this person had her back to me. I saw black shoes and white stockings, the green back of a velvet dress with white bows on the shoulders, and two blond braids. I was looking at a girl, a type of creature I had often seen in church, but apart from two scrawny Nebelmatt sisters who held more in common with mice than with women, I had never been so close to one.

She was bending into a large wooden cage, submerging her shoulders and bringing one leg up to balance, affording me a view of her white stockings from her thin ankle to the curve of her narrow buttocks. With sudden interest, I was aware that a mystery dwelt in that smooth spot where the seams of her stockings met. She dove deeper into the cage, and her dress fell further, like an opened parasol, her legs squirming toward the ceiling. I wanted to touch them. Were they warm or cold? Rough or soft?

"Got you!" she gasped. Her foot kicked in triumph.

The legs came down. The dress fell into place. A shoulder with a soiled white bow was extracted, then another with bow absent, and then golden braids with clinging wisps of hay, a red face smudged with dirt, then two bare arms, two dirty hands, and a snake.

It was as long as my leg and shone oily black in the glimmer of the lamp. The girl swung a braid out of her face, pulled the writhing snake toward her lips, kissed its back, and said, "It's all right, Jean-Jacques. You're free."

I can remember every aspect of that sight. Her freckles. Every speck of dirt on her face. The proud, loving smile for the snake. Perhaps what I see now in my mind's eye is just a memory of a memory of another distant memory, like an old watch that has been repaired so many times no original cog remains. I have called it to mind so often: that girl with messy hair, hands filthy, and a terrified Ringelnatter held against her mouth.

With her lips a mere breath from the snake, she saw me.

In the flicker of the lamp, I watched embarrassment rise to her cheeks. She tried to hide the snake behind her back, but its wriggling was too much for a single hand, and it escaped to the floor. For an instant she paused, considering, then pounced onto knees and elbows, her two hands clutching Jean-Jacques while her braids hung like long ears to the floor. She turned up to me.

"Who are you?" she said. "What are you doing here?"

I was immediately taken with the confidence of her voice, the clear enunciation of her words. No trace of a rural dialect. Instantly, I knew this girl was of better class than even the choirboys who taunted me. No matter how close she stood right now, surely there was no one further from me in the entire world.

She got a firm grip on Jean-Jacques and struggled to her knees, then stood up, holding the snake before her like a priest clasping a chalice filled with wine. She was a head taller than I, and had an extraordinary face, almost like a canvas for emotion: curiosity in the tightness of her brow, caution in the stretch of her eyes, embarrassment in the tuck of her chin, a touch of joy in the broadening of her mouth. She studied my choir robe.

"Are you a monk?" Her tone suggested she preferred snakes to monks.

Again, I said nothing.

"When I am grown up," she said, coming toward me very slowly and yet speaking quickly, "there won't be monks anymore, just *philosophes*, which women can be, even though women cannot run manufactories." When she finished speaking, Jean-Jacques was near my face. He stopped writhing and stared limply into the darkness. The girl looked into my eyes. I retreated a step. She advanced.

Her dress rustled when she moved. Her stiff black shoes creaked. She tapped her teeth together twice. "If you ever tell anyone what you saw, I will bash your face," she said.

Then she walked right past me.

I turned to watch her go, and only then did I notice that she limped. Her right foot was turned inward and her knee did not bend. She glanced backward as she left the room and caught me studying her leg. A flash of hurt joined the battle of her face. "It is cruel to stare," she said.

Then she was gone. I watched the doorway, then closed my eyes so I could run back through her sounds, now stored in my memory. The swish of her dress, the soft snake-charming voice awakened my other senses. Was that her scent of soap and citrus still lingering in the room?

I returned to the main hallway and leaned against the wall until I heard Ueli dragging his feet along the floor, for he had been sent to find me.

We were there to sing a Sunday Vespers—we sang Vivaldi's *Dixit Dominus*, a piece that offered the right virtuosity, harmony, and piety to impress geniuses and wealthy imbeciles alike, and thus to inspire revisions of last wills and testaments in ways most generous to the abbey. The Duft chapel was a dank block of limestone filled with a surfeit of icons and thirty or so worshippers. Feder and I stood shoulder to shoulder at the front of the choir. This evening he did not conceal a needle in his fist and poke it into my arm, or whisper that the abbot had locked Nicolai away for his indecent crimes, both of which were common antics when we practiced. Now, the chapel full with the best St. Gall blood, he smiled like an angel, and gave no sign that he despised me.

Just as we were about to begin, the doors at the back of the chapel opened and in strode the master of the house, Willibald Duft. Not only was the head of the Duft und Söhne textile empire thin, he was short, and so among the other rotund men in the chapel, he had a boyish appearance. He did not pause to cross himself, but only dipped his finger in the stoup and drew a circle in the air, splashing holy water on the floor. His left hand held the now-clean hand of his only child, Amalia Duft, the snake-kisser. She limped along beside him.

They sat beside a woman in the first pew who had the unattractive combination of high, hollow cheeks, thin shoulders, and wide hips, making her appear a sagging, fleshy pyramid resting on the pew. Amalia sat between the two adults. I wrongly took the pear-shaped woman for Amalia's mother and Willibald's wife; instead, I later learned, she was Duft's unmarried sister, Karoline Duft, the chief source of piety in the house and instigator of this particular service.

During the first two movements, I watched these three. The team of tenors and altos fought with each other and with the violins and harpsichord for possession of the chapel, using exaggerated volume and a barely perceptible extension of their notes as weapons. But the war was lost on the crowd; the clamor merely dulled their attention. Some smiled blankly. Others had a dumb look of faked fulfillment on their faces. Several worshippers fell asleep. Duft was staring at his shoes. Beside him, Amalia swung her feet listlessly and made no effort to disguise the boredom on her face. However, it appeared that Karoline Duft could not have been happier if the virtuoso Vivaldi himself had risen from the dead and taken up his violin. She closed her eyes and swayed to some rhythm that had no relation to the actual music. I wondered briefly, *Is she deaf?*

The third movement of that *Dixit Dominus* is two minutes of the most beautiful counterpoint Vivaldi ever wrote for two sopranos. It was perfectly suited to Feder's and my voices, which were not yet brilliant and full, but light and quick. I loved to watch the audience's reaction as Feder began, *Virgam virtutis tuae*, and then, seconds later, I repeated the phrase. It took only this moment to lift the audience out of their torpor.

We sang another phrase in unison before Vivaldi split us apart. Then we were like two dancing sparrows: We climbed in unison. We broke apart, but a moment later the unity was resolved, and we climbed together again. Feder's voice was so nimble it sometimes seemed it might speed away from me. But for a moment we were brothers, and I almost wished I could reach out and embrace him as we sang.

The people in the chapel sat forward and lifted slightly from their seats; the pews creaked beneath them. Duft merely stretched one foot to flick a spot of dirt off the other and yawned, as if he did not hear the music. But Amalia was listening. She stared at me—and in her belly there was a tiny ringing.

The movement finished, and for the first time since we entered the chapel, there was total silence. No shuffling or coughs. No whispers or scolding. Several people wheezed slightly as they exhaled, their jaws hanging limp.

The music continued. The next two movements featured more warring between tenors, bass, violins, and harpsichord, all parties renewed in their inspiration. Then the cornet and organ chorus, limply rewritten for our harpsichord and violins. The short eighth movement began with the kind of plodding violins that Vivaldi used so well to prepare the ear. It calmed the audience, and gave our two gray violins a chance to settle in. Then my soprano solo began, *De Torrente*.

I was a tiny boy, barely half as tall as the man I am now. The choir stood obediently behind me. I was not loud, but my voice filled each corner of that room. My chin quavered as I stretched each syllable to runs of twenty notes or more. To the audience it appeared effort-less—my eyes never tensed, my shoulders didn't rise—but for me, it took the deepest concentration. My slight arms pointed down and slightly forward, and I felt my song in each outstretched finger. My lungs strained, and though my voice was only a tenth as full as it would one day grow to be, it was clear as the mountain air around my mother's church. In the Duft chapel, eyes turned wet. Amalia, in the first row, had creases in her brow; her white fingers clasped the wooden pew. My song ruled her every fiber.

When I finished, there was a silence. Feder was a stiff statue be-side me. Ulrich gaped. He saw me, once again, for the first time. Duft still studied his shoe.

Amalia sat still, pensive and enthralled, as if her snake had sprouted splendid wings and taken flight before her very eyes.

XII.

Afterward, we sat in a tight parlor and feasted. Food and drink were our only payment for singing (Abbot Coelestin of course receiving his by his own arrangements). It seemed everyone had forgotten me, except for Ulrich, whom I caught from time to time staring at my face, willing in vain for its image to summon a memory of my voice. I held a lamb shank in one hand, a chicken wing in the other, and tore at the flesh as if I intended to grow to full size that very night.

"Psst!" I heard a whisper. No one else seemed to hear the voice. I turned toward the door. An eye peeked through. No one had ever wanted to speak to me before, except for Ulrich and Nicolai, so I ignored the voice and turned back to my feast.

"Psst! Monk!" I turned again, and this time I saw Amalia Duft's head poking through the door. "Come!"

I obeyed, but cautiously, well aware by now that behind friendly overtures often lurked cruel tricks. When I reached the door, Amalia tugged me through and shut it behind us. She was wearing a white dressing gown and gazed crossly at my face.

"You're disgusting," she said.

I thought, *Why do people seek me out only to insult me?*

But then it occurred to me that the bottom half of my face was, indeed, tingling with lamb juice and chicken fat. I cleaned it with my choir robe. Amalia groaned and grabbed my wrist. She pulled me down the hall. In a washroom she wiped my face and hands with a soft towel and threw it on the floor.

"Quickly," she said, pulling my sleeve. "I'm supposed to be in bed."

The clangs and drips and chatter of Haus Duft rose and fell as she led me down halls I could never have navigated on my own. We walked at a near run, as she swayed from side to side with her limp. She looked back at me.

"Lots of people fall off roofs," she said. "Matthias von Grubber fell off the same roof as I, but he landed in a pile of manure. I landed on a plough. Karoline says God did it to slow me down, but it does not slow me down, and anyway there is no God."

This last comment made me recoil in shock, but she just tugged me harder. When I still said nothing, she shook her head. "Why don't you talk?"

Because I don't know what to say, I would have said, if I had had the courage.

She just shrugged and continued speaking. "That's fine with me. I hate listening to people. Marie won't shut up. I tried to plug my ears with wax, but she just shouted to be heard. You, of course, you can't keep quiet, but you don't have to talk."

No one had ever spoken so many words to me, apart from Nicolai and Ulrich. It all seemed quite suspicious. I would never find my way back if she abandoned me or, worse, led me to a pack of her spiteful friends. We had not passed a window for a while, and the sounds from the walls grew fainter and fainter. I judged that we had entered an uninhabited wing of Haus Duft.

Finally, she slowed. At the end of a long passage there was a table and, behind it, a set of closed double doors. An old man sat at the table with eyes half closed. A candle, quill, paper, and a silver watch were laid neatly on the table before him.

"Fräulein Duft," he recited as we approached. He wrote something on his paper. I peeked and saw that he had scrawled her name.

"If you don't tell my father we came, Peter," she said, "I will bring you a cigar."

He continued writing.

"Two cigars."

He shook his head. "Accurate data."

I looked at the sheet in front of him. A neat table divided it in two:

Event	Time
Cough (hacking)	20:02 (Duration: 45 seconds)
Cough (clearing)	20:08 (Duration: 2 seconds)
Nurse Blatt enters	20:14
Window opened (Nurse Blatt)	20:15
Window closed (Nurse Blatt)	20:18
Bladder emptied on demand	
Color: Xanthic; Volume: 1/6 Mass	20:20
Cough (hacking)	20:22 (Duration: 31 seconds)
Nurse Blatt leaves	20:25
Visitor (Fräulein Duft)	20:32

As I read this list, a hacking cough came from behind the double doors. Peter looked at his watch. Amalia groaned and grabbed the doorknob.

"Do not interrupt!" he ordered and tilted his ear. When the coughing stopped, he examined his watch. He wrote: "Cough (hacking): 20:34 (Duration: 24 seconds)."

"We're going in," Amalia said. She grabbed two strips of black silk from a pile on the table.

Suddenly the lethargic Peter was gone. Now a gallant knight seemed to have taken his place as he jumped up and clutched my arm. "No!" he said in shock. "Not him!"

"I am admitting him," Amalia said.

Peter looked at her in amazement. He pulled me close and so I smelled his breath, which stank of sour wine. "She cannot admit," he whispered.

Amalia stomped her good foot. "We are going in," she repeated.

The old man pulled me closer. I tried to squirm away, but his grip was too strong. "Do not go in," he hissed into my ear.

Amalia grabbed my other wrist. "Don't listen to him. Father will be pleased."

"Pleased!" said Peter. "Pleased with you destroying experimenting? How is Frau Duft ever to get healthy, then? Tell me that, Fräulein Duft!"

As they both wrenched my arms, I looked from his grimace to her angry face.

"Kick him," she whispered.

So I did. I kicked him in the ankle, and he yelped and released my wrist. He hopped and rubbed his foot. I was flooded with remorse, and would have helped him rub, but Amalia had pushed open the door and now she shoved me through it.

"I'm getting Herr Duft!" Peter yelled. But Amalia shut the door, and we were alone in the dark room.

Not exactly alone—someone else was here. It was a woman, I quickly discerned. She had been coughing, and now she breathed in ragged gasps, which filled her up, until, as if pricked, the air leaked from her lungs. There was a thin candle resting on a table, but my eyes could not see anything outside its halo. The sounds of Haus Duft were silent here. I heard neither the clanging nor the whispers of the walls, nor the city and night winds outside.

I twitched as Amalia tied a strip of silk over my face. It smelled of charcoal.

"It's all right," she said. "We have to wear them so we do not get sick. You get sick if you share breaths with sick people. Mother is sick."

So *this* was Frau Duft on the other side of the room. This frightened me, and I was glad when Amalia took my hand in hers. It was softer than any hand I had ever touched.

As my eyes adjusted to the room, I saw a giant bed. It was so laden with blankets and pillows that, without the sounds of the breathing, I could not have been sure if one or five people lay in it. With the candle behind us, Amalia and I cast a giant shadow on the wall. I held her hand tightly.

"Mother!" Amalia whispered. "Mother, wake up!" She began to lead me toward the bed. I resisted, but she was stronger and more determined.

A crack appeared in the blankets on the bed. A bony hand snaked outward. The fingers were thin and white. Amalia took the hand in hers so she was a link between us.

"Amalia," a throaty whisper said. "What are you doing here? It's late." From a dark hollow in the blankets, I made out the shine of two eyes.

"I brought someone to see you, Mother. A singer." Amalia pulled me a step closer. I watched her, unsure of what to do. She squeezed my hand and nodded. "All right," she whispered. "Sing."

I had been trained in a church choir. We sang sacred music in sacred places. Though we could be rented out for private worship, we never opened our mouths in song unless there was an altar close enough to throw a Bible at. I was not a minstrel, nor a medicine man who knew chants to cure disease.

So I did not sing.

"Please," Amalia said. She squeezed my hand and pressed it to her thumping heart. "We don't have much time. My father is coming."

This seemed like a reason to run, not a reason to sing. Suddenly I was frightened by this girl who kissed snakes and said there was no God. I tried to shake loose from her hand. I was almost free—she was clutching only my index finger in her fist—when the blankets shifted.

I saw Frau Duft's face in the light.

It may seem improbable, but I saw my mother. For a moment I was sure that it was she hiding in those sheets, and I almost cried out with joy. Then I remembered that my mother's face was filthy, and this face, Frau Duft's face, was clean and pale. My mother's skin was hard, like tanned leather, and Frau Duft's was fragile stretched muslin. My mother's hair was tousled and wild, and Frau Duft's was carefully washed and tied behind her head. My mother was strong. Frau Duft was weak. But in those sunken eyes, in that straining lower lip that quivered with exertion, there was an echo of the warmth that I could only recall in my memories of the belfry. At that moment, I would have promised God to close my mouth forever if only my mother could have heard me sing just once.

And so I sang for Frau Duft. I sang from the *Gloria* in Palestrina's *Missa Papae Marcelli*, the piece that had tempted me from Nicolai's room almost two years before. I had never sung in such a small room; the furniture and blankets and curtains swallowed my volume. My breath rippled through the charcoal mask, tickling my nose. I listened for that faint resonance of my voice in those two bodies. In Frau Duft's bony form I heard only the faintest of whispers. But Amalia, who still squeezed my hand, had the gift of those who can hear without ears. Her lips were slightly parted. Her eyes were closed. She pulled back her shoulders. Like a crystal goblet rubbed with a wet finger along its rim, the faintest ringing gradually arose in her—my voice vibrating in the muscles of her neck and upper back. Is this how my mother would have heard my voice?

As Amalia tuned herself to my song, I adjusted the pitch of my notes to her, and so it seemed I held her neck with my own warm hands. I felt, for the first time, that desire to know my voice in her, like the painter who falls in love with his subject because of the power of his own brush.

The *Gloria* is written for a choir, and in the absence of other voices, I repeated myself, dove into the most beautiful of the contraltos' notes, or invented transitions that did not exist. At moments I was silent, and we heard only our breaths: Amalia's light and free, mine eager for air, and Frau Duft's in pain.

I stopped only when we heard footsteps approaching in the passage.

XIII.

"No one move!" Willibald Duft shouted as he ran into the room, frantically tying one of the charcoal masks around his head. He stopped—he seemed slightly disappointed to see that his trespasser was not yet four feet tall. Amalia pinched my elbow, and I gratefully slid behind her. Duft's face slowly faded from violet to red, and he heaved in gulps of air through the mask. He looked angrily past his daughter at me, and then he walked to his wife's side, so carefully you might think he feared harming the air around her.

He touched her cheek with the back of his hand. "Are you all right, my dear?"

"I am fine, Willibald."

Reassured, he turned toward me. His eyes narrowed. "Do you know what you have done?"

I shook my head. I hoped he would not strike me.

"You have interfered with Science," he said. I looked around the room, trying to spot this Science lurking in the shadows.

There were more footsteps scraping their way down the hall. We watched the slouching Peter struggle toward the door, his face as red as Duft's.

"Stop!" Duft yelled.

Peter halted just before crossing the threshold, narrowly escaping interfering with Science himself.

"Father," said Amalia, "we did not do anything—"

"Did not do *anything*?" Duft cried. Then he glanced quickly at his wife and lowered his voice. "You cannot *not* do anything! The moment you breathe in here you do something! Something unknown. Perhaps *unknowable*." He waved his hands, but then froze, and crossed them meekly at his chest, as if suddenly appalled by the incomprehensible consequences of their movement.

Amalia looked proudly past her father. Even through the mask, I saw the bulge of her lower lip curled out in a stubborn pout.

"Amalia, listen to me," Duft said weakly. He took his wife's hand. His daughter still refused his stare. The candle glinted in his eyes, and I saw with amazement that they were filling with tears. "I am trying to understand this, Amalia."

"Willibald," said a soothing voice from the bed, "she is just trying to—"

"Sir," Peter yelled from the hallway, "what about the data?"

Willibald looked toward the door. He nodded. "Good, Peter," he said over my head. "The data must come first."

"The boy was just singing," Frau Duft said. She broke into a cough. Duft looked at her in horror.

Behind me, I heard Peter mumble, ". . . eight . . . nine . . . ten . . . ," and then the scratch of a quill on parchment when she stopped coughing.

"Singing!" Willibald gasped, when the coughing episode was safely recorded. He looked down at me. I knew from Feder and the boys that singing could be silly or even shameful. But for the first time in my life, it occurred to me that singing, like speaking, could be dangerous. "We have never had singing. What if you shocked her heart?" Duft glared at me. I stepped behind Amalia, lightly pressing into her back.

"He did not shock me," Frau Duft said as loud as she could. "It was beautiful."

I wanted to climb into the bed and have her wrap me in her arms.

"I am writing 'Disturbance (singing: possible heart shock),' " was the report from the hallway.

Amalia exhaled loudly through her nose.

"Would someone please close the door?" Frau Duft said.

Amalia quickly obliged. I would have liked to follow her, for she had left me exposed. But Willibald did not attack; he strode up to his wife. "Dear," he said, "we have to eliminate the accidents. Then we can find the cause—and the cure."

"You have said that before," she said wearily. "So many times."

"But something always disturbs us," he said. "Just when we are ready to begin the real analysis."

"Maybe that's my fate. Perhaps I am not supposed to be cured."

"But *Science*, dear."

"Perhaps." She spoke it so despairingly that that one word washed all hope from Duft's face. He shook his head, but I was not sure if he meant to contradict her or fight his tears. I marveled that now he was so shaken when, hours earlier, my singing had moved the entire chapel but had not touched him at all. Amalia lingered near the door and stared at the floor.

Duft wiped his eyes with the back of his hand, and tried to speak. "This time," he said, "I will make sure no one disturbs your isolation."

"No more isolation!" This time, the ailing woman's voice was ten times as strong as her husband's. Even Amalia looked up in surprise, but just then a new fit of coughing began. We bowed our heads in respectful silence until it stopped. The moment Frau Duft had breath again, she spoke. "When I heard this boy's song, I remembered that this world was beautiful once."

I almost began to sing again right then.

"It will be beautiful again, dear, when you are cured."

She shook her head.

Amalia suddenly sprang to life. She limped toward the bed and grabbed my hand. "But maybe this will cure her!" she said.

Duft looked confused. "What will?"

"Him, his singing." She shook my limp arm.

Hope, that beast with a thousand lives, rekindled in Duft's eyes. He looked at me with new interest. "An interesting idea. I had not thought of experimenting with sound. That will be our next line of inquiry, then. But we should start more simply. Tomorrow we will ring a chime."

"I do not want to hear a chime, Willibald."

"It is not about want, my dear. It is about sonic properties."

"Willibald." Her voice was tired.

Duft paced back and forth in a tight pattern by the bed. "It is just a start," he said. "To collect data. Then we will add a second chime, experiment with pitch and volume, and so on."

Amalia dropped my hand. She growled faintly, and then, in desperation, closed her eyes and covered her ears with her hands.

"Am I supposed to waste my life with chimes when a boy can sing like this?" Frau Duft's voice was strong again, and it halted Duft's pacing. "Let him come and sing for me. Do all the tests you want, but let him sing."

Duft frowned. "But . . ." He considered this for a moment, and then shook his head. "He is too impossible to grasp, my dear. A chime is a chime; it is constant. A boy changes, so his voice is never the same from one minute to next. Voltaire says—"

"I want to hear music, Willibald."

Duft began pacing again, more slowly than before, as if he feared that a sudden shaking of the house might knock him over. "Perhaps Peter could learn to play a horn." He looked toward the closed door.

"I am dying, Willibald!"

I started at the word. It was the worst one in the world. Duft froze. He slowly spun to face his wife. Amalia took my hand. She squeezed it, and somehow I knew she wanted me to squeeze it back. I did.

"Please let him come," Frau Duft said. "It will make me happy."

Willibald lifted his mask and wiped his nose with the back of his hand. "Perhaps . . . regimented time . . . durations."

"He is a very quiet boy. Much more quiet than Peter."

"We will have to start slowly."

"Of course."

"In case of negative effects."

"And I will be the scribe," said Amalia, and the light in those blue eyes had begun to glow again. "I can do it better than Peter."

Willibald looked down at his daughter. "You?"

Amalia nodded. She looked at me, but not warmly—it was a challenge, as if to say, *See what you and your voice have done? Are you prepared?*

I looked around and saw that now they all stared at me. How had this happened? Of course I wanted to sing for this kind, ailing woman. And yet this severe and shaky man, this lavish house, this girl who made me tingle when she took my hand—I did not belong here.

"It is settled, then," Duft said. "I will see the abbot tomorrow."

He kissed his wife's forehead through the mask. Then he pushed Amalia and me toward the door.

"Wait," Frau Duft said. We turned.

"What is your name?" she said to me. My mother would have had such a kind voice, too, if she could have spoken.

"He does not speak," Amalia said.

But I could. "Moses," I said, with the voice of a mouse. Amalia's eyes went wide. "*Gute Nacht*, Frau Duft."

XIV.

"Moses," was all the abbot said when he appeared at the door to the practice room late the next morning. He spat my name as if it were something unpleasant sticking to his tongue, and the disgust remained on his face after he expunged it. Ulrich and the boys turned to me—I think I even glimpsed pity on their faces. My feet skated silently across the floor and I slipped through the door without turning my back to the abbot.

I was sure they told him that I had sung in Frau Duft's bedroom. He closed the door and looked down at me. His nose twitched.

"Music," he said, and with every sentence his cold eyes moved closer to my face, "is not a balm. It is not some doctor's tincture. I am building a church, not a hospital! That man is a fool."

He jerked back up and turned to look through a window at the pristine white walls of his church. Their brilliance made him squint.

He raised a finger and put it in my face. "If there weren't so few blasted stonemasons in this city, it would be out of the question. But he says he has them—half a dozen he could loan me. Why is your voice worth so much to him?"

His eyes narrowed as he asked the question, and I felt him trying to read the answer in the soft features of my face.

A novice passed us in the corridor. He bowed at the abbot and tried to scurry past, but the abbot held up a hand to him. "Get me the monk Nicolai," he said. The novice hurried off. The abbot's disapproving gaze returned to me, and remained there until we heard Nicolai's heavy steps rushing down the corridor.

"Father Abbot," he said, his expression concerned. He bowed with his final step. "Is there something wrong?"

The abbot raised his long brow at Nicolai, as if to say, *With those like you in this abbey, need you even ask?*

Instead, he said, very slowly, as if giving an order to a peasant servant, "Each Thursday evening this boy shall sing Vespers at Haus Duft. Be sure to have him clean and dressed to represent the abbey to this city's finest family."

"Of course," said Nicolai. He smiled down at me and tousled my hair. "At Haus Duft! What an honor!" I smiled faintly up at him. "Abbot," Nicolai laid a hand on the abbot's arm, "I will take him there myself."

The abbot recoiled as if Nicolai had burned him. "You will not!"

"It's not far, just . . ." Nicolai wiggled his hand as if it were a fish swimming toward the window. He shrugged. "I could find it."

The abbot's stare was severe. He pointed a finger toward the construction in the square. "I would as soon give this church to the Reformers than have you parade about this city in the evening. *You* sitting in their parlor!" The abbot shuddered visibly.

Nicolai was clearly disappointed, but he laid a hand on my shoulder. "Then I will draw Moses a map."

The abbot looked down at me again. "No, you are correct. He needs an escort." His lips swished about as if he had some sour pastille in his mouth. He nodded. "Brother Dominikus will take him."

That evening Nicolai broke the news to Remus as we sat in Nicolai's cell.

"I am to do what?" The wolf clutched the two halves of his open book as though he would tear them apart. Nicolai paced back and forth in front of him. I sat on the bed.

"Accompany him safely through the hazards of the world," Nicolai said. His hands spread apart a jungle's vines. He pointed. "To Haus Duft."

"Why me?"

"You are the only one brave enough."

"What does Staudach think I am? A mule?"

Nicolai winked at me. "I don't imagine he thinks quite that highly of you."

"I will not do it. I have other things to do." Remus leaned back in his chair. He pressed his book to his chest.

Nicolai looked skeptical. "Other things?" Remus met his gaze with silence. "Oh, Remus, do it for Moses."

"For Moses?" Remus scowled contemptuously. "What does Moses get out of it?"

We both looked up at Nicolai. Though I longed to return to that mysterious, lavish house, I was scared. I, too, would have liked to know why I should go. Nicolai waved his hand at the window. "He will see the world."

"The world is between here and Haus Duft?"

Nicolai stopped in front of the window and peered out as if to examine the path to that house. He shrugged. "Part of it is."

"A very small part."

Nicolai swiped at the air, spreading Remus's confusing fog. "Remus, he has to start somewhere. You don't want him to grow up to be a monk like you, do you?"

Nicolai was as close to a parent as I had those years, and his words surprised me. It was the first time I had considered any future other than a life in the abbey as a monk. Like Remus. Like Nicolai.

Remus looked hard at me. "Why should I care what he becomes?" But when he had said it, he looked at the floor in poorly masked shame, and we all saw that he, too, had become entangled in my life.

Nicolai smiled. "Moses," he said, "don't you see? Remus is afraid."

Remus snorted.

"You see, there are women in that house." Nicolai winked. "Don't worry, I will speak with him. This is a fear he must overcome."

And sure enough, the next Thursday, when Nicolai had fetched me from rehearsal and scrubbed my face and combed my hair, there stood Remus, dressed in hat and cloak and carrying a satchel full of books as though we would be traveling for many days, as if running out of books were tantamount to running out of air. The first day, he carried a map in his hand and at each street corner turned it round and round as if trying to decipher its code. "These damn streets," he mumbled. "They seem to go in circles. Why can't they make them the same as on the map?" I followed patiently a step behind him and listened carefully. In subsequent weeks, we developed a simple pact. He held a book before his eyes and walked. When I heard the butcher's knife, I pushed him right; the blacksmith's hammer, left. When I heard the vendors calling in the market, I led him up the gentle hill.

We entered Haus Duft through the same hallway that had beguiled me before. Imagine a house whose walls were daily stripped and repainted, whose pictures had been newly hung, whose staircases and doorways were added or removed at will. So it was for me in this house of ever-changing sounds. From a spot of wall where one day I heard a hand banging a table, the next week I heard pots clanging, and from another spot where one day I heard the soft whisper of a maid, the next week I heard the husky voice of Karoline Duft.

Every week I was led to a parlor, in which Amalia always sat at a desk beside her father, for my visit invariably coincided with her philosophy lesson, the one subject her father did not entrust to the buxom French nurse Marie. What relief washed across my young friend's face as I entered! In seconds, philosophy washed away, and those cheeks burned. She stood up from her work and greeted Remus, who held up his books to her like a shield. He took a seat as far from Karoline as possible. Then Amalia would nod at me, a dignified, proper hostess, and lead me down a passage. As soon as we were out of her father's and Karoline's hearing, she took my hand and slowed her gait to draw out the walk to her mother's room, for this was the only time during the entire week that either of us was alone with another young person we could call a friend. She did most of the talking, mimicking Karoline's severe reproaches, "That is not done, Amalia Duft, in *this house*," or telling me of how she would escape—to a pirate ship or an Eskimo tribe, or dress up as a boy and study philosophy at a *collège* in Paris. Sometimes she stopped me in the hall, for even our dragging steps were too fast for her bursting mind. One week, she showed me a skull she said was a human's (but that looked more like one of her father's preserved pigs to me). The next week she presented a picture she had drawn of an African king. On another visit, she translated a bloody scene from a Greek epic her father had had her read in French.

Gradually I began to understand that the fall that had maimed her leg had also curtailed her freedom. For example, on one particularly warm evening, after I had sung, Amalia coyly suggested to her father that she would like to see the progress on the church—she would walk with Remus and me to the abbey and return before dark. "I know the way," she said.

Her father was engrossed in business and had merely mumbled, "Fine, dear, that's fine."

But Karoline sniffed her out. She caught us at the door. "Amalia!" she cried. "What are you thinking?"

Amalia told her that she wished to inspect the church.

"Sunday," Karoline said, taking Amalia's hand and leading her back into the house. "Sunday you may go with me."

"But I do not want to go with you!" Amalia snapped. She jerked her hand free.

"Amalia," Karoline admonished in a whisper, "have you forgotten what happened the last time you were out alone?" She looked at Amalia's knee as if the injury glowed through the fabric of her dress. "Do you want another scar?"

Amalia turned red in angry humiliation.

Karoline led her niece away. "Tomorrow," she said as they disappeared into another room, "Marie will take you out in the coach. You don't want everyone to stare at your limp, do you, dear?"

During our second meeting, Amalia led me through the hallways silently, her face sour. She growled slightly as she exhaled. I followed her nervously as she limped ahead of me—until she stopped suddenly in a quiet passage. "I will go no farther," she snapped, "until you say at least six words to me."

I must have looked confused. She poked me in my chest and spoke slowly, as if I were a little child. "That would be one more word than you spoke to my mother."

I tried to speak then, I did—I heard in her plea the same loneliness that dominated my existence—but I could not. I was struck dumb. I stared blankly at the wall behind her, as if the secret text to making friends were written there but recorded in a foreign language. She waited barely thirty seconds before muttering, "Boys are so stupid," and tugged me on.

By the third or fourth visit, I learned that the secret was not necessarily in speaking but in listening. I smiled at the stories she made up, and laughed when she mocked her aunt. She held my hand all the time, and often crowded me against the wall as we ambled, so I had to press against her. We soon found in the warmth of each other's hands, in the rub of shoulders, and even in the occasional hug some small satisfaction of the child's need for touch, which we both missed—me as an orphan, she with an infirm mother and a father who could not embrace without analyzing his love in weights and measures.

When we finally reached her mother's door, Peter always presented Amalia with two charcoal masks, a fresh sheet of paper, a quill, and ink, and asked us to peruse the day's precious data. His attitude toward me had changed entirely since I had begun working with Science, rather than against it. "Affected by the rain?" he'd ask, and examine both my cheeks as if he could discern a swelling. "You haven't eaten any potatoes, have you?" he said of the exotic root. "They give you leprosy, I hope you know." He insisted that I step onto a scale, and he recorded my weight in his notes. Lastly, he always peered into my throat before giving the final nod that we could continue through the door.

Inside, with the ceiling lamp lit, and several candles placed around the room, I could see that Frau Duft's face had once been as beautiful as my mother's, before the skin became stretched across bone and the eyes sank. Her smile was still warm, though, and her voice, despite her hard fits of coughing, calmed me so completely that her room was only the third place on earth, after the belfry and Nicolai's cell, where I truly felt safe.

Amalia placed the quill and paper on a table (she made up the data later) and sat at her mother's side, sometimes even leaning across the bed with her head on her mother's lap so Frau Duft could stroke her hair. For a moment, at least, they were as I always imagined mother and child should be, and not two lonely lives destroyed by disease and separated by Science.

In that bedroom I sang some of the worst performances of my life and some of the best. For, the music we sing in our churches, though often beautiful, is not written for one ten-year-old soprano singing alone in a bedroom. Since Ulrich had no interest in helping me prepare for these private concerts he would never hear himself, as I pieced together my songs I had nothing more than the naïve artistry with which my mother had swung her mallets. I stumbled often, understanding only instinctively how to manage a change of key or the transition from a calm Gregorian chant to florid Vivaldi. What impiety I wrought in that bedroom! I tore down and then rebuilt litanies, cut Psalms in two, mingled Latin and German, mangled both languages, and all of it outside church or chapel, all of it in a small, dimly lit bedroom.

In my later years, I came to appreciate that in Frau Duft's room I gained the important tools I had missed in my training at St. Gall. For in sunny Naples, where boys like me trained in the great Neapolitan *conservatori*, where they learned arias to be sung in San Carlo or Teatro Ducale, they taught not only perfection of breathing, posture, and tone—Ulrich was the greatest maestro of them all in this regard—but also the creativity of the virtuoso. Twenty years later, in rowdy San Carlo, I would stretch an aria of just six sentences to twenty-five minutes; then, after ten minutes of applause, do it again with no repetition. But in Frau Duft's bedroom, I was just beginning to feel how songs were written, and therefore could be unwritten, improved upon, lightened, darkened, stretched, condensed—or turned backward so they mocked themselves. With the same note, I made Frau Duft cry on one occasion; and on another, I made her smile. If I felt like singing high, fast runs and trills, that was fine. If I was in a somber mood, I could start with Nicolai's chants from Vespers and stretch them until Frau Duft and Amalia both had glassy eyes, behind which they dreamed of a perfect world.

When I sang quietly they were silent, except for Frau Duft's wheezing. Then, as my volume increased, I heard my highest notes in the lamp above my head, and once that glass began to ring, I blocked out the sounds of my own mouth, seeking a slightly different timbre. It all depended on the song, or the weather, or that little girl's mercurial moods. Her sound would join my voice like a violin's bow gently drawn across a string, and I struggled to encourage its journeys, crafting my song around her form. She was not aware of it—she could not hear herself, for my voice was so much louder than the faint ringing of her body. She only felt it as a warmth. She hugged herself when my voice rang out. She learned with me, trained every fiber—from her round cheeks to the arches of her feet—to hear the different pitches of my song. And on rare days, when Frau Duft was most alive, I heard in the mother, too, a distant echo of the daughter.

XV.

Ulrich was furious. Of course, if he were sick in bed, the only medicine he would wish to have would be me singing Bach's heretical songs, but this did not stop him from protesting the next time Staudach looked in on our rehearsal. "Abbot," Ulrich whispered so the boys would not hear, "he is crucial to the choir. I have chosen the pieces for *his voice*. I cannot do without him, even for one afternoon."

"It is for the church," the abbot said. "*For the church.*" He twisted the ruby ring on his finger.

"Then send another boy, Abbot. Any boy. Anyone but him."

"What is it about *this boy*?" the abbot said through clamped teeth. He clenched his hands as though he would like to take me in his claws. "Duft would have no other. Of course I tried to send a proper man. And now you say *you* cannot spare him. Why can't you teach the other boys to sing like him?"

With gaping mouth, Ulrich shook his head, lost for what to say. "Abbot," he finally muttered, childlike pleading on his face, "please reconsider."

"For the church," the abbot said flatly. "For now it must be first in all our thoughts."

How could it not have been first in our thoughts? The perfect symmetry of the church's double towers loomed over the Abbey Square. On sunny days, the glare of the white stone made me shield my eyes. "Half a million gulden," Remus hissed one night to Nicolai. "Do you have any idea how much that is?"

"You try to destroy a church eight hundred years old and build a perfect one," Nicolai responded and took a sip of wine. Perched on his chair, his elbow raised, for a moment he was as refined as a prince. "You'd spend all that and more. Staudach probably makes those masons work for nothing more than the security of their souls. They'd make a scoundrel like you pay them double."

"It's not a question of how I'd do it," Remus said. "You're not listening to what I say. None of the monks do."

"I wonder why?" Nicolai winked at me. I suppressed a giggle.

"Every gulden from the pocket of a farmer or a weaver," Remus continued. "Some have nothing to eat after they have paid his taxes. What will he give them in return?"

Nicolai needed to consider only for a moment. "Beauty," he said with a nod, as if this were an incontrovertible reply.

"Beauty?" Remus said. He looked at me. "Beauty?"

We both turned back to Nicolai. I'd never held even one single gulden in my hands. I wanted to know as much as Remus how beauty could be worth half a million.

Nicolai took a deep breath and put down his glass. "Remus," he said. "Moses. Don't think that I like this man. I don't. I loathe him. He's like wine that's drunk ten years too late. But with this church he's got it right. Haven't you seen it?" Nicolai pointed out the window, where even in the dim moonlight the white church shone as if candles burned within its stone. "That's God's work he's doing, and though Staudach may be a fool when it comes to his fellow men, he understands God just fine." Nicolai's face was smooth and joyful as if he'd glimpsed an angel hovering above the church. "God is beautiful. He's perfect. And he inspires us to be beautiful and perfect, too. We're not, of course. And that's exactly why we need beauty in our lives: to remind us how good we could be. That's why we chant. That's why Moses sings. And that's why Staudach is building us a perfect church. For if we know perfect beauty, with our eyes and with our ears, even for a second, we'll come that tiny bit closer to being it ourselves." As Nicolai finished he laid a hand on his heart, and he gave a final nod, to emphasize his sermon. I found myself nodding back, for I wanted nothing more than to be like this beautiful music that I sang, like this perfect church that was rising out of crude blocks of stone.

"What stupid rot," Remus said. He scowled at us both and took up his book again. "Half a million gulden."

. . .

But Nicolai had infected me. Would this church make me pure? I watched it grow with nervous longing, month after month—the towers finished, red tiles laid on the roof. Then it was nearly complete, and news of the inauguration seeped into the abbey like the promise of a miracle. Thousands would come to the event, from the Swiss Confederation and from Austria. Staudach would bless us with a morning Mass. Then we would march throughout the abbey's lands in a procession, before returning for the symbolic completion of the church: the transfer of the abbey's holy relics back into the crypt. And then, when Holy Otmar's head, St. Erasmus's hair, St. Hyacinthus's ribs, and many other scraps of hair and bone were again laid to rest, the day would be crowned with a song of glory: Charpentier's magnificent *Te Deum*. Ulrich had sent to Innsbruck for four renowned soloists to sing the demanding parts. I was to sing in the choir.

But then Staudach read Ulrich's letter to the Innsbruck Kapellmeister and discovered that Ulrich intended a male falsetto for the mezzo-soprano and a musico for soprano. Staudach stormed into the practice room one evening as I rehearsed alone with Ulrich. The choirmaster had me wrapped in an embrace, his head against my chest, his hands fondling the hollows beneath my ears. When Staudach entered, slamming the doors open, he recoiled, and I tumbled off my stool.

"You do not mean a castrate? Not a half-man!" Staudach bellowed, waving Ulrich's letter like a death warrant.

Ulrich sighed, but clearly he was already prepared for this argument. "Yes, Abbot. That is what a musico is. A castrato. An *evirato*." Ulrich nodded at me as if I should agree with him, but my eyes only grew wide as I tried to picture this mysterious being he described.

"In my church?" the abbot stammered. "At its inauguration?"

"They sing in the Sistine Chapel, Abbot."

Staudach's face had grown a deep red. "This church," he said slowly, "*my* church is not the Sistine Chapel, Brother Ulrich."

Ulrich looked down at me as if he sought my opinion on this matter. I cringed from the abbot's attention.

"I could as well preach in front of half an altar," Staudach said, waving the letter again. "Finish only half the roof. Leave out half the pews. Half a man will not sing in my church!"

"Their voices are beautiful—"

"Perfection is beautiful," the abbot said. He stared down Ulrich's protest, as if his words alone could wipe castrati from all the world's churches. He finally looked at me beside my stool and his sneer deepened. "Get a whole man to sing the part."

"Falsetti are unsatisfactory for Charpentier's first soprano," said Ulrich, trying again. "The music is too high. The singer must be . . . angelic. Perhaps we could consider . . . that is . . . perhaps . . . a w-woman?"

Staudach's eyes bulged. Ulrich quickly waved this suggestion off.

"Then just leave it out," Staudach said.

My breath caught in my throat at this. I could see Ulrich trying to hide a similar reaction. "Leave the first soprano out?" he stammered.

"Or sing it lower."

Ulrich was silent. He shook his head.

Staudach tore Ulrich's letter into pieces, spitting out his words with every rip. "I will. Not have. A eunuch. In my church!"

"Abbot, I see no—"

Staudach looked at me. "He can sing it." He said it like an accusation.

At this, Ulrich lost all his composure. He gaped at me, then Staudach. "The boy?" he said in amazement.

"You say he is good."

"Yes. He is great. But—"

Staudach nodded. "Good. Then it is decided."

"But he is not ready to sing with professionals," Ulrich said. "He is ten years old."

Staudach was finished. He pointed at me again. "It is he, Brother Ulrich, or else you rewrite it for a trumpet," he said and stormed out.

· · ·

And so my debut was set: I would sing the soprano of Charpentier's *Te Deum* at the church's inauguration. I ran to tell Nicolai. "Charpentier!" he said. He looked up through his ceiling as if this news had enabled him to see straight to heaven. "Remus! Don't you remember? In Rome!"

Remus shrugged and said he could not be sure. But he smiled at me, which was so rare it made me tingle with shyness. "This is quite an honor, Moses," he said. "You should be very proud."

"You will be great," Nicolai added, and messed my hair.

And then, for the first time in my life, with those two smiling faces staring down at me, I felt that queasy fear well up inside me as I realized that if I could be great, I could also be a disaster. This could be my making—or my undoing.

Ulrich's thinking was much the same. We spent the next months concerned with nothing else. I woke in the middle of the night with the sixth movement's soprano solo in my head, and worried how my voice would fill that giant church. Ulrich feared damage to my tender throat from singing alongside grown men—these men with lungs four or six times as large as mine. But no man has ever lived who understood better than Ulrich how to make a body ring. In the weeks before my debut, his hands petted their encouragement with even more desperation, as he reached deeper and taught me how to sing like a man.

For the inauguration, Staudach awaited eighteen Swiss abbots, as well as the bishops from Konstanz and Petera. "They promise to bring me Diderot's *Encyclopédie*," Remus said, speaking of the Geneva delegation.

"An *encyclopody*?" Nicolai asked, mangling the French. "Is that some kind of bug? Please don't bring it in this room."

And one night, Ulrich managed to terrify me even more. "Moses," he whispered, as if he worried someone might be listening at the door. "I have written to Stuttgart. I want them to know of you. North of the Alps there is no better place for music. They are sending a man, an Italian, who must know something of music or they would not have chosen him." Ulrich reached out and touched my cheek with his finger.

I tensed at the cold and lifeless touch. "Moses, would you like one day to travel to that city with me? Would you like to sing for Duke Karl Eugen?" He finished this speech with his lips not far from mine. I shivered at the thought of going anywhere with him.

Then one day Nicolai appeared at our dormitory room as the boys were readying for bed. He looked very cross. "Moses, come with me," he said, his voice gruff and serious. "Abbot's orders. You're to bring everything you own." For several seconds I couldn't move, but then he winked at me and smiled. "But I'm serious about bringing all your things," he said. "I've got a surprise for you." I gathered up my spare clothes into my arms—I had no other possessions that had escaped the other boys' destruction.

"Have fun," Thomas whispered cruelly as I left, and the last sound I heard was a general snigger. I followed Nicolai up the stairs, and then we passed even his floor and went on to the attic. He opened the door to a tiny room with a bed beneath a square window and nothing but a mirror on the wall.

"Ulrich says an artist needs his peace," said Nicolai, "and he was able to convince the abbot. This is your room! No one may enter without your permission—not even me." Then he kissed me on the forehead and left. He shut the door.

I just stood there, the bundle of clothes in my arms. I stared at the closed door and listened to the silence. *Alone,* I thought, *I have to live alone? Is this what it means to be an artist?*

I dropped my clothes on the floor and the *whoomp* they made seemed a clap of thunder. I climbed onto the bed and pressed my nose up against the window. The new church shimmered in the uneven moonlight. The sight of it cleansed me. It was perfect, and I could be as well. I imagined my voice ringing in its heights. I saw Nicolai and Remus smiling. I even saw the other boys staring at me in admiration. And then I lay down on *my bed*. For the first time in my life, as I crossed into sleep, mine was the only breath I heard.

XVI.

Today it remains an evil, looming presence in my mind, although I haven't seen it for half a century. If an earthquake had knocked Staudach's church to the ground the day before that inauguration, this all would have been so different. But I cannot deceive you. It is perfection embodied in stone. Symmetry rules its architecture. The double towers, pure and white, dominate the city's rooftops. A high rotunda sits exactly in the center, and beneath it, a golden grating splits the church in two perfect halves, just as the world is divided: at the high altar, the shepherds; on the other side, the flock. Great windows of glass are tinted the faintest green, so the brilliant sun shines through them as through a mountain stream. Eighteen white pillars hold the heavens up.

The night before the inauguration, the scaffolding was removed, the red velvet curtains were hung on the confessionals, and the stone floor was polished to a gleam. Staudach unlocked the door through the sacristy to the monks' quarters, and the monks and novices and choirboys poured in as a flood of black. Then I began to understand how architecture is made of sound as much as sight. When the monks crooned at the holy fathers painted on the arched ceiling, the saints crooned back at us. The reverberation of our feet upon the stone consecrated our every step. The oaken choir stalls did not creak even under Nicolai's massive weight. When our knuckles brushed the grating as we pointed into the laymen's nave, the hum of the metal made us feel how solid was this barrier that split them from us. And when Nicolai sang first into the unspoilt heavens, the rumbling of his voice in distant corners made us feel that God, His church, and His music were truly greater than we could know.

I woke eager for the changes that would finally come when my voice sang the most beautiful music of the day. Best of all, my only friend my age, Amalia, would be there to hear it all. And when I was nearly dressed, and the abbey's new bells tolled the beginning of the Mass, my mind recalled the one person who would not be there to hear my completion. I bowed my head and several tears dropped to the floor for my mother.

I listened to the Mass from my window—Ulrich had ordered me to stay in my room and rest my voice. While every Catholic soul for several leagues joined the procession, I strolled alone up and down the abbey's hallways and peeked secretly into monks' cells. I stole food from the empty kitchen. Finally, in the evening, after I heard the crowds returning, warm with food and drink, I sat on my bed and watched my door. Then I heard the thumps of Nicolai running up the stairs. He burst into the room. "It is time!" he shouted. He licked his fingers and slicked down my hair, pinched both my cheeks, then lifted me and flipped me over and spun me about to check for blemishes. Then he carried me out the door. He stopped at the top of the stairs and looked into my eyes. "Moses," he said, his eyes wet with joy, "I thank God every day that he chose me to save you from that river." And then he carried me to the church.

Yet, this time, I found that perfect space far less peaceful than it had been the night before. It was swarming with new faces and buzzing with excited chatter, and I would have been trampled long before I sang, had not Nicolai been my protector. I wrapped my arms around his neck as he carried me from the sacristy and into the mob of monkish black. Almost every face we passed was unknown to me, for I had always stared at knees, and now, looking down at them from Nicolai's height, I could not discern which monk resided in the abbey and which had traveled many miles to be here for the inauguration. The flabby faces of eighteen abbots—a line of mitres in the stalls—chilled my spine. There must have been five hundred monks in all, and also among them I spotted the garb of many priests. For a moment, I imagined I heard my mother's bells ringing a warning, and I looked fearfully for the face of my father. He was not there.

On our side of the grating there were also several guests not in ecclesiastical costume. Among them was Ulrich's Stuttgart ambassador,

Doctor Rapucci. The day before, my maestro had led me to a private
concert for the man. The choirmaster's hand shook in mine as he
guided me through the door, and when the pale doctor approached
me, his thin smile making every hair stand up on my neck, I felt Ulrich gently draw me back, as if he did not want the man to touch me.
"You must sing for him," Ulrich said, nervously, "but just briefly.
Softly. Do not strain your voice." Ulrich stared at the keys as he accompanied me, and then, as soon as I had finished, grabbed my hand
and escorted me out as if he were afraid for me to remain another
minute with this man. Now, in the church, Rapucci gave me a knowing smile, as if he and I shared a secret. And then he disappeared into
the throng.

When Nicolai carried me far enough into the choir, I saw that
this black, holy churning sea was only half the crowd. Across the
grating, the other half of the nave was so awash with the garish mer-
chandise of St. Gall textilers that it made me nauseated to look. In
their pinks and greens and violets, St. Gall's finest souls all seemed
like stuffed dolls dressed up by little girls, chattering noisily. Every
neck bent backward and every finger pointed at the vibrant paintings
on the ceiling.

I turned and found Ulrich's sallow face, which for once was a familiar comfort. The triple choir, tacked together from every passable
voice within a hundred miles, sat in a semicircle in front of the stalls.
Around them were the horns, the strings, and the two massive tim-
pani, which I had at first mistaken for casks of holy wine. In the center
of all of this, the three other soloists were already at their stations.
Gerrit Glomser, bass, stared blankly through the nave, as if this perfect church were a place he had visited many times before. Joseph
Schock was a small-headed, wide-shouldered tenor, who had been kind
to me in rehearsals, but did not seem to see me now, for he had broken
into a sweat and stared at his shaking hands.

But the third soloist, the mezzo-soprano Antonio Bugatti, smiled
kindly at me. Two days before, after I had sung with him for the first
time, I ran to Nicolai's cell to inform my friend of the miracle I had
witnessed—a man who sang a child's high notes, but with the brilliance

and power to match any man's voice I had ever heard. The first time I had heard Bugatti singing, his voice had made my entire body tingle, and I forgot to sing my part. I felt tears in my eyes as I told Nicolai of this beauty.

But my friend had just smiled suspiciously. "I want to see Staudach's falsetto for myself," he said. "The abbot may be fooled, but I can spot an angel." When I asked what he meant, he would not explain further, but promised to carry me to my station on the day of the inauguration so he could see the man up close.

And now, in the church, his task completed, Nicolai smiled as he knelt beside me, pretending to slick down my hair. "Moses," he whispered in my ear, "I was right. Staudach's falsetto is a musico. I can see it."

I looked up at the mezzo-soprano Bugatti, who was as handsome as any man I had ever seen: fined-boned, as delicate in his movements as in his singing. I remembered that Staudach had forbid a musico to sing in his church.

"Nicolai," I whispered, "what's a musico?"

"A musico is a man," said Nicolai, "who is not a man. He has been made into an angel."

I did not see the relics carried to the crypt. I could not see Staudach at his pulpit. I did not listen as he proclaimed to the crowds that this church was the manifestation of God's will on earth, and that we should see in it what we ourselves have the potential to become. I ignored the whispers and the short breaths and the rustling flying at me from all directions. Instead, I stared at Bugatti's long fingers laid upon his knees. Did the man have wings hidden beneath his robe? When the drums began to roll their prelude, Bugatti smiled down at me again, and there was no place I would rather have been than beside him. The horns began to play, and every face in the church, including mine, warmed at the sound of glory.

The bass Glomser sang. He released sounds of such volume it seemed impossible they came out of a single body. The man's voice

filled every corner of the church and silenced every whisper. I heard
his voice ringing in many guts. The echoes from the high rotunda
made his voice possess the church, and I think many believed the Al-
mighty had joined him in his song.

In those first movements, inspired by Glomser's voice, fed at the
day's constant feasting, warmed by the procession's wine, we all filled
the church with our sounds so its windows rang. Ulrich had found
space in my tiny frame; I did not struggle to be heard among these
men. My voice mixed with those of the other soloists like swirls of
precious dye in water, and I knew mine was as fine as any other that
resounded in that church, even as the clear power of Bugatti's mesmerized us all. When I did not sing, I closed my eyes and heard his
voice ringing in my chest. When he was silent, I opened my eyes again
and peered through the grate, seeking in vain for Amalia's face, the
only one I cared to see in that crowd. But she was as obscured to me as
I imagine I was to her.

When the fifth movement ended, Ulrich paused. There was a
sudden, stark quiet in the church. His raised hands held the music
back, and, for a moment, we were all forced to contemplate the emptiness, and made to feel the longing that was Ulrich's curse—his desire for the freshly vanished beauty, just beyond his reach.

Then it was my turn; the sixth movement was my solo. And I sang.
With the perfect hearing that had been my mother's gift, with the tiny
lungs that Ulrich's hands had taught to breathe, with a body that
could ring with song. I sang for Nicolai, for Amalia—and I sang for
my dead mother and for Frau Duft. My voice filled that perfect
church as it fluttered from note to note. When I paused to breathe, I
heard the drawing of a thousand breaths with mine. Then, as I began
again, they held their air for me. My highest notes seemed to lift me
off the ground. Beside me, when I grabbed a secret look, Bugatti's eyes
were closed, a smile on his face. My slight body echoed in the rotunda
and from the deepest recesses of the nave, and so, for the first time in
my life, I felt huge, as huge as Staudach's church.

Then it was over—not even a hundred seconds. No one stirred. The eyes of every monk and singer were fixed upon me, but I knew they stared not at this insignificant boy, but at the voice inside him, which they yearned to hear again. Through the grating, among the crowd of worshippers, I saw one head struggling above the rest, and I glimpsed, for an instant, Amalia standing eagerly upon her pew, until her aunt yanked her down.

Then I looked at Ulrich. His face was ashen. Eyes wide, he had ceased to breathe, as if a knife had been stabbed into his chest.

We feasted again through that evening and long into the night. I crept from table to table and filled my mouth and pockets with food that would have made kings and princes drool. I must have consumed my body weight in roast lamb that day, and where it hid I do not know. Still that little body did not grow.

The wine cellars of the abbey were opened to the visiting and resident monks alike. Midnight found me at my attic window listening to scores of drunken monks in the cloister below, as they celebrated the complete and perfect abbey. From one window, lit like a stage, Nicolai sang French ballads to a crowd that cheered whenever he rhymed. His audience danced in a circle until they collapsed in a drunken pile. Beyond the monastery buildings, the Abbey Square was quiet, the laity long since sent home without food or wine. In the most distant recess of the cloister, I heard Ulrich's voice whispering urgent pleading to the calm nasal drone of the Stuttgart doctor. Opposite them, Remus muttered under the white façade of the new church, where he seemed to be carrying on a debate with a Frenchman, but when I peered into the shadow, I saw no one beside him, just a book clutched before his eyes. From other shadows, I heard seducing whispers. On a night like this, with so many visiting brothers who would never meet one another again, and with wine to dull the conscience, many monks sought to taste the nectars of the world.

I heard frantic praying in slurred tongues. I heard one man

singing my solo in a squeaking whisper. I heard a cask of wine rolled across the cloister. I heard goblets smashed against the walls.

I remember my thoughts exactly: How lucky I am. I want to be a monk.

For the first time since I had come to the monastery, I felt that I belonged. Like the stones of Staudach's church, I had once been low and rough, but now I was formed into something fine and good and holy.

How wrong I was.

XVII.

When he came for me, the cloister was quiet. He held me in his arms, and for a moment I thought he was there just to hold me. I did not like his touch, so I feigned sleep. I only heard his light breath (even with my ear pressed to his shoulder, I could not hear his heart). I felt his gaze upon me. Then something warm and wet fell onto my face. I heard a sob.

With sudden resolve, he swung me into the air. He carried me out of my room and down the stairs, which were lit on each floor by the faint light of the moon through the large windows to the cloister. I lay in his arms as if asleep, and heard the snores that meant we were passing Nicolai's cell. On the first landing, he paused, and this hesitation was so unlike him that I opened my eyes and looked at his face. In the dim moonlight, his pale face appeared bloodless. His eyes shone with tears.

"Ulrich," I said. "Let me go."

"I cannot," he whispered.

I squirmed in his embrace. "Let me go," I repeated, but he shook his head.

"Your voice," he whispered. "We need to preserve your voice."

Preservation was what Duft did to lizards and the heads of bears. Did he mean to cut out my voice and display it in a jar? Or mount it on a wall? I struggled to get free, but he held me tight.

"I am sorry," he whispered. "I am sorry."

His haunted face came so close to mine I thought he might kiss me. I screamed.

But his hand was reaching as soon as my mouth opened, and he covered my mouth and clenched my nose. I could no more breathe than scream as he moved quickly down the stairs and along the empty hallways, past one drunken monk sprawled upon the floor.

Just when I began to lose consciousness, Ulrich removed his hand.

I heaved for air. He whispered, "Keep quiet now. There is no one in this part of the abbey to hear you. You will need your strength." I squirmed and fought to get away, but he clasped me tighter, like a baby he would sooner smother than have stolen.

He brought me to the practice room, brightly lit at this late hour by lamps and candles arranged throughout the room. The harpsichord stood alone in the center, like an altar. It was covered with white linen. Doctor Rapucci, his face marked by that chilling smile, stood beside the harpsichord. He poured wine into a glass goblet and held it before him, like a chalice.

Rapucci took two steps toward us as I fought once again to escape Ulrich's desperate embrace. I tried kicking, but my feet only swung through empty air.

"Have no fear," the doctor said. He spoke with an Italian accent. "I am not going to hurt you."

He came closer, but when I squirmed again he stopped. He shook his head and smiled, as if I were a fool for distrusting him. His thin eyebrows rose, imitating kindness. "Do you know where Stuttgart is, Moses?"

On the back of his white hands, a mass of veins matched the color of the wine.

"It is not far from here—only several days to travel. I hope you will come there someday to visit me. It is beautiful here in the abbey, but nothing like Stuttgart. Have you ever met a duke? Duke Karl Eugen is my employer. If I tell him of your voice, he will let you sleep in the palace. Would you like to sleep in a palace?"

I would not, but I did not speak.

"The duke cares more for beautiful music than anyone in Europe, Moses. More even than your abbot. That is why he brought me to Stuttgart, all the way from Italy. I am a doctor, a doctor for music."

Now he did step forward. I wriggled, but Ulrich's grasp was iron.

"You have a very beautiful voice, Moses. One of the finest I have ever heard. Ulrich has taught you very well. But I can make you even better. Would you like to sing better, Moses?"

My voice is mine! I would have shouted if I had not been so afraid.

Mine! He was only a step away now. I feared Ulrich would hand me over to him.

But Ulrich did not let me go. He just held me more tightly. Rapucci raised the goblet. With his other hand he pinched my chin.

"Open your mouth, Moses. Drink some wine."

His fingers were so cold. I shook my head, and he let me go.

He swore.

Ulrich whispered that I should drink, that it would make me want to sleep. I writhed with all the strength I had.

"Then lay him on the floor," Rapucci said. I kicked and fought until Ulrich sat astride me and pinned my arms to the ground. Doctor Rapucci knelt beside us. "Open your mouth," he instructed sharply.

When I again refused, shaking my head from side to side, clenching my jaw closed, he swore again. He pried at my jaw with his veined fingers until a gap appeared, into which he poured the wine. I choked. It overflowed and ran down my neck. He clamped my mouth and pinched my throat until I swallowed.

"That should be sufficient," he said to Ulrich. The men released me. I coughed and spat.

Yet Rapucci had calculated wrongly. Most of the laudanum-laced wine had escaped my mouth and lay in a puddle on the floor. Though my mind soon began to cloud, and I lost the will to resist them, I did not sleep. I can recall every touch and sound of what followed as if it were a play I have acted a thousand times.

They strip my clothes, and for a moment I feel the cold of the stone floor against my nakedness. I am mesmerized by the ceiling. My fear is soothed; there is something blissful in the pattern of the beams. I should cover myself, but my clothes are gone and I am too weary to seek them.

I am lifted and placed in a basin filled with warm water. I lie there, bathed to the navel. I close my eyes and enjoy the warmth. It seems as if the basin is as huge as a warm ocean. The hard, wooden edge is a soft pillow holding up my head.

Voices speak of minutes.

Knives.

Needles.

I think I will sleep.

I am lifted like a baby, gently dried, and placed facedown upon the harpsichord. My head is toward the keys. When these men speak, the strings resonate with their voices. I want to sing as well, but it is impossible. It seems like such an effort now. I cannot imagine how I ever managed to open my mouth and utter a noise in my life.

Each time I almost fall asleep on the soft sheet, the touch of a cold hand awakens me. It occurs to me that these men, even though one of them is Ulrich, should not touch me. Not in this way. This is not the touch I have come to know so well—Ulrich's hands urging on my voice.

I think, *Call for Nicolai.* I think, *Nicolai will tell them to keep their hands away.* But he is not here. The cold hands lift me and place towels beneath my hips so my naked backside juts into the air. They spread my legs until I think I might split apart. They are hurting me, but I cannot form the words. I moan. They tie my ankles so I cannot close my legs. I feel them touch me where even Ulrich has never dared touch me before.

My hands are still free, and I make them into fists. I begin to weep.

I will be sick.

There is a smell in the air, like something very . . . Cold? Sour? I cannot place it. Something cold and wet strokes my thighs, between my legs. It kneads my testicles and makes me sick. I do not want to be touched there! The harpsichord's strings ring beneath me, but there is no logic in their sound. *I need my voice,* I wish to say. *Do not take it. It is the only thing that makes me pure.* But all that escapes is, "No, no-ooo," as if I am mourning.

A hand pats my head. Ulrich's voice in my ear, "It is all right, Moses. Go back to sleep."

Sleep! Yes, I want to sleep, but the hand is touching me again! *Ulrich!* I try to scream. *Don't take my voice!* But I only manage to say his name; the rest is moans.

"Don't be afraid," he says. "I am here."

I feel sick and so heavy. I cannot move, but I must, or my voice will be gone.

"Hold him!" Rapucci yells. "Put your weight on top of him!"

I cannot get up. There is someone leaning onto me. My chest is crushed. I cannot breathe.

"Hold him tight! He must be perfectly still."

I feel a jolt of pain between my legs. I moan and squirm and cry, and the harpsichord cries with me.

"You have got to hold him!"

I scream.

"For the love of God, Rapucci, what are—"

"Hold him!"

Something is inside me. A hand. Prodding, and searching for my voice! I cough up wine and bits of lamb. Ulrich's fingers stroke my cheek. He is crushing me. Though I struggle, I cannot move.

"Now he must be still or it will kill him!" Rapucci yells, and the low strings of the harpsichord hum.

There is a tug inside me and a jab of pain so sharp I feel it in my toes.

There is no air to breathe anymore. "I had no choice," Ulrich whispers, so softly I am sure not even Rapucci can hear. "Your voice," he murmurs. "Your voice." There is a stinging poke, a tearing between my legs, but suddenly it all seems so far away. I am so tired. I am falling asleep, and my last thought, as Rapucci grunts and Ulrich quietly sobs, is that what these awful men have taken, one day I shall steal it back again.

ACT II

I.

I woke up in my bed. The exhausted abbey was quiet. The fountain babbled in the cloister.

Had it been a dream?

I turned beneath the sheets and felt a tearing between my legs, like hooks fastened tightly to my bowels. My vision fogged with tears. I lay quiet until the pain receded, and then I drew back the coverlet. I was still naked. My child's penis pointed upward. It was purple, and behind it, my testicles were scarlet and seemed twice their normal size. Daggers of red and blue stretched across my inner thighs. But I could see nothing missing. Nothing taken.

Carefully, I reached out a finger and touched my right testicle. The skin was tender, but the rest was numb.

"We need to preserve your voice," Ulrich had said. I pictured myself inside one of Duft's glass jars, singing so no one could hear.

There was a knock at my door. I covered my naked body.

Nicolai did not wait for an answer. He took up half the space of my attic room.

"We should build a new church every week," he said. His eyes were bloodshot and he looked five years older. "God bless Stuckduck and his inaugurations." He grinned, but his smile slowly faded. He studied me. "What's this? Are you sick?"

I nodded.

"No surprise. You need a holiday. I'll tell Ulrich to leave you alone this morning."

I nodded.

Nicolai stood over me. He frowned and stooped down to study my face. "Oh, Moses. You look worse than the Einsiedeln monk who slept in the fountain. Need some food?"

I shook my head.

"Is there something wrong?"

I shook my head. I wanted to tell Nicolai, but now today I am grateful that I could not find the words.

He stood up. "Fine. You should rest, and I will come back later," he said. "And I will bring a juicy steak."

When I did not smile back at him, he gave me a last, suspicious look and left the room. When the door was shut, I twisted so my feet could dangle over the edge of the bed. With each movement, the hooks in my groin tore deeper and I gasped. I stood up, hunched like an old man. Tears ran down my cheeks. I shuffled along the floor and locked the door, something I had never done before. I stood naked in front of my mirror.

I sang the first three notes of the soprano solo from the day before. It was weak and unsure, but it was my voice. It had not been taken from me. A choking sob cut off the song.

Somehow I crept back to my bed and slept.

I heard poundings, yells in my sleep. Someone was chasing me down the abbey's hallways; all the doors were locked and so I could not hide. Then there was a splintering crash and I woke to see my door falling inward, split down the middle. Nicolai stumbled in. Behind him was Remus, with concerned, narrow eyes, and beyond him, Doctor Rapucci held a lamp up to his pallid, frowning face. The doctor pushed past my friends. I cringed as he laid a cold palm on my forehead and then pried open my eye with two fingers.

"He will be fine," he said to Nicolai, who stood like he was ready to take me in his arms. Rapucci pushed him back. "You must leave him alone. He merely has a fever."

My eyelids were so heavy I let them close.

"But he did not wake," Nicolai implored, his voice shaking. "I thought that he was—"

"He is young and strong. Let him sleep," Doctor Rapucci replied sternly. "I will watch him."

"I will watch him," Nicolai said.

"I am a doctor."

I opened my eyes. The room seemed to sway. In the broken doorway, Remus stood silently, ignoring the book in his arms. He watched the men argue over me, suspicion on his face. I wanted to tell Nicolai—even Remus—not to leave me alone with this doctor, but in my haze I couldn't form the words. I was too afraid, and I watched my protectors step over the splinters, their faces imploring me to call them back.

When we were alone, Doctor Rapucci leaned in close. He smiled when he saw I was awake. He put a finger over his thin lips. "You must tell no one what happened last night," he said. "If you do, they will not let you stay here. They will make you leave the abbey, and you will be alone. Trust no one but your friend Ulrich."

I did not wholly understand this warning, but even so, I knew instinctively that he was right.

"Do you understand what I have done, Moses?"

I did not react. In the dim light of the lamp I saw that the same purple veins of his hands interwove his pallid face.

"I have made you a musico."

Me, a musico? That hand twisting and digging inside me had made me like Bugatti? *A musico is a man,* Nicolai had said, *who is not a man. He has been made into an angel.*

"Moses!" Doctor Rapucci was still talking to me. I tried to focus through the fever. "You will notice some changes in your body in the next few weeks," he said. "Do not be alarmed."

Rapucci straightened and blew out the lamp. Faint light filtered in from the hallway.

"One day," Rapucci said from the darkness, "you will have one of the greatest voices in Europe. Do not forget me, Moses. Do not forget who made you what you are."

I closed my eyes.

And I never did forget. Many years later, when my career finally brought me to Karl Eugen's city, I hid a dagger in my cloak and told the impresario I would like to meet Rapucci, Stuttgart's famous "doctor of music." But the man just flushed and shook his head. "Please, sir," he said, "we do not talk of him." I finally plied an elderly stagehand

with wine until he told me what had passed: Rapucci had indeed returned to Stuttgart after my castration, but after two more years in
Karl Eugen's court, castrating boys so the duke could have the only
farm of musici north of the Alps, Rapucci was hanged for fondling a
duchess.

II.

As the pain and fever disappeared, so did my testicles. After a week they were hard kernels. A few days later, I woke up and did my customary reach below the covers—then sat up quickly. I was empty.

It was a simple feat, and it is still done each year by both surgeons and barbers to thousands of boys in Italian lands. Doctor Rapucci had cut the twin forks of my internal spermatic artery. Starved of what they needed to live, my testicles died, and were consumed by my own blood. I noticed no other change, neither in body nor in mind. My voice was as fine and brilliant as it had been at the inauguration, and so, while singing, all I noticed was the sudden lack of those two tiny bells ringing between my legs.

I felt the same. I did not grow wings. I did not grow tall and broad like the musico Bugatti. Yet I knew Rapucci's operation had not failed—Ulrich's pitying glances told me as much. *You do not mean a castrate? Not a half-man!* Staudach had said when Ulrich wished for a musico to sing in his church. I could not fathom what I was, nor what I would become, but I knew that it was something I must hide. I bathed only in the middle of the night, a towel close at hand. I locked my door when I changed my clothes. I never asked Nicolai the purpose of those organs I had lost. I held my secret close, hoping that I could merely forget that awful night and its consequences. For several years it seemed that I could do just that.

About two years after the church was finished, Frau Duft's condition worsened noticeably. It seemed to me that her bones were growing. Her skin tautened, and her chin and eye sockets grew more prominent. Each breath came as though with the help of some invisible hand that crushed the air out of her. Her voice was a whisper, and that warmth she had always spread now cost her so much pain.

Energetic Herr Duft grew sullen. Amalia, who loved that sick woman more than most girls love mothers who can dance and chat nonsense all day, answered her father's anxiety with charm, and attended to the man. "But why did Alexander do everything Aristotle asked?" she'd say. Or, "Moses says he'd like to see the heads," and then she'd poke me until I nodded, even though those vats scared me so. Herr Duft was only roused when he spoke of the fortunes he earned with such ease, or when he discussed his plans to expand his reach eastward, through his correspondence with a Viennese fabric magnate with whom he intended to conquer the fabric-wearing world.

One night as Remus and I arrived in the parlor, Duft was staring out the window, his face gray (which was extraordinary for a man whose standard hue resembled uncooked beef). Amalia stared blankly at a book before her eyes and made no attempt to revive him, nor did she even greet us.

Karoline suddenly swept into the room, as if she had been lurking outside the door, waiting for us to enter. "Not tonight!" she said glibly, as if speaking to two naughty children. "The lady is doing awfully bad. The doctor fears she might *die*." The heavy woman bounced from foot to foot, a clumsy but jubilant dancer. In her eyes I could see she had already begun to dream of the New Frau Duft: more refined, more fertile than the last. She shooed us out the door with a few flips of her wrist. I retreated, but bumped into Remus. Normally he rushed out of the house like a hound released from his cage, but when I looked up, I saw a stubborn anger on his face.

"You jackal," he muttered, just loud enough for all to hear.

"Pardon me?" Karoline Duft asked. But Remus had turned his gaze to admire the blank wall. The severe woman looked down at me, as if I might offer an excuse.

Amalia stared at Remus in admiration.

Suddenly Duft stirred. He seemed to see me for the first time. "Come next week," he said weakly. "She will be better then. With no doubt."

I nodded.

The man stared at me earnestly, as if we were the only ones in the room. "Moses, we just need more time."

Remus laid a hand on my shoulder. We began to back toward the door.

"Voltaire had smallpox once," Duft suddenly said. He stood up and took slow steps and stretched out his hand, stalking me. "Almost killed him. You know what he did? He drank a hundred and twenty pints of lemonade. It cured him." Duft looked at the ceiling and rubbed his lips. I worried he would begin to cry. His voice grew even more feeble, cracking from time to time. "I made her try that, too. But she has not got smallpox, and it only works if you have smallpox. If only she did. Then we would at least know how to fix it. But that's it. Don't you see? Every disease has got a cure to match. Only, the diseases and the cures are all mixed up." He stirred the air up in front of his chest with his hands. "Infinity of diseases. Infinity of cures. *All mixed up.* Even with a society of Aristotles, it would still take forever." He finished his speech so close to me that I heard his toes scrunching in his shoes, which almost touched mine. I nodded up at him.

"Why would God do that?" he whispered down at me. "Why? Why give us a puzzle that is so hard to solve?"

I wished Nicolai were there; he would have had an answer. He never lost sight of the beauty of the world, no matter how obscured was God's great puzzle. But Nicolai was not there, and so Remus laid a hand on Duft's arm, as if to say, *Yes, you are right. It isn't fair.* Then Remus pulled me back, and we retreated down the passage. I watched Duft's silhouette, unmoved, standing on the threshold, as if he planned to wait there until I returned.

Amalia was no longer the little girl who had held my hand in the dark passages. She was taller; one could glimpse the coming woman in her face. But to me she was as kind as ever, for despite the garden parties and lunches with the best of St. Gall's other Catholic girls, I was the only true friend she had in those years. We still lingered in the passages every Thursday on which her mother's health allowed us to visit her. One day she said sadly to me, "Moses, you're so lucky you're not a girl. I hate them. Every girl I've ever met." She bit her lip and tugged at a loose thread on my sleeve. "I never want to see them, but Karoline makes me go. Yesterday I went all the way to Rorschach just so they could insult me." She stuck out her lip and affected a squeaky voice, *"I'm so sorry for you, Amalia. It must be so awful to have a limp. However do you stand it? If I were you I'd just hide in my room all day."* Her cheeks turned red; she was still humiliated by the memory. "It's the boys' fault. It's not as though there are too few of them, but these girls act like there's a thousand of us and just three suitable matches in the world. We can't even get married yet, but all they think about is marriage."

We took several steps and Amalia rubbed her arm absently against mine.

I looked up at her. I dared to speak: "Will you get married?"

Amalia laughed at my serious face. "Of course I will, stupid. Do you think I want to live forever with that witch? I'll marry." She nodded, and stared dreamily down the passage. "But he'll be rich. And dumb. He'll just ride about on his horse and hunt or whatever it is grown men like to do," she said. "He'll do everything I say."

She dreamed of escaping her prison. One day she withdrew a folded sheet of paper. She unfolded a meticulous drawing of the abbey. "I copied it," she said proudly. "Every window, every door. It will be my map, for when I visit you."

"When will you visit me?" I asked.

"Oh," she said, "most likely next week. Certainly before the month is out. Draw an *X* on your room so I know where to find you."

"But they won't let you in," I said. "You're a girl."

"I'm a *Duft*," she said severely.

I studied the monk's dormitories, found the little windows in the roof, and counted carefully from the end.

"That is mine," I said, and with her pencil drew an *X*.

The next week I asked her why she had not come. "I was so busy," she said. "Next week I should manage it. Wait for me in the evening."

I did—every evening for many months, but she never came.

A time came the following summer when extended clear, dry air made Frau Duft's state improve, and I sang to her each week. Then the autumn rains arrived, and once again her condition worsened. For two months I did not sing for her at all. I was again a legitimate choirboy, though I would have preferred the furtive concerts for the two Duftesses to any venue in Europe.

Then one morning, one of the soldiers who guarded the monastery gate appeared in our practice room.

"Moses the choirboy must come with me," he said to Ulrich. "The abbot orders it."

I was terrified. But Ulrich dismissed me to go with the soldier, and instead of the abbot, I found Karoline Duft waiting at the gate.

"Come," she said, and turned on her heel. I walked behind that cone of a woman through the crowded market, which opened for her like the parting of a sea. She said nothing until we had left the busy streets.

"The doctor says she will die," she said, as if she were merely talking about an aged mare whose time had come. "She has asked for you, and he has not refused. I disagree, but he has lost his sense." She walked faster, and I nearly had to run. "A Duft without his sense is not a Duft. That woman has been in bed for seven years. She has but stalled our advance and consumed our wealth. And now she wants a concert." She stopped short and my head bumped her soft behind. She looked down at me. She sniffed. "I suppose you will want your fee."

I had no idea that singers could be paid to sing.

"And you will get it, I am sure. One blessed abbot, and so many souls to burden him. How he bears it, I do not know!"

I was so accustomed to guiding Remus down the streets that when

I heard that butcher's chop, I laid my hand on Karoline's wide hip and pushed.

She yelped and slammed her palm into my ear. "You disgusting child!"

I rubbed my ear as we turned the corner. She massaged her hip as though my touch had burned her. "It is bad enough that this city is full of Reformers. Now even children are molesting women. How could Willibald find a new wife here? He will have to go far away. To Innsbruck. Or Salzburg. I must write a letter tonight."

She turned to shake a finger at me.

"You are a choirboy. You should be the best of all of them, and look at you. In two years you will be looking Amalia up and down, even with her deformation. And she will probably smile back, knowing her." Karoline shook her head in disgust. "One child! And a girl!"

We arrived at Haus Duft, and I entered for the first time through the main doors into the palatial entrance hall. It was a high, two-storied room with a wide double staircase and a huge area of plastered wall, which must have hidden masses of that echoing limestone, because this entrance hall seemed to be the auditorium for the stage of Haus Duft; myriad canals of sound converged in this lobby. The nurse Marie yapped in French to some victim. A piglet squealed. A mop slurped into a bucket. A cleaver split a bone. Two scullery maids chattered. The wind moaned along the roof.

Karoline Duft climbed halfway up the stairs, leaving me dumbfounded at the bottom, immersed in the sounds around me. She turned and snapped down at me. "Close your mouth. You look like an idiot just standing there. Have you never seen such riches before?"

I suppose she meant the thick carpets, oak furniture, and second-rate portraits of Dufts on the wall. For a choirboy from the church of St. Gall, these were mere trifles.

I followed her down ever-twisting hallways, until dutiful Peter came into view, slumped at his station.

"Moses!" He stood like a sentry greeting a general, then realized he had forgotten to record my arrival, checked his watch, and wrote my name before returning to attention. He offered me a charcoal mask.

"Then Science has not yet resigned!" he said. "I knew you would come again. Just in time, too. The doctor says all we can do is pray, but we do not simply pray here in Haus Duft."

"We certainly do!" Karoline snapped.

"I mean," said the faithful scribe, as if noticing the ugly pear for the first time, "Science is our way of praying."

"If there were more prayers and fewer Sciences in this house," said Karoline, "we would not have all these troubles."

"Yes, madam," said Peter. He looked terribly uncomfortable, so he scribbled in his margins, as if he had a very important sum to work out.

"Well, go in," Karoline said to me. "Do not wait for me; I will not risk my vibrant health."

Peter flashed me one final, hopeful look, as if to cheer for Science. Or Music. Or both.

Amalia sat on one side of her mother's bed, Herr Duft on the other. His eyes were filled with tears, but he wiped them away, rising from his chair as I entered. He came to me quickly and tousled my hair. Afterward, his hand remained on my head as if he had forgotten he had placed it there. We stood like this for a minute while he stared glassy-eyed at the door behind me. Amalia sat in her chair and did not look at me either.

"We failed, Moses," Duft finally said. "We tried, but we failed. We did not get enough chances, that's the problem. It's unfair, the way it is. Disease getting all the chances it wants, and we getting so few. If it were the other way around we would stumble on the solution one way or another. However, I do thank you for trying. A noble job you have done."

Amalia looked at her mother's unmoving form in the bed. The sick woman's breath could not even make the coverlet rise and fall.

Duft continued. "Earlier she asked for you, but that is over now.

The doctor says there is no more use for hope. We brought you here for nothing. You may—" His words were suddenly choked off. He covered his mouth, and I saw that his discharging of me was the flag of his surrender, perhaps the first time in seven years when hope had not inflated him to futile action.

I listened to Frau Duft's breaths: quiet and short. Then I looked at my friend again. My vibrant Amalia looked hollow and fragile, and I realized that when this woman was finally gone, the girl's loneliness would be complete. She would have no one left to hold her hand and stroke her hair, nor would she have a friend with whom to boast and dream, for my position at Haus Duft would expire along with her mother.

I, too, began to cry, for the mother and the daughter—but also for myself. Duft, tears in his eyes to match mine, nodded knowingly at me, as if he were finally prepared to begin acknowledging the presence of sadness in the world. He led me to the door.

"Please sing," Amalia said, automatically, without looking up.

"Dear," said Duft, "there is no use. She is not awake."

"Please," she said. Her voice cracked, but she did not cry. I had never seen tears on that face.

And so, against the sense of Science, I began to sing. From that small library of music in my head, I chose sections from Dufay's *Mass for St. Anthony*, a piece written when music was still pure and clear, more like a shallow mountain stream than today's profound musical oceans. Frau Duft had heard it many times, and I knew she loved the *Gloria*.

I sang. Duft stared at his wife's sleeping form. Amalia covered her face with her hands and finally let fall all the tears that had built up during these years of stoic visits. I sang more loudly. The lamp above my head began to ring. Duft's body made no sound. Frau Duft, too, was unreceptive to my voice. But Amalia cried harder, her body opened to my voice, ringing faintly like the lamp above us—a sound she could not hear, but that I hoped she dearly felt like my warm arms around her neck.

She laid her head on the edge of her mother's bed and sobbed.

Then, suddenly, Frau Duft's eyelids fluttered. She looked at me, and as on the first day I had sung for her, I saw again the echo of my mother in those eyes.

She reached out a trembling, bony hand to touch her daughter's sobbing head. Amalia started, sat up, and tried to stop her tears, but there were so many, and they had waited so long to fall. This time she could not hold them back. She took her mother's hand and cried into it, clutching the bone and skin to her wet cheek. Frau Duft could not hold her; even her eyelids were too heavy.

I sang on. My voice was strong, strong enough to hold Amalia while she cried, strong enough to fight with death. I sang louder. My arms were weightless with their ringing; my feet seemed to lift off the floor, so that I was like a bell hanging from the sky. My voice rang not only in the lamp, but louder in Amalia now, and humming in the floorboards, in the ceiling, and in the windowpanes behind the bed.

The walls of that house took up my voice and resounded. Each of those million million tiny shells filled with my voice and passed it on in a chain of song, until the whole house was singing. And then my voice reached farther: into the earth below the house and out into the sky and soon I knew I was making the whole world shake, just as my mother had rung the world with her bells. The shaking was quiet—no one but I could hear it—but everyone in the Duft household could feel it as a warmth that made them smile.

I sang even more loudly, and my voice shook off all the dirt and grime that weighed us down. It shook away sadness and disease. It shook away fear and worry. It shook the meek into courage. The sick rose from their beds. My voice shook the desperation from their eyes. It shook the exhaustion from their bodies, the disease from their lungs. We had again what we had lost.

III.

Frau Duft did not die that day, but it was the last time she heard my voice. A week later, we sang the *Trauermusik* at her funeral.

I was never invited back into Haus Duft. My friendship with Amalia was over—or so it seemed to me in the weeks following the funeral. I did see her frequently, however, for now that her aunt's influence in the household had increased, Amalia was taken to Mass nearly every day. When I sat among the other nonperforming choir-boys near the high altar, I had no chance to approach the grating that split the nave in two; but on those occasions when I sang in the choir, after Mass I stole to the grating's gate near the wall of the church. The gate was always locked and never used. I could hide myself if I pressed up against the stone pillar on which its hinges hung. Through the gate's ornate metalwork I could glimpse her just behind her aunt, among the throng of worshippers passing out the door.

For several months I did no more than peer at her between two golden leaves, but then, one Sunday, I could not resist; I softly sang her name. She looked to her left, her right, behind her. Several other worshippers did as well—thank God her aunt was nearly deaf—and then she passed out the door. I did the same after the next Mass at which I sang, and once again after the next. That third time, I noted that she was walking slowly, waiting to hear her name, and when I whispered it, she turned to look straight at my eye peering through the gate.

The next time I sang, another two weeks later, I did not need to call. I heard Amalia tell her aunt that she wished to look at the plaster relief of St. Gallus, which adorned the wall just outside the gate. Karoline looked up at the statue as if she suspected it of foul play, but as her eyes rested on the face of the abbey's patron saint, she nodded approvingly and passed out the door. Amalia stepped to the relief. If not for the densely woven metalwork of the gate, I could have reached out and touched her shoulder. She bowed her head. For a moment I doubted she knew that I was there.

Then her pious face broke into a grin. "You'll get in trouble," she said.

"So will you."

"But I don't care," she said proudly. "I'm not afraid of her."

"I'm not afraid either," I lied.

She grinned again, and then fought it down. She appeared to have resumed her prayer.

"I'll come every Sunday," she suddenly said aloud.

"Only when I sing. Next time is Pentecost."

"I know when you sing. I can hear you."

"Can you?"

"Yes. Even when twenty other voices sing."

"How do you know it's me?" I asked.

"Don't be stupid. I know." She looked toward my eye. She smiled warmly. "I've got to go." She strode away into the flow of worshippers and out the northern door.

On Pentecost, just as she had promised, when I pressed my eye against the gate, nestled behind the pillar so no monk would see, there she was, telling her aunt she would once again pray before the saint. An approving nod from Karoline.

"I told you I would come," she said.

We spoke for thirty seconds, and then she was gone. The same the next time I sang, and every Sunday after that for many months. We never spoke for long, for fear of being caught, and though I saw all of her there was to see, she saw no more of me than that single eye and scraps of my black choir robe.

"Such a witch," Amalia spat at the back of her withdrawing aunt one Sunday. "Now she says I can't walk to church."

"Why not?" I asked.

" 'Girls of your age should not walk in the streets, even with an escort.' Should I spend my life in the house or in a coach? With her? 'I'll make you into a lady,' she says, *even if it kills me*.' I hope it does. If only each smudge of dirt on my dress would take an hour off her life.

She's just angry that she's a spinster, but that doesn't mean she can make me the lady she wishes she had been." Her face was red with rage.

"I think you're a lady already," I said.

She clenched her teeth, but laughter burst through her nose. She stifled her embarrassment. "How would you know?"

I did not reply then, but I saw every week that what I said was true: she was becoming a lady. The gold of her hair darkened slightly. She'd grown taller. My head would no longer have reached her shoulder, for I was stunted. I had gained no more than an inch a year since Karl Victor had thrown me in the river. I had so little to tell her at our visits, and she so much. "She's been trying for years to prod him gently," she said one Sunday in Lent, "but yesterday she finally got so angry she spoke it straight: 'It's time, Willibald. It is time to find a wife.' Father was shocked! As if he had discovered a thief with a hand in his safe. He looked across the table, to me and then to her. 'A wife?' he said. 'A wife? No, Karoline. I will not remarry. Never.' And when she admonished him, he shouted—he's never shouted like that before—'*I shall never remarry!* Never speak to me of it again.'"

Amalia told me how her father had grown only richer. "Your awful abbot even visited him in our house! I would have hidden in my room, but Karoline made me sit meekly by her side."

And then, when the next Pentecost had come and gone: "I can't stand it any longer, Moses. I hate that house. It's such a prison. I've asked my father if we can travel. Somewhere, anywhere. I would even go with Karoline, but that witch refuses to consider it. 'Soon you'll be married,' she says, 'and then you can travel to your husband's house.'"

In contrast, my life didn't change at all, even as the world changed around me. In the choir, new boys arrived to replace those whose voices had matured. Feder belonged to these who left the choir soon after Frau Duft's death. One day, while rehearsing a new duet, and as all the other boys watched in horror, Feder and I climbed together in complex runs, and time after time, Feder's voice stumbled and could not follow mine.

"He's doing it wrong," Feder snapped at Ulrich, and every boy seated on the floor nodded with wide eyes, unwilling to accept the inevitable.

"Moses sings it perfectly." Ulrich said reprovingly. "He always does." He smiled at me, and I cringed, for I knew that this sort of praise only made the boys hate me more.

"This time he's wrong," Feder claimed.

"Then you sing it alone," Ulrich offered. We all turned to watch Feder, redness creeping up his neck, as he began to sing. The boys clenched their fists and nodded bravely, as if cheering on a horse. He climbed, his nimble tongue slicing every note, and then again, he stumbled; he could not reach the note. He forced his voice, and every boy recoiled as his voice cracked to a screech. There was silence. Feder turned to me and raised a finger, and though I cowered, he could not find a fitting insult. He stalked out of the room.

He stayed with us for several days, singing quietly at the back, glaring at me every second. On the day of Feder's final practice, Ulrich asked me to lead the boys in scales, which were natural and distinct to me as colors are to a painter. For two minutes, the choirmaster listened as I sang and the other boys repeated after me in unison. Feder did not sing. "Continue until I return," Ulrich said and left the room.

As usual, the hierarchy of talent crumbled the moment he was gone. For two or three scales, the boys continued to mimic my notes, but less enthusiastically, and then they began to mill about, until finally I sang alone.

My voice faltered, and I stood silent before them like a king deposed. They did not look at me, but I felt how they despised me. As the boys crowded around Feder, I was reminded that my voice, in all its perfection, meant nothing in the wider world, a world to which the high-born Feder would soon be returning, and into which someday I, too, would be thrust, helpless and inadequate.

Then Feder turned his back to me and withdrew something from beneath his shirt, conspicuously hiding it from my view. The boys crowded closer, instantly hushed by what he held. One or two looked nervously at the door, through which Ulrich would soon return, but most could not divert their eyes from Feder's mysterious treasure. I did not dare approach the group, though of course I was burning with curiosity. I was sure what he held was proof against me.

After several minutes, during which the boys jostled like hogs at a trough, Feder turned toward me. He pressed a small piece of paper to his chest.

"Would you like to see, Moses?" he asked, and beneath his kindness, like a tympano's faint rolling thunder, I heard a threat. But as he stepped forward, I hoped maybe here was a final act of peace. I met him halfway. He smiled and held out the paper to me.

It was a pencil sketch, greasy along the edges from being passed through so many young hands. It showed a woman lying naked on a bed, her legs wide open, a dark cave where they met. Her eyes were impossibly large. They gaped longingly at a man standing above her, from whose midriff extended a giant, bulging penis. Testicles hung beside it, like melons in a sack.

The flush crept up my neck and burned in my cheeks. The boys cackled at the shock on my face. They leaned on one another to keep from falling over as they laughed. Of course, I had heard them discussing such a scene before, but had never pictured it this clearly in my mind. Feder held the picture in front of me for what seemed like hours, but I could not take my eyes from the man, from his organ, from the black hole between the woman's legs. Finally I pulled my eyes away and to the floor.

"Don't you want to look at it some more?" Feder whispered cruelly.

I did. Of course I did, but I knew I could not let them see my eagerness.

"Have you never seen a naked woman before? Do you even know what that is?" Feder said very slowly, as if speaking to an idiot. He pointed between the woman's legs, and the boys behind him erupted in nervous laughter.

I forced myself to look again at the ground. I felt their stares on me like prodding sticks. "Or maybe," he said, and turned to speak with the boys now, "she does not interest him at all. Perhaps it is the man you prefer."

There was no laughter now, just silence.

When I blinked, the slosh of tears seemed so loud I was sure every boy could hear my shame.

"I'm leaving today," Feder finally said, softly enough it seemed he was speaking only to me now. "I am very happy that I will never have to share a choir with someone like you again. I had hoped, however, to be able to stay a little longer—until you finally left. I would have liked to see this abbey just once again how it used to be. Without you. Without those two filthy monks who are your only friends."

I knew that Nicolai and Remus's secret had long since seeped throughout the abbey. The boys had whispered about them, but this was the first time anyone had spoken of it aloud. My shame over this picture and my love for my friends erupted into anger. I snatched the picture out of Feder's hand and tore it in half. I tore it again as he knocked me down, but then I lost the scraps as he kicked me.

The silence was broken. The boys crowded around us, and I could hear the hatred in their voices as they cheered for Feder to "kick the dog." He unleashed the best he had. Blood flowed from my mouth until I was sure I would never breathe again. And all along, as his fury swelled beyond any reason, still I heard them jeering, "Kick him, Feder! It's time he understands! Pay him back!"

For what? I tried to cry. *Pay you back for what?*

The next day he was gone. I remained in the abbey, the oldest, most talented, and least respected choirboy. My life, it seemed to me then, would never change.

IV.

A year after the death of Frau Duft, I began to grow.

It was as if all of that Nebelmatt plunder, all those St. Gall lamb shanks, all that bacon, all that mutton, all that cheese, those almonds, that milk, cider, and wine, had all merely been stored away in my little body, and then, all of a sudden, I discovered all that hidden fuel and used it finally to burst my shell.

It began as a dull pain in my hands and feet during choir practice one day. The ache remained for several weeks, then one morning I awoke to discover it had spread to my knees, my hips, and elbows, and then to all my joints. It hurt so much I could not sleep. The pain spread to my eye sockets, and I imagined my skull would split. In six months my hands and feet had doubled in size; in a year I had grown a head taller.

In the abbey, my growth was viewed with concern, like the gathering of dark clouds. "Hard times to come," Nicolai told me one night in his cell. He told me how my voice would soon crack, and I would no longer be a soprano.

"There is no telling what will happen," he said. "You will probably be a tenor, but maybe a bass." He hoped Ulrich's favor would be enough to find a way for me to stay in the abbey. Staudach, Nicolai said, might not agree to make me a novice, with no wealthy parent to be my benefactor, but he might let me polish silver until my voice developed its final character. "Then," Nicolai said, "we can find the best place for you to begin your career." He nodded knowingly. "Venice, most likely."

"My career?" I asked.

"You do want to be a musician, do you not?"

I considered this. "Like Bugatti?"

"Well," said Nicolai, as he glanced over at Remus, deep in his book, "in a way. Maybe Staudach would let me out to take you on tour. We could sing in all the greatest cathedrals of Europe." Nicolai waved an arm as if those great buildings were lined up on his wall.

I told him I would like that.

"Of course," he said, "the next time I leave these walls, I doubt Stuckduck will let me back in. But then we could start our own monastery—you, me, and Remus." At this, Remus looked up from his book. He snorted, then returned to his pages. Nicolai ignored him. "One thing is sure: if you're allowed to tour the world and become rich and famous, you are not leaving me behind!"

I smiled.

He lay back on his bed and closed his eyes contentedly. "Now we just have to wait for your voice. Be patient."

Many nights I stood naked before the narrow mirror in my attic room and examined the body that seemed every night to have changed. *I have made you a musico*, Rapucci had said, and now there was no doubt. There were Bugatti's long, delicate fingers, his broad, rounded chest, almost like a bird's. My head brushed the slanted ceiling. Bugatti had seemed so tall to me years before, but now I was taller still, taller than all the monks save Nicolai. The novices my age had dark hairs above their lips, I had none. They had Adam's apples jutting from their necks; mine was as smooth as a woman's. My skin was white and pure, with dabs of red on my cheeks, but not a single imperfection, none of the pimples like the other boys. My lips were slightly plump, not unlike a woman's, but no one would ever have mistaken this face for a woman's face. Those eyes were so piercing they made me start each time I glimpsed them in the mirror. But still I looked every night, for I saw in the glass not a man, not a woman, but an angel.

I outgrew that church. I destroyed the choir, because even when I sang at low volume my voice made the other boys' seem narrow and cold. In our brief encounters at the gate, where Amalia still bowed her head and seemed to be in prayer to any who might see her, I longed to hear her praise my singing. "Oh, Moses," she said one Sunday, "my heart flutters when you sing. To think my mother and I used to have you to ourselves." I peered through a higher gap now, looking down upon her beauty. Occasionally, she glanced up, and I saw her trying to discern my shape through the tangles of golden leaves, but she never saw my angelic form. "Touch my hand," she said one day, impetuously, abandoning her pious bow for a moment to reach out to touch the gate. I passed two long, slender fingers through a hole and caressed the soft skin of her hand for an instant. Her cheeks burned as she hurried back to meet her aunt.

Everyone wanted to hear me sing. Even Protestants from the city came to hear our Mass. Eventually, the huge church was too small to sustain the crowds. Staudach portioned the entrance so that the wealthier worshippers, whose favor he required, would be sure of securing pews. The others jostled to stand at the back. The crowd whispered and slept and ate while Staudach preached of God's perfection, but they were silent while I sang.

Then, in a single night, all of this, and much more, did change.

We were in Nicolai's room. Remus was reading gloomily, and Nicolai was regaling me with visions of our future: we would travel Europe together as singer and agent. He had somehow conspired to escape the refectory that night with three pitchers of abbey wine, and having already drunk two of them, he was bleary eyed, and in the best of moods. Now his plan for me had morphed: A palace in Venice would be our home, and from there we would travel to the greatest of Europe's stages. We would take Remus along to carry our bags, he explained, laughing and roaring so loudly I was sure every monk in the passage could hear.

Nicolai had decided that since my voice was so amazingly slow in changing, I would certainly become a tenor. "Tenors are the worst," he said. "They dress like princes, strut around as if their every movement should make ladies swoon, which of course is the case. Everywhere they go they leave a trail of unconscious women in their wake.

You cannot invite them to your dinner parties, because you'd have a pile of guests upon the floor." Suddenly he looked very concerned. "You won't be like that, will you, Moses?"

I shook my head.

"No?" he cried, after downing another goblet of wine. "And why not? What is wrong with making a few women faint? That is what they want. Every woman wants to faint from love at least once in her life. Men want that, too, of course, but their size makes it harder for them to swoon. I've only swooned once before out of love."

"Not for real," Remus said, looking up. "At the Teatro Ducale you were faking."

"I was not."

I glimpsed a suppressed grin on Remus's face. "If you ever really faint," he said, "the world will know. Floors are not built to withstand such stress."

Nicolai shrugged. "He's right. I am not permitted to faint. What I would not give to be a slender lady! Then I could collapse whenever the spirit took me! I would do it all the time." He stood up and gave his best impression of daintiness, his giant hands before his chest like a rabbit's paws. "I would tune my ears and eyes so sharply to beauty in all its forms that I would totter on the edge. All I would need would be a glimpse to make my heart flutter, and I would fall." He looked at me, pretended to fall in love, put a hand to his forehead, and then swooned, carefully, gently, onto the bed. Even so, the bed frame whined. I clapped at his performance. Remus grunted.

"As it is," Nicolai said, reclining on the mattress and staring at the ceiling, "with this frame I need to dull my ears and cloud my eyes so I do not run risks for myself and for mankind. This body is a responsibility." He rubbed his vast gut with two giant hands.

Remus shook his head.

"Don't worry, Moses," Nicolai said, giving his belly a last, loving pat. "Remus worships this form one way or another."

Remus looked up angrily from his book, no grin on his face now. "You need to watch your tongue. That wine is making it loose."

"Oh, dear Remus, we don't have secrets here. Not with Moses. He keeps nothing from us. We keep nothing from him."

"Some things are better left unspoken."

Nicolai nodded up at the ceiling. "You are right, Remus. Some loves cannot be spoken of."

Remus frowned. "Thank you." He shrugged abashedly at me as if to pardon the affront.

"Sometimes only song can do." Nicolai sat up. I smiled. Remus looked pained. We both heard the energy in his voice—the gathering of a storm.

"No, Nicolai. Not now."

"Moses?"

"Yes?" I sat up and placed my hands on my knees, an eager audience.

He poured another goblet of wine and drank it down like water, and then stood in the middle of the room. He swayed from side to side. His eyes were unfocused, but so bright and joyful. "It is time to sing!"

Remus closed his book. "Nicolai, it is too late," he said. He stood. "Moses and I will go."

"It is never too late to sing of love."

"Tonight it is." Remus pointed his book at Nicolai. "Don't give them another reason to hate you, Nicolai."

"Hate me? How could anyone hate me for my love?"

"We will talk about it in the morning."

"When I am not so drunk on love?"

"Among other liquids." Remus nodded at me and beckoned toward the door.

"No!" cried Nicolai, as if I were about to betray him. He raised a finger to keep me in my chair, swaying gently behind it. "A sincere lover never backs down from a declaration of his love. Now I must sing, or else the gods will not believe in my love."

"Please," Remus said earnestly. "Not tonight."

Nicolai looked at me. "Do you see the problem? If I sing they hate me; if I do not, I hate myself." He shrugged. "It is not a difficult choice."

He returned to his wine, poured yet another goblet, took a gulp, and stepped onto his improvised stage. Remus pulled my sleeve. I leaned as if I would get up to leave with him, but I did not. I could not.

Nicolai began extremely quietly: *O cessate di piagarmi, o lasciatemi morir, o lasciatemi morir!* He turned toward me and whispered: "'O release me from this anguish, o let me die, o let me die!' Don't you see, Moses? I'm tortured by love!"

Luc' ingrate, dispietate. He swayed wildly, his arms like branches in the wind. He sang more loudly now, loud enough that other monks must have heard him through the walls. *Più del gelo e più dei marmi fredde e sordi ai miei martir, fredde e sorde ai miei martir.* Nicolai put his hands over his eyes as though he wished to tear them out.

"Okay, Nicolai," said Remus. He tugged harder on my shirt. "That is enough. You have made your point."

Nicolai repeated, *O cessate di piagarmi, o lasciatemi morir, o lasciatemi morir!*

"Moses," Remus said. He shook my arm. "We have to go. He'll stop if we leave."

"That's what they do," Nicolai said to me, as if Remus were not there. "They just repeat the same thing over and over and over and over again. It makes it stronger. And besides, it is not the words that matter. It is the song."

O cessate di piagarmi, o lasciatemi morir, o lasciatemi morir! He sang even more loudly now, and placed his hand over his heart as if it were about to burst. His vibrant bass rang in my stomach. I was sure the whole wing could hear his love song. I couldn't contain the smile growing on my face. I laughed with joy. Nicolai did not have my perfect control of the notes, but he grasped the power of the music.

"You, too, Moses." He reached a hand out to welcome me onto his stage.

"Moses, please," Remus said.

I looked from the one man to the other, Remus with such worry on his face, Nicolai with such joy. It was not a difficult choice to make.

I had never sung in Italian before, but I did my best to imitate Nicolai, two octaves higher. *O cessate di piagarmi, o lasciatemi morir, o lasciatemi morir!*

"Louder!" he yelled, like some pagan priest. "Heaven needs to hear us!"

O cessate di piagarmi, o lasciatemi morir, o lasciatemi morir!

"Together!" He shut his eyes and waved his arms.

O cessate di piagarmi, o lasciatemi morir, o lasciatemi morir!

As I repeated the words again alone, Nicolai improvised, and then he sang a simple bass line while I improvised. We sang the same words over and over, each time further and further from the original until only the words remained the same. The song was no longer about love; now it was about music, about the power of music. Power like Zeus's thunderbolt.

Nicolai sang alone.

We sang together.

I sang alone.

Nicolai laughed while I trilled. I drew out each word to ten, twenty notes, and that single sentence lasted a minute. Nicolai shook his head in admiration. Though Remus crouched as though he wanted to run out of the room, his eyes were riveted on my face, his mouth slightly ajar. I realized in that moment that no one, save for Ulrich, knew the true power of my voice. In church, I had been restrained by those tame, sacred songs. Now I felt the power of this Italian music, so much more potent than even Bach's. I drew a breath into my enormous lungs and I sang. My voice swelled as it climbed. Nicolai's mirror rang with the vibrations of my voice. I sang more loudly. I wanted to shatter every window in the abbey with the beauty of my song. I breathed again, and my voice ebbed, then swelled higher, until I found a note as high and clear as I had ever sung. I held it, my voice vibrating tiny ripples of sound within the larger wave, until that giant breath was gone.

I stopped and gasped for air. It took several seconds until my voice finally dissipated into the night. Then, in the silence, I could see on my friends' faces that in an instant my life had changed.

Nicolai no longer smiled. He held his hand in front of his mouth. His face was white, as though he had seen a ghost. "God forgive us," he said.

Remus stared at the floor.

"What?" I asked. "What is wrong?" But I already knew what was wrong, knew it even though I did not understand it at all.

Nicolai had tears in his eyes. "How could I have been such a fool?" he said.

Remus looked up at me, and his eyes seemed to say, *Moses, it is time for us to stop pretending.* And then he looked back at the floor.

Nicolai stared at me as if my body were dissolving into mist. He took a step toward me and reached out.

I backed away from him. I felt like an animal cornered, as if I could already feel the jaws around my neck.

Nicolai pounced. His huge body pressed me up against the wall. He stank of wine.

"No!" I yelled. I shook my head furiously.

"I am sorry, Moses," he said. "I need to know for sure." He pulled up my shirt.

I tried to push him away, but he was too strong. I felt his hands at my underclothes, and as I squirmed in his grasp, he tore them away, and suddenly I was standing there exposed. Neither monk moved for a long moment; then Nicolai released me. He held out a shaking hand, as if begging me to pardon the assault. His breath was ragged. He clenched and blinked his bloodshot, bleary eyes as though fighting for his fogged, drunken vision to obey him.

Remus stood behind Nicolai. He put his hand on the taller man's shoulder. "Nicolai," he said. "You must—"

Nicolai batted the hand away. He took several slow breaths. Then he looked deep into my eyes. Though I knew the anger there was not for me, I found it terrifying. "Who did it?" he whispered.

"No, Nicolai," Remus said, as calmly as he could.

"Moses, you must tell me. Tell me now."

Remus grasped Nicolai's arm with both his hands. In all our time together, I had never seen him hold Nicolai like that. "Please, Nicolai," he said. He shook the arm. "Nicolai! Please!"

Nicolai suddenly grabbed me by the shoulders. "Ulrich? Was it Ulrich?"

"Nicolai, don't," Remus pleaded. "Not now. Tomorrow. Do nothing rash."

Nicolai shook me as if I were weightless. "Tell me, Moses!" he roared.

Remus's eyes were wet. "Please, Moses," he said. "Do not answer him."

"I vowed to protect him," Nicolai shouted at Remus.

"It is too late," Remus said to me.

"Tell me," Nicolai said. In his eyes was a rage I had never known could exist in this kind man.

I looked from Remus's pleading face back to Nicolai. *Please,* their eyes said. *Please.*

"Ulrich," I said.

Nicolai nodded as he backed away. Remus clutched his sleeve and begged him to stop. Nicolai turned and, with a single, effortless shove, pushed his friend to the floor. Nicolai opened the door, stumbled slightly against the doorframe, and then was gone.

We rushed after him, but though he had drunk so much, he ran quickly through the darkness. He stumbled and fell down the top half-flight of stairs, but was soon on his feet again. His steps echoed through the abbey's halls, and by the time we passed the first floor, other monks were peering out their doors.

"It is nothing," Remus said, waving them back, but that merely convinced them to follow. There was a pounding from the ground floor. We arrived to see Nicolai rushing at Ulrich's door. He bounced off it with a crash, took three steps back—a deep breath—and roared as he ran for it again. He smashed it with his shoulder, tearing it off its hinges. Nicolai stomped into the room, which was lit by a single candle.

Ulrich was expecting this. He had been waiting for five years, and he was already trying to flee. The old man was at his window, gingerly mounting the sill so he could jump down into the dark cloister. But Nicolai was already there, and instead of pulling the choirmaster back into the room, he grabbed him—one hand on his tunic and one seizing the sparse hair on the back of his head—and heaved him through the open window.

Ulrich screamed as he flew. It was an empty, soulless scream. He hit the ground, and I heard ribs cracking, like the splintering of a violin. He wheezed as he gasped for air.

Giant Nicolai followed him through the window. He toppled off the sill as he reached with one foot for the ground, but he was soon on his feet again. He stumbled above the broken man and began to kick him. Ulrich tried to crawl away, but Nicolai's first kick broke his left arm. He fell forward. His face pressed into the grass. He groaned with each blow.

There were monks staring down from every window. Blood seeped from Ulrich's mouth. He spat as he tried to breathe.

I watched from Ulrich's window. I did not avert my eyes. The kicks and screams did not give me any joy—shame was rising up from deep within me, shame that had simmered unseen since Rapucci told me what he had done to me. Shame, because though I did not even understand fully what I had become, I knew it was terrible, terrible enough that this man deserved to die for it.

Beside me, Remus was half out the window, pleading for Nicolai to stop, but the giant only paused to wipe away his tears. Nicolai buried his face in his hands and roared. "Just a boy!" he yelled. "He was just a boy!" And then he kicked the crawling, crying Ulrich again—jolts of pain for every future joy this man had stolen from me. Blood bubbled from Ulrich's mouth as he begged for forgiveness, but Nicolai had none to give.

Four soldiers ran across the cloister. Two held lamps, and the others drew their swords. But when they saw it was not some thief, but only Nicolai, the kindest of the monks, they froze, unsure of what to do.

They shouted at him to stop, waved their swords, but he did not heed them; he could not. One soldier stepped forward and raised his sword, but then he let it fall again. Then the two armed men dropped their blades and all four grabbed the huge monk's arms. They grappled with him, while bloody Ulrich tried again to crawl away. The monks all yelled for Nicolai to stop. "For the love of God, you will kill him!" Now the abbot had come, too. He stood at an open window, yelling down at the soldiers, "Stop him! Use your swords if you must! Stop him!"

But still Nicolai was not done. He struggled with the guards, roaring like a madman. He freed one arm, and instead of using it to beat them back, he took one of the soldiers' lamps and lifted it above the struggle, high above his face. His eyes were lit like two drops of fire. I knew this fury was for me, for my shame, the shame I had secreted away these many years. And though everyone—Remus, the monks, the abbot—was screaming around me, I was silent. I did not ask Nicolai to stop.

He hurled the lamp at broken Ulrich, who had given up on escape. The lamp smashed on the ground, and for a moment Ulrich's face was wet with oil. His eyes stared at me in horror. And then, before he could bat out the flame, his face reddened, and then my teacher burned. He screamed.

V.

"He wishes forgiveness."

Remus spoke for the silent Nicolai once we were alone with the abbot. It was well past midnight now, and the frenzied clerk had lit but a single candle before fleeing from the scene. Placed on Staudach's desk, the flame gave the small abbot a supernatural height. The shadow of his head was huge on the wall and ceiling behind his desk.

"Forgiveness?"

Remus nodded.

Staudach shook his head nervously. "Not from me."

I heard monks chanting in the church, praying for Ulrich's soul, and for Nicolai's. No one would sleep that night. We had all watched Ulrich beat his face with his hands, trying to smother the flames that melted his eyes and skin. None of us had helped him. We merely watched in shocked silence until the flames were out and he lay still on the ground. Then four monks carried his smoking body to the fountain and doused him until the water was red with blood.

"If he dies, you will be hanged," Staudach said.

Though Nicolai stood proud and defiant before the abbot, his breath was shallow, fear in the quivers of its flow.

"Surely, Abbot," said Remus, "even if there is no room for forgiveness, still there can be mercy." Remus stood in front of us at the desk, his moist eyes glinting in the candlelight.

"Mercy?" Staudach shook his head, and the movement was repeated ten times larger in the shadows behind him. "I cannot give mercy to those who wish to destroy this monastery."

"Do not kill a kind man in our name." Remus's voice trembled, as did his hands, half raised in supplication.

"A kind man, you say?" The abbot leaned forward and the shadow of his head doubled on the wall. "Dominikus, a kind man does not beat his brother. A kind man does not set fire to his brother."

"He deserved all that and more," Nicolai said from the shadows. His voice was quiet, but sure.

Staudach turned his eyes to Nicolai and examined him in the dim light. He spoke sharply. "What crime could possibly deserve what you have wrought?"

Nicolai looked blankly at the abbot, but he did not answer.

"Speak!" Staudach ordered.

"I broke an oath."

"You have one vow, and that is to me!" Staudach roared and slapped his desk with a palm. I shrank away. The abbot looked at Remus and then at Nicolai. "Now, which of you will defend this wickedness?"

"You have already pledged to kill me," Nicolai answered. "I will not say."

The cold eyes shifted to the smaller monk. "Dominikus then, speak."

"No, Abbot."

"And you," he finally said to me. "Why are you here? What do you have to say?"

Though I was so much taller than the abbot, I still felt like that tiny child who first stood in this office years ago, the runt he had wished to banish from this very room.

"Speak!"

We were silent. The candle sizzled. Staudach breathed. He looked at Nicolai. "Then you leave me no choice," he said.

Nicolai's hands were shaking.

"He had me castrated," I said.

I felt his eyes slide slowly over my every feature. On his face, first disbelief, then horror. He finally understood why my voice had held so very long.

"Castrated?" he whispered. My friends stared at the candle burning on the desk.

"Where?"

They did not reply.

He turned to me. His throat was tight; he struggled to exhale. He coughed his words: "Speak! Where! Was it in this abbey?"

I so wanted to be strong, but my knees shook as if the ground it-self twitched beneath them.

The abbot rose up and loomed over the candle. "You are a cas-trate? A eunuch?"

I nodded. The abbot's face was as white as the stone of his church. His pectoral cross glimmered in the candle's glow.

"For how long?"

"The inauguration of the church."

"But that was five years ago," Staudach said, terror growing in his voice.

I nodded.

"God have mercy," he whispered. For several seconds he did not move at all. He stared past us. "Death to the castrator," the abbot recited. "Excommunication to all those who aid. That is the law. My law. The pope's law. *It is God's law.*" As if realizing his voice was ris-ing, he cleared his throat and whispered again, "A boy castrated. In my abbey!" Color returned to his face. He glared at Nicolai. "I never wanted him here. I tried to send him away, but you would not let me.

"While the Nuncio slept here? Eighteen abbots! They heard you sing! They will think I ordered it. That I held the knife. They could excommunicate me. Me!" The abbot grasped the cross hanging at his chest.

"They never need to know, Abbot. We will leave," Remus said, stepping forward. "Tonight."

"Yes," said Staudach, nodding, looking through Remus at some distant shadow. "Yes, you must. You and Nicolai both."

"And the boy."

"No!" said Staudach. He reached out as if to grab me. Nicolai clasped my sleeve and pulled me back. "No, he must stay here," the abbot continued, pointing a single, shaking finger at Nicolai and then Remus. "You, you both must leave. You are exiled. If you place a foot on abbey lands again I will hang you for murder and for castration."

"Madness," Remus said.

The abbot nodded, his finger now aimed at Remus's chest. "For both those crimes you both will die, if you ever return here or to any monastery in the Confederation."

Nicolai spoke. "I will not leave Moses here."

"You will!" The abbot strained across his desk.

"I would rather die." Nicolai slowly approached the desk, and I thought that he would overturn it. Staudach shrank back and fell into his chair. He whimpered and held up one hand as if to protect his face. Nicolai grasped the edge of the desk.

"No," I said. They all turned in surprise. "No, Nicolai. You must go."

Nicolai shook his head. "No, Moses. I will not. Not without you."

"I have ordered it!" the abbot yelled.

With the candle behind him, I could not make out Nicolai's face, nor Remus's next to him, though between them I saw clearly the abbot's scowl. For years, this is how I would remember them: their silhouettes standing bravely between me and the abbot, willing to die rather than abandon me.

"Nicolai," I said.

He turned and grabbed my shoulders. "I will not leave you with him," he said, his voice now deep and resonant, as fearless as his chants.

"You must," I whispered, my voice a thousand times weaker than his. "You have no choice."

"I would rather die," Nicolai said.

"And then I will truly be alone."

Nicolai shook his head. He was close enough now that I could see tears filling his eyes. "Moses, I vowed to protect you."

"Someday I will follow you," I said. "I promise."

Remus was at my elbow. "We will go to Melk," he whispered into my ear so the abbot would not hear. "In Austria. You will always have friends as long as we are alive. We will be waiting for you. Come."

I nodded at him, biting my lip. Remus took Nicolai's arm, but the bigger man shrugged him off. He shook his head, his eyes wide.

"Nicolai," I said. He seemed to shatter, and suddenly we were embracing. Now, eight years after he had pulled me from that river,

my head reached above his shoulder, and when he held me, I felt his
warm tears on my brow.

"I am so sorry," he said.

"I . . . I will come and find you," I whispered back. I grasped the
fabric of his tunic in my fists. He hugged me and I knew that he would
never release me unless I let go first, and so I pushed him gently away.
Then Remus conveyed him to the door, and without looking again at
the abbot, they left. Later, I would visit their cells and see that they
had not even paused to collect their things. Nicolai did not make one
last prayer in that church. Remus did not take a single book.

Neither man would ever return to St. Gall or to the Swiss Confederation.

I remained alone with Abbot Coelestin Gugger von Staudach. He
stared at the candle on the table, its flame glowing perfectly like the
world he always longed to realize in this abbey. After several minutes,
he looked up at me. His eyes had lost their coldness, their hatred.

"Come here, my son," he said. He nodded kindly, as if to say, *It is
all over now.*

I hesitated only for a moment. Though I found him repulsive, I
had no one else in the world now. I walked around his desk and stood
beside him in the light of his candle. I bowed my head. His eyes
moved across my face, down along my tall, thin form.

"You wish to go with them, do you not?"

"Yes," I said.

His eyes looked deeply into mine. "Moses, do you know what you
are?"

I did not answer.

He regarded me carefully in the candle's flicker, his gaze sliding
across each feature of my face, then he nodded gravely, as if he were the
bearer of terrible news. His voice was calm and measured once again.
"My son, you are a eunuch. You are not a man. Nor are you a woman.
You are a creature that God never intended to create, and so you are
destined to remain outside God's design. His law says you cannot

marry; nor may you become a priest. This is not cruelty. I expect if you are sincere, you see why it must be so. Moses, your body will not let you be a father. You are weak—a woman's muscles on a man's heavy frame. You cannot work the fields. And your mind is also weak. You will never know manly reason. Did your friends tell you this, Moses?"

I shook my head. Though I had never heard those things said before, I had always feared them.

"They want to help you, but they cannot. They have no roof to sleep under." He waved his hand dismissively. "No abbey will shelter them, for they are sodomites. Any abbot will easily read sin in their faces, as I have, and will turn them away. You could follow them, and you would starve together. Only they are men, Moses, and you are not. People will laugh at you outside these walls. Here we have been deceived by the slow progression of your condition. Only now do I see it clearly in your form. You are an accident of nature, a product of sin rather than of grace."

The abbot looked past me, searching for a solution to my existence in the dark corners of his office. He shook his head. "This is so unfortunate, Moses," he said. "So unfortunate. This world was simply not made for those like you."

I felt a great weakness extending from my center, a vibration that threatened to bring me to my knees. Everything he said was true. How could I deny it? In the abbot's worried face, for the first time, I saw that perhaps he was not so cold and heartless. He was merely a man who worked so hard to put the chaotic world into order. One hundred thousand people depended on his guidance, and now, here he was, hours before dawn, caring for one single soul alone.

His eyes appraised me carefully. "Moses, I cannot keep you here against your will. I will not. The abbey is not a prison. What I said before—that they could not take you with them—I said that for their good and for yours. But now that we are alone, you must make your choice. Go, if you wish; you may still find them. Go and tell them that they must care for you, that they must take you with them. They will not deny you. They will find a way to feed you, they will find a way to care for you, even if it means they will suffer for it."

The abbot was silent. He watched me carefully.

Go? I wanted nothing more. With my friends departed, I already felt the lonely emptiness of the abbey creeping into every room. And out there, two friends who loved me.

Still, the abbot did not speak. His measured breath flowed in, out, in, out.

"I will allow you to stay here, Moses," he finally said. "Those in this abbey have done you a great wrong, and so I shall do what I can to correct it. If you choose it, I will grant you what I denied you years ago: the chance to become a novice and, one day perhaps, a monk. You shall keep your cell. We shall continue to provide for you. I will see that you damage no one with your weakness. No one must know of your imperfection. I alone will know. Moses, I hope you see there is nothing more that I or anyone can offer you."

I pictured Nicolai and Remus, not as I had met them—on the finest stallions, Nicolai with enough abbey coins in his pockets to toss at beggars on the road—but as they were now: stealing through the city, on foot, pockets empty, Remus without a single book to read. How long would Nicolai's strident certainty endure? One day? One week? He had never walked a mile in his life. Would they be the beggars now? Surely they had enough burdens without another, without, as the abbot said, *an accident of nature* to carry with them. Nicolai had done so much for me already: for me he had been exiled from his home.

"Moses," the abbot said. "You must choose."

My nod was slight, but sufficient.

"Good. But you must promise me something, too, Moses."

I looked into his narrow, shining eyes.

"You must promise never to sing again."

VI.

I sealed my pledge to him. He had me kneel before him and he said a prayer and then he nodded kindly at the door. But to me, his prayer seemed an incantation, because everything I heard was changed. The creaking of the door, the hiss of my sliding steps across the empty foyer—for the first time in my life I didn't gain any comfort from these sounds, or any others. Outside, a morning mist hung about the grass in lifeless swirls and dimmed the glimmers of candlelight in the windows of the church. I fell to my knees and was sick there on the grass, heaving until there was nothing left inside me. I cried until the tears were also spent.

But even as I sobbed into my hands, as I told myself I must be thankful for the abbot's gift, my ears strained to hear: the monks chanting into the night, the swoop of a bat chasing an early morning fly. I fought the sounds. I pulled at the cold, damp grass until it came away in clumps. I clawed at the dirt until my fingers bled.

No! Those sounds are not for you. That world is not for you. Do not let it tempt you! These sounds would just make me long for more, long for the mysteries that lay outside those walls, for friends, for love, for my mother's bells, for Nicolai and Remus, and worst of all, it would make me long to sing again.

And so began the most miserable period of my life. I was forbidden to leave the abbey—even to venture into the Abbey Square, where some wandering layman might glimpse my seraphic, imperfect face. During the Holy Offices and Mass, I sat in the novices' stalls, a pillar between me and the greater nave. I never raised my voice in chant or song, never even allowed my silent prayers to rise up inside my head in a memory of what my voice had been. Once or twice I remembered what my friend Amalia had said: "I can hear you. Even when twenty other voices sing." I dreamed of calling to her, in the midst of the others' song; I was sure Staudach would not hear me. But even then shame kept me silent. I never ventured near that gate again.

Staudach had offered me the chance one day to take my vows, and so I donned the novice's habit, which is much like the monk's but lacks the hooded cuculla. (Oh, how I wished for a hood to hide my face!) This would normally have meant studying with the other novices each day under the tutelage of the novice master, Brother Leodegar, but perhaps the abbot feared I would stain the pure noviate pool, for he deemed that I should be a lay monk, untaught. I would require neither Virgil nor St. Aquinas, only obedience and submission.

No novice had been raised this way in the abbey for many years, but Staudach claimed that I could never be a modern monk, who, through learning and piety, could give back to the world. At best, I would be like St. Gall himself: lonely, humble, a hermit.

Throughout this time, I fought with sounds, just as any monk battles with his passions. When I heard the delightful babble of the cloister fountain, I beat it down with prayer. When meat sizzled in the refectory, I fasted. When the mirthful cries of children rose up outside the abbey walls and I could have basked in the warmth of their glee, I exiled myself to some empty cellar and recited the rosary. If my ears began to stray to the charms of the wind along the roofing tiles above my room, I dug my fingernails into the skin of my hand, or pulled the downy hair at the nape of my neck. I found a hairshirt rotting in a cupboard, and its itching fibers distracted me during Offices from the beauty of the chants. I listened in on other men's confessions, heard of the uncontrollable passions stirring in their loins and then, when my turn came, repeated what I had heard, hoping that through this deception I could somehow be absolved for my own sins of sound.

In this manner a year passed, and then another. As Staudach had promised, my condition remained a secret. My speaking voice was high and soft, but other men squeak and whine, so I was not betrayed. My appearance, though striking, was not enough to raise the suspicions of monks who had known me for years.

A new, mediocre choirmaster replaced the supremely talented Ulrich. This Brother Maximilian never spoke with me. No one dared openly discuss the former choirmaster, but I heard whispers. "The abbot sent him to a hospital in Zurich. He'll never get out of his bed again," said one monk. "I heard he's dead," whispered another. But when the monks saw my eyes upon them, they looked shyly at their feet. At first I did not comprehend what this mortified silence meant, but one day, as I shuffled quietly along a corridor, I overheard a conversation between three monks that made me understand that they mistook my shameful secret for another. "A boy brings such disgrace on himself," one monk insisted to the others. "Brother Ulrich allowed himself to be tempted, indeed, and he sinned most gravely, none of us deny that. But that boy was never meant for this abbey. He is a snake in our midst. I expect he wanted . . . to . . . to be *petted*." "Day after day, night after night," agreed another of the monks, "Ulrich had to spend so much time alone with the boy; he was seduced, pure and simple."

There was nothing to mark one day from the next. When I was able to calm my passion for sound, my misery was numbed; I ached only from loneliness. I thought often of Nicolai and Remus, wishing that there was some way of knowing how they fared.

The other novices were not cruel as the choirboys had been, but they were disdainful. They ignored me completely. Their fathers paid a tidy sum so they could be what I had become merely out of pity. They believed me an idiot—an opinion I did nothing to contradict. Instead, I left my cell window open so that pigeons would roost in my ceiling and give me company, but they never came.

I grew to my full height, a head taller than the other monks. My ribs grew and grew. Beneath them, my lungs expanded farther—"The Largest Lungs in Europe," one London reviewer would boast many years later. But my grand stature and bulging chest struck no one in the abbey as majestic or imposing, for I slouched, and was pale and sickly. There were bruises around my eyes from lack of sleep, for I feared to shut them. When I did, I dreamed of my mother's bells, of Nicolai's singing, or of my own voice, ringing to my fingers, and then it hurt so much to wake.

· · ·

There is a single event from that first year after my friends' exile that I need to recount. It was a Sunday in winter. Mass was finished, and on opposite sides of the grating that split the nave in two, laity and monks streamed out of the church. I remained at my place in the novices' stalls, hidden from the worshippers by one of the great white pillars.

"Moses!"

The familiar voice seemed to call from within my head. It filled me with sudden warmth, warmth I had recently felt only in my dreams. Before I could punish myself for enjoying this sound—

"Moses!"

The voice was real, because other monks were turning toward the grating.

I peered around the pillar. She stood at the grating, hands grasping the iron bars and golden vines as though she intended to tear the grating down. The decoration was not so elaborately wrought here as at the gate, and so I saw her face as she moved it from gap to gap, repeating my name into the crowd of monks, who stared at her in amazement. She ignored their shocked faces. It was as if she were seeking me in a forest of unmoving trees.

"Moses? Are you there?" she shouted again, so every ear in the church could hear. Behind her, I heard the voice of Karoline Duft approaching, pushing through the crowd, trying to save the Duft name from everlasting shame.

"Please, Moses," Amalia yelled. "Are you there?"

She had not forgotten me. I felt hope stir from its slumber. I wanted to run to that grating. I wanted to touch my friend's hand.

Amalia slid back along the grating away from her aunt. She peered at every face that stared at her, trying to find the boy she had known among these hooded men. I began to step around the pillar.

Suddenly, he was there, his hand on my shoulder. I turned toward him. The abbatial mitre brought his head as high as mine.

"Remember what you are, Moses," he whispered. "You will only bring shame on her and on the abbey."

I bowed my head. He watched me for a moment more, then glided away. When I looked back again, Karoline Duft had snatched Amalia into the throng.

I redoubled my efforts. I no longer resolved to destroy my passion for the world's sounds like a tree dying slowly for want of water—now, I would strike that tree with lightning, burn it to ashes. I prayed for God to mingle every sound with pain, to make me loathe every note I heard. I drank draughts of tar water on Holy Days so I would be nauseated when the finest singers sang. I did not eat. I paced up and down my room so I would not sleep at night and dream. Then, one early morning, when I could not control my passion, and I found my memory tempting me with luscious symphonies of half-forgotten sounds, I smashed my mirror in fury. I used the icy shards to carve gashes in my arms. Soon my hands were so soaked in blood I could not hold the splinters, but for a moment, one blessed moment, I almost felt content.

But I could not defeat my ears, no more than I could hold my breath until I expired. My heart still beat like a drum, marking the seconds of my life. At night, I awoke and, half-conscious, I broke free and embraced the window's rattle like a lover's voice. Or worse, I woke directly from a dream of my mother's bells or Nicolai's rumbling bass and found my bedclothes wet from sweat, and the echoes of my dreams still ringing in my ears. In these moments, I closed my eyes and unlocked the library of my memory, and my imagination sampled the pleasures of every sound I had ever heard. My heart soared. Hope that I could be happy in this beautiful world began to reawaken inside of me.

Until I opened my eyes and found myself in my cell, in my prison, in this imperfect body, and once more I loathed myself for dreaming.

One night I resolved to take the final step. I stole a quill from a monk. I sat upon my bed, no light in my room save the block of moonlight cast upon the floor. I turned the quill over and over in my hands and imagined its golden tip passing through the drumheads of my ears. I sat there a long time, waiting for some reason not to do what I had planned, but instead of rebelling, the sounds in my memory seemed to slowly fade, acquiescing for the first time since I had begun to fight them down. The abbey and the city grew quiet in the early hours of the morning, and then it seemed to me that the whisper of that wooden wand sliding through my hands was the only sound in the world.

When my ears had given up any trace of struggle, I raised the quill to my right ear and prepared to stab myself into silence.

Three times in my life my dead mother called me with a bell. This night was the first: the abbey's bell struck two. Two strident peals just as I would maim my most exquisite sense. Into the bleak silence of the world, the two strikes woke my ears. They clung to the subsiding rings for ten, twenty seconds until I heard just faint echoes from the distant city.

Deaf like you, mother, I would have been.

I heard the whispering of her dancing feet on that wooden floor. I heard her body ringing with her bells. Oh, her prison had been worse than mine! My evil father lurking near her day and night. Yet she had reveled in every sound that she could grasp with the fibers of her body. And I—so blessed with perfect ears—was now ready to destroy them.

The quill clattered to the floor and I stared at it as if it were a blood-soaked knife. Suddenly the air felt so close in my narrow room; I could not breathe. I threw open the door, but the hallway seemed even more confining. The walls and ceiling were closing in. I turned about, dashed across my room, and leapt to my window. I could barely squeeze my shoulders through. The night air was so sweet, the heavens so far away, and I drank my fill of the cool summer's night, but still I needed to escape. And so I clambered through, squatted on the sill, and clung to the wooden frame so I would not topple to the cloister far below. The infinite space above me pulled me farther from my prison. I needed to be free! I let go of my hold and slithered up the tiles of the steep roof until I lay heaving across the peak.

The white abbey shone in the moonlight. The streets of the city were black chasms between rows of gray roofs. I listened to the world.

Somewhere, a loose shutter swung open and banged against a house. A dog barked. A rat scurried along the street and paused to chew a rotten scrap. Liquid seeped between the cobblestones and tinkled into the gutter. Footsteps creaked inside a house. The light wind hummed as it wound through the alleys. Somewhere a door opened, whimpering on its hinges. Rats and cats and dogs ruled the warm night, picked at refuse, snapped at one another. I heard the city sleeping. I heard the heavy breathing of fat men, the sighs of women. I heard snores. I heard people babble desires in their sleep.

The world was huge again, and I had ears for its every sound.

VII.

I could have been a great cat burglar if God had endowed me with a love of silver rather than a love of sounds.

Every night, I escaped my prison—and soon found that I was not the first to do so. Go and look in any of the so-called Great Monasteries of Europe. The ground is gently hollowed beneath a gate, a lock bent on a low window. Moreover, in the cellars there are secret tunnels and hidden doors, supposedly known only to the abbot, but these are found by any monk stirred by lust or curiosity—and all of us were stirred, all but those with shrunken souls.

In bad weather I would risk one of the paths frequented by other monks. My preference was for a tunnel in the medieval foundation of the stables, carved by centuries of stable boys too lazy to walk around to the gate. But when the ground was dry of rain and snow, and the wind did not blow fiercely, I scrambled up the roof. At first I took short, terrified steps along the rounded tiles at the peak; later I bounded. At the end of the wing, I crept down the roof and dropped to the top of the medieval tower, which was all that remained of the old, imperfect abbey. There I passed below windows of the abbatial apartments, in which a lamp gleamed from dusk till dawn. Thank God the abbot never came to his window to ponder the imperfect world.

I darted along the wall that separated the abbey from the Protestant town. Houses were built flush against it, so I slid down their uneven roofs and leapt to the ground below.

Then I was free.

Free only to hide, of course, but in any shadow I desired. I stole a cuculla and kept the hood pulled over my brow, so no one would see my pale face shining from its depths. I directed my ears to approaching footsteps, to the turn of a key, to a sleepless sigh emitted from an open window. The tolling of the church's bells was my compass, and each hour I would scrutinize their volume and tone to decipher my position. Without them, I would have been lost among the convoluted streets, deprived as I was by the daytime sounds such as those that had guided Remus and me to Haus Duft.

Landscapes of sound, like paintings, are composed of layers. The wind forms the foundation, which is not a sound, technically, but creates sound as it plays the city: it clangs a loose shutter, hums in a keyhole, makes a whistle of the tin knife coat of arms that hangs above the butcher's shop. With the wind come those other sounds of weather: The rain patters on the cobblestones, it drips off eaves, it rushes in gutters. Sleet hisses. Snow dampens other sounds with its blanket. The earth shifts. Houses creak.

On top of these are the sounds that feed upon the silence of dying and decay: the jaws of rats, dogs, and maggots; the bubbling streams of wash water and urine steaming in gutters; the piles of rotting scraps of food that cackle for the patient listener; the heaps of warm manure that sizzle their putrescence; the flit of falling leaves; the dirt settling on a fresh grave. In the twilight, winged beasts feast on the dead and dying: the flutter of the bat, the graceless clap of the alighting pigeon's wings, the mosquito's tenor, the fat fly's ecstatic hum as he hops from shit to urine. No sound was ugly. I laid my ear to graves. I crouched at piles of manure. I followed the streams of urine along the gutters.

"In an opera, Moses, there are two kinds of songs," Nicolai had instructed me one night years before, pacing back and forth in his cell, a glass of wine waving in his hand, spilling crimson drops on the creamy, priceless rug. "Pay attention, Moses, you will need this in your future. *Recitatives*, the first, move the story forward. Sometimes, in recitatives, the music starts and flows like speech. We hear information that some composer thinks we need." He held up a finger. "In recitatives, sometimes I fall asleep. But that's alright. Nothing to be ashamed of. Because no one goes to opera to hear these songs, my friend. They go to opera for the arias. Arias wrench my eyes wide open. Pure passion, pure music—no other consideration."

I had stored this teaching away, never thinking I would need it, much less outside of any theater. But on my nightly outings I soon realized that I could divide the human sounds of night into Nicolai's two categories of opera songs. On the stage of life, you can hear recitatives from the street on a warm night, and in winter you need no more than climb through a window or pick a lock and enter a front hallway. They, like their cousins in the world of opera, are the sounds that propel our life. They are the snore, the steady breath, the rasp, the rolling over groan, the dream babble. They are the hissing above a chamber pot, the trumpet of a congested nose. They are the chop of wood and the stoking of the fire in the winter, the kneading of dough in the dark hours of the morning. The recitatives of our nights are the turning of the page by a sleepless hand, the pacing of the sleepless foot. They are disgusting. They are dull. They are repetitive, ignored, unheard. They are necessary.

For many weeks I heard these sounds. I sat on vacant staircases, ate scraps of food in empty kitchens while the occupants slept above. I slipped into children's rooms, leaned over cribs and drifted on their soft, calming breaths. The more I listened to these sounds the smaller I became; the world became large—and what a comfort this was to me. I became a ghost. It was not hands and faces and naked flesh that interested me. I wanted only sound. I slid through windows or crept down hallways, and I felt as guiltless as the angels who look in on our dreams.

It was several weeks before I recognized another level: the aria of the night. To hear this you must be lucky, or else very bold. For people hide these sounds as they hide the most private patches of their flesh. To hear aria on a hot night, pull yourself up to an open window. Or, when it is colder, find an unlocked door—or learn to pick the lock by the sounds it makes when prodded with pins. Do not stop in the front hallway, but climb the stairs, crawl along the floor until you can place your ear against a door. Or, better yet, if you find occupants still busy washing, hide beneath their bed or in their wardrobe. If not that, then climb onto a roof and pry up the tiles until you find a hole through which you may mine the sounds below. Only ghosts, angels, and thieves have a right to aria.

Crying has a thousand forms: the baby's needful whine, the sickly moan, the lonesome sob. Some cry into the mute of a pillow or press a fist against their teeth so they snort their sadness. Some sadnesses are floods of tears and snot spat out. Some are dry, raspy creatures that desiccate a heart. Sadness can sound like giving birth to an unwanted child. These species are impartial; the stoic, wrinkled man may drool and beat his forehead, while his frail granddaughter's sorrow may merely make her shudder.

The sounds of hatred—part of any night—are, in their most spectacular form, the shouts and clanging swords the Neapolitan stage mimics so well. The angry slap and drunken fist count, too, and they are far more common. Insult and reproach are as common to a bedroom as the bed. I heard bones cracked, blood dripped upon the floor, clothing ripped. Though I could listen to sobbing for hours—I was always in awe of the depths of sorrow in this world—when slaps and insults flew, I bit my fist to endure them.

Or course, it is for love that opera lives, for which its temples are built in every city. And soon I was like those mobs of Italian men who go without supper for a week so they can afford a single ticket. I strained for the most sublime of all: the arias of love. I crept into bedrooms, hid in closets (and crept out only when sleep had come for good). The shy giggle. The urging murmur. The whisper of a hand on bare skin. The matching of the breaths. The warming of the exhalations until they seemed to whisper *Hot! Hot! Hot!* The kiss whose pitch deepened as it moved from lip to neck to breast.

I should stop here. Close the curtain. Love is allowed on the stages of Europe only because the most indecent sounds have been translated into Italian. Although the pope rewards the castrato's aching love song with gold, the woman who puts her hand between her legs and moans in the presence of the Holy See will find herself in prison. But I must tell you of these illicit sounds, for listening to love helped me finally piece together what I was—and what I lacked. When kisses turned to gropes, and the breath was joined by other steady rhythms (the drum of the headboard, the sibilance of the sheets, the synchronized sighs), I did not excuse myself. My ears pursued the sounds of those bodies like one of Herr Duft's microscopes focusing on the eye of a flea. I heard the crack of clenched toes, hands that kneaded breast and buttocks with a sound like the tightening of a leathern belt. Chest against chest was the slip of dry skin and the slide of sweat, the slap of breasts, the grind of rib against rib.

Lovemaking is like singing. At the first breath—the first thrust—the body is asleep to sound. Sighs and moans die in the throat. But as the tempo quickens, pleasure radiates, and the body tunes to its reception. Soon the sighs enter the chest, and though they may be no louder, the sighs are fuller; the moaner moans to her fingertips.

I could not know then that in lovemaking one feels a magic touch—I could have as easily understood the undulations of a hawk's wings in soaring flight—so I thought at first that it was this song the lovers sought. They moved together, moaned together, gasped together. They whispered *Yes! Yes!* in each other's ears, and shuddered from head to toe in their united song. I heard that when they came to rest—silent but for their racing breaths and hearts—their ecstasy was the same as mine in song, a body unified for a single purpose, ringing with its beauty.

It was in the sounds of the lovers' arias that I finally understood what Nicolai had told me so many years before, sitting with him on his horse: the union of two halves in love. I understood this when I heard the ecstatic cries of union in those houses, but also because I heard my own soul call out, *Please! Please! I, too, wish to be loved! I wish to be complete!* But, so, too, did I understand my tragedy: that because of my imperfection, love for me was impossible. All at once, the musico's exchange made sense. We had given up this song of union for a song that we must sing alone.

VIII.

During my nocturnal ramblings there was one house I often passed, longed to explore, but never entered: Haus Duft. Even from the outside I heard echoes of those beguiling sounds and knew I would be lost in its labyrinthine halls, or worse, tricked into thinking a room was empty, only to find evil Aunt Karoline lurking behind the door.

But sometimes I hovered in the shadows and observed a lighted window for a time, hoping for a glimpse of Amalia's form. And what if she had appeared? What if she had gazed out at the night? Only this: I would have retreated even more deeply into the darkness that concealed me.

It was outside Haus Duft one night that I discovered I was not this city's only ghost.

I was in the shadows watching a lighted window, hoping to discern the hint of long, hay-colored hair, or of a limping shadow. My ears flitted from a skittering rat to scattering leaves to a chicken that had escaped her coop and wandered dumbly through the streets.

Suddenly, in the corner of my eye, I saw a figure dart into a doorway. What seemed impossible was that this figure made no sound. I retreated into my shadow and waited. I heard nothing. Assuming I had imagined the vision, I moved farther down the street, ready to retreat to the abbey. Just before I turned a corner, I looked back. A dark form was moving noiselessly among the darkened houses. It made no sounds at all that I could hear. It was as terrifying to me as if I had seen a man step through a solid wall.

I fled.

I rushed down an alley, then turned again and again, until I was sure I had lost the soundless apparition. It was autumn, and the shuttered windows blocked the city's sleeping breaths. I heard only those sounds of decay, muted by the cold, and the whistling, sighing wind. Farther along the alley from whence I had come, a window was lit. It would expose anything that should approach me. I had seen only a vagrant, I told myself. The wind had stolen his sounds. I was the city's only ghost.

Then I heard the rough tap of wood against stone from beyond the window. I listened for footsteps or a breath. I heard nothing but tapping. It was repeated with perfect regularity, like the clicking of the clock's cogs in Staudach's northern tower.

I saw the silhouette of a man. He hunched to one side and limped quickly down the alley. He wore a long black robe. A hood hid his face. From the way he tapped the street with his stick, I saw that he was blind. Then he stopped. He stood before the lighted window. He straightened and turned his head back and forth, listening.

There was something familiar in this gesture; I knew this man. It was indeed a ghost.

I ran. I turned down narrow alleys without knowing where they led. I did not care if I was seen or heard. Each time I stopped, I heard the tapping behind me; it seemed to tap into my very skull. I ran like a startled foal, crashing into walls, tripping over the uneven street, skinning my hands on the cobblestones.

I ended in a blind alley. I pawed the high wall for a way out, found none, and so I turned around and listened. *Tap. Tap. Tap.* I crouched behind some rotting barrels and willed my sounds to disappear. My breath was only the slightest whisper, but my heart still beat like a drum. *Tap. Tap. Tap.* The sound passed the opening of the alley. The ghost paused there. The wind gathered at the end of the alley, whining around the barrels.

The cane had turned and now tapped down the alley toward me. It was less urgent now. *Tap.* It clicked once as I inhaled in terror. *Tap.* Once as I exhaled.

Tap.

When the figure drew closer, I discerned faint footsteps, quiet as my own when I crossed roofs and escaped from bedrooms. It was not a ghost, but a man whose feet did indeed touch the ground. This did not comfort me.

The cane and the steps stopped. The wind flapped his robe. His breath was softer than mine.

I stood. I stumbled into the barrels. They broke apart, strewing rotten wood across the alley. He came closer, swinging his cane at my feet. I backed up against the wall. When his cane swung for my feet, I darted past him, but his ear was faster. A hand grabbed my sleeve and jerked with such force that I lost my footing. He dragged me toward him. I fought against his grasp, but he dropped his cane—it clattered to the ground—and clutched me with both hands.

"Let me go!" I yelled. He was old and crippled, but to him I was no stronger than a screaming child. One hand drew back his hood. Our faces were inches apart. Even in the dim light, I could make out every ravaged feature. He had no hair left at all. His skin was mottled red, with patches of whiteness like the gristle of raw lamb. His left cheek was taut and smooth, like thin muslin that would rip at a needle's touch. His right cheek was bubbled and scarred. His eye sockets were empty; his eyelids, wrinkled flaps of skin.

"I found you," Ulrich said.

"Who is there?" someone cried from a window in the alley.

"Come with me," Ulrich whispered. "My house is near."

I struggled to get free.

"I will not let you go again," he said. He grabbed me again with both hands. "I do not care if they find us, though we will both be punished."

"Who is there? We are armed!" the voice cried.

"Come!" Ulrich snapped. He held me by the sleeve and tugged. I was as submissive as I had been when he had carried me down so many midnight hallways. Though I was taller than he now, I could not muster the courage to strike the crippled man.

He tapped his way up the alley. He wove us expertly through the streets, and so I saw that his memory for shape was far better than his memory for sound. We came to a square with a three-spouted fountain, and he pushed me into a doorway of a narrow house. He unlocked the door and pushed me inside.

The house had only one room on the ground floor. It was extraordinarily neat, with a single chair at a small table, and a bed pressed into a corner. There was no decoration on the walls, no other furniture, no lamps or candles of any kind. The only light came from the glow of coals in a stove. A steep flight of stairs led upward into darkness. The bed was neatly made, the chair centered at the table. There were no stray ashes around the stove, no scraps of food on the ground. The stone floor gleamed.

He locked the door and put the key in his pocket.

"Unlock the door," I said.

His head rose as if he could see me with his empty eyes. "Your voice is so much the same," he said. "But stronger."

"Unlock it," I said.

"If I unlock it, will you leave?"

"If I wish."

He considered for a moment, then he unlocked the door. He walked to me, reached out until he found my chest, and slipped the key into my pocket.

"That is your key," he said. "This is your house. If you wish."

"I do not."

He said nothing. The coals crackled in the stove like ice.

I walked past him to the door. Our backs were to each other when he spoke.

"When I recovered sufficiently to walk, Abbot Coelestin gave me a bag of gold. He said he would hang me for your castration if I ever returned to this city. Then he had me sent to Zurich. I was pushed off the wagon and left by the lake. I did not even have a staff. I listened to the wagon vanish. The waves upon the lake. Passing horses. Vendors from a nearby market. I have never heard such an empty world. If I had possessed a pistol I would have put it to my head."

I heard the pleading in his voice, but still, I reached for the door handle.

Ulrich continued: " 'A coach,' I shouted. 'Get me a coach!' "

My teacher's cold and eager voice chilled my spine. He took two steps toward me. I feared his gentle touch now with as much revulsion as I had as a child.

"Moses, Nicolai should have taken my ears! He could have cut them off, and I would have thanked him as I screamed. But blindness is the devil's curse! All I do is hear. I hear ants crawl across my floor. I hear the earth settle beneath my feet. I hear my scars fester as I try to sleep. I hear you, Moses. I, too, wander at night, for I, too, must stay hidden. I have followed you. I have heard your step, your breath. That breath I taught to breathe."

I turned around and saw tears flowing from where his eyes used to be. He reached out a hand as if he wished to touch my arm. I shied away.

"But what is there to hear? I heard beauty in this world once, but the noises of this dreadful city remind me every moment what I have lost. Moses, I so want to hear you sing again. Please."

He paused. I could not take my eyes off his burnt head, which shone crimson in the coals' light. He wiped his face of tears.

"Moses, please—"

"I no longer sing," I said abruptly. "The abbot forbids it."

"The abbot is a fool."

"The abbot has been kind to me," I said, with anger in my voice. "He has made me a novice. I shall one day be a monk."

Ulrich opened his mouth to speak, but then he stopped. His face twitched as he considered what I had said.

"That is . . . fortunate . . . for you," he said, but I heard in his hesitation that he was disguising what he truly thought. "You plan to stay here, then? Forever, in this city?"

"Where else do I have to go?"

I saw surprise on the blind man's face, but he quickly stifled it. "The abbot is very generous," he said. "This is a difficult world for those like you. The abbey can offer you much luxury."

"I do not desire luxury. I merely wish to be left alone."

"Good," he said. He nodded. A trembling hand reached out and found my sleeve, but so lightly I could have pulled away. With his other hand he patted my arm, like an uncle might, one who was un-used to children. "Moses," he continued. "Let me offer you then the one thing the abbot cannot. Then you will have all that you desire. You will forever be content."

"What could you offer me?"

"Sing," he said very quietly.

I jerked my arm away and took several steps back.

"Please listen," he said quietly, struggling to control his fervor. He shuffled toward me, trying to regain his hold. "Please sing here. Here in this house. At night, instead of wandering the streets. I will not tell you what to sing. I will not speak. I will only sit and listen."

I opened the door.

"Please, Moses. Sing," he whispered like a prayer.

I turned to look at him for what I hoped would be the last time. Then I said, "How can you ask that?"

"Moses!"

"You ruined me."

"I . . . I . . . had no . . ." He could not finish.

"I will never sing again," I said. "Not for you. Not for anyone."

IX.

I was the city's silent ghost, haunting the streets and houses, collecting every sound but my own, for I made no sounds. I was as content as I had been at any time since the exile of my friends. I had come to terms with my plight, accepted that God had not intended the gift of joy for those with my imperfection. I was just nineteen years old, but I had already given up on the world. And I would still be there today—an elderly, silent ghost—if an angel had not brought me back to life.

My resurrection came by surprise. One early morning, I slid along the abbey's roof back toward my window, careful not to make a sound. I softly touched my foot to my windowsill and crouched, ready to drop onto my bed. I blocked the starlight from the room.

As I cast this shadow across my floor, I heard a sigh. It was so quiet that most would not have heard it, but to me it was as instructive as a portrait. I recognized the lungs that pushed the air, the throat that molded its intent.

I did not move. I could not have been more frightened if I'd heard a lion standing there.

"Moses," she said. "Is that you?"

I did not answer. I crouched on my windowsill and tried to blend in with the night. She stepped across my room. She wore a black cuculla, just like mine. But her hood was down. In the darkness, I could see only the outlines of her face, the gleam of her golden hair.

I climbed down onto the bed, stepped down to the floor. The top of her head reached my chin.

"Moses?"

I listened to her breathe. Her exhalations were damp and warm.

"Won't you speak to me?"

I heard her bite her lip.

"What a fool I am," she said. "I am so ashamed."

She turned to go. I listened to her shoes upon the floor. I heard the fabric rustle across her back.

"Wait," I whispered, as softly as that tiny boy.

She turned. She waited. I did not speak. I tried to hear her heart. It was too faint to hear from across the room, but I was too frightened to take a step.

"Wait," I said again. "Do not go."

For several seconds we just stood there in the dark.

"Do you have a candle?" she finally asked. "A lamp?"

"No."

"How do you see?"

"I do not need to see."

"I want to see your face," she said. "For five years I have seen nothing more than your eye and some fingers through that awful gate. You have grown so much taller."

I closed my eyes and wished the world would freeze but leave me with her sounds.

"Do you not want to see me?" she asked.

"I saw you," I replied. "Every time we spoke. And last year, too. In the church."

I heard humiliation seize her breath. After several seconds she spoke. "If you were there, why did you not answer me?"

I did not answer now because I could not tell her the truth.

"I wanted to see you," she said. "I want to see you now. It has been so long. I have always thought that you were my friend. My only friend. Have you forgotten me?"

"No," I whispered. "I have not forgotten you at all."

She moved lightly across the floor. I cowered in my hood, so she would not see my face, would not read my imperfection in its smooth curves. She was only inches away. I could hear her heart now, like a drum. Each beat shook some withered part of me alive. I suddenly noticed how small my attic room was, how my head almost brushed the slanting ceiling. If I had reached out my arms I could have touched both walls. My tunic was suddenly so tight I could not breathe.

"Can I see your face?" She reached up a hand and touched my hood. I took her hand in mine so she could not uncover me.

"Please do not," I said. When I let go of her hand, she released the fabric, but her hand stayed near my face.

"I should not have come."

Her breath had changed. It was even warmer now; her throat was tighter. She swallowed.

"Months ago I stole this robe from my father's factory. I thought, I'll disguise myself in it. I thought, I'll go see Moses. I found this. Do you remember it?" The crackle of unfolding paper. I could see little in the darkness; it was some kind of drawing. "The X still marks your room."

I recalled those two naïve children chatting in the hallway. How I wished we were there again!

"Moses," she continued, "when I lie in bed and try to think of one happy thing in my life, I think of you. Once a week, every Thursday, Karoline visits her aunt in Bruggen. The house is so empty—I can do as I wish for once. I always think: but what is it that I wish to do? Twice, I've come as far as the church before turning back, this robe beneath my arm. Tonight I could not stop. I climbed that grating. I don't think anyone saw me, but in any case I do not care. Moses, how could I not come?"

We stood like that for several seconds, her hand still raised before me, as though she meant to bless me. Then, with a ragged inhalation, as if she could not resist the urge, she reached forward and her finger touched my chin. It traced the line of my jaw. She laid her palm against my cheek, then moved her fingers across my lips, and I felt my warm breath reflected by her fingers.

"My God," she whispered. "I am such a fool."

Both our hearts were racing. I heard the moisture of her mouth as she swallowed again. Her hand reached behind my ear. Fingers ran through my hair, and then she was pulling my face toward hers, and I felt her lips touch mine. My lips did not respond to hers, but my ears heard every note of the kiss: the parting of her lips, their soft tug on mine, their release.

She stepped back in shame. But as she began to take another step—perhaps even to run away forever—my arms rose. One hand held her shoulder, the other her hip. I did not embrace her, or even draw her toward me, but simply held her, as if I held a fragile treasure in my hands.

She exhaled, and then breathed in and out again. Each heartbeat, almost identical to the last, was a new and beautiful sound to me, and I found myself slowly moving closer, my arms snaking around her back to bring her sounds to me.

She sighed, and the gentle humming in her lungs sent a shiver of ecstasy up my back. I pulled her even closer. The softness of her breasts pressed against my chest, and below, her ribs touched mine. When she sighed again, the vibration passed from her body and into mine, and I felt her in my lungs. She pressed her cheek against my shoulder, her head under my jaw. Now each sweet exhalation was captured in my neck.

I could not stand it anymore. I began to sing a single note, softly at first, but I could barely resist using all the power of those lungs. It had been so long—more than three years since I had sung. The familiar tingle of the note spread outward from my neck, into my chest and jaw, until I was ringing once again. The song passed directly from my chest to hers. My voice was still a whisper, but I heard the resonance of it in her neck, in the muscles of her back, as if she were a bell I had gently tapped with a mallet of the softest felt.

I sang more loudly and held her more tightly. I lay a finger on each rib of her back, so I could feel my voice as it passed through her.

And then I heard a footstep in the hallway. I cut off my voice, as if a hand had grabbed my throat. Someone had heard me singing and was standing in the hall, just outside my room.

"What's wrong?" she whispered.

"Someone's there," I said.

Whoever it was took two more steps toward my door, and waited. I held my finger to her lips.

After several seconds, the footsteps retreated down the hallway.

"Come with me." I led her toward the window.

"Up there?"

"I will hold your hand."

I climbed out, and then lifted her up so her feet were on the sill, and she could look down to the cloister. Her hand tightened around mine. It was a moonless night, so my face remained safely in shadow. The city was pure blackness beyond the white abbey. The fountain in the cloister babbled. The wind rustled like thin silk drawn over the roof. A pigeon hooted. A cart rolled down a distant street.

I helped her crawl to the peak, and then we stood, hands in hands, and I walked backward and she forward, her lame leg shuffling. We slid down the tower, past the abbot's windows, and crept along the wall to descend into the city. Haus Duft was the one place I could surely find, for I had visited it almost every night this past year, though I had not entered it. I led her through the dark streets, guiding my way by the tone of my feet upon the cobbles, and the murmur of the wind. We did not even whisper—not, I think, because we feared being overheard but because both of us felt this was a dream, and any noise would startle us awake. She held my arm lightly until we reached Haus Duft, a black shadow in the night.

I stepped behind her, held her arms below her shoulders, and whispered in her ear. "At this spot," I said. "In one week. I will be here." With a gentle push, I led her to the house's garden gate and then released her.

She turned around once more, but I was gone. I had vanished like a ghost.

X.

The night after Amalia's visit, I stole away to Ulrich's house. I used the key he had placed in my pocket. I did not knock. At first, from the utter lack of human sounds, I was sure the old man had died from his rotting flesh, but when I entered the room, the glowing coals in the stove illuminated the former choirmaster at the table. His empty eye sockets pointed down at his hands crossed before him. His festering skull was bare.

He did not react, but I was sure he heard me. He made no more sound than a corpse. I had brought a candle, and I lit it from the coals. Then I climbed the stairs. He did not move his head.

A layer of dust on the fourth step indicated the reach of Ulrich's fastidious neatness. No one had climbed this far in a year or more. On the next floor, a long hallway was littered with chairs, rolled up rugs, broken picture frames, shattered vases, and a pile of tarnished silver, all of which blocked the four doors leading off the hallway. Upon closer inspection I found the chairs and rugs and frames were also soiled by many stains. Dirt? Blood? I gagged and quickly backed away from the revolting mess, following the dusty stairs to a final story, where they terminated on a landing with a door. I opened it.

This space below the roof was a single long room. The ceiling sloped down so that my head just grazed the beams as I stepped to the broad windows at the far end. Dust covered every surface.

An unlit stove stood by the door, and there was an old bed near the window littered with yellowed books and papers. In the center of the room stood a rectangular table, at which ten guests could have comfortably dined, had it not been caked with grime and covered with jars and other refuse. Studying it more closely, I found various knives and brushes strewn across the table, and saw that the glass jars were filled with paints—mostly open to the air and dried out, but some still sealed, and in these jars, the paints had settled into layers like specimens of sand. On the walls, unframed canvases covered every square inch of space. More paintings were stacked in the corners, likely a hundred of them in all, some as large as the portrait of Staudach hanging in the abbey's library, some as small as the tiny icon of Mary that had always hung above Nicolai's bed.

They were portraits. Each pictured only a single face, and I could tell immediately the same hand had painted them all. The lines were careless, yet as I waved my candle in front of the canvases, I immediately felt a familiarity with these pictures—more than most real faces had ever given me.

One woman's face I found often repeated: here large, there in miniature, here in a ball gown, there, at the end of the room by the bed, in nothing but her pale skin. On this final canvas she sat in a chair, in a formal pose unsuited to nudity. I stared at her naked body. This woman—no, this picture of this woman—caught my breath. I heard her. Was it her voice or her breath or the gliding of one smooth thigh against the other? I heard all of those sounds in a rush of noise that passed through me like a gale.

I looked over my shoulder. Was she with me in the room?

But I was alone.

Soon the room seemed noisy. With each glimpse, each painting whispered to me. I removed many of them and turned them so they faced the wall, but I left three portraits of this enchanting woman's face, and the one of her seated naked.

I threw the jars and brushes to the street below. The jars exploded in multicolored splats. Candlelight appeared in the houses across the street, and I heard one woman shriek, "My God! The ghost!" Shutters were latched and doors chained. I aimed the jars at the shutters themselves, leaving green and blue streaks on the houses across from Ulrich's. One stray, red jar stained the fountain bloody. Soon I had cleared the room of all but the paintings, the long table, and the bed. I beat the mattress until the room was hazy with dust.

I had intended to ignore Ulrich, but back downstairs I noticed the anatomical perfection of his ears, so conspicuous amid the wreckage of his face. Suddenly, he raised his head. I found myself staring at his empty eyes.

"He was a tailor like his father," Ulrich said. "He never told them he was painting their faces. Only his wife knew. But then she died."

Dead? I thought, knowing instinctively that Ulrich spoke of the woman in the paintings. How can she be dead?

"She died in childbirth, and took the child with her to the grave. He did not cry at the funeral, I was told. They all thought him heartless." Ulrich's empty eyes twitched as he spoke. "After the funeral, he came home, here, alone, and he cut into a vein. He took one of his brushes and painted her picture with his blood. Not on a canvas, but here, in this room. On the walls, on the floor, on the windows." Ulrich turned his face as if he could see the remains of the blood. "They found him on the floor covered in blood from head to foot, the paintbrush still in his hand. They said her ghost had made him do it—angry that he had not cried for her. No one would clean the blood." I looked for traces of the painter's blood on the floor and walls, but every inch of the room had been scrubbed immaculately. "They think her ghost still lives here. When I asked after the house, his father's agent begged me not to buy it. Said it should rather be burned. It cost me nearly nothing."

Ulrich's empty eyes pointed at my face. "I thought it would be no trouble. I had time to clean—all the time in the world. What I could not see could not disgust me. But there is so much blood. No matter how much I clean, I can still smell it rotting. I feel it lodged in the creases of my fingers." He held out his dry, cracked hands toward my candle. They were as white as the patches on his face.

"Have you seen his pictures?" he asked.

"Yes."

"Was she beautiful?"

"Yes."

Ulrich nodded slowly, deep in thought. "Do you know why he did it?"

"He loved her," I said.

Ulrich gave an empty chuckle without smiling. "You are like the abbot," he said. "He wanted us to love God, but instead he built a beautiful church for us to love. He let you sing, and we loved your song. Moses, we love what we see, what we hear, what we touch. A beautiful woman's body in candlelight. The sound of your voice.

"But then those things are gone," he continued, "and we are emptier than before. If that is love, then love is our curse. Love is like the blood that dripped from that painter's vein, Moses. We lovers are all fools. Better we should all seek that thing we love and destroy it, before it is too late."

XI.

From the broom closet on the second floor of the abbey, I stole all
the tools I needed to dust, sweep, and mop that attic room until the
specks of paint, which dotted the floorboards like scars of some in-
curable disease, shone like Staudach's gold leafing. I stole sheets,
feather beds, pillows, and tablecloths from the abbey. Soon that attic
room was fit for lovers once again.

Twice I came in the night to find Ulrich on his knees, scrubbing
at a stain he imagined on the spotless floor. I merely stepped over
him. I did not interrupt his work.

A week later, the night of our rendezvous, was cold and rainy—
October's worst. I sneaked through the tunnel in the stables as soon
as the city was quiet enough that I could slip from shadow to shadow
unseen. I stole to Ulrich's house and lit the coal in the stove. Then
back into the wet night, where for two hours I circled Haus Duft,
watching as the lights in the windows were gradually extinguished,
until, when the abbey's clock tolled midnight, Haus Duft was a solid
black edifice on every side.

Once I chased after a scullery maid, sneaking out on her own
mission of love, but I quickly heard in the evenness of her step that
was not my Amalia. At one o'clock the rain intensified, and even
though I huddled in shadows that offered some shelter, my habit soon
smelled like a flock of Nebelmatt sheep.

In my memory, she enters like the ringing of a bell; all the tones of
her body fill the night with sudden warmth. My teeth cease to chatter.
My toes stop aching with cold. But my memory must lie, for I know
sound better than that. It must have been only a hint: the scuffing of

her lame leg, the turn of the key in that garden gate, perhaps the whisper of my name hushed into the night.

I did not run to her, or call to her. I was terrified. But of what? This should be the second-act finale: The lovers have escaped their respective prisons, the love nest awaits. They may embrace until the pink fingers of morning crawl across the sky! This is no time for terror!

Do not believe what you learn in opera. Love is not the mere opening of two souls' doors. Nor is it a palliative to the troubled heart; it is a stimulant. Under its influence, that heart grows until each tiny imperfection glows with painful evidence. And the castrato's imperfection is not tiny. I knew enough from my nocturnal wanderings to understand I was engaged in the greatest of deceits. In this unhappy world, where we are all incomplete, I had lost the gift that could make us whole again.

And suddenly, there was my other half, beautiful and limping through the rain.

Some honorable part of my soul—a part I have since tried to starve of food and light—did speak then, as I hid from her in my shadow. It told me to go back to my abbey room and seek there whatever comfort I wished in life. This part quoted the abbot's words to me again. *You are an accident of nature, a product of sin rather than of grace. Do not burden others with your tragedy*, this voice inside me said. *Leave her in this rain. Do not share your misfortune—you shall never gain it back again.*

But another part—the ardent part who loved and yearned—said: *Her! Her! Her!* He forgot the rain, the cold. With her this close, the world was so warm.

And so, like a thief, as she called my name and sought me with her eyes, I hid from her ears. My feet made no sound as they slid across the wet cobblestones. I did not call to her. Then I took from within my habit—where I had hidden it from the rain, against my chest—the flag of my deceit.

It was a strip of soft red silk, stolen from the abbot's private store, where one day it was to have been part of the rarest vestments. I held it in both hands as I crept behind her—matching her steps with my longer strides—until I was so close I heard the drops of rain patter on her shoulder. Any man spotting us from his window would have assumed I was about to strangle her.

I raised the silk high and then drew it tight, just as it reached her eyes.

She screamed, of course. Yet I was afraid she would tear away the blindfold and see my face, and read in my soft features all my shame. So I tightened the silk yet more, and pulled her toward me, hoping the touch of my body—which was wet and cold, and stank of sheep— would calm her.

It did not. She screamed again.

"Amalia," I said. "It is Moses. Do not be afraid." This was, at least, a better strategy. She did not scream, but still her hands struggled at the silk, which must have pressed painfully into her eyes.

"It is Moses," I said again.

She ceased to pull intently at the blindfold, and I relaxed my hold.

"Moses?" she asked.

"Yes," I said. "It is I."

"What are you doing?"

I chose silence. A light flickered on in the house nearest us, its inhabitants woken by her scream.

"Moses, please let me go."

"You cannot take off the blindfold," I blurted.

"Why?"

"You cannot see me." The light grew brighter and then shrank to the point of a single candle at one of the windows.

"Why can't I see you?"

"Quickly," I said. "Someone is there." A window began to creak open. I tied the blindfold behind her head. To my relief, she did not pull it off. I took her hand and led her up the street. She walked with her other hand out to ward off obstacles. We turned toward the narrower lanes of Ulrich's quarter.

"Moses," she said. "This is silly."

Silly it was not, but how could I convince her?

She squeezed my hand, just like that little girl had squeezed my hand years before as she led me through an unfamiliar world. "There has to be a reason."

Why did she need a reason? I would have let her blindfold me forever without a word. I could not say: If you see my face, you will see in my features that I am not the perfect other half of you that God meant for me to be. You will see I am broken, and you will not love me. I could not say: That man you see now, in your mind, that perfect man—he is the real me.

And so I said, "If you see me, I will disappear." It was not a lie.

"But that is impossible," she said.

"Please, Amalia. Believe me."

She placed her hand on my shoulder, and I felt in the touch a probing, as if she were trying to see with her hands, to know me by the rise and fall of the bones of my shoulder. I squirmed under her touch.

"Are we going to walk through the rain all night?" she asked.

"No," I said. "We are going somewhere."

"Then I can take my blindfold off?"

"No."

"When can I take it off?" Her hand moved along my shoulder.

"You cannot take it off."

"Not ever?"

"Not when you are with me."

"Or you will disappear?" Her fingers probed along the muscles to my neck.

"Yes."

"But I thought *you* were Orpheus."

"What?"

"You have got the story wrong, Moses."

"What story?"

"Orpheus and Eurydice."

"Who are they?"

"Do you learn nothing in that abbey? Orpheus was the son of a king and of the muse Calliope," she recited as if reading from a book.

Her hand explored the knobs of my spine. "A man like no other: beautiful and strong. But more, he was the greatest musician who ever lived. Eurydice was his wife," she said. She stopped us. She turned me toward her so she could explore my neck with both her hands. "Eurydice dies, yet Orpheus tames the Furies in the underworld with his song and gets her back, but on one condition: He cannot look at her until they leave the underworld. If he does, she dies again, and he loses her forever. Is that how it is?"

"Yes," I said, the words *A man like no other*, echoing in my head. My deceit was complete.

"Then *you* need the blindfold, Orpheus."

"You don't want me to look at you?" I asked, sensing a compromise.

"Of course I do. I want you to look at me," she said. She tilted her head upward, a hint of a smile playing on her lips. "Fine," she continued. She held my head firmly in both hands. "I will wear the blindfold. But you have to let me touch you. Stop squirming."

Her hands began to explore where my shame was hiding: in the slight roundness of my cheeks, in my delicate nose, in my narrow brow, in my skin as soft and hairless as a baby's. Her hands touched all of these, and then touched them again as rain made my face and her hands cold and wet. Her left hand found my throat—where my Adam's apple should have been—and rested there.

"What are you afraid of?" she asked.

"Afraid?"

"Your heart beats as if you were afraid of me."

I listened to my heart and tried to slow it. But it would not obey me now. I gently pushed her probing hands away and nudged her forward into the night.

Soon I heard the three-spouted fountain and was relieved that we were going in the right direction. When I stopped her in front of Ulrich's door, she turned her head as if trying to see through the blindfold. I unlocked the door and led Amalia into Ulrich's room. He sat at his table, with his head bowed as usual, but when we entered, his head shot up in surprise. I was worried she would hear him, but he made no more sound than the smoke swirling about the stove door.

"Come with me," I said, as Ulrich's empty eyes followed us across the room.

Climbing to the attic in the darkness, I was as blind as she. My right hand held her right hand, my left supported the small of her back so she would not fall. The steep stairs were awkward for her lame knee, which did not bend.

On the landing, I groped for the door—found it on my third lunge—and opened it. Warm air dried our cold faces. The glow from the stove was enough for me to see the black of the big table, the white of the bed, and the dark rectangles of the woman's portraits on the wall.

"Moses?"

My hand on the small of her back, I pressed Amalia into the room and closed the door behind us.

Behind that door, at first, is merely silence. We face the stove, drips fall off my sopping sleeves and make puddles on the floor. I turn and look at her; the red silk blindfold, stained crimson by the rain, dangles down her back and mingles with her hair. She seems mesmerized by the heat, as if the hot coals draw her toward it.

Does she hear her aunt Karoline's prophecies of dishonor cawing in her head? *Who is this man?* she must wonder. *Who hides behind this blindfold? Is this the answer to my loneliness? What happened to that girl who sat for so many patient hours beside her mother's bed? Am I trying to revive that girl tonight? Or am I about to lose her?*

And in my head: *My body is misery. It cannot love and it cannot be loved. How dare I lie to her? How dare I bring her to this awful house? I should pull that blindfold from her eyes—before she truly falls in love.* I almost do this.

I hear the creak of the floorboards when she shifts her weight, the regular hush of the rain on the roof above our heads. In one corner, water seeps through a hole in the roof and drips into a puddle on the floor. And I do not remove her blindfold.

What saves me from exposing myself to her—saves me from her pity—is a drop of rainwater. It collects on the wet wisps of hair by her ear and slides down her cheek, along her jaw. It must tickle, because she raises a finger, and I hear that finger wipe her smooth, wet skin, so the raindrop balances on her knuckle. And then, like a sound from heaven, she kisses that raindrop.

Her lips envelop her finger. I move closer. Her breath, still deep from the climb up the stairs, hurts me, it is so lovely. I reach out my hand and stroke her chin, where moments before her finger rescued that raindrop, and I hear her skin like a warm wind passing through grasses. I realize it is the sound of my skin, too, brushing against hers.

Her breath hardens into a sigh.

Her cold fingers find the damp skin of my neck. I shudder as they creep into my hair. She tugs so hard it hurts, and her mouth tenses as if she feels the pain, too. But then her lips relax and she is pulling my face toward hers. It is an unlearned, frantic kiss, which mingles our sounds. I feel the vibration of her moan in the tip of my tongue.

She claws at my hood as if to tear it off. I lift it over my head and drop it. Then she pulls at my tunic. As I help her lift her dress, I place my head to her chest. *Thump-thump, thump-thump.* Her hands are shaking as she loosens her corset and kicks out of those last scraps of fine white fabric. Then she wears nothing but the red blindfold. Her pale, damp skin shivers, but I look a moment more before I embrace her.

I press my head to her chest to come as close as I can to that heart, and then I hear her breath in her lungs. It moans like a wind through a giant, damp cavern, and on every inhalation it climbs higher toward a sigh.

The first chilly touch of the abbey's fine bed linen makes us draw in our breaths, but then it is so warm, and we are floating in it, fumbling for each other. She paws at my chest as if she has never known how large a body is. She reaches for the last bit of clothing I wear—a cloth wrapped tightly around my middle, like a bandage—but I draw her hand away, for there I will not let her touch.

She gasps when my hand strays below her navel. When I kiss her shoulder she exhales. The sounds she makes seem to come from inside my head. She gasps again. My hands graze across her breasts, feel the soft curve of her belly. They squeeze the protruding bones of her hip. Her breath is like weeping as my finger traces the scar that runs from the middle of her calf upward over her knee to the soft inside of her thigh. Her hands pull at mine, but I do not need the guide because her breath, her gasps and moans, guide me. She plays me with her sounds, and I play her with my touch. And as she begins to shudder under my hands, I press my ear to her hot moan so no drop of her sound escapes me.

XII.

One night every week I was alive.

I prayed that Karoline's ailing aunt would not pass away, and for one blissful year, at least, my prayers were answered. Every Thursday, as soon as it was dark, Amalia and I both escaped our respective prisons. I was there to grab her hand and lead her to our room as soon as the blindfold was fixed around her head. Ulrich was always at his table, his head bowed as if he were asleep. I knew he was not asleep, and that he heard our every noise. But I soon forgot him, and he was no more to me than a statue in that house.

Those Thursday nights on which Karoline had to forgo her weekly journey due to snow or some other impediment, Amalia left a note for me on a windowsill. She had given me a key, with which I slipped into the Duft garden and up against the house. I dreaded to reach my hand up to the cold stone sill; my heart ached if I found a scrap of paper there. Then I would wander the streets alone, hunting sounds that reminded me of her.

In the attic room, I lay beside her on that bed, and she would hold my ear or my hair, lay a hand on my cheek or on my chest, as if without it I would float away. "Sing, Moses," she asked, and even though I had sworn to Ulrich in this very house that I would never do so, I found myself singing again. Whatever came to me: the Masses Ulrich had taught me and that I had sung for Frau Duft, or the monks' chants, or Nicolai's pastorals (Amalia laughed at my arbitrary pronunciation of the French), or Bach's cantatas, or improvisations on all of these. Sometimes I merely sang notes that would have seemed unconnected to anyone but Amalia and me.

I watched her lay supine, and at my first notes she would gently raise her chin and arch her toes, slightly turn her feet outward, then inward and then outward again, like a violinist twisting his tuning pegs. She did not even realize she was doing this until I told her, but she did it without fail. It pleased her.

Then I always closed my eyes. We both were blinded as I pressed my ear to every inch of her skin so I could hear what rang beneath it. Her body was my bell.

She tried several times to remove the bandage-like cloth that protected my secret. But I stopped her. She thought I was protecting her chastity (for which she mounted no defense). I certainly had nothing of the sort in mind. Any forbearance was due only to my castration. There are rumors of castrati who can still commit the act of love. Don't believe them. We are cut too early.

Amalia was the first person I ever told of my mother. "We slept on straw," I said one night, and watched her face for repulsion. There was none. "We ate with our hands. She bathed me in a stream. I wore scraps of fabric which before had been some farmer's undergarment." Still, she did not shy away from me. She lay beside me and ran a finger up and down my arm, which tickled at the elbow. "Amalia," I said. "Doesn't this surprise you?"

"Surprise me?" she said. She laid her ear on my arm, as if listening to my muscles tremble. "No."

My neck grew hot. So she had always thought I was a dirty peasant?

"You see," she said, kissing my wrist, tasting it, "I thought at first you were just like those other boys who wanted to be monks. I thought you had some rich father who loved God and wished for you to be like the abbot. What you tell me now explains why I liked you so. If you had told me you were a peasant orphan maybe I wouldn't have been so mean. I would have helped you more. As it was, I just thought you were stupid."

She bit into my forearm.

My life outside that room stood still. Staudach saw no rush for me to take my vows, so I remained a neglected novice who attended only enough Holy Offices to avoid notice. If my life in the abbey was to change, I would need to take action, but I did not desire change. I was ready to grow old in that room.

But upon Amalia, the only daughter of the wealthiest man St. Gall had ever known, the world intended to act. Suitors were a constant hassle. She wove elegant condemnations of their faults that, for a time, convinced even Karoline that Amalia had a discerning eye for the Perfect Man.

"Karoline has simply intensified her search," Amalia told me one Thursday night. "The paper she has wasted sending for her 'applicants'! 'One more year,' she says, 'at the very most. If you can't decide, then your father must!' At this Father snorted. 'Patience, Karoline,' he said. 'We will find a fit; there always is a perfect fit.'"

We laughed at all of this, knowing that no perfect fit would ever come along.

But then:

"Marry me," she said one night.

Suddenly, I could not breathe. I did not move. I said nothing. I felt as if any sound might reveal my deceit and my shame.

"Moses?" she asked.

"Yes?"

"I asked you to marry me."

"I cannot."

"Why not?" she asked. She laughed. "Because you are a monk? Moses, you do not even know the Bible. You spend every night with a woman. You—"

"It is not that, Amalia."

"Then why?"

I thanked God for that blindfold then, for she could not see me shaking with the fear of all I stood to lose.

"I cannot."

"But why not?" she said, no longer flippant.

"Please, do not ask me."

She must have heard my sincerity, for she did not press me.

"I see," she said. "Fine, I do not need to marry you. We will run away. I am tired of my days away from you. We can go to Zurich. Or to Stuttgart. Orpheus, you could sing."

"Please do not call me that."

"Why not? To me you are Orpheus. My Orpheus."

I shook my head, though she could not see it. This name was a symbol of how terribly I had deceived her—and how much I had deceived myself. For what she desired was what I desired: To run away, to flee Staudach and Ulrich and our daytime prisons. To be one as man and wife. I wanted it as badly as she did, perhaps more.

"Please do not ask me to run away," I said. "It cannot be."

"I do not mind being poor," she said.

"Never ask me that again," I said as forcefully as I had ever spoken. I choked back my tears.

For several minutes we were both quiet. Then her hand began to feel along my chest, my neck, my chin. She touched my lips, and then she wet her finger on my tongue.

"I want to see you, Moses," she said. "I want to see you with my eyes."

"You cannot," I said. "As long as you love me, you cannot."

XIII.

Soon, the future began to weigh on us like stacks of books piled upon a harpsichord. When I sang, I had to force air from my lungs to feel my voice ring in my knees and elbows. My hands and feet were clenched so tightly they would not resound if placed against a bell. I ground my ear against Amalia's chest to hear her heart.

Only in the heights of our ecstasy did this weight seem to lift, and so our need for the touch and sound of each other's bodies became a frantic hunger. While we were apart, I both longed for her and hated myself, and I resolved the next week to pull off that blindfold. But from the moment we entered the room, her hands pressed and groped at my body as if she sought some opening in my flesh. I heard the gradual tuning of her fibers until that beautiful body rang like a bell hung from heaven. Only then did bliss overcome me and I was sure this love we felt was real. Every doubt vanished.

But by the summer of 1761, twelve years after my arrival at the abbey, nine years after my castration, four years after Nicolai's exile, and one full year after Amalia's foray into my attic room, I knew that this could not go on. I was anguished.

"His name is Anton Riecher," she said one night as we lay in bed. She sprawled supine, her left hand clasping my wrist. My back was pressed against the wall. "'Anton *Josef* Riecher,' Karoline says, as if a third name makes all the difference. '*Count* Sebastian Riecher's eldest son,' she adds to anyone who will listen, even though the man just bought the title several years ago. Have you heard of him?" She squeezed my wrist.

Except for the composers whose music Ulrich had brought to me, I had never heard of any living person but those residing in St. Gall. "No," I said.

"Father has been in correspondence with him for many years. He's to Vienna what my father is to Saint Gall—the empress wears Sebastian Riecher's cloth, as do Austria's peasants. I suppose he's actually even richer than my father, Count Riecher is. Vienna is awfully large." There was some hint of condescension, of knowing more than me about important persons, which, in all our nights, had been absent until now. She waved her hand glibly through the air. "I wonder how the son of such a wealthy man must act," she continued. "Like a prince, I suppose. Anyhow, we soon will know. He's traveling all this way just to meet *me*. He should be here in a matter of days."

I pictured Anton Riecher as handsome as Nicolai, proud as Staudach, and as rich as Willibald Duft. As I pieced together this caricature of greatness, my attention was riveted to his center, which held his greatest advantage over me.

"Father and Karoline are determined that I marry him," Amalia said. "Father says it is of course up to me, but that nothing could be better for his dealings, and Karoline says such a match is extraordinary. She says that I am *engaged*, though I have not even met him yet. They have told him about . . . about my leg, and he writes that the selection of a wife for him is not about such trivialities."

I lay still. It was as if I had heard a tempest coming and saw no better plan than to lie close to the earth and cover my head.

"Moses?" she said. "Did you hear me?"

"Yes," I said.

"He will inherit the whole Riecher fortune when his father dies, just as I will inherit the whole of Duft und Söhne, even though I cannot run it. You see how it makes sense, then? We would be the greatest textile family in the world—or at least outside England, and maybe some other places. We would go to Vienna, where Empress Maria Theresa lives. I would be free of this city, of that prison of a house. I would never see blasted Karoline again. I could do anything I wanted."

In a crescent around her navel, the tiny golden hairs stood up and glimmered in the candlelight, as if a cool wind had awoken them.

"Our children would have to be Riechers, because they cannot be Dufts."

I tried to quiet my breath.

"Moses, are you not listening?" She sat up and pointed her blindfolded eyes at me.

"I am."

"Then why don't you say something?"

I felt as if time slowed then, and I had an eternity to give her an answer.

"Moses, what should I do?" she asked.

"Marry him," I said. No words had ever tasted so bitter.

She said nothing for a long time. Her hand held the red silk and it seemed that she would pull it away. I did not tell her to stop. Perhaps she felt my weakness, for she withdrew her hand.

She began to sob, and wet crimson patches blossomed on the silk. I listened to her sadness: the sobs, the soft gasps, the wetness in her nose and mouth. For an instant, I wished she would pull off that blindfold and see me for the weak half-man that I was. I lay there, her sobs jabbing me like hundreds of tiny daggers.

"You are weak, Moses," she said. She turned her back to me, and I so wanted to press my ear into the hollow track of her spine, but I sensed this was forbidden to me now. With her bare feet, she felt for the floor. She stood, naked, her hands sweeping the air before her. She stumbled forward and knocked over one of the chairs at the artist's paint-blistered table. She clutched the table's edge and worked her way around it, the muscles of her back and buttocks twitching as she fought to balance herself. She had only to withdraw the blindfold and it all would have been so easy. But she would not make the choice for me.

She turned back toward me. "You do love me," she said. "And that just makes you weaker. I don't know what you are so afraid of, Moses, but no one should be so afraid of anything." She tried again to find a place to step, but she could not, and she almost fell. "Do you know why I always need to touch you?" she said as soon as she had caught her balance. "Because if I let go I just see that little boy who did not reach my shoulder. Perhaps I am in love with a ghost." I watched her struggle, and never had I wanted to be strong, to be a real man. But

I was paralyzed with grief. And fear. She stumbled and fell to her knees and crawled along the floor until she reached the wall.

"Say something," she yelled. As she stood up again, her hands came upon the canvas of the painter's naked wife. I noticed for the first time how similar they were—they could have been sisters, or the same angel sent to two different men.

"Say something!" she yelled again.

I am sorry, I mouthed, but I could not say it.

"Say something!" But the command dissolved into sobs. The soft insides of her naked thighs shook as she cried, and she tensed suddenly from heel to neck. She tore the painting off the wall. She threw it toward the bed. The frame splintered as it hit the floor in front of me, and I jumped. Amalia leaned against the wall and cried in wild gasps. She slid down the wall until she sat against the floor and embraced her knees. Still, she did not tear off that blindfold, just as her hands had never unwrapped the bandage around my middle.

I brought her clothes and helped her dress in silence. As I led her home that morning, I heard that something inside her had broken. I wanted to return to our attic room and press my ear to every inch of her flesh until I could repair it.

As we approached Haus Duft, Amalia stopped us before the gate. I did not like this change in our habits, and I gently led her on, but she resisted. For several seconds we stood without moving. A cock crowed in a nearby yard. I looked up nervously at the house. I thought I glimpsed movement at a window.

"Someone might see us," I whispered. "The sky is turning gray."

Abruptly, she turned toward me. "No more," she said. "I will not do it anymore." She reached up and slid her thumb beneath the blindfold, drawing it up. Every muscle in my body tensed.

She lifted the blindfold off. I could not move. I could not breathe. Her eyes were closed.

She held the blindfold out and dropped it. I was too slow; it fluttered to the ground.

Still, she did not open her eyes. "Moses, I will not wear it again," she said. "Not ever. Next week I will see you with my eyes. If you come."

Her hand felt its way up my arm, along my shoulder and my neck until it found my cheek, her thumb resting on my lower lip. Her palm lingered.

"Goodnight, Orpheus," she whispered.

I could not find my voice to reply.

She turned to the gate, and I knew her eyes were open, for she walked with a sure step. She did not look back, and though I could have called her to me then, I let her go.

XIV.

Do not think me such a coward to suppose I retrieved that blindfold, cleaned off the dirt, and hoped to make her wear it again. I left it in the street for the horses to trample.

As I endured the week of Holy Offices, I knew my deceit was at an end. She would know I was a castrate—even if she somehow did not read it in the softness of my face, I would tell her. Though I fought back visions of her laughter cruel as that of Feder and the other choirboys, in my heart I knew she would not be spiteful.

She might insist it made no difference. That she loved me as much as ever. This she might even believe. But I knew different. Orpheus was a man and I was not. If I took her back to that attic, we would both blush. We would stare at the spots of paint on the table and not know what to say. If our eyes met, we would smile shyly. Would she hug me like a sister?

I ached with regret as I sat in the stalls, oblivious to the chanting around me. The only sounds I heard were those in my memory that I treasured most, which soon I would have no right to hear. Yet, as the week wore on, I noticed an eagerness growing inside me. Soon someone would share my secret.

When the sun had finally set on that last day of waiting, I lit a candle and stood before the remaining shards of mirror on my wall. I had bathed, scrubbing off every speck of dirt. Since the last time I observed my own reflection, my eye sockets had lost their dark circles. My cheeks had grown fuller and gained a healthy flush.

Out in the city, I circled Haus Duft twice, waiting for the lights to extinguish. I tried to mine the sounds from within, but they still beguiled me. I heard the clangs of kitchens where I knew the sleeping quarters to be, excited talk from a room whose window was dark.

The last light was extinguished just after the abbey's bell struck midnight. I hid outside the garden gate, listening for the creaking

hinge. She did not come. At one, I grew impatient and resolved to see
if she had left a note. I withdrew the key she had given me, opened the
gate, and crept to the garden window.

What disappointment I felt to find a slip of paper on that sill! I
retrieved it and tilted it toward the moonlight. I almost had to touch
it to my nose to read it:

My dearest Moses,

*How glad I will be in the morning when I find no note on this windowsill
and know that you have come. I so want to see you with my eyes! I can think of
nothing else. But tonight it is not to be. There is something about. Karoline is a
crafty witch—she left for Bruggen, but then I heard her in the cellar. I dare not
come. But next week she shall be gone again, and I will be out in the night, gazing
at my Orpheus.*

A.

I pressed the note to my chest, as if her voice could caress me
through the ink. Another whole week! How could I fight back my
doubts so long?

Then I heard a door open into the garden.

She had come after all! I nearly leapt out into view, but I did not
want to frighten her, not on this night with so much at stake.

"Amalia," I whispered.

There was a gasp, and I realized in an instant that I had made a
most terrible mistake. That heavy breath was not Amalia's.

"Did you hear that!" said Karoline Duft. "I told you I saw something coming through the gate. I have the eyes of a cat. We will catch
this scoundrel yet."

I had not seen her for several years, but I immediately knew that silhouette stamping into the garden, though now her hips were so wide
one could have believed she hid her brother's fortune in her underclothes. She whipped her narrow head from side to side as if she
wished to shake something loose inside of it.

With a thump of boots, two men—the abbot's soldiers both of them—stepped into the garden behind her. They moved slowly.

"He is here," she said. "In this garden. Find him."

They looked languidly behind bushes as she pulled up her skirts and hunted. She was the loudest cat ever known to nature, snapping limbs off shrubs, huffing with the effort, cursing quietly with whatever air remained.

I did not move. I prayed that they would search in the other direction first, so I could dart across the garden and out the gate, but the soldiers poked the hedges along the garden wall with their bludgeons, and Karoline drew nearer to me. Then she was upon me; her hips blackened out the night.

"Come out!" she instructed. "You are apprehended!"

I did come out. I sprang around her so silently and swiftly she squeaked and fell onto her soft behind. I darted for the gate. But a soldier waited there, and as I passed him, he raised his forearm and caught my throat. I fell to the ground. I choked and gasped and was sure I would never breathe again. A boot pinned my chest to the ground.

I heard her thumps along the ground. Then her white face appeared above me, partially obscured by the planet of her waist.

"A monk!" she cried.

"No, madam," said the second soldier, whose weary face joined the two others staring down at me. "Just a novice."

"Wickedness!" she said, and shook her finger as if she would drive the stuff out of my filthy soul. "But you shall not stain this house! Not while I am alive! These eyes are always watching. I saw the guilt in her eyes! Wickedness! Evil! And a monk! You wait until the abbot hears of this!"

"And he will," said the soldier with his boot grinding into my chest. "First thing in the morning."

"In the morning!" Karoline said. "Take me to him now!"

"Madam, the abbot is asleep."

In the moonlight, I saw Karoline regard the soldier with as much scorn as she had just regarded me. "This is not some profanity with a parlor maid," she said slowly. "He threatens the reputation of a fam-

ily of first importance to the abbot. This boy threatens an engagement of first importance to this city. Take me to the abbot now."

The soldier sighed, so softly I was sure only I had heard it. He
grabbed my elbow and lifted me as if I were made of straw. "Any trouble and I'll twist off your arm," he said, and twisted once to confirm
his proficiency in such procedures. He pushed me toward the gate.

"Give me that." Karoline snatched the letter I still held in my
hand. I had not thought to hide it.

She read it.

"I can make nothing of this foul gibberish," she said, "but it does
seem best we leave this note where you found it. She need not know
you were here at all. A little disappointment will do her good."

Karoline stomped through the low bushes below the window and
laid the note back on the sill. I thought to call to my love, to shout
that I had indeed come to show my face, and that I would come again,
and again, even if it meant my death. I turned and opened my mouth
to sing, "Am—"

That soldier clamped a gloved hand over my mouth. "Keep quiet.
You've disturbed enough sleep for one night."

He dragged me silently through the streets, while the other soldier rushed to wake the abbot.

XV.

In a windowless cellar of the Abbey of St. Gall, there is a cell where a monk, having enough of the vicissitudes of the world, may withdraw into his own for a time. The door has a gap along the floor so food may be slid inside without disturbing his peace. A hole at one end of the short room drains the occupant's refuse into the river. This monk may sing or pray or cry out his deepest sorrows without the slightest fear of being heard, for stone walls and several thick oaken doors separate him from the dormitories above.

In our modern age, with scant esteem of silly mystics, this cell is seldom used. A mold grows along the cold, damp floor. I imagine I was its first tenant in a dozen years or more.

The abbot was kind enough to visit me after several days. This visit did not require the interruption of meditation or holy prayers, for I was using the hours of my solitude in other ways. I had curled up into a ball and cried. I had erupted in fits of anger and pounded my hands against the door until I bruised my palms. Using Europe's largest lungs, I screamed for them to let me out. When, after many hours, my first meal arrived—light and bland, according to the needs of monkish introspection—I dashed it against the walls in fury, and then slept an exhausted and troubled sleep in the remains. I dreamed of Amalia fiercely ringing my mother's bells.

When the abbot finally came, my strength was much diminished. I am ashamed to say I accepted the cup he held to my lips, and no water had ever tasted so sweet. He propped me against the wall, and a soldier brought a stool so the abbot might sit beside me. He fed me figs that tasted as if they were soaked in blood. I ate them greedily.

"You must use this time, my son," he said, "for reflection. I regret to tell you that you will have to remain here some days more."

He must have seen the terror in my eyes, for he smiled that avuncular smile. "It is for your own good. Though you have threatened both the abbey's reputation and the reputation of this city's finest family, do not think I am cold to your own welfare."

He placed a new fig in my mouth, forcing it between my lips. "It is for your welfare that I am here today. You see, were you any other novice, Moses, I would still be speaking with you now, but our conversation would be different. If I were speaking to a boy who would one day become a man, I would ask him to search within his soul and ask himself whether he is prepared for the vows before him. Whether he is prepared to forsake worldly love for a higher one. He might tell me that he is not, and then, in that case, I would suggest he seek another calling.

"But, Moses," he continued softly, "for you, all of this is different. There is no other calling. You can have what I have offered you or you can have misery. For you, worldly love is mere deception. And so I cannot offer you the choice that novices have been offered in this abbey for a thousand years. The choice has been made for you already."

He offered me another fig, but now I closed my lips tight. I told myself I would accept no more benevolence from this awful man who kept me from my love. Nevertheless, he held the fig against my lips, patiently waiting for me to open them.

"I have spoken with Karoline Duft at great length. Great length. You may be relieved to know I have told her nothing of your"—here he let pass a respectful pause, and I cringed—"condition. She is very concerned about the honor of her respected family, and wishes, as I do, for the greatest discretion in all of this. She is doubly concerned about the approaching marriage of her niece, the girl who, it seems, you have deceived. She says this girl has been mysteriously resisting the wishes of her father, which was what first awakened Karoline's suspicions. Karoline believes she finally knows why the girl did not wish to marry: she was besotted with another *man*."

He drew the fig back from my lips, and as I opened my eyes, I felt the blood once again flow in my veins. *She is mine*, I wanted to scream at him, though I knew I would sound the world's biggest fool. *Mine!*

Finally, he placed the rejected fig back in the bowl. He took a deep breath, and when he spoke again, his voice was slightly tinged by anger.

"How could you be so cruel, Moses? Surely you knew of such a marriage? She is a fine girl, from the best family in the abbey's lands. He is a noble man of great standing in one of Europe's greatest cities. My son, they will be happy."

He sighed, waiting for my reply. I was silent. He shook his head in dismay.

"Was it jealousy? Did you loathe her because she was rich and educated? Or do you have secret reasons for your wickedness? At first, when I was informed that a novice had been up to such impropriety, I did not think for a moment it could be you. *You* last of all. But then I reconsidered. After all, they love your voices in Europe's most depraved cities. Did you sing to her? It must be that. That naïve girl spellbound by your voice. I thank God that years ago I stopped your singing in my church."

The abbot stood. He stepped toward the door and then turned again toward me. The hem of his cuculla hissed across the floor. Every word he said was true, and yet an anger had begun to pulse inside of me. How dare he disrespect those sounds I treasured most? "Misery, for you and for whomever you deceive," he continued. "I hope you see that now. It is fortunate there seems to be no permanent damage. Of course, the Duft woman is so worried that you have spoilt the girl for her husband. She asked me if there were some remedy the abbey's physicians might provide." The abbot drew tight his lips to contain his laugh. "I told her that would be unnecessary, but she remains unappeased. So it must be. But I trust the husband will not be *disappointed*."

I flushed in shame, and prayed the abbot could not see it in the dark.

"However, she was even more concerned that the girl would refuse the connection out of lingering"—he waved his hand in the air, searching disdainfully for the right word—"*attachment* to you, and in this, I am pleased to say, I was able to comfort her. The matter was easily settled."

I sat up.

"You see, the girl knows nothing of what has passed. And so I wrote a letter to Herr Willibald Duft, informing him of the death of the choirboy who, years ago, sang for his ailing wife. I explained you had fallen off a roof. I could not fathom why you were up there in the middle of the night. I trust he will share this regretful news with his daughter; Karoline Duft will see to that." He bowed his head humbly. "Perhaps what I have reported is only half true, and there is some shame in this." His head snapped up. "But it corrects your far greater deception. It is better for you, for her, and for all of us—"

"No," I pleaded. I crouched on my hands and knees, trying to stand. I felt so weak. "You must let me speak—"

The abbot ignored me. "It seems the girl wants nothing more now than to escape this city. The wedding is tomorrow. Here, in our church. I myself will wed them."

I tried to stand. The abbot watched me struggle. He shook his head as if pity overwhelmed him. Then he raised his foot and placed his shoe on my shoulder. A slight shove was all it took to knock me down.

He left the cell, but he spoke through the last crack before shutting the door. "Truth, no matter how unfortunate, is always preferable to deception, Moses. I will let you out when it is safe for you—and for her."

In the dark, I tried to call for help, but I could only moan. After several hours someone slid food beneath the door. I struggled to crawl across the floor and stuff it into my mouth. I had to grow strong again. In the blackness of the cell, I lost any sense of time; it slowed and sped. In hours or days, I heard the stamping feet and chatter of a thousand people, and I knew they were arriving for the wedding. I struggled to my feet. I yelled that there was a fire, a flood, that I was sick, that I wished to confess my sins, but no one came except to deliver food. I yelled for Amalia. I had told her she must marry, but now a sickness crept up inside of me. *No!* I would have said, if only she could have heard. *My ears tell me that we have made a grave mistake! We love each other, you and I! Stop! I am not dead!*

I lost track of minutes and hours. My ears rebelled against my other senses. *You fool!* they said. *You fool!* The sounds of the festivities seeped into my cell. I covered my ears and screamed, but that just made every sound even louder, for they did not come from the church above, but from deep within my head. They were there when I paced the cell awake; they were there when I tossed on the floor wracked by nightmares. Karl Victor at the pulpit. Bugatti singing for the lovers. Nicolai and Remus in the smiling crowd. Those bells of my childhood ringing through the world. Amalia in her husband's arms. Everyone had forgotten me.

Finally, the door opened. "You may return to your own cell," the abbot said. His lip rose slightly in disgust at what he saw. Two soldiers stood behind him, but I was prepared to best all three. Only I needed an answer first.

"Has the wedding happened?" I asked. My voice was cracked and hoarse. "Is it too late?"

The abbot shook his head sadly. "But dear boy," he said, "that was three weeks ago."

XVI.

The soldiers lifted me off my knees and dragged me behind the abbot out of the cellars. When we reached the ground floor of the dormitories, the abbot stopped and turned. The soldiers dropped me to the wooden floor. I knelt and looked up at the abbot.

"You must bathe," he said. "Change your clothes. Should you wish to confess your sins, you may come to me."

There was no fatherly smile now, just disgust at what he saw in the light: my filthy clothes, my pallid skin, and my other deficiencies.

I lunged at him. He was not expecting this, and so my pounce toppled him backward. Few sounds in my life have I enjoyed as much as the pleasant thump of his skull on the oaken floor. He yelled. He cursed. He raised his hands before his eyes in fear that I would try to gouge them out. But that would have to wait for another day. The soldiers grasped for me as I took off. My legs were long, my body light, and they were armed and muscled. And more: love blew at my back. The soldiers had no chance to catch me as I darted into the cloister. I was through the gate and into the Abbey Square before they could raise an alarm.

It was mid-morning in early autumn. The hundred persons crossing to the abbot's palace, loitering in the sun, or accessing the perfect church all turned to watch the filthy novice monk—his lanky legs barely touching the ground, like an alighting bird's—race across the square. Three soldiers chased me now, but I left them far behind.

They called to a fourth soldier who stood blocking the gate to the city.

"Knock him out," one yelled.

"Tried to murder the abbot," another called.

The soldier at the gate was young, dull-eyed, and built like a bear, with shoulders twice as wide as mine, though he was not as tall. He smiled and bared his claws.

Ten strides shy of this single strapping youth, I inhaled the deepest breath I could, and when I exhaled, I sang the most awful screeching devilish scream. I twisted up my face. I spread my long arms like a dragon's wings. My scream was so loud and harsh that every person in the square covered his ears. The oaf at the gate stumbled back in fright, sure that I was a demon who had escaped from hell. He held his hands before his face. I only touched him lightly on the arm as I flew past, but he recoiled as if my touch had burned him.

There were people on the streets!

My first reaction entering that daylit city for the first time in years was not unlike the man who comes home to find his rooms overrun by mice. These streets had been mine and hers alone! How I wished these people would again retreat into their houses. They drove carriages and oxcarts filled with bolts of white linen. Their clothes were fine and clean. They stared at the filthy monster. Children pointed with pink fingers.

The soldiers had lost me, or given up the chase, when I arrived at Haus Duft. I banged my fists on the stately front doors until the elderly porter opened them. I grabbed his velvet coat with one hand and tugged his silly cravat with the other.

"Call Amalia," I said. "I must speak with her immediately."

I saw he could not concentrate on my words as long as he was being choked, so I released him and smoothed out his fabrics. He stared at me as if I were a wolf, distracted by my filthy face and odor.

"Fräulein Amalia Duft," I said, calm and patient as a schoolmaster.

"Fräulein Duft," he repeated unsteadily. Then a light came into his eyes. "*Frau Riecher* now," he said. He shook his head. "But she left for Vienna ten days ago."

I backed away, and he did not miss his chance. He slammed the door in my face.

I stumbled through the city. I had only one place in the world left to go.

As soon as I had unlocked the door, I heard a chair knocked over.

The old, scarred man had leapt up in surprise. "Where have you been?" Ulrich yelled. He grasped the table as if the earth quaked around him. "Where is she? What has happened?"

I walked across the room and began to climb the stairs.

"Moses!" he called after me. "Tell me there is nothing wrong! Where is she?"

In our room, where we had spent our nights, I pressed my teary face to the sheets. I cried until I drifted into dreams of her.

When I finally opened my eyes again, it was nearly dark, and her scent had been slaughtered by my stink. I hunted the room for other remains, but there was nothing. I had found and lost the world's greatest treasure: the sounds of love.

In the last of the evening's pinkish light, I saw the painter's wife in her portrait. It still lay on the floor where Amalia had dashed it in her anger. I hugged the canvas to my chest and remembered then that in his sadness, the painter had painted her portrait with his blood. If only I could drain mine with song!

I stepped to the window and punched through it. The broken glass tinkled in the street below like falling ice. I broke off a large shard and sat on the bed, the portrait between my feet. I would slice my veins and die here on this bed.

But suddenly Ulrich stood at the door.

"What are you doing here!" I roared, furious that he would dare to pollute our sanctuary.

"Please," he said. "I have waited every night for a month. I must know. Is she . . . is she dead?"

"It is nothing to you!" I yelled. "Get out or I will knock you down the stairs!"

But he took another skating step into the room, his hands stretched before him. "I listened to you," he said. "Every night. I heard you sing. I heard her ringing with your voice."

No words had ever been more repulsive to my ears. I stood up. I lifted a chair from the table and heaved it across the room. He heard the whoosh of air and held up his arm. The chair grazed his arm, knocked him back, but he did not fall.

"Just tell me and I will leave," he said. "Is she dead?"

"As good as dead," I yelled. "Married and gone to Vienna. Now go."

But he did not move. He reached out a hand as if for something to lean upon, but found nothing.

"Not dead?" he said, as if to himself.

"Get out!" I yelled again.

"But then," he said as I laid my hands on another chair. "Why are you here?"

I hurled the chair across the table. This time, it glanced off his head. He stumbled back and fell, without so much as a groan. He sat by the door. His sealed eyes stared at me.

"Moses. Why have you not gone after her?" he murmured.

That he should ask such a stupid thing angered me even more.

"She called you her Orpheus."

This only brought back the cold guilt of my deceit. "And that," I said, lifting another chair, "is exactly what I can never be."

I thought then how this man huddled on the floor now was the architect of my tragedy—and yet to kill the pathetic, broken Ulrich would be such small recompense for all that I had lost. I dropped the chair, and he did not even cringe at the noise.

"Leave me be," I said. I turned my back and hid my face in my hands.

There was such a silence I feared I may have killed him after all. But when I turned, he still sat there, his head gently shaking. "I have wronged you," he said.

"That you did," I replied.

"No," he said. "Not that. Of course there is that as well, but that is so long ago, and I have asked God every day to forgive me for it. What I speak of is another wrong, one that carries to this day."

He was climbing to his feet. Blood traced a line from his temple to his chin. He held out a hand for some support.

"Moses, when I finally found you again, I so feared that you would leave this city, that I would never hear your voice again. I knew I would never find you if you left. And so, when you told me of the shame the abbot used to keep you here, I did not contradict him. He fears that you will tell others what happened in his abbey, and because of this, he has lied to you. I, too, in my silence, have lied to you."

I watched him, confused. He reached out and shuffled toward the table.

"Yes, the world is indeed a difficult place for those like you. If the abbot has told you that you may not marry, that you may not become a priest, here he has not lied. If he has told you that simple men will laugh when they hear you are not a man, that they will not let you live among them without ridicule, that is also true."

He had one hand on the table now. I felt a warm prickling along my neck.

Ulrich crept as he spoke, "But there is more he did not say. More that I would have told you if I had not feared that I would never hear you sing again. Moses, beyond these villages where you will find no friends, there are cities that even the abbot does not comprehend."

I saw that his hands shook as they slid along the edge of the table. "In those cities they can be cruel as well—but there, you will sing. You will tame them with your voice. They will give you gold and make you rich. Moses, you must know that Vienna is such a place."

He reached the end of the table. He released it. A hand reached for my face. "She called you Orpheus!" he said again, as if this were reason enough to travel across worlds. He took another sliding step toward me; the white and cracked hand strained for my face. "I heard it all, every note of every night. Hate me for it! Kill me! I don't care anymore. But, Moses, you, too, heard it all! When you came tonight alone, I thought that she was dead. Only death would have explained it to me, but even death was not enough to stop Orpheus! Moses! Your Eurydice is alive!"

When his hand reached my cheek, I did not shy from his touch. He gasped, as though the feel of my skin awakened in him a million faint memories of my voice.

"But I am not Orpheus," I said weakly.

His hands felt along my jaw. He ran them down my long, noble neck. One hand paused briefly to hold the place where the treasure of

my voice lay hidden in my throat. Then he felt the contours of my
bulging chest, below which breathed lungs twelve times as large as the
ones he had touched years before.

"Yes," he said. "Yes, you are."

One last time he laid a hand upon my throat, his touch as light as
silk. "Go!" he whispered. "Go!"

ACT III

I.

I did not even pause to wash the prison grime from off my face. I left that blind man in the attic. He fell to his knees and called for me to sing one final time. I did not.

I strode out of the city at dusk, and then asked the first farmer I met which way was Austria. He looked me over, for he had certainly never seen such a large man with such a boyish face, and I felt a shadow of the old shame. But then he rubbed his chin, and we both turned twice around. He finally pointed toward the distant Rhine. "That way," he said. Then he shrugged and turned back to his plough.

And so I walked until I reached the great river at dawn. I had never heard its copious waters tinkling along the gentle banks, though I had spent twelve years not five leagues away. I followed its stream, for it made sense to me that this magical Vienna must be where this river's crystal waters had their source. I carried on like this for several days, watching the horizon for a glittering city.

Of course, in my total ignorance of geography, I did not notice as the Rhine curved back on itself and led me southwest. And so for several days I climbed into the mountains, my face aglow with hope, my back toward the object of my heart. I stole food at night from the finest houses I passed—stealing as well their sounds—and shared my plunder among any poor, kind peasants I encountered.

One of the poorest and kindest of these, an ancient man who had long ago been a soldier, finally said to me, "Boy, you are a fool." He shook his head. "Head west a lifetime and you won't get near Vienna. East, boy. It's east you want!" He took me by the shoulders and turned me about like a doll.

"Each day, head for the morning sun," he whispered into my ear from behind. "Rest at noon, then follow your shadow in the evening." He pushed me off, and I stumbled back down the same road I had climbed. And so I pillaged the same fine houses again, was cheered by my same peasant friends. I followed my sage's rule, and asked every friendly face how I might find the Holy Roman empress.

Thank God I was a fool! Otherwise, I never would have had the strength even to begin such a journey. My memory conjured Amalia's sounds from around every bend, and so I did not give up even when my bare feet began to bleed, when it got so cold my fingers ached, when a column of Austrian soldiers knocked me into the mud.

The snows closed the Arlberg Pass and kept me in Bludenz for the winter. I swept dust and polished floors for a blind widow who heard me sleeping in her cellar, and heard something in my voice to pity. She bought me shoes and clothes that made me a good imitation of a man. I crossed the pass as soon as the snow melted, and rode a trader's cart down to Innsbruck. In the early summer, time seemed to run ahead of me as I descended the mountains to the plains, so that centuries passed as I left the rough footpaths behind for the towpaths of the canals. Then I found the widest river God could ever build.

I asked a passing man what this river might be called and if it might lead me to my goal.

"It is the Danube," he said. "And if you are a fish, you might yet reach Vienna before autumn." I sat on the banks and watched the gentle current. I chewed on the last scraps of a stolen salted ham. My feet ached. I resolved to walk no more, but to find a way to float down this massive river, for my love was as plentiful as its waters.

I waved at every passing boat, large and small. I yelled, "Are you going downstream?" as if the direction of their bows were not proof enough. Some shook their heads; others pretended not to hear. None stopped to take me as their passenger. Then I looked at my reflection in the waters, and what I saw surprised me. I had not bathed since the widow's house in winter, some four months hence. I tried to wipe off the thickest dirt with the cloudy water, but that only streaked the mud along my cheeks, like the stripes of a savage's war paint.

Finally, at dusk, a narrow boat weighed down with sacks of grain drifted downstream. It was a sorry sight. Its hull showed as many patches as the clothing of its captain, who stood at the stern languidly pushing his pole into the shallow water. A lanky boy, all bones and pimples, sat dumbly at the bow. I felt down to my tired toes that this was the ship for me. I jumped up and paced beside them on the bank.

I sang a simple song.

The captain jabbed his pole into the mud of the bank, as if twisting a dagger into a wound. The boat swung around on this anchor. The man's jaw hung open, like his son's. They did not move, just listened, mesmerized.

I finished singing, but they did not close their jaws, and so I began another song. While they listened in dumb amazement, I stepped into the muddy river, waded to their boat, and climbed aboard.

From the moment I stepped on the swaying craft, I knew that boats were not for me—first an uneasy swaying in my belly, as if I had sipped a bubbly drink. I stopped singing and clamped my mouth for fear of losing my dinner with my song. As the boatman recommenced his languid stirring of the soup, I was paralyzed by sickness, and collapsed into the sacks. I thought to shout for them to throw me on the bank, but stopped myself, for just then we began to drift slowly downstream, and through the fog of nausea, my heart cried out in joy, *Amalia, I am coming!*

II.

I slept among the sacks of buckwheat for several days in a nauseous fog, until, one morning, I was awakened by my mother. Or so it seemed. *Get up!* she cried into my queasy trance. *Get up! It is time! It is time!* Her call was a massive, booming ring. The instant I heard it, I knew it was meant for me—she was calling me a second time.

I leapt up like a general roused by a bugle's call. I struggled out from the buckwheat embrace and jumped to my feet. Nausea hit me like a horse's kick, and I collapsed again.

The heavens boomed again, and so, for my mother, I stumbled up and almost fell into the stinking water, but the boatman's son hugged me with two bony arms. He handed me a pail, which I took, thinking it to be a tool for getting to the distant shore, but then I saw the compassion in his face. "Go ahead," he said, helping me lift the rancid-smelling pail to my mouth, "let it out. You'll feel much better after."

"No!" I shouted, and pointed at the sky. "Listen!"

The boy looked at his father, who shrugged.

"Please," I said. "Take me to the shore!"

The river was very crowded here, with barges and smaller boats, and was much narrower. We were in the center of a city. On both sides the muddy banks had been replaced by a stone quay alive with movement. The booming resounded again, even louder and more lasting, and the next round began even before the last had faded. Now it sounded like a giant's footsteps running across the heavens.

"Hurry!" I shouted at my captain.

The fool was as languid as the current. I sprang to the bow and leaned over so I could paddle with the pail. I had nearly forgotten my nausea. The pimply boy stood beside me.

"Are you," he asked, and tapped a finger on my temple, "not well?"

I threw up my hands. If his dull ears could not comprehend the significance of the sound, I could not explain it to him in an instant. Finally, we approached the high quay, which was crowded with more people than I had ever seen—all of St. Gall packed together in a narrow space. Men and horses and carts jostled not to be pushed into the fetid water. That boom passed again through the world. The surface of the river rippled, some men covered their ears, but not one of them looked up (though one laden mule bellowed anxiously at the sky, as if beseeching it not to fall).

We seemed close enough to the stony edge, and so I leapt, but no one had ever explained to me Newton's Laws of Motion. As I sprang, my momentum stopped the boat's, and so my leap was more up than out. I only just snatched the quay as I dropped past it and my legs submerged to my knees in that foul stew. I could not find a hold, and would have slipped and drowned had not that pimpled boy wrenched my shirt and helped me climb back aboard the boat.

He began a lecture about the dangers of swimming in the Donaukanal, but I had no time for this; by my calculations I had wasted several years already and had mere minutes left before that sound would disappear. And it was calling me! I leapt again, this time landing within the throng.

My brow banged against a brute who clutched a live chicken in each bulging hand, one of which he swung at me as I darted off. I ran along the crowded quay, which was hemmed in by the highest wall I had ever seen—higher than Staudach's palace, and without a single window. The booming came from the other side of these ramparts, and so I climbed between a horse and his moving cart and toward a tunnel packed with people.

So many sounds! The one-eyed idiot's howling, the rattle of the coppers in the leper's wooden bowl, the creak of a warped wagon wheel, the hissing of a black cat plucked of half its fur by some disease. As I pushed through the tunnel, I heard voices more diverse than I had imagined could exist on one earth, all shouting to be heard above the din: the gargle of Hungarian, the buzz of Czech, the choke of Dutch, mesmerizing French, Italian as if someone were bouncing a ball against my head. It was dark in the tunnel, but I was the tallest in the crowd, and I saw into the meat market on the other side. I had never heard such slaughter: cleavers chopped through the thick legs of cows; blades scraped along the scales of fish; a goat squealed against a rope as it was tugged toward its murder; a woman with arms as thick as posts deboned a sheep and slapped the slabs of meat onto a blood-drenched table; a child split intestines with a rusty knife; a one-legged man sprawled in front of a mound of offal and swung his cane at birds that tried to snatch at eyes and hooves.

And still, that booming.

It was louder on this side of the ramparts. I felt it in my toes, along my back. I chased it up a wide street of palaces, every one as grand and high as Staudach's abbey. I heard harpsichords ringing out of windows, the clink of crystal and the clang of silver. The street was laid with even cobbles. I timed my strides to the booming, leaping every fourth step so that the sound hit me as I hung in flight. I dissected its million tones. I heard the high notes in the tight muscles of my calves, and the low notes in my arms, which swung awkwardly at my sides like broken wings.

As I ran, the palaces grew larger and more ornate, the cobbles more regular, the smells less obnoxious. The street narrowed, then widened, and I saw a vast square ahead. Here every person blocked their ears against the sound, and rushed where they were going, as if trying to outrun a hailstorm. I burst out into the largest square I had ever seen, and beheld a dark building so huge it was a mountain. I looked up into the sun, toward that sound that shook my heart, and perceived a shadowy pillar that I knew I must climb. I ran inside the black mountain. I pushed aside wrinkled grandmothers, mourning widows. I knocked a general to his knees, splashed holy water upon the floor. Windowpanes as red as blood cast the pale faces pink. Except for the constant booming, my footfalls upon the black-and-white-checkered floor were the loudest sound in what I realized was a vast church. I stopped in the center of the nave and looked up at the ceiling. It was like the ceiling of a forest: looming gray pillars split into intertwining branches of stone that could have held up the sky.

I would have climbed the pillars and hung upon their branches, but then I saw a small man, and behind him a narrow door. The tired, dull look upon the man's face recalled instantly for me the dutiful Peter standing guard so many years ago before Frau Duft's sickroom.

Through the open door I saw a staircase. I ran, gathering speed as I crossed the church. The small man saw me coming, for his eyes widened at my charge and his tongue began to work nervously inside his mouth. He held up his hands—a bear defending his cave. Yet, a tiny bear, a cub, not half my size, and so at the last instant, as I bore down to plaster him upon the stairs, he looked absently toward the altar and stepped aside. I ducked to save my head and charged up the winding stairs.

"Sir," he called behind me, "you cannot go there. Your ears—"

I wound up and up, my head spinning, but I had to hurry. I burst out into a square room and saw sixteen men, their backs to me, ears stuffed and bound with cloth, pulling on sixteen ropes hanging through the ceiling. They tugged until they sat upon the floor. The boom sounded, shaking all my inner organs. Then the ropes pulled taut and these sixteen men held tight and, in perfect unity, like Russian ballerinas, leapt fifteen feet above the floor. When they were at the peak, the boom resounded again.

But I gave this scene no more than a glance. I dashed up an even tighter flight of stairs, so steep I climbed with both my hands and feet.

Then I reached the top and burst out into a room with four sides open to the sky. There she was: the Pummerin, the empire's greatest bell, cast from 208 Turkish cannons. She was twice my height. She had a clapper as long and thick as a tree trunk. The ropes of those sixteen men were wound here into a single strand that turned a wheel twenty feet across. As it turned, she rocked. She cut the air like the bow of a rushing ship. At the height of each swing, the sound bow on the inside of her lower lip slammed against the clapper and her strike tone—a perfect, strident B—boomed across that city.

I stepped below her. The clapper hung inches in front of my face. I saw that they had wrapped it in leathern padding to dampen the bell's massive ring. I wished to tear off the padding so I could hear her as she was meant to sound, but when the clapper was struck, it jumped and writhed, and I saw that if I touched it I would quickly be wanting of fingers. But I promised then I would come back someday to set her free. The bell's lips whooshed just above my hair. If I had jumped up, she would have snatched off my head.

I closed my eyes. The force of her wind made me sway from side to side. My jaw hung loose, my arms limp, my hands open. Her sound touched me everywhere. It tickled the insides of my thighs and shook my eyelids. My fingers buzzed. My muscles—tight from walking, from sleeping under bushes, from my loneliness—were pried apart, made again to ring. Wherever I had become stiff, she made me soft again. I admired her many tones like the infinity of a sunset's hues. There were my mother's bells, just waves in this massive ocean.

Her booming softened.

I opened my eyes to see that her swinging was much reduced; the sixteen men had released their ropes. For many minutes her momentum still made her strike the clapper. Then, even when she ceased to touch the clapper, a ringing lingered in her body for several minutes more, and the only sound was the whooshing of the air before her as she gently rocked—until that ceased as well, and my breath, and the city's din far below, were the only sounds moving in the air.

Then I heard footsteps. A hand grasped my shoulder and gently turned me about.

It was the guard. I stared across his balding head, on which drops of sweat were gathering. It was several minutes before his heaving breath let him speak.

"Not allowed up here," he yelled and moved his lips carefully for me to read, assuming that I was deaf. But I saw his lips only at the edge of my vision, because my eyes were fixed on the scene behind him. I laid a hand on his shoulder so I would not fall. He led me to the edge.

Our arms around each other's shoulders, we peered down at a city more magnificent than any in my wildest imaginings. Wide

streets, crowded with horses and carriages and people like tiny ants,
led off in every direction from the square. Rectangular palaces with
flower-filled courtyards were jumbled between these arteries. In the
distance, high ramparts bound it all together in a many-pointed star.
And beyond these ramparts, still more city, as far as the green hills in
the distance.

"My God," I said to the man who held me up. "What is this
place?"

"This, sir," he said, as if speaking to an idiot, "this is Her Majesty's city. This is Vienna."

And so, finally, after nearly a year of travel, I had arrived in the same
city as my lover. But just then a devilish voice, silent all these months,
suddenly whispered in my ear, "But how do you know she still loves
you? She is married to *a man!*"

I must admit, I had not expected Vienna to be quite so big, quite
so full of people who, when I stumbled into them, looked at my rags
and dirty face as if I were an animal who had lost his forest. But then
I closed my eyes and let the city's sounds pass me by, and I recalled all
our secret sounds of love, and my faith was reconfirmed.

All day I wandered the inner city searching for any trace of her
sounds, and happily collecting others while I meandered. I turned
around only when I came to a dead end, or else to one of those gates
that would lead me out of this magic place. Only once did I dare
glimpse what lay beyond the walls; I stumbled out of the Stubentor
across the footbridge to the green glacis, that parklike field that sur-
rounds the ramparts so Her Majesty's troops may slaughter invaders
with their guns. The silence was to me unbearable: birds chirped and
two horses chewed their oats.

Back inside the gates, I marveled at the rush of people: magis-
trates and officers and secretaries in their carriages or on their giant
horses, clerks and pages on foot. Columns of soldiers marched up
and down the streets, the gaunt and haggard ones overjoyed at their
return alive from the war with Prussia, their vigorous replacements

downcast at their prospects for the cold winter ahead. I stood at a smallish square and in a single glance took in a waif begging for coppers, a one-legged graybeard lurching on his crutch, a minister so corpulent his stallion sagged. A lady peeked out of a carriage with a nose like an eagle's beak. I soon learned that, provided I stayed out of people's way—a difficult task, to be sure—no one wasted a moment's glance on me, neither on my filth nor on the angelic face that hid beneath it.

I stood outside some of the most magnificent palaces and tried to mine the sounds from within. I heard whispers of a singing girl, of a French lesson, of the toil of maids and cooks and porters. Most of all, I noticed the amazing quiet of these stunning structures. Their hinges did not groan. The wheels of the carriages that rolled out their gates did not creak. The feet of their maids did not seem to touch the ground. When I heard voices through an open window, they were never urgent or enflamed.

I understood nothing of the city except that it was surrounded on all sides by ramparts, that it sloped slightly downward toward the stink of the markets and the river, upward toward the most magnificent of the palaces, and that in its center stood this giant black church, the Stephansdom, in whose high south tower hung that greatest bell, whose ringing was the biggest sound I had ever heard, bigger even than the ringing of my mother's largest bell.

If I found a door ajar, I walked through it. Once I was chased out by a wrinkled woman with a cleaver in her hand, but in others I had more luck. I crept into pantries—my bounty was a loaf of bread, half a cold turkey, two sausages, three boiled carrots, and a lump of cake. Then I went still farther, up wide, curving stairs; into empty bedrooms with bulging mattresses; up, up to tiny attic rooms (one in which a young student slept, his snores stinking of spirits). I poked my head out of any high window I could find, and peered across rooftops, half hoping to glimpse my beloved locked away in a tower, half hoping to hear, *Moses! Moses!* whispered in the wind.

But soon I realized that my haphazard methods were clearly not suited to such a task as finding one beautiful girl in a teeming metropolis. As evening came on, I began to ask passersby where I might find this Anton Riecher.

I probably should have found the chance to bathe before I began my directed search, though such careful planning would have disrupted much of what later came to pass that first miraculous night in Vienna. I still had the sludge stripes on my face, long, dirty nails, hair like the tentacles of a swamp plant. My trousers were torn from knee to ankle and one shoe's sole flapped like a hound's flopping tongue each time I stepped. So my inquiries were met only with disgusted stares. Finally, I selected a page who seemed in such a hurry that I had to block his path with my long arms. He swung his glove at me, but clearly feared to dirty it on my face.

"Please help me, and I will go away," I begged. I told him what I sought. "It is a mission of love," I added.

He looked me up and down. Then he named two streets and told me to seek where they crossed.

"And in what part of the city might I begin my search?" I asked.

He looked at me as if I were indeed a fool. "Go to the Stephansdom," he said, pointing up at the black tower in the sky, "and consider whether you might not be better served within its walls. Should you still wish to find the Riecher Palace, you will not have to travel far."

I should have known! I had wandered the city for a day, when in fact she was just where I had begun. My mother and that bell had called me to her! If only I had eyes like my ears, I might have spied her from that tower. In a half hour, I had found the intersection the page had named, and then, looking up, I beheld the Riecher Palace, as grand and perfect as Staudach's church.

III.

It had grown quite dark. The Riecher Palace was squeezed between two larger, but less pristine façades, so all I saw of the grand building was its face, with two lit windows in the second floor its glowing eyes, and its closed black gate its fearsome mouth.

The large gate, built to accommodate the empire's largest carriages, had a tiny door cut into it for wretches like me. As I approached the gate, I did not consider what I was doing. I knocked.

There was no answer. Then I noticed a string dangling beside the gate, not unlike a pull rope for a bell. I pulled it. Somewhere deep inside I heard a chime. Fascinated as always by any ringing thing, I pulled it again, and tried to judge the size, shape, and metal of the bell; then I pulled it again, and guessed the chime's proximity. I pulled it in quick succession, and played a simple rhythm. *Bing, bing, bing–bing. Bing, bing, bing–bing.*

This is not done was the first lesson I learned when an ogre of a man peered out the tiny door. He did not have to explain in words; the glow in his eyes sufficed. I released the rope and smiled innocently. I stepped toward him. He did not smile back.

"Good evening, sir," I said.

"Away with you," he replied.

"You see," I said, "I need to speak with Amalia Duft, er, Riecher. She lives inside." I pointed up at the house.

"If you ever pull that rope again," he said, evidently not comprehending my request, "I will twist it around your neck." His head was awfully large. I spied the shadow of some massive shoulders, and no neck in between.

"Just for a few moments," I said, "just to say—" I stopped, because in fact, I did not know what I would say to her. During those many months of travel, I had pictured it somewhat differently. I had pictured that it would be she greeting me at the door. "Let us fly," I

would have said, and we would have flown. Simple—no need for elo-
quence. But now, with an ogre blocking my way, what message could I
send her? For example, *Tell her that the man she loves is not dead* would not
suffice. I knew enough to know that illicit acts of love are best handled
tête-à-tête.

But I could not give up so easily.

"Might I show you something?" I asked the ogre. I pointed up the
street. "Something that will interest you. *Very much.*"

When he stepped through the door, he had to turn his shoulders
to fit. When he stood on his hind legs, his head looked down at mine.
I quickly gathered he had not come through to examine whatever
tantalizing distraction I had promised. Rather, he wished to give me
a message. He beckoned that I should lean closer. When I did so, he
grabbed my hair and snarled in my ear, "I do not like your face. If I
ever see it here again, I will change its proportions to better suit me."

But my hair was so greasy, he could not get a firm grip. I twisted
away and, like a graceful dancer, darted through the door. I was just
about to close it and lock him out when he grabbed my ankle. He
dragged me back out and held me up like a giant catfish he had caught
in the river. Then he hurled me into the street and shut the door
behind him.

I stood. The brute had skinned my elbow on the street. The front
gate was now firmly locked. I could not ring the bell again or he
would make me ugly, and even if I were lucky enough to get past this
man, I knew I would then meet whoever guarded the next circle of
this fine house: a butler, or perhaps some male Riecher who would
wish to know my business. If I told them why I was there, at best they
would throw me out; at worst, lock me up and spirit Amalia away to
some distant place where I might never find her again.

No, I decided, I had acted rashly. I must get into the house some
other way.

The ground-floor windows were sealed with ornate bars of iron;
the higher ones were not, but they were certainly firmly locked, and
in any case, I had no means of reaching them. I saw that the Riecher
Palace was a prison, and my love was trapped inside.

I turned away, discouraged, but then I considered: What would brave Nicolai have done? This set my imagination loose. I wove fantasies: costuming myself as a chimney sweep, or stealing a sow from the market and delivering it to the kitchen before hiding in a closet, or shooting the ogre with a poison-tipped arrow that would make him sleep. But all these notions made me shake my head; they all contained the same fault. Namely, to do them, I lacked resources. I did not even have a clean pair of trousers, nor had I yet even discovered a place to steal them.

Little did I suspect then that within a day I would have the means of entering the Riecher Palace, and not through some subterfuge, but by invitation from the very mistress of the house.

Follow me that miraculous evening as I turn at the Schottentor back up the Schottengasse and into the heart of the inner city. I strolled blindly, listening to the clink of silver against Vienna's finest teeth emanating from the elegant residences along the street, when a carriage overtook me, then stopped some twenty paces in front of me. I paid it no mind, even as a man descended, sent the carriage off, and remained in my path as I approached.

I was a few strides away when he began to laugh, at first snorting through his nose in a disbelieving way, then, when I came closer, with a full-bellied guffaw that rather frightened me. From his deep, easy breath, I knew he must be either a musician or a dancer—and he was too fat to be a dancer. In the darkness I could see that his round, red face was flushed either with goodwill or with wine.

"Orpheus," the man said. "You have outdone yourself."

IV.

The man looked earnestly at me, but could not hold the scowl, and broke once more into a guffaw as he came close. He leaned close and sniffed my collar; revulsion pulled him back. But then, much to my surprise, he buried his face in my shoulder and inhaled my stink as if I were a rose.

"Only a son of Garrick," he said with a squeak, as if his lungs would never inhale another breath, "would dare to smell that bad. What have you done? Slept the day in a Spittelberg brothel? Let me see your hands."

I held up my dirty hands and splayed my fingers for him to see the scum growing between them.

"Oh, God," he said. "Those hands are worth as much as these ears." He tugged at his own earlobes. Then he pinched my neck. "And this throat, which seems to have caught a rash from that shirt you found in the river, is worth ten times more. Durazzo will be furious. But as a statement, it is effective. Farewell, artifice!"

The man squinted at me in the dark, as if surprised that my nose was so large. Thank God I didn't say a word. A single word, "Hello" or even "What?" would have cut off this interaction as abruptly as it had begun. But fortunately silence was still my natural state, and this man shook off his doubt and said, "Let us, then, enter your house not as master and friend, but as artists." He put a hand on my filthy rags and pushed me toward a stately house made of stone, wedged between two palaces. He rang the bell. A very tall, broad servant—the kind only the Bohemian farms can raise—opened the door.

"Oh!" exclaimed the servant.

"Oh?" said my escort admonishingly. "Oh? Is that how you speak to genius?" The servant retreated several paces and bumped against a wall. He forced himself into a slight bow.

"Ch-Chevalier Gluck," he mumbled. "They are waiting for . . . for you."

"And we shall not disappoint them!" cried this Gluck, and poked an elbow in my ribs. The servant mastered himself and began to lead us deeper into the lavish house, whose scent of lavender could not conquer mine.

Gluck chuckled in my ear. "Your own Boris thinks you are a tramp," he whispered.

I rather agreed with insightful Boris, but he did not even turn to stare as he led us up the wide carpeted stairs, where the sound of mirthful laughter rose occasionally above the low din of serious conversation. Boris ushered us through double doors, and I found myself in the midst of my first soirée.

There were some twenty men in the ballroom, and a smattering of women, too. Even the youngest men had flowing white hair, and every nose in the room seemed pointed, though I soon realized this had more to do with a general raising of the chins. These men and women chatted in dense circles, speaking in such sharp whispers that I was sure I had interrupted a diplomatic conference of utmost gravity. A group of four men standing near a harpsichord seemed to be some kind of commanding ministers, for when they made any exclamation, eyes around the room looked expectantly, almost hopefully, in their direction.

Our entry disturbed this equilibrium. As Gluck strode across to the group of four, from around the room came "ooh!" and "ahh!" as if a peacock had just opened its tail. Glasses were raised, each higher than the next.

And then every eye took me in as well. Glasses fell. The room was silent.

Finally, one of the four men stepped forward. "*Chevalier Gluck, qui est-il?*"

I still had no French, but it was clear to me that the entire room wished to know what this vagrant was doing in their midst. Gluck smiled slyly. He eyed his audience sternly, pausing first on each of the four important men, "Signor Calzabigi, Signor Angiolini, Signor

Quaglio, Superintendent Durazzo, ladies and gentlemen." He pointed a finger at me. "This is the future of our art."

He let this statement settle, pacing slowly once around me, studying my tattered rags as if they were the most elegant clothes he had ever laid his eyes upon. "No peacock feathers, no diamond-studded vests, no paint upon his face. He does not look the clown. Take one look at him, and you understand his message." He raised one finger at the ceiling. "Artifice is not art."

Gluck nodded gravely and walked forward and then back to me as he stared down each guest like a father might his misbehaving children. "For this opera, we are not reviving the Orpheus that every audience has heard a hundred times. Not the Orpheus of Naples, nor of Venice. No. I turn away from that. With my music, with Signor Calzabigi's stunning libretto, we call instead to that Orpheus who lived long ago, who did not wear feathers in his hair, who sang the most beautiful music that ever was, and most important, who felt passion that was real and true." Gluck looked at the ceiling and spread his arms in supplication. "Orpheus!" he cried. "Come sing for us! We wish to know of love! Of greatest sadness and of greatest joy! With your music, fill our hearts!"

For several seconds Gluck let silence reign, and then the stern eye returned to the crowd. "In October, Orpheus will rise again as none of you has ever heard him. For not only do we have the libretto and the music to awaken his spirit, we have as well the singer to channel his voice. Tonight humility disguises him, but you all know him. Ladies and gentlemen, your host, our Orpheus, Europe's greatest voice, Gaetano Guadagni."

With a sweep of his hand he presented me to the crowd, and their shocked faces melted into delight as they made themselves recognize this famous Gaetano Guadagni, whoever he was, under the layers of grime on my face. They clapped their hands, and as they did, I understood with sudden dread that the room had been inflated with an expectation, like a bubble about to burst with a violent *pop!* I did not smile as they clapped, and they clapped more loudly in response, and so I resolved to run. I took two steps backward, but just then I heard

my escape blocked by approaching footsteps. I turned to see a man
enter. The sight of him explained everything—at least to me.

Gaetano Guadagni was fifteen years older than I, but we shared
the same ageless face. He stood only to my ear, but we both had that
angelic stature that made crowds think him six feet tall and think me
seven. Like me, he had the castrato's birdlike chest and the grace of
a body not weighed down by manly muscle. Twins we were not, but
brothers we could have been. That night my youth was distorted by
grime, and in his long brocaded coat he appeared a king.

He seemed to float into the room. If everyone had hushed when
they saw me, now that they saw Guadagni—and me next to him—they did
not even breathe. The famous castrato showed no alarm at this vagrant
in his house; for a moment he considered his audience with a generous, knowing smile. Then he looked at me carefully from head to foot.

"Chevalier," he said in strongly accented German, "have you found
me a replacement?"

Gluck's ruddy face had turned scarlet. "You impostor!" he gasped
at me. He shook one fist and held the other against his chest as if his
heart might burst from embarrassment. I stepped backward again and
would have crashed into the castrato had he not evaded me with his
dancer's agility. He held up a hand to soothe the composer's rage.

"You mistook him for me?" Guadagni asked as he circled back,
placing himself between Gluck and me. I began to inch toward the
door.

"He was loitering outside your door. He deceived me."

"A cunning disguise," Guadagni said, and pursed his lips so his
audience might know that they were permitted to laugh.

"I will throw him out myself," said Gluck, and reached for me.

"*Non!*" Guadagni shouted. Gluck froze. Guadagni did not even
turn to confirm that the composer had obeyed his command. The
singer simply laid his palm against his chest, as if feeling for his
pulse; the red arrowheads of his painted nails sparkled. "I never forsake a brother of the knife," he said quietly.

He bowed his head and his hand remained upon his heart. Every
eye in the room marveled at his compassion.

"Boris!" he called in his soft ringing voice. Boris appeared from where he had been lurking outside the open door.

"Give this man a bath, some clothes, and food. I think only your clothes will fit him."

Boris betrayed nothing more than a horrified swallow. He did not glance at me as he led me out of the room and down a passage. "Wait here," he ordered. For twenty minutes, I perched there like a statue, afraid that with any movement my grime would stain the white walls. Which way was the door? Finally, Boris returned with a pile of clothes over his arm.

"Follow me," he said, his voice devoid of both respect and scorn. He led me down a narrow flight of wooden stairs to a servants' washroom in the cellar. A wooden tub was half-filled with water, which Boris could certainly have heated more, but since it was the first warm water my skin had touched in months, I did not think to complain. I shut the door and barricaded it with a wooden chest before I stripped off my filthy rags and submerged myself.

Fair skin appeared beneath layers of grime. I massaged soap into my hands until the pads of my fingers were wrinkled pink ovals. My hair lost the weight of a year of oil and, when it dried, fluffed up into a downy halo as fine as a hatchling's plume.

When I was sure I had scrubbed every inch of skin, I stepped out of the bath and stood in front of the mirror. I examined my entire naked body. No castrato is a muscular man, but after a year of trekking along the Alps, my hairless body had a nymphic litheness. I saw in my thighs a glimpse of those other naked legs against which I had pressed my ears that year in Ulrich's attic. The jutting bones within my chest and pelvis were a man's bones, but my skin's milky, fleshy tone was similar to the one I had so often kissed.

I was hairless, yet now cleansed of grime, a golden down shone under my arms, above my lips, and in an arrow pointing downward from my navel. When I raised my arm, the movement rippled over my round chest, across my long stomach, and dissipated in my thighs. My year of walking had firmed up the stature that Ulrich had worked so hard to train. The castrato in the mirror did not look frail. His feet were anchored to the floor, and his shoulders seemed to hang from some unseen string tied in heaven. It was a noble body, with one single flaw at its center.

A brother of the knife, Guadagni had called me—the recognition I had always feared. He did not even have to hear me sing. I had seen it in him, too. I had seen a shadow of that other musico, Antonio Bugatti. Their soft, angelic faces, their grace, their smooth voices—all were signs that marked my body, too. *Orpheus.* The name still echoed in my ears. *Orpheus.* And looking at this naked angel in the glass, I thought proudly that if Guadagni could be Orpheus for an empire, surely I could be Orpheus for a single woman.

Boris's trousers were almost long enough, but I could not button the waistcoat over my chest. My wrists poked out of the jacket. I had to leave the painful shoes unlaced. I studied myself in the mirror. I had never looked so handsome.

In the passage, a platter awaited me with a plate of dry bread and scraps of meat—a meager meal for someone of my thieving ways. I skipped up the stairs. No longer the invasive tramp, I could find my own way out.

The house Guadagni occupied was laid with carpets on the wooden floors and gold-framed landscapes on the walls. It was quiet, as if every guest had left during my bath and the servants had been sent to bed. I found the front door, grasped the polished brass handle, and prepared to slip out unseen. But then I heard a sound that made me draw in my breath.

A harpsichord began to play. I heard at once that a master sat at the keyboard. I drifted on the sound, away from the door, up the flight of stairs, quickly, silently, anxious that any sound I made would stop this music.

As I neared the open door from which the music filtered—that same room as before, I realized—I found Boris and the other servants crouched around its frame, hidden from those inside the room. They did not react when I joined them, for their bodies strained to hear. Through the doorway, I heard creaking chairs and shuffling feet beneath the clear notes of the harpsichord.

I needed to know who was at the keyboard. I probably would have stumbled through the door and upset the evening—for a second time—had I not heard a sound that stunned me even more: Gaetano Guadagni began to sing.

Che puro ciel! Che chiaro sol! Che nuova serena luce è questa mai!

What warmth! I closed my eyes and exhaled every drop of air from the recesses of my lungs. I crowded with all the servants until we pressed against one another like a litter of piglets jostling toward a row of nipples. As one mass, we crept closer toward the doorway. I peered around to see Guadagni standing before the rapt crowd, Gluck behind him seated at the harpsichord.

Guadagni waved his hands as he sang, his long fingers describing ebbs and swells just as his voice did. In its delicate moments, he held me rigid as I strained to hear, and then, in its massive moments, I felt as if I might collapse under the force of his voice's brilliance. Guadagni gazed toward a corner of the room, and I saw in his eyes that there was his Eurydice, soon to be his again. *Find her!* the music said to me. *Find her!* It swept away any fear that lingered in the shadows of my soul. Warm tears stained my now-clean face.

As Guadagni cut off the final exclamation—*Euridice dov'è!*—the tug of his voice was violent, and only Boris's strength kept us from all falling into the ballroom. The guests began to applaud; the servants shook off their trance and scurried away. My reaction was not so trained: from the moment Guadagni ceased to sing, I felt that warmth recede. Fear crept back out of the shadows. With each moment, I grew less and less sure that I would win what I most desired. I needed to hear this music again, needed to learn to sing it myself, and here were two masters who could teach me.

I felt Boris's hand on my arm trying to pull me away from the door, and I sensed he was whispering something in my ear, asking whether I was such an idiot as to interrupt the evening a second time. I was. I strained against his pull.

But Boris could not tolerate another interruption, least of all by a fool wearing his clothes, and so he yanked at my shoulder. I twisted and strained until he finally lost his grip. He fell backward and toppled a vase off its stand. I stumbled into the ballroom.

In servant's clothes, tears streaming down my cheeks, I tumbled into their party as if I had just fallen down a staircase. The applause stopped. They stared at me, but this time their gaze was different. Surprise did not fade to repulsion, but to admiration—admiration of my beauty.

I took several steps toward Guadagni, and everyone saw the two castrati alongside each other—me a younger, taller mirror of Guadagni. His soft, angelic face, fine bones, and gentle green eyes were all that I had despised in myself.

I tried to gather words, but all I could manage was to clench and unclench my fists before my face, as if trying to grasp some elusive speck of magic dust floating in the air.

"Your Orpheus has returned, Chevalier Gluck," Guadagni said and laughed. The audience laughed as well.

The composer glared at me from the harpsichord. Boris returned and clamped a hand on my arm.

"Wait," Guadagni said to his servant, not moving from his stage. "Perhaps this is our opportunity, Chevalier, in Mademoiselle Bianchi's absence, to let our audience hear a duet from act three."

"Him?" Gluck sputtered. "Eurydice?"

"Can you sing soprano?" he asked me.

I nodded. Gluck raised more objections, but an Italian phrase cut him off, and the chatter in the room made it clear the guests would happily listen to Guadagni sing with a goat. Guadagni retrieved some papers and handed me a score. I eagerly looked it over and was instantly flooded with disappointment.

"But it's . . . I can't . . ." I stammered.

"It is too high for him." Gluck's stool squealed along the floor as he stood up, his palms raised as if to push me from the room.

"No," I said. "It is not too high."

"Then what is the problem?" Guadagni asked.

"It is the words," I said. "They are not Latin."

Guadagni pursed his lips, and everyone saw him contain his laugh.

"Is it Italian?" I asked.

Guadagni nodded. "It is indeed."

"I don't speak Italian," I said. A hush came over the room. "I wouldn't know how to say the words."

Guadagni took the papers from my hands, gently, as if they were a treasure he was recovering from a child's grasp. "You do not speak Italian?" he asked quietly, but loud enough that every straining ear could hear. "But you are a castrato."

I nodded. My face reddened despite his dispassion.

"That is impossible," Guadagni said. "In which houses have you sung?"

"Houses?"

"Theaters."

"I have never sung in a theater."

"Where, then, did you learn to sing?"

"At the monastery," I said. "The Abbey of Saint Gall."

Guadagni turned to Gluck. "Where is that?"

"In the Swiss Confederation," Gluck said. I nodded.

"But they do not have musici in German lands," Guadagni said, amazed. Gluck shook his head slightly in confirmation. Suddenly Guadagni's face brightened. He smiled at me. "But this is extraordinary. How long have you been in Vienna?"

"I came today."

"Today!"

Guadagni began to laugh, and his laughter was as powerful as his song. Soon everyone in the room was laughing with him at this amazing musico who did not speak Italian, who came from a land where his kind did not exist. Boris seemed to think this a good opportunity to sneak me out, and this time I let myself be pulled away.

But Guadagni simply held up a hand. Boris and I froze, and the audience hushed at once. Guadagni's disdaining eye passed over each of his guests, as if seeking a single noble heart among these vultures. "I, like this poor musico," he said, "had no *conservatorio* to make me what I am today. I taught myself. And I will not abandon him.

"Tomorrow," he said to me, "you shall come to the Burgtheater. You shall be the student of Gaetano Guadagni."

V.

"A visitor to the city, sir, are you not? May I be of service?" the boy had said after I had risen the next morning from my hard bed upon the quay and turned three complete rotations, with but one question in my head.

"In fact," I said, "you can. Are you a native of these parts?"

"My uncle's cousin is practically the king," he said proudly, sticking out his chest, which was so very scrawny I could have encircled it with my hands. I wondered when he had eaten last.

"That is good," I said. "I am in need of directions. Could you help me find this theater—the Burgtheater it is called."

"The Kaiserliches und Königliches Theater an der Burg," he recited with a nod. "Michaelerplatz. Let Lothar be your guide."

I did so. I marched after him through the sleeping city just after dawn, up the gentle hill, that black church looming to our left through the morning fog, everywhere freckles of damp manure sprinkled across the cobbles. We never turned left or right, and the palaces grew in size and ornament.

After no more than ten minutes we broke out into a square. "Michaelerplatz," Lothar said, and bowed.

I gaped. In the near distance, the jutting rooflines of the largest buildings I had ever seen cut sharply against the brightening sky. In the square itself: some sort of ornate palace with domes and statues of white warriors high above us.

"My God," I said to my guide, pointing up at the edifice. "Is that the theater?"

"No," he said. "That's the winter riding school—for princesses and their ponies. That's your theater." I followed his extended digit past the sharp edge of this riding school—which seemed to end abruptly, as if cut by a blade from heaven—down, down to a windowless stone box nestled in a corner. In St. Gall it would have been something to consider, but here, it was . . .

"Rather small, isn't it?" I said.

Lothar scowled up at me. "The greatest theater in the empire. Fourteen hundred people fit inside."

"It doesn't look like a theater." The front was windowless, doorless.

"Used to be a *Ballhaus*."

"A ballroom?"

"Ball *court*. So the princes could play with balls. Now it's a theater. It could be the devil's gate for all I care. I'll never be let inside."

I advanced into the square. The palaces behind my theater loomed even larger.

"Satisfied?" Lothar asked. "Satisfied with my service?"

I nodded absently.

"Two kreuzer," he said.

"What?" I inquired.

"My fee. You owe me two kreuzer."

"What for?"

"For the service."

"But it was nothing. Any fool could have found the way."

"Any fool but you. Two kreuzer."

"But—"

"Two kreuzer." He held out his hand and advanced.

"I haven't got a pfennig."

"I'll bite your ankle." He bared his teeth—yellow, but sharp enough to do the job. I backed away.

"Nothing!" I cried. "I'm as poor as you."

He looked me up and down as if noticing for the first time how poorly my clothes fit. He scowled at my poverty. "Then give me your shoes," he said.

"No!"

He dove for them and pried one off while I hopped away, but he soon tripped me up, and though he was but half my size, he snatched the other off as well. But I fastened a pair of fingers into each and held on for my life, tumbling forward while he backed away. The little beast dragged me across the square.

He grinned.

He bit my hand.

I roared and wriggled, and this dislodged the only thing in my pocket, a fat wedge of sweaty cheese, the last of my stolen victuals.

Lothar's eyes popped. He released the shoes and leapt for the cheese. He tore at it with his teeth. I gave halfhearted chase for my breakfast, but it scampered off.

I dusted off Boris's clothes and recovered a button from the dirt. Lothar had left a cheesish waft in his wake, and my belly rumbled. I looked about me and read the architecture well: Michaelerplatz is not a good place for trespassing unless one has a taste for imperial dungeons. And so I turned back to the rather unimpressive theater. It was as out of place as a wrinkled grandmother in the center of a lavish ball.

I felt the first pulses of love for it flutter in my heart.

I approached. Though the front was blank, around the corner rose two high oak doors, the only thing about this building that seemed appropriately grand for the first theater of an empire. I knocked on these imposing doors, but my pounding barely raised a thump. The doors did not swing open.

For an hour I paced along the three sides of the theater. So little to hear; the imperium lived at night. An occasional carriage rolled through Michaelerplatz. A mule struggled before its cart piled high with cantaloupes. Behind the theater, through a gate, I glimpsed the vacant Castle Square, but each time I ambled close, thinking I might slip in, the guard there raised his eyebrows: *I'd like for you to try*. I turned on my heel.

But then, at the end of that hour, I saw something odd. There was a miniature square metal door on the front of the theater, at about the height of my hip. Suddenly this door swung open. Out of it two arms appeared. A head slid out after. The arms continued to the ground, where they pretended to be feet. The feet, meanwhile, emerged from

the door, and a heel—like the palm of a hand—firmly shut it. Then this
collection of hands and feet righted itself to a proper standing man
and scurried off. I would have been sure that it was only a boy I saw, for
it stood no higher than shrewd Lothar, but this imp had had a manly
beard and a mass of hair.

Once he was out of sight, I inspected the tiny door, which I now
identified as an abandoned coal chute. I pried with my fingernails. I
attempted to slide it up or down or to the side. But I could not open it.
I had been doing this for several minutes when I heard an angry cry.

"Hey! Don't touch that!"

I turned and saw that the little bearded man was back. There was
something rodent-like about him. His hair and beard were chestnut,
as were the tufts of hair that spilled out of his open shirt. He was thin
and muscular. His lips were perpetually pursed. He had black beads
of eyes and not much head behind his ears. He held a loaf of bread in
one hand and a piece of sausage in the other. The sausage was as thick
as his arm; the loaf, as round as his halo of hair.

"That," he pointed with the sausage, "is the empress's door." He
bit savagely into the meat. "You want to lose your head?"

I told him I did not want to lose my head, but I needed to get inside the theater. I told him I was Gaetano Guadagni's new pupil.

He eyed me up and down.

"You got no balls?"

I turned red and did not reply.

"Suit yourself," he said. He dealt the door a tremendous whack,
and it popped open. He placed the bread and sausage in the chute.
Then, as if he were merely bending over to pick up a copper, he flipped
himself so that his feet were just above my waist and his hands upon the
ground. His knees bent backward and his feet disappeared into the
dark chute, where they caught hold of some sort of ladder. Then, step-
by-step, he pulled his torso into the hole. When only his head and arms
remained, I touched his shoulder.

"All right," I said. "It is as you say."

"Did it hurt to cut them off?" he asked.

"Yes," I said. "It did."

His eyes bulged as he lay on his back there in his tunnel, as if it were a burrow. His head seemed screwed directly onto his shoulders, dispensing with a neck. His arms were as taut as tree branches. "Do you know what I would do if someone tried to cut off my balls?"

I did not ask.

"I would tell the empress, and she would hang him."

"Why would the empress protect you?" I asked.

"She is my employer. I work for the empress."

"What is she like?" I asked.

"She has sixteen children. She named all eleven daughters Maria, after her."

I nodded. "Have you ever met her?"

"See her all the time. She comes to the theater."

"But have you shaken her hand?"

"Don't be daft," he said.

He began to slowly slide deeper into the chute. "Name's Tasso," he said, as his head began to disappear. "Want some breakfast?"

I did.

"Just make sure you come feet first," he yelled from somewhere in the hole. His voice was muffled.

I considered for a moment how I could manage this acrobatic feat, and then gave it up and climbed in headfirst. The cave was roomy enough for me to crawl in on my elbows, and at first was not very steeply inclined, but once I had climbed entirely into the hole, I could barely stop myself from sliding. Then I lost control altogether. As I slid through the dark chute, I yelled and held my hands out before me. I crashed into the ground and was soon bunched up like a sausage stuffed into a jar. I looked up past my knees to see a dim light and the silhouette of the little man dismally shaking his head.

I panicked, whimpered and squirmed about. "Help!" I shouted.

"Stop that wriggling!" Tasso shouted from above. He tied a rope around my ankles. I heard the creak of pulleys and then he hauled me out of the hole, the rope tearing at my skin. Finally, I tumbled out of the opening and onto the old ball court floor.

I lay in a large room with an extremely low ceiling. Tasso could just brush his fingers against it when he stood with his arms extended. I had to squat so I would not hit my head. The little man shook a finger in my face. "Coal chutes feet first," he said. "Always. Lucky I was here."

He stood up and brought over his miniature stool, then gave me half the bread and somewhat less than half of what remained of the sausage.

"How do you piss?" he asked as soon as I had accepted his offering.

I told him that urination caused me no difficulty and that I did not care for more of his questions. Yet I ate his food greedily as I looked around his cave. A single candle was the only light. There was a small unlit stove, and next to it was a child's cot neatly decked with blankets. This took up only a tiny corner of the vast space. The rest was filled with ominous shadows, which resembled tools of torture in a dungeon. Laid horizontal at the height of Tasso's waist, a wooden axle ran the entire length of the room—from the coal chute toward the middle of the ball court—like a ship's mast laid on its side. At its midpoint, a winch protruded with a crown of spikes. Ropes fed off the axle, threaded blocks at the edges of the room, and disappeared through the ceiling. At the room's far end was a Tasso-size capstan with more blocks and more ropes running every which way. There were also eight devices that looked like torture beds of different sizes, each with many ropes and blocks around it. The sound of our chewing echoed in the dark corners, as if rats lurked amid the machinery.

"What is this place?" I asked Tasso as we finished eating.

"See for yourself." He leapt up and tumbled over the main axle. He walked on his hands for a moment, snaked a foot into a loop of rope, and tugged it downward. As his foot came down and his head went up, a trap opened in the ceiling above the largest of the wooden torture beds. I saw a square of black sky.

"Sit," he said. I climbed over the axle and through the web of ropes and sat on the bed, which hung freely. Tasso sped across the room yanking on a rope. I watched the line tighten through a set of blocks. I shouted as the bed suddenly shot upward, and then every-thing was dark.

I clambered to stand in the pitch blackness, blindly waving my hands before my face. Nothing there. I tapped my foot against the wooden floor. The tap reverberated into the darkness. I heard that I was in a giant cavern.

I could not resist. I sang an arpeggio into the dark.

Architects: Do not build a concert hall for the listeners—so they are comfortable, so they can see the stage, so they feel honored in their seats. Such halls should be burned to the ground for idolatry. The only temples left standing should be ones to worship song.

In the architecture of song, *time* is the fundamental consideration. In those temples built to other idols—a Notre Dame, a St. Peter's, or even Staudach's church—a song may reverberate in the heavens of that space for as long as ten seconds. This may give the audience a fear and love for God and for His church, but in those ten seconds, song grows old and muddled, like a soft, tasteless apple. In contrast, when singing in your parlors or your dining rooms, there is the opposite problem: the song impacts walls and rugs and dinner plates so quickly it has no time to ripen before it dies.

Now consider the great hall, which at this moment in our narra-tive I had met for the first time in my life. Here the life span of sound is so ideally contained there is no premature, tragic death, and there is no old age; sound lives for a perfect three seconds. Three seconds of vivid youth.

This Theater an der Burg is perhaps the holiest of our temples. The geometrics of *Jeu de Paume* are ideal for song. Uniquely, its two lev-els of loges and double gallery above are constructed entirely of wood, no stone at all, and so even with six hundred people seated in them, they mimic an instrument's resonating wooden body. The room is narrow and long—not round as in the other great opera halls—and so song, like the *Jeu de Paume* ball from a princess to her cousin, is con-veyed along the room until it bounces off the loges' gentle curves.

I saw none of this at the time; I only heard it. But as I slid carefully forward toward the edge of the stage, Tasso scurried about behind me with a flaming wick in his hand. He scampered up embedded
ladders, igniting the lamps of the wing lighting panels. The theater
began to glow.

A double gallery ringed the theater on three sides just below the
ornately painted ceiling. Below these were two levels of tiny rooms,
like prison cells with one open wall, each accessible by a single door.
On the floor of the theater, at the back, stood several rows of backless
benches and, in front of these, two dozen rows of velvet chairs.

"Where does the empress sit?" I asked.

"Over there." Tasso pointed a thumb at the largest of the rooms
to my left. "So she can enter from the palace."

"And who sits here?" I asked, pointing at the rows of seats below
me on the floor.

"Loudmouths," the little man replied. He clung to a ladder twice
my height above the stage. "Show-offs. We call it the Ox Pen. Talk
louder in those seats than the actors on the stage."

"What about those benches way up near the ceiling? Can you see
anything from there?" I pointed up at the distant galleries.

"Not half the stage," Tasso said. "*Le Paradis*, they call it, perhaps
because it's nearer to the sky than to the stage."

"But why do they shut people up in these little rooms?" I said.
"So they don't talk?"

He snorted. "*Loges*," he corrected. "And the doors aren't for keeping the rich ones in; they're for keeping the poor ones out. Ready?"

"Ready for what?" I asked, and turned about as the light faded
from gold to red.

I found myself in burning hell. Hell was a cave. Frozen tongues of
fire. Pillars of gnarled stone. A tunnel that led to some bright opening, as distant as a star.

Tasso's head appeared through one of the traps, a marmot peek-
ing from its burrow. I looked up at the red lamps. "Tinted glass," he

explained. "Ready for the next?" he asked. His head was gone before I could nod assent.

I heard the patter of his steps and the groan of the axle below my feet. All at once—fast enough to miss if I had blinked—we left the dismal cave for idyllic fields. Trees bent over a spring. A field of soft grass invited me to sleep. Just as when Guadagni sang, hope filled my heart. In such a place Amalia and I would one day be together.

Tasso's head poked through another hole. "See?" was all he said.

"You did all that?" I asked, and pointed at the canvas backdrop.

"Ba!" he said. "Takes an army to do all that. Quaglio takes the credit. No one mentions Tasso. He just pulls the ropes."

"What is it like," I asked him, "to see an opera?"

"Don't know," he said. "I can't see anything from down here."

"You've never seen one?"

He shook his head. "Don't care to."

"Don't care to!" I said. "Someday I will sing for you of love. Then you will change your mind."

He blinked again. "Love?" he said.

"Yes," I said, as proudly as I could. "Love."

He grunted. "I've got better ways to spend my time." He disappeared into his hole.

VI.

At nine, three sullen stagehands arrived. After that, Tasso never left his cave. His head poked through a trap and he shouted, "Grease every groove as though the empress were coming. Durazzo will be here in three hours with the maestro! The slightest squeak and he'll want your heads!" The three men slunk about en masse, as if shackles bound them together by their ankles. At eleven, the German theater company appeared. They rehearsed for an hour, and for the first twenty minutes I was allowed to sit in the Ox Pen and watch, but the scenes caused in me such fits of teary laughter that the sullen director snapped, "Get out! And don't come back until you can contain your noise."

At twelve the French company strode into the theater, interrupting the rehearsal with their loud voices. Their acting seemed a dull affair to me, and I expect I would have found it so even if I had understood the French. At one, the stage was taken by Angiolini's ballet, which was wonderful in glimpses, and I would have watched forever if only Angiolini had not stopped his dancers every second step to swear at them in his delightful Italian.

No sign of Tasso, but when they yelled, "Lights!" the footlight elevator rose like the sun upon the actors. "Curtain!"—and the curtain closed as if by magic. I did not see my new friend's face again until the great men of Vienna's theater arrived at three and Tasso's head peered through a trap to nod at his masters, whom I recognized from the previous evening. Then Tasso was gone, and I heard only the softest shushing of lines below the stage as Durazzo, Gluck, and Calzabigi nodded and rubbed their chins when Quaglio yelled, "All right, now give us Greece." "The Caves. The Caves!" "The Fields! Hurry, man. These are important men you're keeping waiting!" The scenes changed smoothly, squeaklessly. These important men considered each setting with frowns; their thumbs pressing white dents into their chins. Each man found a token item that displeased him. Quaglio promised changes.

Finally, at four, Guadagni arrived. I jumped up to greet him, but he strode past me and the other men; he had eyes only for the stage.

"Yes," he murmured, when Tasso had raised the red lights on the Caves. "Hmm. Yes." Then he closed his eyes and we all watched as he swayed back and forth in the aisle, as if in his mind he summoned a vision of the future of this opera. He opened his eyes and nodded, and the other men nodded back at him. Then he climbed onto the stage and paced several circles. He waved his hand to a tune in his head, and the four older men hummed in satisfaction. "Now give me the Fields," Guadagni ordered to the air. I heard Tasso scurrying as fast as he could below the stage. The backdrop fell, the new wing frames slid into place, the fiery glow became evening sun. Guadagni turned slowly around, and then shook his head. "No," he said. "No."

"What is wrong?" Quaglio asked, a meek servant to a prince.

"*It* is wrong," said Guadagni. He waved his hand and turned away from the fine paintings, as if he could not bear to look at them.

"Wrong how?" Quaglio begged, walking toward the stage, but Guadagni swiftly descended and passed Quaglio in the central aisle. The scene painter called after the singer, "How is it wrong?"

Guadagni stopped, but did not turn. He shook his head. "I sing," he said quietly. He looked over his shoulder in the general direction of Quaglio. "You paint."

Guadagni strode toward the exit. Gluck called after him, "But don't you want to see the others—Greece, the Temple?"

Guadagni continued on. "Not today," he called flatly. "Not today."

"But when?" Gluck's voice grew desperate. "Time for changes is running short!"

But Guadagni did not seem to hear the question. He made for the foyer. I came out of the shadows and stepped into his path. "Will you not sing?" I asked. Still, he did not stop, and so I had to stumble backward to avoid a collision. I bounced off seats and then bumped into the door. For one heart-wrenching moment, I worried his offer the night before had only been a cruel jest.

Guadagni peered at my face, annoyed at the interruption. "Ah!" he finally said, and his sudden smile warmed my fears. "Our Swiss musico!" He took my arm and pulled me gently away from the door so he could open it. "Sing? Today?" He sniffed. "No, not today. Not tomorrow. Not next week. Late September, perhaps. Perhaps only in October." He pointed slyly back at the men still gaping in his direction. "My first lesson to you: Never give them all they want or they will gobble you up like their *Knödel*. Never let them think that they have tamed you, *mio fratello*. Never." He pulled me gently into the small foyer and then pinched my arm. "The brave hunting dog, as soon as he is cut, lies quietly in the corner. *Purtroppo*, that is what so many of us become: Titillate a princess before dinner with our song so we may drink her wine; titillate her after dinner with our fingers so we may share her feather bed."

Guadagni shook his head and held a finger before my face. "I am different. When a duchess asks me to sing for her, I tell her I have no time. When a prince asks, I am ill. It is part of the hunt. And for whom there is no kill, the hunt is all. Come."

He led me to the exit. Through thick doors I could detect the sounds of a hungry mob: fingers scraped the wood, women snarled at each other, voices called, "*Gaetano, mio Gaetano!*" Four imperial soldiers stood ready to protect us from the throng.

"Let them touch you," Guadagni instructed. "But never let them hold on to you." He nodded, and the doors opened.

The women and men who waited outside were not the peasants with whom I had shared my bed upon the quay. The women wore magnificent dresses. Gold and the finest jewels flashed on their necks. Behind the throng stood a line of carriages from which ladies of the highest class peeked through lace curtains.

Guadagni stepped into their midst. The soldiers encircled us and held back the crowd just far enough so straining hands could graze the great musico. Guadagni seemed to see every hand—even those behind him—and he brushed every one. Some fingers he took in his for an instant. But no hand that tried to grab him—to possess him—none of these found their hold. Clenched fists thrust forward scraps of paper, love verses scrawled on every one.

Fingers pinched me.

They plucked out my hair.

They tore my clothes so that they might press the shreds of Boris's coat against their lips, merely because I walked beside the great castrato. Hungry mouths seemed to gag on lolling tongues as they reached for us like peasants lunging for bread amid a famine. Most faces were women's, but the occasional man struggled amid the crowd; some of these wore carnival masks to hide their faces. One masked man proffered a ruby ring. Guadagni kissed the gem and placed it in his pocket. Ladies screeched as others pushed them back. One greedy madam pulled another's hair. Carriage axles creaked as packs of sisters strained out the doors.

Guadagni selected one carriage from the fray. Inside the doorway, a woman signaled to him with none of the urgency of the others, as if merely calling to a waiter. Guadagni bowed and kissed her hand. She did not even seem to feel his touch, but looked past his bowed head at all those worshippers who envied her advantage. She was beautiful—her gown was of fine green silk, jewels glittered at her neck, no feature on her face betrayed a single imperfection—but her white skin gave me the impression of being cold, and I was sure that a single finger of hers placed upon my neck would have made me shudder with chills. She was not young, but her smooth, expressionless face and brow rendered her ageless.

"You will come to hear me sing the new *Orpheus*?" Guadagni asked.

"Of course," the woman said. "Our loge is always full when Guadagni sings."

He bowed.

"And who is this?" she asked and looked at me. The guards held back the crowd, but still some hungry girl plucked at my untucked shirt.

"This, countess," Guadagni said, as if unveiling a treasure, "this is my new pupil."

Was that a wink from my teacher to this woman? I did not like her grin. Guadagni turned to me. "May I present Countess Riecher, the most charming woman in Vienna."

I had begun to bow, but my head shot up when I heard the name. I studied her face. Her cold green eyes seemed to clench my gaze in theirs.

"I hope he sings better than your last," she said with a grin.

I listened into the darkness of her carriage. Was there a breath?

Guadagni gave her an earnest look and shrugged. "*Non parla italiano.*"

The countess shook her head and gave Guadagni a disapproving look.

"So," she said to me in German, "how is it to have such an eminent teacher?"

Did her son have eyes like these? And these hands she clasped before her—had they touched my love today?

"Does he speak any language at all?" she asked Guadagni.

"He appears to be enchanted by your beauty, Countess."

She shook her head and gave me an amused smile. Then she turned back to Guadagni. "I must have you sing," she said. "I am having a little party."

"I am terribly busy, Madame."

"In three weeks," she said. She handed Guadagni a slip of paper. He unfolded it, and I saw that only a number was written on it. I thought I glimpsed surprise flash across the singer's face.

"Most people write me love poems," he said, "to gain my favor."

She shrugged. "Let this be a testimony of my affection, then, which runs so very deep." She spoke without emotion.

"I will consider it," Guadagni said. He placed the slip of paper in his pocket. She held out her hand for Guadagni to kiss again. He kept his eyes on hers as he bent forward.

She smiled at me once again; a tongue flashed along her thin lips. "Of course, if you do come, bring your charming student." Then she sat back and vanished into her carriage, and as it pulled away, the throng again consumed us. This time, I was too stunned to fend off the hands. My shirt was torn from beneath my coat as I listened to every Riecher sound: the click of the closing carriage door, her curt instructions to her driver, the snap of the whip, the clack of the wheels on each cobblestone.

Guadagni watched her go. "She is grotesque," he said quietly, brushing off the hands all around us. "But she is so very, very rich. I suppose I must bless her party with my voice."

Guadagni's immediate concern upon leaving the Burgtheater was that I should be properly attired as a student of the great castrato. His Italian tailor cut me several of the fine, long brocaded coats that are the castrato's uniform. In the mirror, I studied myself as the tailor worked with gold thread—I soon had monkeys dancing across my chest.

"Perfect," Guadagni said when I was properly adorned with gold and velvet, and with pointed shoes. "Exquisite."

That very first evening, as we drove in his carriage back to his lavish home, which was also to be my home in Vienna, I asked him when he would begin to teach me Italian so I could sing his opera. He suppressed a smile and averted his gaze out the window of his coach. "Be patient," he said. "Be patient. You have so much to learn. Singing will come later. You see, before they will ever let you on their stages, before they will even listen to you sing, they must believe in *you*." He examined me closely, up and down, and with this final word, his large nostrils flared. "You must be a musico before you can sing like one."

We drew up to his house.

"But I am," I muttered shyly, "I am a musico."

"No," he chastised. He tisked his tongue. "You are a castrate." His stare dared me to dispute this claim. Boris opened the door to the carriage. "I am a musico."

"If you would teach me Italian I cou—"

He raised a finger to cut me off. "I will teach you what you must know," he said, and then he let me follow him into his house.

. . .

I was his shadow. Just as he never went anywhere without his fine clothes, his noble carriage, and the amused smirk always on his face, he never went anywhere now without me trailing behind him, like those fluffy *chiens* French ladies haul behind them on a leash.

For two weeks he did not perform, and his only lesson to me was that he was the greatest creature on this earth. I slept at his house, dined with him, followed him about Vienna when it was, for him, convenient; he sent me away when his hunt required intimacy. I carried his coat when it was warm, and opened doors when no porter was available. I entered soirées at his elbow, until the admiring crowds drove us apart.

At our first soirée, after I had been swept away to an empty corner, he suddenly appeared holding the arms of two sisters—some dumb daughters of a duke. Their twin stubby noses seemed to droop as he passed them over to me, but when he was gone again into the crowd, they turned to me with matching smiles that said, *Make us yours.*

Comment t'appelles-tu? said the one who was only slightly less homely than her sister.

I squinted at her, willing my ears to dissect this simple question that might be the secret to my escape. But it was no use.

"Ah," I offered. "Hmm." The two sisters giggled and rubbed more warmly against my chest. I tried retreating, but soon they had me pinned up against the wall. I caught the sight of my master in the crowd. He winked at me.

I closed my eyes and pretended I was a bell hanging silently in the corner. When I opened my eyes again, the soirée was half-empty and the two sisters had found some more willing prey.

Not for one second had I lost sight of my goal. Through my new teacher I would gain entry to my Amalia's prison, but three weeks seemed an eternity to wait, so I did not give up the idea of succeeding by other means. In the morning, when Guadagni slept, or when he sent me away, I loitered up the street from the Riecher Palace, hoping I would glimpse her in one of the carriages leaving the gate. I fantasized running alongside it singing a secret message. "Stop the carriage!" she would yell, then descend and we would embrace there in the street, as every other poor wretch in Vienna applauded our reunion.

Alas, this never was to be. The carriage's curtains were always closed, and no brilliant blue eyes ever peeked from between them. Sometimes at night I stole to the palace and examined the exterior for some new method of stealing in. But I found it better sealed than any house in St. Gall. One night I tried to climb the walls to see if an upper window could be forced. When I was twice my height from the ground my fingers failed. In the morning my ankle was blue and swollen.

Every day, at midday, for two blessed hours, my master sang. Mostly he practiced from Gluck's new *Orpheus,* repeating the arias and recitatives again and again until he found that precision for which he was renowned. Sometimes he chose other arias, often from Handel, which he wished to keep sharpened so they would be available if he needed a weapon in his hunt. I lay upon my divan and listened to his extraordinary phrasing filtering throughout the house. I committed the music to memory while humble Boris brought me tea and cakes. "Yes, sir," he said when I asked for another cup. "No, sir," he said when I asked if he'd sit and drink with me. In just several days, I had gone from a peasant wretch far below him to a second master distantly above. *Camaraderie,* said his every detached look, *we shall never have.*

Guadagni's singing still touched me deeply, but soon the arias moved me in the form they should have taken—would have taken—if I had sung them. My well-trained ears recognized Guadagni's deficiencies, which were in fact many, and so what I finally heard was a murky amalgamation of his song and the song of my imagination. I would have sung them myself, perhaps even been imprudent enough to show Guadagni that I could sing, but though my ears captured the sounds, the transfer to my lips and tongue would take time. I needed to learn Italian, to read it so I could grasp its forms and meanings. Yet my only teacher kept this from me. I would need to find another.

Then one day I did: a wolf sulking in a corner.

VII.

I was walking in the Innenstadt, lost in those labyrinthine streets. I had lurked outside the Riecher Palace until noon when I decided to attempt a more direct route home. Now I was so lost I had certainly already missed my master, off to dine with a princess and her sister. I hoped for a familiar landmark, or even cunning Lothar, but the street was empty—or nearly empty, for a single man was waiting in a doorway with a book held close to his face. I could see nothing of his skin except for his hairy hands. He wore clothes that would have been respectable, but they were rumpled and fitted his thin hips like a sack drawn tight about his waist. I paid him no heed, until I passed by him, at which point he gave a throat-clearing cough and slurped his air like it was a liquid.

This sound!

It filled me with such joy, like the sun bursting through the clouds in cold winter. I tore the book from his face and leapt upon him. He thought me a thug and tried to beat me back. But I held him tight.

"Remus!" I cried. "It's really you!"

It was my friend! That ugly scowl! That tousled hair! That twisted nose! I called his name again in joy. That name, which only two people had ever used to address him, was like a spell. The scowl melted. The face that was never happy nor sad was suddenly both at once, and he pressed his face into my collar. I sobbed into his disheveled hair as if I had a lake to draw upon for tears.

"Moses! You are here!"

"And you as well!" I said. "In Vienna!"

"At Melk they would not have us. Staudach must have sent a letter. We tried to send you messages, but I fear they were intercepted."

"They were," I said.

"Thank God I found you now! The world is so huge!"

"There is so much to tell you!" I said.

"Look at your clothes," he exclaimed, pushing me away so he could take in my brocaded coat, then hugged me close again. He was older—with his gray hair, there was no doubt of that—but I was sure he had never looked so good. For once there was color in his face.

"And Nicolai! Where is Nicolai?" I looked around hopefully, as if I expected him to leap out from a doorway singing a merry ballad.

Remus's smile hardened. He nodded gravely. "He is here," he said.

His tone alarmed me. "Remus, what is wrong?"

Remus looked up and down the street, and the old Remus, who would not look into my eye, was back. "Nicolai is much changed. He is ill."

"Ill?" I said, unable to believe that any sickness could infect the bear. "But he will soon get better?"

Remus shook his head and looked away. He was silent.

"Tell me, Remus. I am his friend."

Remus nodded. "I promise to tell you all. But first, it is best you see him. Judge it for yourself. Seeing you will certainly cheer his spirits."

"Then he has not forgotten me?"

"Forgotten you?" Remus laughed, and it was so sharp and sad—I could not recall ever having heard the man laugh—that it disturbed me. He put a hand on my arm, and turned me down the street. "No, he has not forgotten you. Come, I am waiting for my student to open his door, but he has been out drinking and will not wake up to learn his Latin. He will not tell his father, and so I will be paid. No one loses, except Saint Augustine."

These five years had changed Remus. He strode quickly, and did not hesitate as he led me left and right through the winding streets. "This belongs to Prince Lainberg," he said, pointing at a palace with dusty windows. "And that monstrosity," he shook his head at a new palace with marble horses rearing from each corner, "belongs to Count Kursky. That one, Prince Barhainy; there, Count von Palm."

"How can there be so many princes and counts of just one city?" I asked him.

He laughed. "No, Moses. Not one city. *One empire.* And even for that there are too many. Some rule land far away; some actually occasionally visit there. Others couldn't find their estates on a map. Still others have no land at all, just the title. People will do so much to be a count. And so now, when the empress needs money for her war, this city is bursting with them."

Remus led me out of the palace gate and across the green glacis for the first time since I had arrived in the city. We left the stone palaces of the Innenstadt behind for the half-timbered houses of the Vorstädte. Here the streets were narrower, the human sounds less refined: children ran about without shoes while their mothers scolded them from open windows; men spat in the street rather than dirty a spittoon; cows were allowed to forage in mounds of refuse piled in the street instead of being tied up in a yard.

Remus led me to a part of the city that I could identify by its most infamous sound: the urgings of the ladies beckoning from the doorways and windows of the decrepit taverns that lined the main street of the quarter. Remus saw me staring in mortification at each waving dame. "Welcome to Spittelberg," he said. "Our home for the past three years. Indeed, there is no better place for us, for there is no place on earth farther from Staudach's abbey." He waved his hand at the street in proof of what he claimed. Women threw buckets of dirty wash water directly in our path. Men pushed handcarts laden with sour-smelling cabbage. Above all, the streets were full of children. They poured out of the houses, screamed from open windows, poked sticks into the rotting scraps along the street. In the late summer warmth, few wore shirts and none wore shoes. One young girl sat upon and tickled another, who must have been her younger sister, for they both had flaming reddish hair. Four boys stood on the mound of a collapsed tavern and shouted about the rules of a game I could not understand. "He's tapped," one yelled. "Three stones! Three!"

Remus's hand touched my elbow, bringing me back to him. "It wasn't always so. A hundred years ago, traders from the south and east stopped here when they came to the imperial city. This muddy street was paved with cobbles. These gray taverns were brightly painted.

Wagons jammed in every courtyard. But the Turkish army laid siege here, for eight months in 1683. They took everything of value, and destroyed most of what was not." Remus gestured at an abandoned tavern. Nothing remained but the drab façade. On the other side of the vacant windows several dirty boys were smashing the rubble into dust. "Just stay out of the lanes at night," Remus continued. "And if you have any coins, watch your pockets."

We came to several lanes leading up a hill, and at the corner of one of these we stopped before a house of just two floors. It was in better care than many of the houses in the quarter, though it leaned slightly to the side. The ground floor was some kind of public house, with a single word printed above the door: *Kaffee*.

"In here," Remus said. The sole room was crowded with men on benches. They all drank the same steaming liquid, with a pungent, earthy smell. It seemed a magic brew, for they were all possessed by the same wide-eyed vivacity. They pounded on the tables and spat urgent monologues into each other's ears. At the back of all of this, a raven-haired man played the sorcerer; he ground beans, as black as death, into a fine powder before mixing it with steaming water from a samovar.

I followed Remus to a staircase at the back. My friend stopped and put a hand on my shoulder. "Do not be alarmed," he said, alarming me. "There are good days and bad ones."

We climbed the narrow, winding stairs. Remus opened the door and bade me pass into their three rooms: a parlor, and a separate bedroom for each man—all added together, still smaller than Nicolai's cell at the abbey. In the parlor the ceiling continued to the beams of the high, slanting roof. There was an empty fireplace against one wall. Thick curtains covered the three small windows, so only a dim, indirect glow illuminated the room. Stacks of books were piled on the tables and on the floor along the walls. The close air smelled like drying hay.

Someone sat in an armchair, his back to us, but he was such a large man that even in the dark I could see it was my friend.

"Nicolai!" I said with all anxiety gone from my voice. I crossed around the chair so I could examine his face.

I have since seen that hideous visage in dark corners of so many cities: its swollen roundness; the traces of sores that have long since healed into scars; the soft, deformed nose, as if its cartilage has been eaten away by maggots. He was still a large man, but now he was round where before he had been square. His hair and beard were gray, and his skin was pale.

"Who's there?" he asked. His eyes pointed toward me, but the flutter of his eyelids betrayed their failure. I must have seemed a shadow to him.

"I will open the curtains so you may see for yourself," I said, trying to keep my voice warm and firm.

"No!" he cried as I reached for the drapes. Remus shook his head and whispered that Nicolai's ruined eyes could not bear the light.

And so I knelt at my old friend's side, held his arm, and brought my face so close to his that I perceived the spongy pallor of those syphilitic gummas beneath his skin. His eyes struggled to focus on my face. Suddenly he inhaled. He raised a shaking hand to touch my cheek.

"Can it be true? Remus, tell me this is real!"

"Nicolai, it is really he. Moses has come to Vienna."

"God bless us!" Nicolai cried and took my head in both his swollen hands and drew me to his chest. He sobbed onto my hair, and I cried onto his chest, and then he lifted my face so he could look at me again. He studied each of my features with those clouded eyes until he had them memorized.

"You have grown as beautiful as I have grown ugly," he said.

I did not know what to say, for indeed, he could not have walked down the street without people staring at him as at a monster. I, however, felt no repulsion, and I told him so.

"I have deserved all this and more," he said.

"Nonsense," I said. "That is nonsense."

Nicolai looked at Remus and then back at me. "I have nothing to do all day but sit here and think how I have failed the only two friends I ever had."

"Nicolai," said Remus sharply, "do not begin this now. Not yet. Let us be happy today. Moses is finally back with us."

"And I have wanted nothing more than that," said Nicolai, tears appearing in his eyes, "so I can tell him how sorry I am for what I did. For what I failed to do."

"Failed?" I said. "Nicolai, you were a father to me. You saved my life! I have never blamed you for anything."

He shook his head. "I never should have left you with that man. We should have left the abbey years before. The world was open to us, and we missed our chance."

"Nicolai," Remus begged, "not now. You will—"

"We should have left!" Nicolai roared at his friend and then covered his eyes with his soft, swollen hands. Remus bowed his head.

Nicolai's hands soon moved from his face to his temples, and I heard his breath constrict as a headache came upon him, as those soft growths within his brain became engorged with blood. A dismal whining emanated from his tightened throat, like the heaves of a choking man.

I took his arm and tried to soothe him. "Nicolai, is there something I can do?"

But Remus knew the only cure, and he went to fetch the tincture of laudanum that had become Nicolai's only relief from the pains. My touch had no effect other than to reopen Nicolai's eyes. One of his hands left his temple and clutched my wrist so tightly I feared he would crush it.

"Please forgive me," he said.

"There is nothing to forgive."

Then Remus was there, pouring the tincture into his mouth. Nicolai lapped it eagerly. Soon his eyes had faded even more, and then they closed. He slumped in his chair.

Remus and I stood face-to-face beside our friend for several minutes, then Remus lifted a pillow and propped Nicolai's drooping head. His hand lingered on his friend's cheek, as much a loving gesture from the man as I had ever glimpsed.

Remus smiled sadly. "It is good that you are here, Moses," he said.

I embraced him. His body was tense, unyielding to my touch, but his hand on my arm did not release me for several seconds. As he did, he wiped tears from his eyes and looked away, as if ashamed. I led him to the small, cluttered table. He sat in one chair and I took the other.

For several minutes neither of us spoke.

"Forty-five years," Remus suddenly began. "It is almost hard to fathom. He spent more than forty-five years in that abbey, and for almost all of them he spoke of leaving. It was a miracle they even took him in—this child left in their church one night. The abbey has never been an orphanage and yet, for Nicolai they made an exception.

"When I first met him he was already a giant. He was the only novice who would speak with me. I found his yearning for the wider world so irresistible—we must have talked about seeing it nearly every day for thirty years. Thirty years! And always, at the end, it was always on my account that we stayed—my books, my need for quiet. We never even left the city. And when we finally left, went to Rome, every day, from the very first, I wanted to turn back, even though I loved every minute of it. God, I was so happy at the Vatican! But I told him every day, 'Nicolai, we must go home,' I said. 'I want to go home!' "

Remus placed a hand against his mouth. He took a deep breath before he continued.

"You see, I never comprehended our situation. I was such a fool. It was only when they turned us away at Melk that I suddenly understood: we had stayed at the abbey *for him*, not for me. That day, as we walked down to the Danube after being turned away, I was seized with terror. 'Nicolai, we must go back!' I cried. 'Back to the mountains. Some monastery will take us in!' I would have gone anywhere, to any rotting sty that called itself an abbey. No books? I did not care. I would have lived with him in a secluded cave. 'We'll find another abbey,' I said. 'Staudach can't have written to them all.' 'Nonsense,' he replied. 'Don't you see! God has sent us to Vienna! We are free! Finally free!' Moses, these words were like a curse to me, a sentence passed."

Remus was silent for several seconds. He looked me in my eyes. It may have been the first time in my life I had looked so deeply into his. The tears seemed so out of place on that grim face. "He made me lose my faith in God, Moses," he whispered, leaning closer. "That same holiness for which I worshipped him from the first day we met— when I was fifteen, and my father paid to have his stunted son put away for life in the abbey—that same holiness summoned the devil in this city. He killed a man. Do not tell him. He does not remember. A man had called a whore a whore, and then spat in her face. Nicolai threw this man into the street. One kick was all it took to break his neck. Everyone cheered and bought him drinks while I dragged the body to the river.

"They loved him. He drank the dukes' champagne and the peasants' Schnapps. We did not need money. He had his smile and his laugh. "Saint Benedict and his wolf!" they would cry from windows of palaces, and no matter how late it was, we would have to stop for a drink. For a song. Often he would stay the night. Men, women. Princes, whores. He had love enough for all of them.

"When the sores came, suddenly he was dead to them. One lover sent him a doctor, who filled him so full of mercury that he could not eat for a month. The rest forgot him, even when he pounded on their doors. Finally he just stayed here, never going out. He would stare at a new sore for hours and watch it come. He watched his beauty fade, staring in his mirror for hours every day.

"And then one day, after a year of this, the sores were gone. And though he was ugly, he shouted in the street, invaded parties and yelled, 'I am cured!' But he was not cured. His eyes began to cloud and grew sensitive even to the faintest light. Then the lumps began—on his arms, in his neck—and with them the pains. I would wake up to hear his moaning. His nose began to soften. The bones seemed to dissolve. He would simply hold it in his fingers."

Remus turned, and we both looked at our sleeping friend. The large armchair seemed intended for a child—the giant's arms spilled over, his knees splayed. The pillow had slipped away, his head had fallen forward.

"And you were all alone," I said.

Remus nodded. "But isn't that what I had wished for? He and I alone? Our lonely cave? Perhaps we got all that we deserved."

VIII.

When the weather was fine and Guadagni had no other distraction, he ordered me into his carriage and had his coachman convey us to the Prater or to some other royal park to which he was granted entry, and we drove for hours along the roads the emperor had constructed for his hunt. I hated these days, for it meant that I had no chance to stalk the streets around the Riecher Palace. While we drove about, I always feared it would be this day, of all days, that my beloved would take a few steps in the street.

But one such afternoon, deep in the Prater's woods, the birdcalls in the trees and the carriage wheels on the gravel my only distractions, I resolved to show my master that I, too, had a brain. I, too, had an ardent heart. I would raise the issue of most profound importance to us both. I asked Guadagni, "Signor, who castrated you?"

I held my breath, awaiting his reaction. He closed his eyes and slowly shook his head.

"*Mio fratello*," he said, "that is the one question you must never ask a musico."

I apologized and shut my mouth.

But then he smiled. "I am sorry," he said. "How are you to know such rules? You, of all people, deserve an answer. And so I give you one: Italy castrated me."

I pictured an army of Rapuccis swarming across the Italian lands commanded by some evil king with a mitre on his head. But this was not what my master meant. He held up a finger.

"*Mio fratello*, castrates are as old as the knives that cut them—no culture is free from this barbarism—but those like you and me are a class alone among the castrates. Consider: in ancient Egypt, Greece, and Rome, in India and in Islamic lands, the castrating cut has always been an insult. To be cut was to be reduced from man to something less—something simple, something tame.

"In London," he continued, "a man once showed me an account of the Chinese eunuchs, who comprise a class of servants in that land. After the affair is done, these boys receive their pickled members in an earthen jar. They keep this jar with them always. They store it on a shelf. *Pao* they call it. When they seek promotion, or change employment, they bring this *Pao* to their new employer, who lifts the lid and inspects what the man has lost, as if it were evidence of his character."

I swallowed, tugged at my collar. Guadagni laughed. "Does that disgust you?" he asked. "Why should it disgust you?"

"They must keep . . . it," I muttered. "In a jar?"

"Yes," he said. "In spirits. I suppose they change the liquid once a year so it does not cloud. One wants to see it *clearly*."

"Please don't talk of that," I begged.

He chuckled. "Fine," he said. "No more pickled *Pao*. I'll tell you instead of Greece and Rome, those civilizations of renown. There they cut boys like trimming shrubs—fifty or more at a time, though a score of every batch died of their wounds. *Cut to the belly* they called it; just a tiny hole remained. This mutilation made them tame, it was thought, and so they were the most desirable kind of slave. They did not dig holes or wash floors. Dressed in gold, their bodies slicked with oil, they fed their masters, poured wine, massaged aging backs. Their bodies were vessels for their masters to enjoy. Nero is perhaps the most infamous such master. He had a boy slave, Sporus, whom he loved above all the rest. An innocent, beautiful child. He instructed his surgeon to cut off every sign of Sporus's manly organ, and when the boy had healed, Nero dressed him in a bridal veil and married the little eunuch. Then he deflowered him on the imperial bed."

Now I could hardly breathe. I had known that many boys had suffered a fate as bad as mine, but now I saw that many had suffered worse—much, much worse.

"Might we stop a moment," I asked weakly. "I would like to walk about."

"But that is nothing," my master ploughed forth, his constant voice seemed to pin me to the seat. "Nero and his Sporus. Quite gentle in fact, when one considers other examples. Read the Book of Matthew. The apostle honors the noble 'eunuchs who have made *themselves* eunuchs.' God! It is one thing to have another do the cutting, quite another to do it to *oneself*. And how many have sliced themselves with daggers after Matthew's wisdom? Thousands. Scholars, mystics, fools. I've read of one ecstatic rite, in ancient Anatolia: on 'The Day of Blood,' men gathered on a mountain and, together, praying to some kind, caring god, mutilated themselves with scraps of broken pottery."

I opened the door to have some air, even though the carriage still bounced along. Light rain pattered on my shoes, but the air was like a cool, damp cloth on my burning brow.

Guadagni laughed and tugged at a lock of my hair, like an older brother might. "*Mio fratello*, don't give it a second thought! Don't you see? Those poor wretches have nothing to do with us. We are a different class—what made them despised as slaves makes us revered as gods. Even you, though you may not be rich, or known by anyone. No one will ever make you show them what you lost. You will never be inspected by your employer. You will never be ordered to lie face-down upon a bed. Your pain vanished years ago; you won't die from your wound."

He took my hand in his and held it up to the light. "Look, *mio fratello*, look what this cut has given you. No man has such beautiful hands. Such elegant fingers. And look at this." He touched his own cheek, lightly painted to enhance its natural glow. "No man has pure skin like that; pimples are the scourge only of the uncastrated. More, look how short they are and how tall we stand." He placed his hands on his breast, which bulged in the brocaded coat. "Does any man have such a chest? My lungs are twice the size of the world's best uncastrated singer. I have the cruel cut to thank for that as well. It was the magic of the cut that made our ribs grow so long. And there's more: our greatest treasure lies hidden until we sing." He held up a finger and gazed at me, as if daring me to guess where it would point. He finally pointed to the middle of his neck. "*They* have that ugly jabbing thing, *la pomme d'Adam*, jutting from their throat. And to think that crooked protrusion is where their voice begins! As unsuited to singing as a violin with a splintered neck." He massaged his own neck now as if it were the spine of a cat. "In contrast, our voice boxes remained undescended, hanging where God placed them.

"Don't you see!" he exclaimed. He clasped my arm. "Our singing makes us so different from those castrates of other ages. They were cut because they were poor, or beautiful, or unlucky. I was cut because, as a boy, I sang like a nightingale. And so now, here in Vienna, they ask me to be their Orpheus! I have sung Orlando, Solomon, Julius Caesar. These are gods among men! I am not their slave. I am not their servant. I am their hero. I am their angel. I am the one they dream of when they fall asleep at night. Oh, and how easy it is for them to love me! Love between a woman and a normal man is tedious at its best, filthy and shameful at its worst. But when I am with them, their desire becomes a torrent. There is no fear to hold them back; there will be no children conceived this night, no forced marriage will occur, no everlasting shame. They know that in the morning the memory of their pleasure will be pure, without regret. God does not disapprove of an angel taking part in their lustful dreams. And so I play not only Orpheus, but Bacchus, too. Occasionally their stupid husbands sneer at me—I hear them say my sword cannot stab—but it is they who are the fools. For that pelvis-thrusting poke, which they think their greatest feat, can be replaced, reproduced, improved upon."

Guadagni smirked, as if recalling a recent example of this boast. He stared out the window until his grin faded, and then turned back to me. "What was your question? Oh, yes: my castrator. I told you that Italy made me what I am. I cannot merely blame my father, nor the *buffo* company he sold me to, nor the barber they paid to cut me. Surely, I hope that all these men are in hell, but that would be little compensation, both for me, and for you, and for the thousands of other boys cut every year in Italian lands. *Mio fratello*, we were cut for the beauty of our voices. We were cut because every night in every Italian city, angels sing upon the stage and every man who has a son goes home thinking, *Could my son be an angel, too?*"

The cool air had calmed my swoon, and I raised my eyes again to my master. That smooth face was as collected as it ever was upon the stage, but I had heard a faint tremor in his voice. Now he looked out of the window as though he spoke no longer to me but only to himself. "I often ask myself," he said, "as I take my bows, how many boys have I castrated with my voice tonight?"

IX.

When I asked Remus to teach me Italian, he took the request with surprising gravity. We began to study for two hours every day on which I could manage to be away from Guadagni. Remus was an even more demanding teacher of language than Ulrich had been of song; he saw through words and sentences to some secret structure beyond the grasp of my mind, where different languages connected in mathematical simplicity. Yet the building blocks of language are not words but sounds, and there was my gift: I recognized the basic sounds immediately, and though after two weeks Dante still made no coherent sense, as I recited, I began to grasp occasional clumps of meaning—a king pickled in swill; a bellowing Sicilian bull; a thousand choking, purple faces.

"His Italian is better than yours already, Remus," Nicolai soon jested from his chair.

"Accent is not relevant," Remus countered, "if he doesn't know what he is saying."

"I don't understand it all either," Nicolai said from the shadows, for we burned only a single candle on account of his eyes, "but what he reads is beautiful. Something about deepest love?"

"Lechery and lust," Remus said flatly. " 'Groaning, tears, laments. They suffer here who sinned in carnal things. With never ease from pain nor hope of rest.' "

"How lucky we are to have you, Remus," Nicolai replied. "Otherwise we would all mistake the basest lust for truest love."

"Keep reading, Moses. Don't let him distract you."

"Is there any true love at all in that rotten book?" Nicolai asked.

"In all its forms," Remus retorted. "Sundered hearts, unquenchable passion, idealizations from afar."

"Get another book," Nicolai said disdainfully. "I want love here and now. Dante is dead. Hell is so far away. Can't someone tell me of something I could almost taste?"

"Read, Moses."

I opened the book again, but my hands were shaking. *Tell them! Now! Tell them of her!* I so wanted to, but I could not. They would not laugh at me, I knew, but I was afraid to read astonishment in their eyes. *You? In love? You?*

They would not say it, but it would be said.

One evening, when the Burgtheater had neither theater, nor opera, nor ballet on its program, I persuaded Tasso to leave his cave and join us in Spittelberg. He scampered behind me through the streets, staying in the shadows, as if he feared some hawk might swoop down and snatch him up.

When I led the little man up the stairs and into the dim parlor, he stopped at the threshold and examined the room as a man judging whether the ship he is about to board will float. Remus greeted us and offered Tasso his hand, but the stagehand did not take it. He peered around Remus at the massive shape in the chair.

"Just two men," Tasso asked, "alone?"

"It is just the two of us," Remus answered.

"No women?"

"No."

Tasso peered up at Remus. His nose twitched.

Nicolai called without turning. "Moses, is this that little man you told us you would bring one day to meet us?"

"Yes," I said uncomfortably. "This is Tasso. From the theater."

"Come in," yelled Nicolai. "Come in! Is it true you know the empress? Tell us of her daughters!"

Tasso looked up at Remus. He stuck a thumb toward Nicolai. "What's wrong with your husband?"

"He is not my husband," Remus said angrily. I had never seen him turn so red. "He is sick."

"Sick in the head," Tasso said, and then walked past Remus into the room.

"Moses," said Nicolai, "I like this mousy man."

Tasso sat beside Nicolai, in Remus's chair.

"This calls for celebration!" Nicolai said. "Moses, sing! No, no, wait—something to get us in the mood. Remus, go downstairs and tell Herr Kost we'd like his blackest stuff."

Remus reappeared a few minutes later carefully balancing four cups of steaming, black liquid, like the tar pools in Dante's hell.

"Sugar," Nicolai instructed us. "That's the secret to getting it down your throat."

We dissolved several lumps in each cup. Tasso held his nose while he drank. I could only get it down after doubling the sugar—enough to turn it into sweet sludge. But after ingested, it took only a minute for the magic to work its power: The dim room pulsed. I thought I would never need to sleep again. Tasso giggled secretively.

Nicolai shook his head as if a bumblebee buzzed about inside it.

"Sing for us, Moses," Remus said. I smiled. Never once in all the years I'd known him had he asked me to sing before, and now, this potion throbbing in my veins, I wanted to let the ringing out.

I stood before them and showered my three friends with song. Nicolai reclined and closed his eyes. Tasso swung his feet, which reached but halfway to the floor. Remus leaned against the wall, swayed a foot with the music, joyful tears in his eyes.

X.

At last it was September, and the night of Countess Riecher's engagement. Guadagni dressed me in red velvet with golden lions roaring from my breast.

"Why so anxious?" my mentor asked as we rumbled through the Vienna night in his coach. "They will not ask you to sing." His face was calm, his clothes refined.

"I'm not anxious," I said. I twirled a button on my coat. It popped off in my hand.

He shook his head. "Just try not to be such a bore," he said. "The hunt, *mio fratello*, the hunt is all."

We passed through the gate into the outer courtyard, and the Riechers' ogre—who, not two months before, had thrown me in the street and promised to smash my face should we ever meet again—himself opened our carriage door. I was so afraid of him I missed the stair and fell. He caught me in his white-gloved hands. He held me up, our faces as close as lovers'. Recognition, shock. He stifled it. "Sir" was all he said, and set me gently on my feet again.

Guadagni led me into the palace, which made Haus Duft in St. Gall seem like a caveman's dwelling—walnut floors, red silk-covered walls, every doorframe and table embellished with gold. In the foyer, a grand staircase led up to the higher stories of the house. I lingered there, listening for the sounds I wished to hear, but Guadagni pulled on my sleeve.

I entered the ballroom just behind him. I stumbled into him as he stopped to bow. "You fool," he hissed through his smile as everyone turned to see us. I smiled and bent slightly at the waist, as if I had a stomachache. Then he began his dance—women giggled as he kissed their hands, men blushed and swallowed when he winked at them.

I stumbled around the room, jostled and elbowed about like a log drifting down a stream. I tried to hear it all. Men's heels clicked on the hard walnut floor. The white toes of women's shoes shushed on the frilly hems of gowns. "I can't bear visiting my estate," said one prince. "So far from what really *matters*." "Coal is converted into steam," described another. "Or is it steam into coal?" I tumbled into a circle of wrinkled widows, who grunted and conveyed me on to a set of ladies with overpainted faces. "I don't understand it," one of them said. "In the country they have fields, houses, water to clean their children, but they all insist on living *here*." And then, farther on, were several girls admiring a newly made duke. "Father said the title cost him a fortune," one whispered, while the others licked their lips. "Oh, but how I'd love to be a duchess." I glimpsed Countess Riecher sweeping through the crowd—yearning looks followed in her wake. A man with medals on his chest held up a hand and stumbled after her. "Oh, countess," he said. "Might I just have a minute of—"

My ears strained to hear the voice, or the laugh, or the sigh that matched those stored in the precious recess of my mind. I did not hear them. Twice I ran into a wall, and remained there like an automaton, until I was taken arm-in-arm by some intriguer and led back to my master. He smiled and thanked them, then grumbled at me to go away.

And then, there she was.

In fact, my eyes found her first: her hair tied up in a golden crown. I peered across the ballroom, over all that powdered hair and frilly muslin and coats stuck with golden medals gifted by the empress, all of it swirling like translucent, lifeless fog. My ears strained for her precious sounds, but she stood silently among a group of men at the top of a set of stairs, on a gallery that overlooked the ballroom.

A jeweled hand grabbed my arm, "You're rather pale," the woman said, poking her beak up into my face. "Are you ill? Have a sip of wine." I let her place the glass to my lips and I drank, but then I pushed myself off her arm and took shuffling steps to the stairs as though I walked on ice.

Amalia glowed among those men like a burning coal half-buried in spent ashes. They argued, they gestured, they nodded violently, and though she just gazed past them, unenthralled, it was she they spoke to, she they wished to reach with their words. "Oh, do come," one fat man said. "Do come. You must." Another nodded as if this were the greatest wisdom he'd ever heard. *Among us someone is alive!* their hungry gawking said. She smiled politely, her shoulders back, as if she were merely posing for a portrait. Her white gown, tied below the breast with a violet bow, hid all her curves. It was she, and yet something was vastly different. I could not place it. *Speak!* I prayed, *Let me hear you laugh!*

I glided up the stairs, masking my sounds as I had when stealing into those St. Gall houses late at night. Her neck was so long. That spot below her ears, where her pinned-up hair terminated in an arrow of soft, blond down, was where I most wished to press my ear.

I circled around behind her, and for a moment we stood just inches apart. I heard her breath—the drawing in deep within her nose, the parting of her lips, the warm exhalation through her mouth, the soft gown against her skin as her shoulders rose and fell.

Then she and a younger man from the group moved down the stairs. He put a hand across her back to guide her: Anton Riecher, I realized, and I found myself admiring even his trimmed eyebrows, the whiteness of his teeth. He was as much a man as I had feared: elegant and tall. His dominant brow and deep-set eyes made him handsome, but also somehow sleepy, as if his soft steps were pointed toward his bed. For several minutes I stalked behind them, my ears tuned to their every sound. When Anton met a guest, he offered his hand as though he merely sought a place to rest it for a while. When spoken to, he gave successive nods that bowed him closer and closer to the speaker's mouth until he seemed ready to lay himself in their arms. He rose again only when he was ready to speak himself, which he did slowly, with great emphasis. "I have heard so much about you from my mother. How nice it is to finally make your acquaintance," he said to one officer. "It is fascinating what you say," to a man of business. "From what I understand, Vienna needs more men just like you."

He occasionally whispered in Amalia's ear. "No man has a more beautiful wife in this room than I," he said. "They are all saying it, you realize." "Has anyone ever thrown you such a party? All for you," he said a few minutes later, "and, of course, for me." She let herself be guided by his hand as if she were a sleepwalker. And while I ached to hear her voice, Amalia never spoke; upon meeting a new guest, the canvas of her face softened slightly, then swiftly returned to a portrait of quiet patience.

I took a glass of champagne and held it before me—a slender sapling to hide behind. I stepped within a few paces of her. I waved the glass back and forth before me and fixed my eyes on her. Her husband was deep in talk, so he did not look in my direction, but finally I managed to distract her. Our eyes met for the first time since we were children. My blood warmed ten degrees.

Her eyes were blank. She did not know me. A stranger stood before her.

But it is I! I almost yelled. *Your lover of so many nights!* But had I done so I would have lost her once again. Instead, I smiled. I waved. I nodded my head. She blushed and turned away.

"Not that one, you fool." My teacher was suddenly beside me, whispering in my ear. "That one is reserved for the masters of the hunt. First, you have no hope. Such a woman would not even converse with you. Second," he murmured, "if the Riecher woman glimpses how your eyes rest on her jewel, she will carve them out."

I begged my master at least to introduce me, but he shook his head and clucked his tongue. "I must say, at the very least, your eye is good. She is indeed the finest catch in the room. But give it up. She is not for you." Guadagni smiled again at Amalia. "Though perhaps, when the time is right, I will show you how it would be done. But not now. Now is time to strike elsewhere."

He swept across the room, and his purposeful glide was enough to signal his intention to the room. The crowd hushed and gathered around the harpsichord at the end of the ballroom. Gluck himself appeared and sat at the keyboard.

The ballroom filled with the sounds of shifting feet, with the rustle of fabric as an audience condensed, with soft cries of "Guadagni! He's going to sing!" I closed my eyes for a moment to block it out. To me, there was just one person in that ballroom, and she was silent.

As Guadagni began the aria "Armida dispietata!" from *Rinaldo*, I left the stairs and joined the crowd. I pushed through them. I pressed my elbows into ladies' backs, stood in front of stooping generals, tugged on sleeves. I did not care for these people any more than for trees in a forest.

Then I was behind her once again, so close I could have kissed the down of her neck. Her husband—he was almost as tall as I—stood beside her, but they did not touch. I closed my eyes. In her neck, in the soft hollows behind her jaw, I heard the whispering resonance of Guadagni's song. It took all of my concentration to hold the sound, and I seized at it, seizing for her.

But then I could not help myself. Guadagni's voice was too weak. It played that body so inexpertly, and so I opened my throat just a hair; the slightest sound escaped. No one heard my voice above the music, but the faint sound caressed her. It touched the long, narrow muscles on the backs of her arms, and her arms moved slightly outward, like wings awakening. She sighed. For the first time that night, her breath deepened, and I heard that she had awoken to Guadagni's song. I released her to it. She rang.

But then, she began to cry. A sob escaped with her exhalation. Though she pressed her thumb to her lips, she could not stifle the soft moan, which grabbed my heart and strangled it. The sadness stored inside of her—her body bound up tightly—was released by the music ringing through us. Then, she could take no more. She pushed through the crowd and dashed from the room, limping now.

I looked at Guadagni. The great castrato watched her run, and smiled as he sang, for he had made ten thousand other women cry as well, and here, he thought, was one more soul he owned.

Anton also watched his wife depart, and then, when she was gone, he turned and his gaze alighted on my face. Perhaps I looked alarmed, because he smiled kindly, as if to say, *Oh well, there is indeed sadness in this world. But you and I, at least, are content.*

I saw my chance. I retreated, backing through the crowd.

I followed her.

XI.

I was that well-trained ghost. My breaths were quiet draughts of air. I listened for advancing feet, but the house was empty; even the servants were listening to Guadagni sing. In the foyer, I looked up the grand staircase. I heard her uneven steps far above, so I began to climb. The thick carpet muted every step. The railing did not creak. Around me, lamps hissed. Up one flight, I paused. There were so many rooms in the house, enough for a Riecher army. Ancient portraits hung on every wall, and I felt the eyes of dead Riechers watching me.

On the top floor, I closed my eyes. I heard muffled sobbing to my left. After several paces, the passage turned. I saw a long wing and knew this must be where Anton and Amalia made their home.

The last door was ajar, and I rushed toward it like a thirsty man for a spring. I would hold her in my arms! But I forced myself to slow—already servants were clunking up the stairs; the brief recital was finished. Reason held me back: I could not startle her; a scream would endanger all my plans. I slipped lightly into her room.

She was lying on her bed, her hand upon her face, her gown spilling across her.

I halted at the threshold. I suddenly comprehended what had changed: the shape of her body. The thin muslin gown lay flat against her now and I saw that her belly curved where once it had been flat.

A sudden heat washed over me, for this was too much to comprehend in an instant: the child growing inside of her, the act that had created it, the future family it represented. *Your body will not let you be a father*, the abbot had said so many years before, and here, now, the evidence of my inadequacy lay before me, so unmistakable. For several seconds I could not breathe. She cried violent sobs into her hands, the sadness pouring out of her now, and gradually my ears overcame my eyes. I recalled that silent woman in the ballroom, as unresponsive as a muffled bell. These tears were for me! This propelled me another silent step into the room. I opened my arms. *But I am alive!* I would exclaim.

But already I had delayed too long. I heard Anton's slow steps coming up the stairs. He whistled Handel's aria out of tune. I could not have him find me here. I retreated swiftly into the passage and slipped through the next door, just as his merry whistle rounded the corner.

The door did not lead to an exit, but to another room. It was dark, but I could see I was in a nursery. I looked frantically for another way out, my stomach churning, but I could see that the only other door connected to Amalia's room.

"What a singer!" I heard Anton shout from the other side of the door. "A voice like sunshine in the summer!"

I heard her rustle on the bed, and was sure she was wiping that beautiful face of tears.

"Feeling ill again, are you?" he said.

"You need not concern yourself."

"The music?" he asked disbelievingly. "Can it really be the music?"

"I said you need not concern yourself."

I crept to the door and peered through the keyhole. Anton stood in the middle of the room, as if in front of him was a line he was not permitted to cross—an abyss. He shook his head. "Really, this is something you must overcome."

"I shall not overcome it," she said, hotly. "I have told you that before."

"Amalia, don't be foolish," he admonished. "No one hates beautiful music."

"You cannot change me."

His eyes hardened, and a smile flashed across his face. *Oh*, it seemed to say, *I get everything I want. You'll see.*

"Fine," he said. "I will not try to change it. Hate every sound you hear if you must. But, Amalia, really, you must be reasonable. One cannot always enjoy oneself. One has responsibilities."

I heard the sound of her shifting on the bed. Was she sitting up now? "Anton, when you took me from my father's house," she said, "do you remember what you said? 'Anything you want. In Vienna you shall be free.'"

"And free you are," he said, still smiling, but his anger was not far below the surface. "Is there anything I deny you?"

"You deny me the freedom to walk about the city. To take a carriage on my own."

"Amalia, indeed! You are a lady. A Riecher. We are not in some Swiss mountain village. Look around you! I give you all that you could want. That carriage you complain of is as fine as any prince's. This house, these clothes! Gaetano Guadagni singing *for you*. And more. At this premiere you will sit before them all, and they—"

"What are you talking about? What premiere?"

Anton flinched. He had misspoken.

"Answer me." The bed creaked as she stood.

"The new *Orpheus*, of course," he said flippantly. "Surely you have heard it discussed."

"But we cannot go." Her voice was flat, afraid.

"And why not?" An innocent, tender smile.

"Because we are leaving."

Anton shook his head, the condescending smile grew only wider. "Amalia," he said.

"You promised me we would leave Vienna!" she shouted with sudden violence. She took several steps toward him, coming into my view. Her eyes were still red from tears, but anger was the dominant emotion now.

He retreated a small step backward. "You are not in a state to travel."

"Anton! That is why I wished to leave a month ago!" Her hands grasped the fabric of her gown below her breast as if she would tear it.

"In any case, now it is too late." He tried to take her hands, but she cast him away.

"It is not!" For a moment her face tensed and she fought back tears. "I must get out of this city before the baby comes." She pointed an accusing finger in his face. "You promised me we would spend the winter in the country."

"But my mother—"

"Goddamn your mother!"

"Amalia!" He grabbed her arm and shook her violently. He drew his other hand up to his ear, as if about to strike her.

I clutched the door's handle. *If he dares*, I thought.

But she just looked at his cocked hand. Her eyes were ice.

His body trembled with fury. But he released her. Still, she did not shy away, but stared into his eyes.

"It is not possible to leave just yet," he said as calmly as he could. "My mother wishes to have us here for several more weeks—"

Amalia enunciated every word. "I will not be her fattened sow to par—"

"Amalia, you are no longer in Saint Gall," he said censoriously. "This is Vienna. You are a Riecher. You must comprehend your situation. The Riecher family will have *an heir*. This is most evident in your person, and at the premiere the empress will sit opposite our loge. You cannot blame my mother for the fate you have chosen."

These words seemed to strike her painfully. The ice in her eyes melted into tears.

"No," she said quietly, shaking her head sadly, biting her lip. "No, I can't. I have only God to blame for that."

"If you are unhappy, Amalia," he said disapprovingly, "search inside your own heart for the cause."

"I know perfectly well why I am unhappy," she said, and turned her shoulder to him, her back to me. He watched her with repulsion. But then he mastered himself, and took her hand.

"I have promised my mother that we will attend the premiere in three weeks' time."

She pulled back her hand. "You should not have promised her. You know it is torture to me. I will not go."

"You must," he said. "If you anger her, she will never allow us to leave."

She turned to him, now some terror in her eyes. *"Allow us to leave? Does she rule our lives?"*

"Show more respect!" They held each other's gaze, and again, it was his that faltered. He stared angrily at the wall. She studied him. Finally, she shook her head slightly from side to side.

"If I agree to go," she said carefully, "we can leave the very next day?"

"Yes, of course," he said quickly.

"If our things are packed," she said, "and everything is prepared for our departure, I will go to the premiere, though I will hate every moment. But if I feel I cannot trust your promise, I will complain of cramps." She walked toward her bed, limping. When his eyes gazed at her uneven hips, I again saw that repulsion on his face.

"Fine," he said flatly. "I hope you see now that there was no reason to speak to me in such violent tones."

I heard her whisper then, "I so wish my child's father were not a sheep."

"What was that?"

"Nothing. You can leave me now." She waved him off.

"Leave you? I came to fetch you. The concert is finished. You can return." There was no trace of that condescending smile on his face.

"I do not wish to return," she said.

"You must."

She turned to stare him down, but she looked tired now. "I will follow you soon," she said.

"I will wait."

Wait he did, until she had cleaned her face of tears and anger. He took her arm gently in his and led her out the door, as if she were blind and he her only eyes.

When I returned downstairs, Guadagni grabbed my hand as soon as I had entered the ballroom. "Where have you been? There are two ladies waiting in the coach," he whispered in my ear. "I will teach you much tonight." He pulled me out into the air.

But once in the coach, he placed me on the seat opposite him, so I could observe him between the two rosy ladies. One woman gazed with hungry eyes as he stroked the other's thigh. He kissed the hungry one on her cheek to calm her, which set the other climbing onto his lap. He pushed her down. "Patience," he insisted. "Is that any way for a princess to behave?"

When we reached his house, he leaned over and whispered into my ear, "These two will fight like cats tonight. Ride the coach about for a while. Come back when it is light."

For an hour the coachman drove me around the city, and I mused over my failure. Would I ever have another chance? I cursed myself for being so slow to act. I promised that I would never doubt her love again.

But even as I grew more and more disheartened about my chances of winning her back, there was some flame growing gradually inside of me, until I found myself smiling.

A child! She would have a child!

I had first reacted to this with a jabbing at the deepest center of my shame, but now, as that initial sting receded, this coming life seemed a hopeful omen.

I so wish my child's father were not a sheep, she had said.

Finally, I told the coachman to take me to Spittelberg. He took me as far as the Burggasse before he said he would not break a wheel on the pitted street. I descended and walked from there.

In the early morning, the sky was already turning gray. The filthy streets were as silent as I had ever heard them. No ladies beckoned from the windows of the decrepit taverns. In his coffeehouse, Herr Kost slept upon a bench. I did not wake him as I glided up the stairs.

One resident of Spittelberg was awake: Nicolai sat in his chair at an open window. I sat beside him, and we stared together down the Burggasse toward the city. The street's few remaining cobblestones poked out of the earth like old, crooked teeth. In the taverns, few lamps still burned, and in those windows grime coated the panes like frost.

"I like to sit here and breathe the air," Nicolai said, "before the sun comes up and hurts my eyes. There are just a few more minutes now. Then I will close the curtains for the day."

I did not say anything, and so he probed, "Are you out late or up early?"

"Out late."

"Guadagni take you to a party?"

I nodded. Two dogs moved out of the shadows and poked at the islands of rotting refuse in the street. We sat for several minutes more before I had the courage to speak.

"Nicolai, do you remember when you told me that love was the meeting of two halves?"

Nicolai shrugged. The gentle light of the rising sun made his bulbous face seem even softer, like a mold of warm wax. "Did I say that? I suppose I could have. I've certainly said even more foolish things in all these years," he told the open window. "In any case, it would be so easy if it were true. Love like a meeting of lock and key! No, Moses. Any man who says that is a fool. I found my other half decades ago and look how I have hurt him. I should have left him alone."

Someone opened a door at one of the taverns and lurched off toward the city. The gray sky now had hints of pink along its surface, like the sheen of oil on a puddle.

"Nicolai," I said. "I am in love."

When he regarded me, his dulled eyes squinting in an effort to read my face, there was that astonishment I had so feared to see upon his face. From me, he never expected such a confession. But it did not wound me as I had expected, because with the surprise was also the purest joy.

"In love!" he said.

And so I told him all: of that high-born girl and her dying mother, of the young woman who stole into the abbey, of our nights in that attic room. I told him how she did not know my face, just my voice, how she called me her Orpheus. I told him also of the fool I had been, how I had missed my chance, how she had married the great Anton Riecher of Vienna. How she would soon have a child. I told him how she thought me dead, but loved me still.

"But now you have a second chance!" he said, and his hope was so hot it warmed my own. "Orpheus can save his Eurydice!"

Shamefaced, I told him of my failure at the party, and how I feared that I would never breach that prison of a house again, where she was locked away. How, soon, she would be leaving for the country.

"Then we cannot delay!" he exclaimed. "We will get into that house if we must knock down its walls!"

I thanked him for his courage, though I knew only a fool would try what he suggested. But I had one last idea. "She will be at the premiere of the opera in three weeks. If I could conspire some way to get her a message there, I could tell her to slip away. Perhaps we could escape." My voice shook as I told my friend of my hope. Would he think it foolish?

"You will steal her at the opera!" he exclaimed and looked so intently into the dawn it was as if he saw a vision of the two of us in the pink swirls of the sky.

Excitement swelled within me, like a drumroll slowly building. I would be her Orpheus and spirit her away! But I calmed my heart. "Nicolai," I said. "Caution is of first importance. If Countess Riecher suspects anything, I might never see her again."

"Caution?" he said. He considered. "Perhaps we should ask Remus for his advice."

I helped Nicolai struggle into Remus's room. A narrow bed filled up most of the space, piles of books the rest. Nicolai tripped over some of these, half-fell onto the bed, and at the crack of the bed frame, Remus jerked awake just in time to avoid being crushed by Nicolai, who flailed about like a giant fish trying to flip back into its stream. When he had finally righted himself on the bed, he felt for Remus's shirt. He shook the smaller man. "Remus, wake up! Moses is in love! In love! Wake up!"

"I am awake," Remus said, pushing Nicolai's hands away from his throat. "You've seen to that."

"Then get up and dance about! It's true—and she loves him, too!

For years they held secret trysts in an attic room and he sang for her until she cried. She is as beautiful as a princess, and best of all she's here, right here in Vienna! Married to an evil man. We've got to save her and reunite them." Nicolai fairly swooned.

"He's . . . he's not exactly evil," I muttered.

"Oh, and I almost forgot the most romantic part," Nicolai added. His hands had left the still-startled Remus and were reaching into space, trying to grasp some distant sun. "She doesn't know his face."

"Doesn't know his face?" Remus asked.

"She wore a *blindfold*."

"A blindfold? Why?" Remus turned to me, and my neck grew hot.

"It doesn't matter why," Nicolai said. "The important part is that she knows his voice, knows it better than most know their lover's face. All he needs to do is speak—or sing! Then he'll have her back and they can flee!"

Nicolai swung his arm and tried to point toward our distant escape. He knocked over Remus's unlit lamp. The glass shattered on the floor.

"Would you be still!" Remus yelled.

"How can I—"

"And be quiet! I need to speak to Moses." Remus regarded me gravely. "Is what he says true?"

"He's not an evil man, this Anton," I said. "The rest is mostly true. She does not love him. That I know."

"And you are sure she loves you?" he asked. "Moses, this is a dangerous thing. Will she really betray her husband and his family?"

They both waited for my answer. A moment was all I needed to review the history of our love in sounds. "I am sure," I said. Nicolai clapped his hands, and even Remus smiled.

"Then I will write a note," he said.

"A note?" Nicolai asked. "But Remus, your writing is so dull."

"That does not bear," he said. "It is simply done. It will merely relay the facts. Moses is alive. He, too, is at the opera. She should slip away at a certain moment."

"When Orpheus looks into Eurydice's eyes!" whispered Nicolai.

"Or another moment," Remus said. "It makes no difference."

"*It makes no difference*," Nicolai chastised. "Remus, these books you read are wasted on you." But Nicolai smiled with the jest. Suddenly, though, his face darkened. "But Remus, there is a problem with your plan. Something you have overlooked. How will she get the note?"

Remus nodded knowingly at me.

"Moses will lay it in her hands himself."

"Me?"

"Yes," said Remus. "You are Guadagni's student, his messenger. You alone can gain entry to any loge at the opera. You could deliver a letter to the empress. You will tell anyone who asks that you carry a letter to the lady from the virtuoso himself. They will think he admired her from the stage."

"Remus," said Nicolai, "this is genius!"

Remus smiled proudly.

And so our plan was set. I needed only wait for the premiere.

XII.

I first met the goddess of love one afternoon while Tasso and Gluck were trying to teach her to fly. As my teacher and I entered the theater, plump Lucia Clavarau stood in the middle of the stage with miniature wings affixed to her back. "My God," Guadagni muttered. "Don't they know a boar with wings is still a boar?"

"But you're so small," she said to Tasso, when he had her strapped into the harness, "you will dro—"

She let out a shrill soprano scream as Tasso set loose the weight to lift her into the sky. She swung across the stage.

"Don't squirm!" Tasso shouted.

"Let me down!" she yelled.

Tasso yanked another line and she arced, screaming and thrashing, back across the stage.

"Let her down," Gluck said to Tasso. "She looks more like an insect than the god of love. We'll put her on a pedestal."

Orpheus's bride, Marianna Bianchi, was slight and pale, with a gorgeous voice that quickly brought tears to my eyes. In all my life I'd so rarely heard a woman sing, and I was suddenly sure my mother would have sung like that. During rehearsals each afternoon, I sat with Tasso, or in the wings waiting to receive my teacher. My Italian was good enough now, and Calzabigi's simple enough, that after the first week of rehearsals I not only understood the story but could sing along with Guadagni under my breath. I noticed both the beauty and the flaws of his voice.

"Master," I said very carefully one evening as we returned to his house, "it is such an honor to hear you sing."

He bowed perfunctorily from his seat.

"I wondered if I might, though, ask you one question."

He raised his brow.

"The first two acts are so exquisite, don't you think that the third act is too . . . too . . ."

"Too what?" he snapped.

I sought the correct word to describe the phenomenon. "Too . . . too . . . loud?"

"Too *loud*?" He turned, and the ferocious glint in his eye made me lean back against the door.

"Not too loud, exactly," I retreated. "But . . . but *only* loud. You have the finest voice I have ever heard, Master, but, well, perhaps if you held back at places, at others your limited volume would be more convincing."

"Limited volume?" Guadagni peered at me as if he were witnessing some disgusting maggot crawling out of my nose.

"Well, very ample. But—"

He leaned forward. I realized he was shaking from his very core. "How dare you! *You!*" he shouted. "You know nothing! Nothing!"

"I am sorry." I waved my hands, hoping to put off his attack. "I should not have—"

His anger lifted him off his seat so that he towered above me. "You know less of opera than the idiot princes at these parties. You are some choir singer cut for someone's perverse enjoyment. Someone's eunuch pet escaped." He took several deep breaths. When he spoke, his velvet voice rippled with fury. "Never"—his face came so close to mine I thought he would bite me—"never again tell me what you think."

I never did, but later, so many others would. He would return to London, and though at first they greeted him as a victorious son returned, his voice failed to be what they had dreamed it was. He fled to Padua and obscurity, where he died a pauper, his fortune spread among the castrated wretches who surrounded him as his students. His only joy, in his final years, was the routine staging of a solo puppet show of Gluck's great opera, which would be remembered as his finest achievement.

You have certainly read much about the premiere of this opera. In mere weeks all of Europe knew of Guadagni and Gluck's success. However, I must disappoint you: none of it is true. Not only are all accounts mistaken, because on that celebrated night in October 1762 events proceeded contrary to official history, they are doubly mistaken, because that night was not, in fact, the premiere at all. The true premiere took place several days in advance. The empress was not present, nor even the composer. In fact, the venue was a cramped parlor in Spittelberg. The official audience numbered only three: one stunted stagehand who had no Italian and who, until two months before, had thought Orpheus a species of flower; one syphilitic former monk; and a bookish wolf who knew two dozen versions of the Orpheus tale and could recite Ovid's or Virgil's in any language one could name.

I fetched four cups of black magic. I turned Nicolai's chair toward my makeshift stage at the empty fireplace. I bid Remus close his book. I told Tasso that Orpheus was the greatest musician ever, and that he had lived a long, long time ago, but that tonight I would bring him back to life. I explained that my beloved wife, Eurydice, was dead.

"Then what's the point?" Tasso said. "Why don't you sing of something else instead?"

Nicolai shook his head. I began.

It was not the greatest performance of my life. The orchestra and the chorus played only in my head, and so my audience heard long periods of silence. When I began, in fact, I held my fists against my heart and did not move—as I had seen Guadagni do on his stage—for the entire four minutes of the opening *coro*. My audience heard only my three cries of *Euridice!* which I sang, as Gluck had instructed Guadagni, "as if someone were sawing through your bones." Nicolai stiffened with each cry, and Tasso's eyes widened from their beads.

It was a warm night, and the windows were open. Occasional infant cries, drunken curses, sweet enticements, and moans of pleasure filtered through the air and reminded me that this was a place where one need not hide his sounds. Mine would simply mingle with all the others. Who would care to listen?

But I was wrong: As I sang to the giant, the wolf, and the dwarf in that parlor, calling my dead bride, families left their crowded tables and stepped to their windows, trying to identify the mourner. The children in the streets ceased their play. Men put down their ale and looked up at the sky. These cries to my beloved awoke every heart in that quarter.

I did not realize then I was being heard outside the room. In the theater of my mind, the chorus left the stage, and I, Orpheus, stood there alone. Eurydice had been cruelly taken from me to a wakeless death. I sang out to her. Then, as the orchestra swelled, I felt my sadness turn to an anger purer than any I had ever known. I hated those greedy gods for what they had stolen from me.

My hands tingled as I sang. When I again opened my eyes, Tasso was cowering in his chair under the power of my voice. My curses rattled the empty cups resting on the table. Downstairs, in the coffeehouse, the men had ceased to debate.

Finished singing, I gasped for air. Nicolai clapped his round hands together. Remus shook his head in wonder. Tasso looked from one man to the next; he clenched and unclenched his fists.

"I can't sing the duets alone," I said. Tasso's brow tightened as if he smelled a cheat. "But I'll tell you what you miss," I continued. "My sadness is so great that Jove has pitied me. He sends Amor, the goddess of love, to tell me that if I can placate the Furies in the underworld with my song, I may have my Eurydice back."

Tasso pressed his palms together and looked at Remus, who was the expert on these things. When Remus nodded confirmation, Tasso grunted.

"I knew she wasn't really dead!" he said.

"She is," I said. "But I can save her!"

"All right," he said. "I am ready." He clutched both armrests as if he feared that whatever followed would throw him from his chair.

"But there is a condition," I said.

Tasso's face hardened. "A condition?" he repeated.

"Yes, Amor says once I have her back, I cannot look at her until we leave the caves beyond the River Styx."

"But why?"

"That is the will of the gods."

"But it's not fair!"

"The gods are not fair."

"But you will get her back, won't you?"

"You must listen."

"Then begin already!" he barked.

I sang. In my mind, I descended to the Stygian Caves. Angiolini's Furies danced about me. I begged them to pity me, but they only swarmed and shouted to frighten me away. But they could not scare me, for their hell was nothing like the lonely hell inside my heart. I sang to them: you would not be so cruel if only you knew the depths of my love.

Nicolai's face was wet. He wiped the tears with the back of a swollen hand. Outside, the street was quiet, too; a crowd had gathered below our window. Drivers shouted because their carriages could not struggle past, and men elbowed to stand closer to the window. Finally, on the stage, the Furies suspended their dance. The demons backed away, amazed that love like this could exist in hell. They let me pass.

The gates to the underworld slid open.

I paused. There was silence in the parlor. Remus swallowed, and Nicolai wiped his brow with his sleeve. Tasso chewed his lip. I did not keep them waiting. I began that aria that had tempted me into Guadagni's ballroom two months before. I left the dark, fiery caves for the warm and bright Elysian Fields. The sky was clear, and hope filled my heart. In my mind, I heard the soothing notes of Gluck's oboe.

My song was a warm blanket to lay over my friends. I wanted to soothe them as the music soothed me. I wanted them to feel the hope that was in my heart. Tasso pursed his lips, and Nicolai closed his eyes as if basking in the warmth of my voice. Remus's brow was smooth, his eyes so calm. I had never seen him look so handsome.

Outside the night was silent. This aria would change the street; I would never walk it again without people staring, without whispers: He is the one who sang that autumn night. He made us stop and listen. He made us shiver. He made my mother smile. He made our ailing father leave the bed and listen at the window. He is our Orpheus! How Gluck would have hated me, spoiling his genius on such simple ears.

And then there she was, in my mind, the shadow of her form. I reached out my arm, but just as she came into the light—before I saw her face—I turned away, for I could not look at her, or she would die again.

When I finished the aria, Nicolai's breath was a gentle wave; his eyes remained closed. He could have been asleep. Tasso leaned close. "Is she back?" he whispered. He did not wish to disturb the night.

"Yes," I said. I lifted my hand. "I hold her here. She is alive again, but I cannot look at her, or she will die."

Tasso breathed in sharply.

"She does not understand," I said. "She thinks I have ceased to love her. It is so painful. She sings that she would rather die again than live without my love. It is like a dagger in my heart. I wish to tell her that the gods keep me from looking into her eyes. There is nowhere I would rather look! But I cannot say a word about my pact, or it is broken, and she will die again."

"Sing the rest in German," Tasso said. "I cannot wait for the explanation."

"Tasso," I said gently. "It will not fit the music."

Remus motioned to Tasso to sit on the arm of his chair. He said he would whisper a translation in his ear.

I closed my eyes. Tongues of fire licked the walls. I held her hand in mine, but still she was so distant. *Hurry! Hurry!* We had to escape these horrid caves, get back into the light, so I could see her face. This place would kill us both. But grief had made her weak. She collapsed on her knees and begged me to look into her eyes.

My senses cracked. I would go mad if this torment did not end! My voice strained with terror. I felt the tendons bulging in my neck.

I opened my eyes. In the parlor, Remus's lips whispered at Tasso's ear. Nicolai's eyes were wide and focused on my face. I had no choice! I could not bear her pain!

I broke my promise. I looked into her eyes, and for a single instant Eurydice knew I loved her. And then Jove's will was done: she died.

Tasso stared at my feet, where he saw Eurydice, dead upon the floor. He looked up at my face in shock, his beady eyes now shiny jewels, polished by his tears. The city outside was still, but I was now aware of the many breaths. I knew there were eyes peering up at the window, hoping the song was not yet over.

Gluck's strings began again in my head—the first notes of "Che farò senza Euridice?" I had never felt such sadness.

I rang. I was a bell cast from ice.

Tasso leaned forward from his seat, caring no more to hear Remus's translation. Nicolai cried into his hands. Remus sat upright, his eyes shut. In the streets there was much weeping. Children clutched their mothers. Whores at their windows leaned against their sills, straining to see my face, for there was hope in this song. If Orpheus, in his sadness, could summon up this hope, so could they, too. And, as I sang, they clenched their fists and cried.

When I was finished, I leaned against the wall.

"Is it over?" Tasso whispered.

I shook my head, but I could not speak. *Of course it is not over*, I would have said. But it was too much. I recalled that my own Eurydice slept not far away. I could not breathe. My head began to spin. And then I was on my knees. The last thing I saw was Nicolai, eyes closed, a giant, calm smile on his face, as if he had glimpsed an angel.

Then I let myself fall into the blackness.

Tasso was my hero. He leapt from Remus's chair and caught me before my temple smashed into the fireplace. He laid my head gently in his lap and stroked my brow.

As I began to recover, I heard him ask Remus, "Is that it? Is it over?"

"Yes," Remus said. "Orpheus has lost Eurydice again and forever. According to Virgil, he mourns for many months, singing such beautiful laments that all the animals of the forest come to hear him. But this angers the Ciconian women, who do not believe in such love. They tear him to pieces. As his dismembered head floats down the Hebrus, he calls Eurydice's name."

Tasso sighed. "But how can that be?" he asked. "He loved her so much."

"It matters not," Remus said. "The gods are not so merciful."

"That's not true!" I gasped. "His love is heard!"

Tasso held me down, worried I would faint again, but he smiled broadly at Remus. "I was sure it could not end like that!"

Remus shrugged. "But that is how it ends," he said. "Of course there are other versions. In Ovid, it is the Thracian women who dismember him."

"No," I said. I struggled up against Tasso's resisting hand. "I am sure. Orpheus tries to kill himself, but Amor intervenes. Orpheus's lament has moved her, and Amor brings Eurydice back to life and takes them to the Temple of Love. That is where it ends! With a ballet!"

Tasso's eyes were glassy. "Yes, the temple!" he said. "The final backdrop! It is true. I've seen it!"

Remus shrugged. "Then Calzabigi and Gluck have changed the story," he said.

"And what's wrong with that?" Tasso asked. He huffed, and his lower lip stayed hung in defiance of the learned man.

"The story is more than two thousand years old," Remus said. "One of our oldest myths. It makes no sense if the gods keep giving Orpheus more chances. They become merciful to absurdity."

Tasso's face was angry. "You just don't believe in love." He jabbed a short finger at Remus.

Remus smiled kindly. He shrugged, and was about to answer, but did not have the chance, for at that moment Nicolai spoke. "I believe in love," he said. I had assumed the giant was dozing, but he sat upright in his chair, looking stronger than I'd seen him since I had arrived in Vienna. "And to prove it," he continued, "I am coming to the premiere."

The candle's light seemed to flare up and illuminate his smile.

"The premiere?" muttered Remus. "What do you mean the—"

"Yes!" I said and jumped up, still dizzy from my spell, and stepped to Nicolai's chair. "You must—you of all people deserve to be in that crowd. You shall—" I cut myself off, realizing only then the many obstacles. Nicolai's grin did not fade. "But . . . but how will your eyes bear the light?"

"You will put a sack over my head and parade me through the streets like the sinner that I am," he said. "But in the theater, where I will sit, it will be dark."

Remus shook his head. "No. It is light throughout the theater," he said. "So all may see the empress."

"Not light everywhere," said Nicolai. "Not beneath the stage."

Tasso sprang to his feet. "No," he said. "No, no, that is not permitted." He waved his hands, clawing at the air. "The empress would have my head."

"Don't worry about your head," Nicolai said with a smile. "It is your heart we want!"

Tasso's glance darted from Nicolai, to Remus, then to me. He looked at the door—his escape. He chewed his lip, but then he looked back at the spot where I had sung, and his face brightened.

"But you must promise not to touch a thing," he warned.

"You can tie my hands behind my back," said Nicolai. "I need nothing but my ears. That, my dear Tasso, I promise you."

XIII.

It was the fifth of October, 1762—barely forty years ago today if we count revolutions of the sun, but so much longer by any other scale. We were so young. Little Napoleon still needed seven years before he was ready to be born, and another thirty to conquer France. That year Robespierre and his Terror cried in a Calais crib. Frederick the Great was just Frederick then. America was a far-off place where cotton grew, not a nation that would embarrass George III with revolution. Bach and Vivaldi were still our heroes. No one had ever heard of Beethoven; he was not yet alive. Little Mozart was six and, in fact, was that night just ten miles from where this history unfolded, speeding toward the imperial city to play his tiny violin for the empress. Today, Amadeus is already fifteen years dead, though he will outlive us all.

The year 1762 was still one full of dreamers. And one of the most faithful dreamers had a sack over his head that October evening. He was being shoved foot first into a coal chute, which, though it may have been the widest coal chute in the empire, was not quite wide enough for this dreamer, large as a bear. His two friends pushed with a violence that made several well-dressed passersby pause in consternation. Then there was a tearing of cloth, a thick pop, and our dreamer slid into the chute.

I left my friends in Tasso's cave and raced back into the theater. My master had sent me for his wine and would scold me if I tarried any longer. The small foyer was so full that the rumbling voices shook the floor. The entrance was split. To one side the common people jostled. They waved their tickets like flags, for these tickets—which would allow them to peer down from the galleries or to sit upon the hard benches at the rear—let them breathe the same air as the empress, be

seen with her, and be seen with those who were seen with her. These
men, accompanied by their wives, were simple lawyers, secretaries,
physicians, craftsmen. They waited impatiently, while on the other
side, a stream of nobles, their faces known to all, strolled through the
entrance.

I, too, knew them well by now. There was His Excellency Duke
Herberstin and his eight daughters, all dumb, plain, and highly
sought as wives. Behind them, the Spanish ambassador, Duke Agil-
iar, was clearly in a sour mood, for he had agreed to share his loge
with the tedious Prince Galizin of Russia. General Braun was in
Prussia dying of gangrene, but his wife was here, with a smile on her
face. Old Duke Grundacker Staremberg waited perplexed for a son
or grandson to lead him to his loge; he could not find it anymore
alone. Though Duchess Hazfelda arrived in one of the finest carriages, she could not afford the four hundred gulden for her loge this
season, and so she entered behind Princess Lobkovitz, who had taken
pity and let the dumpy duchess sit behind her tallest son. Among the
parade of peach muslin and powdered wigs were also those, like Herr
Buthon with his stunning child bride, who had no title; Buthon had
never bothered to purchase one.

I darted through the foyer with Guadagni's wine held before me,
my other hand fending off princesses. There was lace, frills, the glit-
ter of many medals. I was nauseated with their swaying. I closed my
eyes for just an instant. I felt wine splash on my wrist.

The crowds lingered in the passages outside their loges, chattering, rubbing up against one another in the narrow space. I squeezed
along the wall, trying not to brush the wide gowns with my clumsy
knees. More wine swished past the rim—oh my, a bloody stain on a
dowager's behind! At last, I cleared the last loge and reached the stage
door.

Here, there was even more excitement. At the end of the former
ball court there was little space for all the secret machinations that go
on behind a stage. Musicians streamed past with instruments held to
their shoulders, like soldiers bearing guns. Tasso's stagehands filled
the lamps with oil, greased the wing frame grooves. They swept the

stage one final time; should Guadagni stumble and trip, he would surely feed them to the bears at the empress's menagerie. Furies smeared black greasepaint on their faces. Tasso poked his head up through a trap and shouted, "If any of you touch Quaglio's scenes, I will bite off your filthy fingers!"

Signora Clavarau trilled arpeggios in her cramped dressing room, while in Signora Bianchi's room, I saw through the cracked door that Eurydice was being smeared with white paint so she would look properly dead in the opera's first scene. I had spilled half the wine by then, and protected the remains as I would my very blood.

Guadagni had the only room larger than a closet. I knocked, and though he did not answer, I entered. Anyone else who dared step inside would have been cursed, but he wanted me here—the way he looked up expectantly told me this. He sat with his back to me and considered me in his mirror. I was shocked by the reflection—his eyelids gently curled, his wrinkles smoothed by cream—because he looked ten years younger. For a moment, I thought I was looking at myself in the mirror.

But then he spoke. It was not my voice. "Was the empire out of wine?"

I shook my head and handed him the glass. He took a sip and set it aside. He looked in the mirror. Gluck had carried through with his plans; there were no peacock feathers, no gold lace, no wig. Orpheus wore a simple white tunic, opened at his rounded chest.

I stood behind him. He stared at himself as he inhaled through flared nostrils and then closed his eyes and formed his mouth into a tight circle, exhaling as if softly blowing out a candle. He had to let the sadness grow, he had told me, if he was to make us know it with his song.

My toes twitched inside my shoes.

"Signor," I finally asked, unable to stand it anymore. "Do you need me?"

"Do you have somewhere else to go?"

"No," I said. "I do not wish to disturb you, that is all. Shall I wait outside?"

He paused, but I knew he would never admit to needing me beside him. "Very well," he said.

I stepped outside and nearly collided with four bearers holding Eurydice's funeral bier. I ducked and grabbed a skinny boy—he seemed to be rushing about with no job to do—and ordered him to stand outside Guadagni's door and holler into Tasso's cave if the singer called for me.

"And why should I?" the boy said. Though I towered over him, he glared up at me as if I were beneath him.

I fished in my pockets. Empty. I promised him twenty pfennig. He nodded and took his station, and I dived into an open trap.

Below the stage, in Tasso's cave, Nicolai was reclining on the remains of Tasso's cot. I smiled, for though he had crushed it into a dozen pieces, he seemed at ease. Remus sat beside him on the floor, leaning up against the cold iron stove. Tasso skittered all about this dark room, checking lines, greasing blocks. Then he leapt and hoisted his head up through a trap to yell at the dull stagehands to light the lamps, and then he hung there, a body without a head, jerking in horror as they nearly set the curtain afire. Nicolai did not seem to notice that the little man was busy; he wanted to know about every line, every trap.

"And what about the capstan at the front?" he asked. "Does that raise the empress's gown, so all can see her skirts?"

"That is the footlight elevator!" Tasso growled, disdainful of Nicolai's ignorance.

"And that rope?" Nicolai said, squinting in the light of the dim lamp.

"Works the central trap!"

"Amazing," Nicolai said to Remus, "how much he knows."

Remus looked at Nicolai with distrust. "Do not touch a thing!" he whispered, so Tasso did not hear.

Nicolai held up his hands. Tasso had not, in the end, insisted that they be bound. "I am as innocent as the empress."

I was so happy to see Nicolai beaming. I hugged him as I crawled past.

"Where are you going?" he asked.

"To see," I said over my shoulder. "To see!"

A few days earlier, I had discovered a tiny peephole that Tasso used to peer out at Gluck. I crawled to it now and peered out. I had never seen so magnificent a gathering. In the Ox Pen, a crowd of the finest men in the world conversed loudly. Those in the loges must have heard every word, which was, of course, the intention. Above them, the candle-laden chandelier tinkled with the resonance of so many voices.

To my left was the royal loge, just beyond the orchestra. It was distinguished tonight by a crimson awning, as if a drizzle were expected in the theater. In the center, buxom and rosy, sat that great woman, mother of sixteen children and an empire. Her cheeks shone as if someone had slapped them. Beside her, the emperor—his nose bulbous, his mouth thin and narrow—was a pale, drab figure. They were surrounded by a halo of their children.

But I was not at this peephole to see the empress.

Hundreds of eyes peered down from the double gallery of *Le Paradis*, as though they were considering a leap. Perhaps they would have risked the injury, but landing on a duchess would mean eternal banishment from the theater.

My ears searched all the theater's sounds. *She must be here, she must.*

The orchestra began to tune in discordant chaos. The loges were filling up. Most sat six: three along the railing, three behind. (What coordination was needed to see the stage from that second row!) Surplus sons and daughters stood behind their older siblings. There was a lamp burning in every box, so every loge appeared itself a stage.

And then, opposite the empress on the second tier, they entered. They were so close I made out the sharp tendons of Countess Riecher's neck as she led Count Riecher in. Then Amalia entered before Anton—and my heart soared! *She is here!* Four other Riecher offspring followed, but I had eyes only for Amalia, round and glowing, the most beautiful specimen Countess Riecher ever had to display, no matter how many children she had borne herself. Amalia was given the honored third seat in the front row of the family's loge. Anton sat behind her. He placed a hand on her shoulder and smiled as if to say, *See? See how right I was?*

I was certain she would soon be mine again. When Orpheus looked into Eurydice's eyes, Amor would be as kind to us as she was to those fabled lovers on the stage.

Then the urchin I'd asked to stand watch outside my master's door yelled into the cave, "Guadagni calls his boy!" The little wretch stood above the trap, his hand outstretched for his reward. I smiled and told him I would pay him on the morrow. He grinned and tripped me as I passed.

I stumbled to Guadagni's door just as he opened it. He wore his coat across his shoulders, his face serene. "I am ready," he said.

I nodded, but was unsure what to do. I turned to the crowd of stagehands standing in dumb admiration of the singer. "He is ready," I said.

For the first time in my life, the world reacted to my words with instant obedience. The fervor subsided. Like giant bats, Furies flew off to hide in the recesses of the wings. Stagehands took their stations and were still. The chorus rushed onto the stage. Eurydice climbed onto her bier and was dead. Behind the curtain, all was silent as Gaetano Guadagni strode onto the stage.

I followed him. My footsteps felt so heavy I was sure the empress herself could hear them. The clamor of the audience behind the curtain was like a foreign army waiting at a gate—please wait for me to flee! Guadagni stood in the middle of the stage. He placed his fists across his chest. Sorrow was painted on his face.

He nodded to me.

What was I to do? I looked to my left, my right. Every stagehand and chorus singer stared at me, but their blank stares were no help. *Do it*, the stares said. *Everyone is waiting for you to do your job.*

Do what? Leave? Peek through the curtain and tell Gluck all was ready? No one had told me anything! I had never before attended an opera!

Then I realized—his coat. It was Guadagni's coat, not Orpheus's. I took it as if I were removing a blanket from a sleeping baby.

I rushed off the stage as applause began. Gluck tapped twice for attention and began the overture. Still, Guadagni did not move. His head was bowed. The footlights at the lip of the stage were just partly raised, so his face was dimly lit. Behind him, the choir of mourners were as still as a painting of a funeral.

The overture ended. The curtain parted.

Gluck's music became a sad march. Beside me, the bearers lifted Eurydice's bier and slowly advanced onstage. Guadagni stayed bowed until the chorus began their song. Then his head rose until his eyes focused on his love, dead before him.

He sang her name.

I had woken Spittelberg with that call. As his voice filled the theater, Guadagni woke fourteen hundred hearts. For an instant his echo rang from every corner. He sang again, his voice more sorrowful, and the wooden loges and crystal chandeliers resonated with her name, silencing the shuffling feet and nervous hands.

I had seen it so many times in rehearsal, but now it was a magic rite—this crowd assembled, their scents of rose and jasmine; this dead woman on her bier; the stifling heat of the lamps and fourteen hundred bodies; Guadagni's voice even more brilliant than I had ever heard it—all this summoned the immortal lovers back to life. Tears shone on mine and many other faces as Orpheus sang his lament, as Jove heard his call and sent Amor to him. Soon Guadagni and Clavarau's voices mingled in the cavern of the theater. My heart swelled. He would gain her back! He would save Eurydice from death.

When the curtain closed, I rushed to Guadagni with the coat, but he shook his head. The theater erupted in applause. Four times Guadagni stepped through the curtain to take his bows. Still they applauded, but he strode to his dressing room.

Tasso's head peeked through a trap, and when the singer's door closed, the stagehand sprang to action. I heard the spinning of blocks, the creaking of the axle's turning, the tensing of lines—and as if by magic, the wing frames slid on their tracks. The backdrop fell.

Red-tinted glass moved before the lamps, turning the stage a flickering red. It was the cave beyond the River Styx, where Orpheus would tame the Furies.

Gluck began act two.

The black-faced Furies danced. Their ankles cracked as they jerked and writhed. The sounds of a harp made them freeze, for hope and love were forbidden in their cave. They cursed the man who dared bring beauty to the underworld. They sang more loudly to overpower Orpheus's harp. Guadagni's door opened as the harp sounded a second time. He shrugged off his coat, not even glancing at me, and marched onstage. I tried to catch the coat, but it fell to the floor.

The Furies danced about Orpheus, trying to frighten him away.

He stood calmly, though—a still tree in a gale of whipping branches. His love knew no fear, and his lone voice was stronger than the chorus. It thickened the air in the theater when it rang, and the audience knew these demons had no chance against his powers. Their voices grew meek. Their dance grew calm. They let him pass, and watched in awe as he disappeared in the shadows.

Guadagni left the stage, and I was there to receive him.

The curtains closed only for a moment. Tasso spun his winch and set loose the backdrop. The dark red wing frames vanished, and blue, blue sky took their place. The red-tinted glass fell away. When the curtain parted again, Tasso had brought heaven to the empire.

Angiolini's ballet warmed the audience's eyes. Guadagni stood beside me in the wing, his head bowed as if he were asleep. His broad shoulders rose and fell. The ballet ended, and the chorus gathered to watch the hero enter.

When the oboe's first notes filled the theater like a ray of sunshine, Gaetano Guadagni glided back onto the stage. Orpheus stopped at the exact spot on the stage where he had begun this opera in his misery. Now, with each breath, he inflated. The audience knew something was gathering inside him. They sat forward, eager to share this joy.

The aria poured from his precious throat, and my body tingled with its warmth. I grew, both up and out, as expectation filled me, but I was careful not to make a sound as I climbed down into Tasso's cave. The three men were lying beside each other on the floor, gazing at the ceiling as if through the dark wood they might see the golden swirls of Guadagni's voice spreading across the stage. Truly, my master's voice—too weak for explosive passion—was made for the serenity of this aria.

I crawled beneath the web of ropes to the peephole. Gluck's face shone with sweat as he beamed at his creation. Behind him, in the Ox Pen, they stared up at Orpheus without blinking, faces slack. The royal family sat so still I could have been looking at a portrait. There was no breath of movement from *Le Paradis*, just the glint of wet eyes.

Amalia! She gripped the railing in front of her and sat upright, tense. The music hurt her, and she bit her lip, for surely a thousand faces would turn if Countess Riecher's daughter-in-law lost her composure. She wiped a tear with a white-gloved hand, then pressed a knuckle against her trembling chin.

Anton placed a hand on his wife's shoulder. She stiffened. She took several breaths. She took his fingers in hers—but just long enough to lift his hand off her shoulder and release it. Anton withdrew his arm and returned his attention to the stage.

Countess Riecher cast a disapproving look, but Amalia did not seem to see it. She looked blankly at the loges across the theater, breathing shallowly and steadily until Guadagni had finished his song.

Soon you will love music again, I whispered, and I crawled away from the peephole.

Guadagni took his bows and walked to his dressing room. It was time to deliver the note, but the singer had left the door ajar behind him. With great reluctance I followed him.

"Signora Clavarau sings like a cow," he said. There was no truth in this statement; she had sung beautifully. But I nodded. He took a sip of wine.

Gluck barged in. The composer smiled at me and looked as though he would embrace me, then realized I was not the one he sought. He pushed past me to Guadagni.

"What a success!" Gluck shouted.

Guadagni nodded.

"Wait until they hear the third act! Orpheus shall live again!" Gluck eyed Guadagni's glass. "May I?" he asked, and before waiting for an answer, he gulped down the rest of Guadagni's wine. I prayed I would not be sent for more. "I am off to the count's box," the composer said.

"Send her majesty my respects," Guadagni replied.

Gluck disappeared to speak with Count Durazzo, whose loge was adjacent to the empress's. I slid toward the door. "I will be outside," I said. "If you need me."

"No," he said. "Stay. Shut the door."

I did, wishing I were on the other side, and then returned to stand behind my master. He studied me in the mirror.

Suddenly he reached up a hand and held it over his shoulder. I realized he meant me to place my hand in his. He pressed my hand to his shoulder.

"It is good we found each other," he said. "This world is not a friendly place, least of all for us."

Us? I thought. *But we are not the same.*

"*Mio fratello,*" he continued. "I am sorry if I wounded you the other night. It was rash. In your ignorance, you thought that you could help. I am sure you will never make the mistake again. I see that now, and so I regret my words. You see, I have had many students in the past. In the end, they left me, or I sent them away. I never found a single one I could trust completely. Until I found you. You are different."

My hand was sweating. *Let me leave!*

"Sooner or later, they all became wolves. They wanted what I had. You are different. You want nothing except to hear me sing. Is that right? Is there anything else you desire? Simply tell me and I will give it to you."

"Nothing," I said. *After tonight I will never see you again.*

He smiled and squeezed my hand tightly. "I thought so. Know that you can trust me, too. I will never abandon you. When I leave Vienna, you will accompany me. We shall stay teacher and student forever."

I mumbled my thanks, and he smiled graciously. "Now leave me," he said. "I must return to Orpheus. Before this final act is through, Vienna will know that Orpheus lives again."

I backed away quietly, like a nurse from a sleeping child she fears to wake, but when I had shut his door, I darted to the nearest trap. "The note!" I cried into the darkness. "The note!"

Nicolai had insisted on holding it, saying he wished his heart to be warmed once more by such ardent love as ours. When I called into the substage, Remus retrieved the piece of paper and passed it up. It was less royal-looking now, creased along one corner, and Nicolai's sweaty grip seemed to have smudged the waxen seal, which Remus had applied hours earlier. But that was no matter. I flew into the corridor and did not give my doubts a second thought.

It seemed half of Vienna was milling about in the passages. At least four dukes and a prince cursed me for elbowing them in their ample guts even before I made it to the stairs. I heard the slurping of wine as if tongues were lolling in my ear. Finally, I made it to the Riecher loge. The door stood open, several men fighting to poke their heads inside, trying to gain an audience with one of Vienna's greatest families.

"Pardon me," I said, pushing one man aside whose head was down near my elbow. The next man resisted, even when I trod on his foot. I tugged his coattail. When he turned to confront me, I slipped by.

"A message for Amalia"—I choked back her former name— "Riecher."

There was an awkward silence, and I realized I had yelled this rather loudly. I blushed. Heads turned not only in the loge, but across the theater. The cold moon of Countess Riecher's face was upon me. Amalia turned as well, and my heart raced. She stared at me—for this voice had reminded her of one she knew.

"From Gaetano Guadagni," I said, as quietly as I could. Amalia's eyes rested a moment more on me, but then her imploring stare grew dark; her ears had fooled her. She turned away as a hand wiped away a tear.

Countess Riecher frowned, even as everyone else within hearing grinned.

"Give it to me," the matriarch said. She reached out three white fingers, tensed like a bird's claws.

"I am to lay it only in the lady's hand," I recited, just as Remus had instructed.

Someone muttered about the castrate's gall.

"Let her have it," said the dignified Count Riecher, without looking at me. "It is harmless admiration. After all, the man is a soldier without his sword."

This brought general laughter to the loge. Even Countess Riecher smiled cautiously. They all looked at Amalia, whose hands remained in her lap. Her back was still toward me, her head only half-turned.

"My dear," Anton whispered in her ear, "you cannot refuse it. Do take it as an honor. He has admired you from the stage."

She shook her head. "I do not want it," she said.

Before I could object, Anton grabbed the note. He fumbled with the seal, broke it, and started to unfold the paper.

"No," I said uselessly from the door. A brief vision: I leap upon him and tear—

But Amalia turned and snatched the note. "It is not for you to read," she said. This brought another snigger from Count Riecher, followed carefully by those around him.

Amalia opened the letter and began to read silently. I had read it a dozen times that day and knew every word:

Dear Amalia,

It is of greatest importance that you show no surprise at what you are about to read. I am alive—your Moses. I love you still, and have come to take you away, if you will still have me. When Orpheus looks into Eurydice's eyes, make some excuse and slip out. I will be waiting outside the theater.

Tell them you find this letter most appalling. Return it.

Moses

I watched her eyes examine the paper. Her performance was most extraordinary. That canvas that had always poorly hid the turbulent emotions below showed only confusion, then a flash of repulsion. Then annoyance. She looked angrily at me.

"What is the meaning of this?" she demanded. I was not as accomplished an actor as she, but I managed a shrug.

Then, to my horror, she turned the letter around and showed it to everyone in the loge.

The paper was blank. Anton took the letter from her hands and examined both sides. There was nothing hidden on its creamy surface.

"Explain this," Count Riecher ordered.

"Look at his face," Anton said. "White as a sheet. Guadagni's eunuch is as shocked as we."

I glimpsed angry embarrassment on Amalia's face before she turned away. Her husband petted her shoulder.

"Get out," Countess Riecher ordered. And I was conveyed away by eager hands, as lifeless as a paper doll.

XIV.

I sank into the substage just as Gluck took his place for act three. Remus awaited my report, but when he saw my ashen face, he knew something had gone wrong.

"It was blank," I said. "The words had washed away."

"What?" Remus cried, slamming his forehead with his fist. I told him exactly what had happened, the miracle of the empty paper.

"But that is impossible," Remus whispered, as the orchestra began.

"You must have used magic ink," Nicolai berated.

"I used the same ink I always use," said Remus. "How could this have happened?"

"Lie down," Nicolai told me. He took my hand. "We will think of another plan. We still have time. If nothing else, at the close of the opera, we will send Remus to deliver another message."

Remus's eyes grew wide in horror.

"Lie still," Nicolai said to us. "The music will tell us what to do."

In act three, the lovers were alone in the Stygian Caves. Her hand was in his; his eyes were averted from the danger of her face. There were no Furies, no chorus, no dancers. Vines grappled for the lovers. Rocks were strewn about the ground. The dim and flickering footlights threw grotesque shadows on the backdrop. The audience listened and prayed that Orpheus would find strength to escape his destiny.

I, too, prayed for my destiny. Could it really be only loss and failure? She had slipped away again, and if I could not find some way to show myself, tomorrow she would leave. Would I follow her? Of course I would. I would follow her even if it meant chasing her forever, like a pilgrim chasing the horizon.

The lovers stood upon the stage above us. Cracks between the floorboards shone golden gashes, and Orpheus sang that Eurydice must hurry. She asked him why he would not embrace her. What had become of her bewitching beauty? What had happened to his love?

But Orpheus could not answer, even though the audience knew he would have penetrated a thousand hells to save her.

Tasso sat on his stool like a statue, contemplating the lamp's tiny flame. The rigging was like a spider's web about his head. Only when Orpheus and Eurydice passed above him did he look up, like a man hearing a mouse in his ceiling.

I closed my eyes. The violins' bodies rang with Eurydice's voice, which was clear and strong, even though she lacked the will to lift her feet. In the audience, many bodies were tuned to Guadagni's voice, and so, though he sang his part alone, the impression was of many people humming with him. If Gluck had ears to hear this, he would have hung his audience like bells from the ceiling, so the beauty of his music would have overwhelmed their every fiber.

On the stage, Eurydice was begging Orpheus to look at her, if only for a moment. Her singing was high and piercing; I felt it in the soft skin behind my ears, like the tickle of a feather. To Orpheus, these cries were sharp daggers in his back. His will was breaking. I had seen this rehearsed many times, so I knew Eurydice stood just behind him. He faced the audience, eyes closed.

As the two lovers sang—her pleas to him, his cries to the gods—Guadagni's voice began to lose its perfection. He could not push more hurt into these notes. He tried to sing louder, but he could not, and so I heard that his voice had begun to lose its fluid ebb and swell. Now it was all just forceful swell. I heard a thump near the front of the stage. Eurydice had dropped to her knees. She could not take another step. If he does not love her, he should leave her in this awful cave.

He could not stand to refuse her. How could the gods have demanded anything so cruel? He would look into her eyes.

I turned to Nicolai, expecting to see him crying at the music, but to my surprise, there was no grief on his face. He had propped himself on one elbow and was staring intently through the substage. I thought I saw a smile flash across his face. His eyes were clouded, but he was absorbed by the music, as if he were struggling to understand every word the lovers sang.

Orpheus called to his beloved wife so he might embrace her, and just as his will was finally broken—

Nicolai sat up. He groaned with the effort, and Remus turned, concerned. But Nicolai was not in pain. He reached into his coat and withdrew a folded paper. It was nearly identical to the note he had given me before. He handed it to me. "Moses," he said. "I am sorry. I have deceived you."

This note was tidily creased, its blue seal perfectly round—just as Remus had made it. I broke it open. Here was the letter I had been meant to deliver. I looked up into Nicolai's foggy eyes. Why had my friend betrayed me? There was an odd smile on his face.

"Moses," he whispered. "Don't you see? Love like yours is not meant for paper. Not with the beauty of your voice."

I trembled. I had no idea what he meant. He smiled. Above us the floorboards creaked as Eurydice stood to embrace her lover. Orpheus began to turn his head. The two lovers stepped toward each other.

Nicolai began to crawl through the cave.

"Nicolai!" Remus whispered. But Nicolai did not seem to hear him.

Orpheus and Eurydice embraced. She saw in his eyes that he loved her. They were blissful for a single moment, then she died in his arms.

The theater was silent. Orpheus had killed his Eurydice. No one breathed. No one moved. There was nothing more to hope for.

But here in the substage, in the soft glow of the lamp, Nicolai was crawling through Tasso's cave, grunting with each movement. Remus followed him, tried to grasp his foot, tried to stop Hope before it ruined this evening, before it angered the empress, before it got them cast out of this city just as Fury had gotten them cast out of St. Gall. Tasso, too, realized that something was amiss. His paws shook before his chest. He scuttered to the giant's side and hissed, "Be still!"

I could not move. I was bewildered. What destiny had Nicolai dreamed for me?

Orpheus laid his dead wife on the stage and stood above her. The orchestra did not play. They waited for the master to sing.

Nicolai peered upward at the stage—looking, listening. A creaking. Guadagni was stepping backward, away from this corpse of his dead bride. Nicolai crawled with him, his face inches below Guadagni's steps. Nicolai sniffed. Remus held Nicolai's foot with both hands and Tasso pushed on Nicolai's shoulders. But Nicolai, his face raised to the creaking steps above, was stronger than them both.

Guadagni stopped his retreat, pausing at the center of the stage to begin the greatest aria of this opera—

And Nicolai pounced. He dragged Remus and Tasso with him as if they were mere scarves tied about his neck. His hand stretched for a line. His fingers grasped the rope. He pulled.

The trap below Orpheus's feet opened.

Gaetano Guadagni fell heavily into the substage, and Nicolai was on top of him before the singer could scream. He pinned Guadagni to the floor, held a huge hand over his mouth. Then Nicolai turned to me. He jerked his head up—toward that square hole in the sky above him, through which the dusty theater light was pouring.

He squinted, for the light hurt his ruined eyes, and he said, "Please, Moses. Please. Deliver your message."

XV.

I could not move.

There? I thought. *Up there?*

Then Remus looked at his giant friend—his companion of thirty years—and shook his head. He shrugged. This had gone too far already. No time to change the course.

He was a ravenous wolf. He darted toward me and tore off my coat and collar. He ripped my shirt down the front so it resembled Orpheus's tunic. I had no time to think as he hauled me toward the trap.

"Turn down the lights," Remus hissed at Tasso. Tasso, who had not moved since the great castrato fell, leapt to the capstan at the order, like a sailor in a tempest heeding his captain's command.

I crouched below the trap. Remus held his hands intertwined at his waist. Nicolai smiled, his eyes full of tears, his palm still smothering Guadagni's terrified face. Remus nodded. "Hurry, Moses," he whispered.

It seemed like a small step to place my foot in Remus's hands, and so I did. I grabbed the edges of the stage floor. I thought, *I can still turn back.* But Remus—what strength you had!

He growled, and I was lifted up. The theater fell around me. I took a step.

I was onstage.

At my feet, the corpse of someone else's lover. In front of me, fourteen hundred pairs of eyes. I swayed gently from side to side. The theater was silent.

Had they noticed? Seen their hero fall? Realized that he had returned taller, younger, more in love? Tasso had lowered the floorlights, and so I was lit only from the side. When I looked into that sea of eyes, there was no suspicion or anger. Instead, they stared with the enchanted eyes of children. The eyes said, *Orpheus! Sing for us! Sing!*

I glanced at the empress. She gazed as if she knew me well. Gluck

squinted, unsure of what he saw, yet his raised hands were poised—
ready to lead the orchestra the moment Orpheus began to sing.

Then I found Amalia. We looked into each other's eyes, but she
did not know me. She did not seem to breathe. She was a statue.

I formed my lips into a tight circle and exhaled. To my ears, the
sound was a gale in the silent theater. I blew until my shoulders
crumpled above my lungs. Then my giant ribs rebounded. I opened
wide my mouth and the air streamed down my throat. I grew taller
and wider. Air rushed into my lungs, tearing at the muscles between
my ribs.

I sang.

Ahimè! Dove trascorsi! Ove mi spinse un delirio d'amor!

"Alas! What have I done? Where has love's madness led me?"

It seemed like barely a whisper, but my voice washed over the theater. Gluck sucked his breath and jerked apart his raised hands. On
his face, shock replaced suspicion. The empress's tight lips parted.
Everyone in the theater shifted minutely in wonder. Some sat straighter.
Others sagged, as if a support had been removed. Hands clenched
the railings. Heels scraped the floor. In *Le Paradis*, four hundred necks
stretched closer to the ceiling.

Amalia's hands left the railing and held her cheeks. Inside her, a
sudden storm. She was the only one in that audience who had heard
this voice before. With those first notes, she told herself it was some
cruel trick, her foolish, hopeful imagination—but still, all those walls
burst. She blinked away the tears, and when she looked at me again
with clear eyes, and I returned her gaze, she saw that this musico before her on the stage was her Moses—and she understood it all.

Gluck had hesitated for an instant, his hands still raised. He
stared at me. His eyes wide, for a ghost stood before him. Gluck heard
the music he had written, sung as in his dreams.

In a moment Gluck is again the great maestro. His hands cut the air.
The orchestra obeys, and the violins' bows strike their strings. I feel
their sound in my chest. When I sing now my voice is huge. It bounces

off the walls and returns from every corner. Gluck sways backward as if a wind is blowing. His eyes are closed.

Then there is a pause—silence. Gluck's raised hands seem to control not only his orchestra but every person in the theater. His thumbs, pressed against his forefingers, clasp every breath. When he splays apart his fingers, fourteen hundred shoulders drop. And then, as he rises on his toes and lifts his hands as high as he can reach, fourteen hundred pairs of lungs expand. Gluck's arms cut the air.

I feel naked on the stage, but I want Amalia to see every curve of my face. The empress's lips are still parted, as though she is thirsty. I begin Orpheus's great lament as Guadagni would have; each note cut with the sharpest knife.

Many eyes close. Bodies gently twist. They thirst for Orpheus's pure sadness. It seems the empress cannot breathe. Her mouth is wide open. Tears collect in her eyes. When my music swells, many pull back their heads as they squirm to feel my song through their bodies. Gluck's eyes are closed. His arms swoop like wings. But he has not lost control. His movements are precise. His musicians respond to his every move so intently it is as if he is a sorcerer who has bewitched them. I, too, let myself be guided by the meter of his movements. He is the master of this music.

I sing.

Amalia's hands grip the railing. She leans forward and presses her round belly to the wood, which rings with my voice.

And then it is over. There is a hum in the room; my voice is still a whisper in every chest. The orchestra ceases to play. Gluck opens his eyes and beams once more at the ghost he has summoned back to life.

I step back and fall.

XVI.

In the cave, Nicolai was holding a shocked Guadagni like a baby in his arms. He placed him on the elevator and whispered in broken Italian that it was time to sing again, no one had noticed anything amiss, so Guadagni could rest easy; he was still the night's hero. Then he gave the man two hard slaps.

"*Tutto bene!*" Nicolai said. Tasso yanked a rope, and the elevator rose. Gaetano Guadagni ascended back onto the stage.

I slid out the chute and ran around to the theater's entrance. This time, I would not miss her. I seized the heavy door and in my mind a lovely vision of Amalia was waiting there in the foyer, her arms spread to embrace me—

But the door swung open and slammed into my face.

It knocked me down the short stairs. I lay on the street, staring up at the night.

She would have thrown herself at me, but her state forbade it, so she clambered down until she could kneel beside me. Then she kissed me and looked, finally, deeply, into my eyes.

She helped me up. For a minute we clung to each other.

"You're alive!" she said.

"I am!" I said.

"You're alive!" she said again, and we would have carried on just like that, her hands stroking each inch of me that they could reach, my arms holding her warm body to mine, locking us together.

"You're alive!" she said one final time, tears staining my shirt with transparent streaks.

"I'm sorry—" I began, but she shook her head and pressed a finger to my lips.

"Moses," she said. "There is no time. We've got to hurry. They . . . she'll . . ." She took my hand and pulled me into the square, her eyes hunting for a coach to hide in. I let myself be dragged as I took one last look over my shoulder at that theater.

I heard a sound from within, like the rushing of a river.

They were clapping. The empress and emperor, the dukes, the princes, and all those people in the galleries, they were cheering my voice. With his bows, Gaetano Guadagni was collecting my applause. A smile crept onto my face as I stumbled blindly after Amalia. One booming voice yelled, *Evviva il coltello! Il benedetto coltello!* and the noise swelled, cheers now adding to the thunder.

Amalia heard it, too. We stopped.

Standing alone with her in that empty square, I took the first bow of my career as she laughed and clapped for me. Inside the theater, the applause did not end, and so I bowed again and again, up and down, like a toy on a string. Then she took my hand again. *Come!* and we rushed away.

We climbed into a carriage and sped to the Riecher Palace. As Orpheus and Eurydice vanished into the Temple of Love on the stage, and Anton left his loge to seek his wife (who had whispered to him that she felt ill and would take a few steps in the passage), Amalia told me, "Hide your face." We passed by the ogre into the Riecher courtyard.

"But why here?" I begged her. "Please, anywhere but here."

"You'll see," she said.

She left the carriage and strode into the house as if nothing were out of order. A porter opened the door for her and looked out. I drew back the curtain to hide myself. But too late? Had he glimpsed my face?

I heard a noise, and peeked out the other window to see the ogre himself considering our carriage. *My God*, I thought. *If he sees my face, all is lost. She'll hunt us down.*

"Is there anyone inside?" the ogre asked the driver.

"Yes," the driver murmured. "A gentleman."

"A gentleman? Are you sure?"

"Am I sure? Don't I know who's in my carriage?"

"Who is he?"

"Didn't see. Too dark."

The ogre approached the door. He considered it. He breathed five times, each exhalation like that of a bull about to charge. Then he knocked twice, each blow falling like a hammer.

"Who is there?" he demanded.

I fastened the door, as silently as I could.

"Open this door!" The door bowed as he pulled on it.

"Mind yourself! That's my door!" the driver said.

"I'll smash your window if he doesn't open it this minute."

I cowered in the corner. The door bowed again, the hinges groaned.

"What are you doing?" Amalia shouted from afar.

"Madame," the ogre said sternly, "I wish to know who is inside this carriage. Where is Herr Anton Riecher?"

I heard her steps slowly crossing the courtyard. When I peeked out between the curtains, she was standing so close to him her rounded belly brushed his thighs. She wore a heavy cloak now across her shoulders.

"You disrespectful brute," she said. She poked him in his chest, and he retreated two steps. "In this carriage sits a kind old man disfigured in the war—of course he will not show his face to a boor like you. And where is Anton? I'll tell you that. He's waiting for us at the Count Nadasty's—every minute angrier that you are keeping me."

I slipped open the clasp just as she reached to open the door. We sat as still as corpses until our driver had escaped the gate. Then we both exhaled.

"I hope she burns every dress she bought me," Amalia said. "And says curses on my name."

She passed a small, intricate chest into my lap; it could have contained a little Bible. I opened it.

Ten stacks, each with twenty ten-gulden golden coins, two thousand gulden in all. I gaped. I had never even held a single gulden in my hand.

"On my last day in Saint Gall," she said, "Father came into my room. I'd thought him so happy about my marriage, but he paced nervously back and forth. When I asked him what was wrong, he put this in my hands. 'In case,' he said, 'someday you wish to come home.' And then added, for the sake of propriety, 'To visit, that is, I mean.' Two thousand gulden for a visit!"

I closed the box.

"It is enough," she said, "for wherever we wish to run. But run we must. When she returns and hears that I have been there, they will not believe me lost or kidnapped. They will not seek a wife and daughter. They will hunt a traitor."

For two hours we rode around Vienna, considering our options for escape. We changed carriages twice, to be sure we could not be tracked.

"The roads leading away from Vienna will not be safe," she said. "Count Riecher has agents in every direction. It is better that we hide here for a time and prepare some means of disguise."

I agreed. A pregnant lady—and one as striking as my Amalia—would be hard to disguise in the inns of surrounding towns, and she could not sleep in a coach. If we tried to flee the city, in but a single day I would be in that ogre's hands.

I told her I knew where we could hide.

"It is quite small," I said as our carriage navigated the mounds of refuse on the Burggasse in Spittelberg. "And the air can be rather close. It is noisy. But the walls are solid. The furniture is soft, though worn."

"Oh, Moses," she said, "I told you, I do not care."

"It will not be what you are used to," I said, thinking of the riches of the Riecher Palace and Haus Duft.

"What I am used to is a witch who watches over me day and night.

What I am used to is a husband with no will of his own. The only reason I am pregnant is because she ordered it."

The carriage bounced as it ran over a loose cobble, or perhaps a dog. When the coachman said he would go no farther, I offered to pay him double. He brought us to the coffeehouse door.

"Here it is," I said, humiliated by how small the building now seemed. It could have been a set piece on Tasso's stage. Amalia drew her cloak's hood low across her brow. I held the chest of coins in one hand while I helped her out of the carriage. She was strong, but her back was sore from the hours sitting on the hard seats of the loge and carriage, and her limp was much more pronounced as we walked across the pitted street to the door.

It was past midnight now—an illicit time of day in this quarter—and so the passersby stared at the ground rather than look us in the eye. The coffeehouse was almost empty. Four men, ruddy with drink, sipped at their bitter, dark medicine, staring at Amalia as if she were a fantastic vision conjured by the potion. Scrupulous Herr Kost looked at his shoes, certain he was not meant to witness this fine lady entering his establishment.

We climbed the stairs to my friends' rooms. Remus leapt from his chair. Nicolai struggled to his feet. I beamed at them, and relief washed across their faces.

"Praise God," Remus said, like a worried mother. He clasped his hands before his chest when I appeared in the doorway, though as Amalia entered behind me and drew back her hood, his grin faded to a nervous nod of greeting.

But Nicolai's smile only grew when his weak eyes discerned a female shadow. "Welcome to the Temple of Love!" he shouted. Remus's face paled another shade, while mine reddened in humiliation. Only Amalia smiled. Then she looked closely at Remus.

"My God!" she said. "It's the wolfish monk!"

"Hello, Fräulein Duft." He bowed.

"Actually, they call me Frau Riecher now," she said. "But tonight I wish to be a Duft again."

"In this house you can have whatever name you wish," Nicolai said. He took her hand in his two giant ones, as if he meant to warm it.

"Friends," I said. "May we stay here for some time?"

Nicolai pressed Amalia's hand to his cheek. "As long as you wish!" he exclaimed.

"Thank you," she said. She smiled. She looked around the shabby room. To my relief, no disgust appeared on her face.

"You may have Remus's room," Nicolai said gallantly. "He can curl up out here with his books."

"I don't want to be any trouble," Amalia said.

"It is no trouble," said Remus.

"It won't be for long," I said.

"I pray it is!" said Nicolai.

"We are going to Venice!" I blurted.

"To Venice?" said Nicolai. His eyes were huge.

"Moses will sing in the opera," said Amalia.

"Yes!" shouted Nicolai. "In Teatro San Benedetto!"

"And you two as well," I said. "You must come with us!"

Nicolai clasped his round hands below his chin. Tears welled in his eyes. "Venice! My dream come true! Of course we will!"

For a moment Remus did not speak. His face was like a cloud over the sunshine of our future. "Remus," Nicolai said, "don't be such a bore."

"Nicolai cannot travel to Venice," Remus said to Amalia. "He is sick."

"I went to the theater tonight!" Nicolai's smile was stubborn. "You can place a sack over my head so I miss the sun."

"Nicolai, Venice is four hundred miles from here, across the Alps. You can't possibly ride a horse. In any case, we have no funds for such a journey."

"Yes, we do!" I said. I took the chest from beneath my arm and set loose the lid. The gold glittered in the candlelight.

"My God," whispered Remus.

"What is it?" asked Nicolai, trying to focus his eyes on the gold. "Is it on fire?"

"Moses and Amalia have a fortune," Remus told him. "More money than you've touched in your lifetime."

Nicolai gasped.

"We will buy a coach," I said. "We will build Nicolai a bed inside it."

"You see, we need you," Amalia explained. "Here in Austria, you must be our disguise. And in Italy, no one will believe that Moses is my husband."

"I will be your husband!" Nicolai said.

Now Amalia did blush.

"We were thinking," I said, "that Remus could be her father. Her husband, we will say, is away in the war."

"I could be an uncle, then."

"We thought you could be a patient," Amalia said. Then she looked at Remus. "My father's patient."

"A rich patient, then," Nicolai said.

"A rich patient," I confirmed.

Just then we heard footsteps on the stairs. Remus looked toward the door, blood draining from his face. Nicolai reached out a long arm and herded Amalia and me behind him, squaring himself against the threat coming up the stairs.

But I just smiled: my ears heard more than theirs. When the door finally opened, and Nicolai lumbered forward in attack, the invader barely reached his waist.

Tasso's face was red and coated with sweat from running through the city. He rubbed his paws together in relief when he saw me.

"Guadagni is looking for you!" Tasso said between breaths. "He jumped out of the shadows as I was sweeping up the stage. Grabbed me by the throat. Said Durazzo would banish me from the theater!"

"What will you do?" I asked.

The little man smiled and shook his head. "I kicked him in the shin and laughed at his threats," he boasted. "I heard Durazzo himself congratulate Guadagni. The superintendent said that what you sang was the greatest song ever sung in the empress's theater. They think it was he, so Guadagni can't say a word! But he asked me where you were hiding. I said you are his student; he should know."

"Thank you," I said.

"And I'll kick him again tomorrow," Tasso boasted.

Amalia took my arm and stepped out from behind Nicolai. Tasso jumped. "But that means we must both stay hidden until we can leave the city," she said to me.

"Tasso," I said. "This is Amalia."

The little man looked her up and down. When his eyes fell upon her rounded belly he let out a squeak with an intake of air. We had told him nothing of our plan, and he turned to each of us now with looks of rage such as I had never before seen on his little face. I feared for a moment that he would go himself to seek Guadagni and Countess Riecher.

He swung the door closed behind him; it clattered against the misshapen frame. He shook his head at each of his friends and then he stepped to Amalia's side and clasped her wrist. His head just reached her elbow. He raised her arm and, taking it in both hands above his head—like a waiter carrying a platter—he led her first toward the door, then bent around Nicolai, past a stack of books, between two upturned coffee cups, and around a dark stain on the carpet, until he had positioned her before Nicolai's armchair. Then he turned back to us. We had not moved. He scowled. "Get over here," he spat. "Right this minute." He pointed at the floor beside her. When I arrived, he helped me lower her slowly, gingerly, into the comfort of the chair. He removed her shoes and ordered, "Rub her feet."

Tasso nodded as I provided the outlines and Nicolai the color of all that had led to our current state and all that was to come. The little man's head lowered as we spoke, so when we finished, it was as if he were asleep. For a moment we were silent, perplexed.

It was Amalia who understood. "Tasso, will you come, too?"

He looked up at her. "I might," he said.

"But Tasso," I said, "you would not leave the theater!"

He shrugged. "There are other theaters."

"That there are!" said Nicolai, throwing out his arms. Remus cringed as Nicolai's fingers grazed his ear. "And we shall need someone to drive our carriage! Tasso, can you swing a whip?"

"Horses are violent, stupid beasts," he said. "But I know how to drive them."

So it was settled. We would stay in Spittelberg for a month or two—only long enough for the baby to be born—and then, in our disguise as patient and his entourage, we would travel together across the Alps to Venice. We cleaned Remus's boxy room of books and dust, so Amalia would be comfortable. It was nearly dawn before I lay down beside her on the bed and we stared into each other's eyes.

"You're alive," she whispered for the hundredth time that night. She ran her hand through my hair and studied every feature of my face. "When I dreamed of you I had to dream of that little boy, or else a shadow. I should be angry: you lied to me for years, you fool."

"But I . . ." I began, and though she gave me time to speak, I could not find the words to name my excuse, or the nerve to utter them. When I finally averted my eyes in embarrassment, she smiled and pulled my face to hers.

We finally fell asleep. I slept beside her in the narrow bed until I rolled off onto the floor, where a blanket awaited me. So it was every night. The room had no decoration except a single small window, so the next day Nicolai hung a cross above the bed, and Tasso appeared with silken curtains, which he had made from costume scraps he salvaged at the theater. Remus slept on the divan; his snoring kept us all awake, but we did not mind, for, as we lay awake, we dreamed of our happy Venetian future: gulls crying above canals, gondolas bumping on the quays, echoes of opera in the air.

XVII.

Remus and Tasso found a decrepit stagecoach rotting behind one of Spittelberg's decrepit taverns. I went with them to view it, and I was greatly discouraged by its disrepair: only one wheel that was round, flecks of peeling paint, no glass in the windows.

"We need the gold only until we reach Venice," Remus pointed out. "Afterward Moses will sing. Why not buy something more . . . intact?"

"Something newer?" I suggested.

Tasso looked up at me, and then at Remus. He shook his head. Then he swung the door back and forth on its one remaining hinge. It whined like a drunk soprano. "No," he said. "We'll take this one," he said. "Go and pay the price."

Tasso was a genius. Remus and I were merely his dim-witted stagehands as he built onto the still-stable frame the most convincing doctor's coach ever forged. When finished, it was massive and dark, with small windows hung with gray curtains. Inside, we installed a large bed on springs for Nicolai, a curtained one for Amalia and her baby, and six hooks for hammocks, should we not find a tavern any night along our journey. Tasso nailed a small stove to the floor and bored a hole in the ceiling for a chimney. Despite the carriage's bulk, on its new leaf springs the ride was as smooth as on a feather bed. The large wheels I painted black and gold.

When Tasso mounted to his perch, Remus pointed out a curious illusion: the little man appeared normal-size and the massive contraption seemed twice as large as the empress's grandest coach. We bought the four largest, tamest gray mares we could find, and boarded them at the tavern with the coach until we were ready to depart. Straining his eyes in his chair, Nicolai painted a sign that read: "Dr. Remus Mönch: Beware of Terrible Diseases." We hung the sign on the coach's door.

We bought Amalia peasants' clothes, and dirtied them with charcoal, so she would not raise suspicion. In the early mornings, when we did not so much fear a sighting, Amalia put on her cloak and we walked about to breathe the fresh air. I led her around mounds of rotting cabbage. We talked about our future: of Italy and its cities; of Paris and distant England; of the greatest opera houses in the world, whose names we recited to each other like magic spells: Teatro San Carlo, Teatro della Pergola, Teatro San Benedetto, Teatro Capranica, Teatro Comunale, Teatro Regio, Covent Garden, die Hofoper. Children were our only companions on the street. As soon as the sun was up they climbed into the windows of the abandoned houses, skipped down the lanes, were shooed out of doors by their mothers. Older children towed chains of younger siblings behind them. As the children raced around us, I found myself examining every smiling face. Would ours be like him? Or like her?

One day Amalia told me she wished to take a short journey into the city to purchase a gift for Nicolai. The day before, she had borrowed the numbered strip of linen Tasso used to measure lengths and wound it around Nicolai's head, scribbling figures on a scrap of paper. She tied her hair back with a scarf and smudged her face with ash until she appeared some serving wench, and we traveled through the palace gate to the *Fischmarkt*, where she told me to wait in the carriage.

She disappeared into a shop, with a sign that read, "Linsen." The stink of fish wafted on the chilly air and made me nauseated. I looked up and down the street for Countess Riecher's ogre or some other spy who would steal my love away. An old man pushed a creaking cart piled high with greasy lumps of soap. A dirty boy held drooping broadsheets in his hand and shouted, "Defeat in Silesia! War surely to end!" Another woman entered the lenses shop with a thick cloak about her ears, and I was suddenly convinced it was Countess Riecher herself. But just as I summoned the courage to confront her, Amalia came outside, her rosy cheeks looking very satisfied indeed. She held a small package underneath her arm.

That afternoon she unveiled her gift: a pair of round, smoky lenses hung on wire frames.

"Sit still," she said to Nicolai as he tried to reach out and feel the contraption with his clumsy hands. "Let me put them on your face."

His eyes became two black ovals, with strips of black leather around them to block out the light. Nicolai cooed, even though in the parlor's dim light he surely could not see a thing. He stood up. Amalia drew back the curtains. The late afternoon light streamed in, and for the first time in several years, Nicolai did not recoil.

He gasped with delight and waved his hand before his face, as if the lenses enabled him to see spirits flying about the air that were invisible to us. He stepped to the window and stood there as a massive silhouette, his arms outstretched to embrace the streaming sun. "A miracle!" he said.

A miracle it was not, just another gift of Science, and neither was it the perfect solution. When he wore the glasses, he could see only as well at sunny noon as others could see at midnight. "No, no," he replied to Remus's assertions that he was deceiving us. "I can see as well as I ever could. Like a bat."

Amalia shrugged and whispered to me, "It's just smoky window glass. But why tell him?"

Nicolai cavorted about the apartment as if he saw every pile of Remus's books, every table, every cup of coffee or wine, and so when he upended these, which he often did, he'd exclaim, "Oh, so clumsy. I'll have to be more careful of my fat feet in the future." He ordered Remus to accompany him while he strolled about the quarter. "Even ugly monsters," he said, "shock no one in the company of expensive doctors."

When her baby moved, Amalia placed my hand on her body so I could feel it, too. When the baby was long silent, and I saw her gently prodding, hoping to awaken some sign of life, I drew her hand away and pressed my ear to her belly. I listened to the miniature heart beating twice as quickly as its mother's. One day, as I sang for her an echo of the heart, *thump-thump-thump-thump-thump-thump*, she took my head in both her hands and pulled me to her face until our noses touched. "Moses," she said. "He shall call you Father."

I blushed and turned away, but was secretly thrilled by the idea. *Father*, I repeated to myself the next time I was alone. *Father*.

From then on, every day when I sang to Amalia I sang as much to our child in the womb. I secretly hoped that my voice would penetrate to its tiny ears as the sound of my mother's bells had penetrated to mine. Could I be as much a father to this child as the bells had been to me?

One night, dressing for bed, I stood before Amalia in our cramped room. She studied me in the candlelight: my long arms and round chest. In the cold air the skin of my hairless stomach tightened into the dimples of an eggshell. Her eyes fell momentarily on the bandage I still always wore around my middle, and then quickly flickered to my face. But I had caught that furtive glance, and as our eyes met, she blushed.

I unwrapped the bandage. The cold air chilled the damp skin below. I could not bring myself to look down; that shame would have been too much. But Amalia did not avert her eyes. She held out her hand, and naked, with tremendous relief, I climbed beneath her blankets. She nestled in my arms.

"Amalia," I blurted after several minutes.

"What is it, Moses?" I heard in her confusion that she had been asleep.

"I will not let it happen to him."

"What are you talking about?"

"If it is a boy—our son. I will not let it happen to him as it did to me."

"Oh, Moses. Don't be silly. Of course it won't."

I soon heard in her lengthening breath that she had faded back to sleep, but I lay awake for many minutes.

I would protect him—or her, son or daughter, it did not matter—I would protect that child from the evil that had befallen me and all the other evils that lurked in the world. But I would never mention it again, not even to Amalia. It would be my secret pact: If I could do it—if I could be a father to this child growing in her belly—then my shame about my own imperfection would finally fade away to nothing.

Though I could never unbreak what had been broken, I would stop mourning all that I had lost.

And so we went into cold November. Our days seemed so light and easy; we almost forgot that there was anyone or anything in the world to fear. We forgot that we shared a city with people who hated us very much, for Spittelberg was our haven, and the men and women who populated these streets were as distant from the Riechers' soirées and Guadagni's concerts as dirt is from the sky.

XVIII.

"Something is different, Moses," Amalia said one morning. She had grown fully round, and her swollen fibers dampened her body's ringing. Her limp was visible even when she shuffled slowly along the floor. Now she stood, and her thin gown washed over her belly like a cascade over rocks. I saw that the bulge of her child had dropped.

"Does it hurt?" I asked.

"No," she said. She placed her hands alongside her belly. "It does not hurt at all."

But that afternoon, the hurt began—a dull, creeping pain. I heard it in the sharpness of her breath as she moved. "I am fine," she kept telling us as we stared in dumb terror. Remus, Nicolai, and I sat before her in the parlor. I asked Amalia if she would like some tea, or apples from the fruit seller, or for Remus to read aloud to her, or for Nicolai to tell her again how life is in Italy, or—

"Just hold my hand and ask me no more questions," she said. But then she huffed like someone was pressing a hand on her gut. She propped up from the chair on extended arms and raised her belly, as if she were trying to lift her baby toward the ceiling.

I tried to help her lift it.

"Let go of me!" she yelled between gasps.

Remus jumped up and backed toward the door. "I'd better get Tasso," he muttered, and rushed out faster than I'd ever seen him move.

When Tasso arrived, the stagehand ran up the stairs, leaving Remus far behind. The little man was the oldest of thirteen children; birth had been as much a custom in his house as Lent. He rubbed Amalia's hands between his paws and told her it would still be many hours before she delivered—we would wait before sending for the *Hebamme*. "Stand beside her," he ordered, "hold her hand." I did as he said. The room began to spin.

"For God's sake, Moses," Remus said, "you have to breathe, or else you'll faint."

Amalia rubbed the back of my hand against her hot cheek. "Moses," she said, "you mustn't worry. It will be fine."

But I did worry. My ribs refused to expand, and I could breathe only by raising my shoulders. I chewed my lip until it bled. I swooned to one knee; Remus brought me a chair. Then Amalia was rubbing *my* hand.

"Are all his kind that frail?" I heard Tasso whisper to Nicolai.

"No, no," Nicolai murmured back. "He's always been like this. Even before he was . . . well, you know. I suppose it was rather his childhood in the mountains—living too close to the sun."

Tasso studied me and nodded.

After several hours, Amalia's pains grew stronger. "I think," she said, gasping, squeezing her eyes shut, "I might like to lie in the bed."

We all jumped up, but Tasso nodded to me. "Only you." So I helped her to her bed as Tasso scampered down the stairs and into the street to fetch the *Hebamme*.

"Sing for me, Moses," Amalia said. I knelt beside her and chose one of the sacred songs I had performed for her mother, and suddenly I could breathe again. She closed her eyes, and her toes moved up and down as she worked my voice through her swollen legs. She sighed as it vibrated along her back and loosened her gut. Her breathing slowed, and she opened her eyes again and smiled. *This is all I ever wanted*, her look said to me, and as I knelt there in that cramped room as if singing a prayer, with the din of clinking coffee cups through the flimsy floor and the acrid taste of wood smoke on my tongue, I realized what a gift I had received. *Let the future come!* I thought, as proud and hopeful as I had ever been.

Then, as if she had seen a hostile ghost looming behind my head, her eyes widened and her face tightened. Her body lost my voice, like a hand muting a violin's strings. She reached below the curve of her belly and gasped.

In thirty seconds it was over, but flashes of the anxious girl I had met so many years ago were closer to the surface now. "Oh, Moses," she said, "this will hurt." I placed a cool towel on her brow, and searched for words to comfort her, but I was lost.

She took my hand. "I am so afraid it will have Anton's face," she said. "I want our child to grow up like you instead."

This was the first time she had mentioned such fears. I took her hand and kissed it. "I have a secret," I told her. "I had a father. He was the most awful man I have ever known. He was ugly. And very mean. And so, unless you see that awful man in me, do not fear for this baby. I cannot say what this child will become, but I promise you, it will not be like the father."

She squeezed my hand, and I was happy to see that this comforted her—even as the next pain made her clench her eyes and groan. When it ended, the door opened and Tasso ushered in the *Hebamme*. She was tall and thin, with wiry gray hair. She frowned at the overcrowded room. But that was all. Many *Hebamme* from the Innenstadt would have gaped and fled from this scene: a lady alone with four men, none of them the father! But this woman—hardened by these streets of brothels, by mere children becoming mothers, by women who would like to kill the nascent being inside of them—she asked no questions.

She glanced at me, and must have clearly read my terror. She told Tasso to boil water, fetch sheets and towels, and get her a table so she could lay out her tools. And then she gave a final order. "Take this man," she nodded in my direction, "out of this room and do not let him back until the child comes."

Amalia struggled to sit up, but the *Hebamme* forced her down. Our eyes met. I had never seen such fear on her face.

"Moses!" she said.

"It will be fine," I said, my throat so tight it was a whisper. "I will be right outside."

Tasso nudged me out.

He deposited me in a chair, and we all sat in the parlor, trembling in the silence of the dim room—the occasional slamming of the coffeehouse door, the frequent squeal of a child in the street, the regular exclamations of pain penetrating the flimsy door.

"Now we just sit and wa—" Remus started, but he stopped because I had shot up in my chair.

I heard the slow footsteps up the stairs a moment before the others. We had never had a visitor before. I did not want one now.

"Who is it?" Tasso murmured.

"I will make them go away," Remus said, leaping up. "They must not—"

He had no time. The handle turned. The door opened. A tall figure shrouded by a hood stepped gently inside and slowly closed the door behind him. Then, as though on a stage, very slowly, Gaetano Guadagni reached up his two perfect hands and drew back his cloak. He considered his meager audience. When he saw me, he smiled, as if in great relief.

"*Mio fratello*," he said.

XIX.

The parlor had never seemed so small. Guadagni's brilliant eyes considered the tattered curtains, the dusty books stacked along the walls, the mismatched furniture, as if each object whispered to him secrets about the men inhabiting these rooms. Finally he turned to me.

"You hide yourself well," he said. "It is fortunate for me that you surround yourself with quite"—he gestured around the room—"*conspicuous* persons, who have been very active today." He smiled at Tasso. "Who was that woman whom you just escorted here, might I ask?" The little man crossed his arms and stared at the floor.

There was a loud groan from Amalia's room, and the firm, deep voice of the *Hebamme* in response.

Only Guadagni turned to look at the door. "Moses will come to see you," Remus said, "at another time. Or you may come visit. But today we are indisposed."

"No, no," Guadagni said absently, still watching the bedroom door. "Another visit is not necessary. I will not be long. I only wish to say goodbye to my student. Then I will leave."

"Goodbye," I said.

Guadagni smiled at me and shook his head at my naïveté. He stepped forward, until he stood inside our circle, Nicolai to his left, Remus and Tasso to his right, me seated before him. "Of course, I did not want to take my leave," he said, "without discussing what has passed between us. I am sure the stagehand has told you that the aria you stole made quite an impact."

"Moses is a far better singer than you," Nicolai said suddenly. Guadagni did not appear affected by this outburst, but he studied Nicolai closely, as if noticing his deformities for the first time. He raised his eyebrows.

"Moses," he said, weighing my name this first time it had passed his lips, "before I take my leave, before I let a man like this"—he showed a palm to Nicolai—"inflate your ambitions, I wish to give you some advice. I have sung opera since I was ten. I have sung on rotting stages in remote Italian villages. I have sung in Covent Garden. You are not the first student who left my care thinking he was greater than the teacher. And what became of them? I do not know. I have never heard the name of a single one again." He shrugged and looked again toward Amalia's door. "I imagine they sing somewhere. The choirs of rural churches, or travel in *buffa* companies. I know how they live, for I once lived like that. They sing upon a tiny outdoor stage, and people cheer their voices. They make men cry. Then, the concert ends. The audience leaves, and as they walk home through the streets, some of these men from the audience who laughed and cried at the song, they hold their hands over their parts"—he looked down pointedly at my groin, then returned his eyes to my face—"and pretend to sing like little girls."

Nicolai shook his head defiantly from his chair, but Guadagni had eyes only for me.

I looked at the singer's feet.

"Moses," he continued, "do you think these poor singers have no talent? Is that why they rot in nameless villages? *Moses*," he called my name softly and I looked up. He shook his head sadly. "Oh yes, they have talent! They have great voices, like yours and mine. They could make the empress cry, as you did, if only they could make her *believe in them*." His face grew dark. "But don't think it is an accident that they sleep in wagons and I sleep in one of Vienna's finest houses. It is not an accident."

Amalia began moaning again, and Guadagni stopped, glaring at the door as if her suffering were like a hacking cough in his theater. "It is not an accident at all," he continued, much more hotly now. "Singing is only the gateway to our profession. Moses, I explained all this, but you did not listen. You would not have done such a *stupid* thing if you had understood—" Guadagni paused, willing himself to control the anger growing in his voice, but my ears told me more; he was also afraid of something in this room. With a shaking hand, he patted the pocket of his cloak. He took a slow, deep breath.

"They do not love us for our singing," he began again. He took another step forward. "You have a fine voice, Moses—"

"He has the best voice I have ever heard," Nicolai broke in, waving a finger that was adequate to stop Guadagni in his tracks.

"A fine voice," Guadagni said. He nodded respectfully. "Any *buffa* company will be pleased to have you. Good thing," he looked about the room, "that you seem well used to the conditions of that life."

"Please leave," I said.

"But I would have taught you to be a musico!" The sudden force of his words made me cringe, as if he meant to strike me. When I looked up, I saw that he shook with fury.

Very quietly, I said, "You did not teach me anything."

"It is time for you to leave," Remus said.

Guadagni whirled around. "I will leave when I am ready!" He closed his eyes for a moment. Then he turned back to me and pointed a shaking finger. "They thought they heard *me sing*. If they had known it was you, they would have laughed. And the empress's soldiers would have chased you from the stage. It was your voice, but it was *me* they cheered."

"Nonsense," Nicolai muttered.

Guadagni swung his arm and slapped Nicolai with the back of his hand. His long fingers left four white shafts across Nicolai's cheek and temple. Nicolai's new lenses flew off his face and shattered on the floor.

"I created Orpheus," Guadagni roared, and his voice in the small parlor made the room tremble. "I brought his spirit back to life! And this boy, this *amateur*, stole his voice from me!"

Nicolai squinted, but he did not shy from the light. Slowly, he began to struggle out of his chair to his feet. He rose above the singer. Guadagni stumbled back until he hit the wall and then fumbled at his cloak. As Nicolai approached him, he withdrew a pistol and pointed it at the giant.

Nicolai laughed and reared to his full height. "Go ahead," he said. "Make sure you do not miss."

Remus pulled Nicolai's arm. "Nicolai, sit down."

The pistol shook. Guadagni kept it pointed at Nicolai but turned to me. "I am so much more than a voice, and you are nothing more than a thief."

For a brief moment, I felt sympathy for the man. He was correct: I had robbed him. I had stolen from him what every virtuoso needs: the faith that no one in this world could perform better. He held the pistol loosely, inexpertly. He would not shoot us; he merely needed to make us listen.

"Is this all you came to say?" I asked carefully.

"I came to tell you to leave this city. I do not want you here."

Just then, the moans began once more. I dug my fingers into my thighs. Tasso jumped up from his seat. When Amalia was quiet again, the pistol shook more violently in Guadagni's hand. His eyes jumped from each man in the room to the next. He finally firmly grasped the meaning of these cries. He was looking for the father.

"We are leaving Vienna," I said. I tried to speak forcefully to divert him, but my voice was a dry whisper.

"When?" he said.

"Very soon."

He nodded, but he was distracted. His face drained of color. "My God," he whispered. "It can't be."

"Get out!" howled Nicolai, struggling from Remus's grasp and toward the pistol, which now trembled more than ever.

Guadagni backed away. "Is it true?" he muttered. "Is that the Riecher girl?"

None of us replied. Nicolai froze his assault.

"She ran away with you?" he asked me. His red lips and piercing eyes were the only color in his face.

Just then, Amalia screamed. There was such pain in her voice that I jumped and rushed for the door, but Remus grabbed my arm and held me back.

When her scream faded, Guadagni was standing at the door to the stairs. "You are all damned," he said, and then he fled.

Only Nicolai reacted. But he was no longer the man who had raced through the abbey toward Ulrich's room years before. He lumbered down the stairs. Remus, Tasso, and I went to the window. We saw the singer bolt into the street and disappear amid the throng. It was several seconds before Nicolai followed, and when he burst into the afternoon sunshine, without his lenses, he cried out and tore at his eyes. Beside me, Remus gasped as we watched Nicolai clutch his head and fall to his knees on the street below.

XX.

I stood at Amalia's door as the others helped Nicolai back up the stairs. They placed him in his chair. "No!" he cried, pressing the heels of his palms against his temples. "No, no, no!" Remus brought him wine laced with laudanum, but Nicolai batted it away, and the glass smashed on the floor.

"Will he tell her? Will the Riecher woman come?" Tasso whispered to Remus, thinking I could not hear.

"I think she will."

"Why?" he asked. "It is not her child."

"If it is a boy, it will be her eldest son's eldest son—one day Count Riecher. And it will be the Duft heir as well. She will try to take him."

"But we will not let her," Tasso said.

Remus did not answer. He came to me and, placing his hands on my shoulders, led me back to my chair. Nicolai exhaled rhythmically, trying to drive the pain from his head.

"Remus," I said. "What will we do?"

"I do not know."

"If she tries to take the child," Nicolai said, "I will kill her."

She did come, an hour later, and she did not come alone.

It was growing dark outside. Four soldiers rode with her carriage. "Move aside!" they shouted. "Move, you cur!" They thumped their bludgeons against their palms and whisked them through the air at anyone too slow to make way for the horses. Tasso watched them from the window. The carriage's springs creaked as it struggled over the pits and mounds in the street. Then all was silent, except for the snorting of the four stallions.

"The carriage door has opened," Tasso whispered. "Someone is getting out."

I heard her shoe step on the narrow stair of her carriage and her gown rustle as she lifted it over the filthy street. The heavy footsteps of a soldier stepped before her, opening the door to the coffeehouse. "Clear out, you swine," he yelled. "A lady wishes to enter." Benches scraped along the floor. Patrons struggled with their coats. Three coffee cups shattered on the planks. The men hurried into the street.

We all heard the footsteps: the heavy boots of two of the soldiers, the click of Countess Riecher's heels—and another shuffling step I could not identify. They climbed the stairs. The door slammed open into the wall. A soldier, his hand on his sword, quickly took stock of the room, but soon deemed us a pathetic foe. Nicolai balanced his head between two fingers. Tasso stood defeated by the window. Remus looked at his hands in his lap.

When Countess Riecher stepped into the room, the swishing of her pristine gown and cloak around our slanted door, the tap of her toes on our creaking floor, every single hair on her head tied up in perfect order—all this made it all too clear how foolish we had been. Behind her came the second soldier, and then a pale, plump woman—a nurse—who cowered like a timid hound dragged forward on a lead.

Countess Riecher glared at me. "Is what the castrate says true?" she demanded. "Is she here?" She stepped forward, and Nicolai's shattered lenses crunched beneath her shoes.

"Answer me," she said.

I shook my head, but at that moment we all heard a moan, and it climbed into a scream, as if someone had pressed a knife into my lover's belly. The nurse's eyes grew wider, and I froze, the sound tearing through my head.

Countess Riecher's expression was blank. She waited for the yelling to subside. "Very well," she said, "I will see for myself what unfortunate creature is making that noise." She stepped around Nicolai toward Amalia's door.

Remus blocked her path. He was no taller than she, and at that moment seemed twice as frail. "No," he said. He held up his hands.

"Move aside," she said.

"There is no need for you to go inside. You know it is whom you seek, but she needs nothing more to alarm her at present."

She examined his face, but did not push past. He offered her a seat. She waved him off. "I will stand until it is born. Then I can leave this filthy place."

"We will not let you take it," Nicolai's deep voice growled, his palms still pressed into his temples. His eyes were closed.

Countess Riecher turned to face Nicolai in his chair. "You will not *let* me?"

Nicolai did not say anything, but I was afraid his quivering hands would crush his own head.

Countess Riecher frowned, looking around the room. She shook her head and snorted. "I can have you arrested this very minute. All four of you." She laughed coldly. "I do not even need your names. I can have you hanged for abducting her, before the sun comes up to-morrow." She stared at Tasso, and though he matched her gaze, he was shaking. "Are you all such fools? Did you really mean to steal this child and raise him here, in this hovel? Why? Because"—she pointed at the bedroom door and spat her words—"that *impudent* girl told you she wished it so?"

Guadagni must have told her that she should direct her anger at me, for now she glared at me. I wished I held a knife. I would have killed her then.

She continued: "She has no right to choose what happens to that child. It will be a *Riecher*." She looked me up and down. She shook her head.

She bid the soldiers to guard the door to Amalia's room. "Sit," she ordered Remus.

He did.

She looked fiercely at each of us in turn: Tasso's stunted limbs, Nicolai's deformed face, ugly Remus. Then me. "A castrate," she hissed. "For you she left our house? Left my son?" She smiled cru-elly. "Oh, I hope you have a pretty, pretty voice. In twenty years, when she is miserable and lonely, I hope its faint memory will comfort her."

I did not answer. I felt her stare like a cold finger across my face, probing for each proof of my inadequacy.

"I give you a choice, then," she continued. She turned about and waved her hand dismissively. "We will wait until the baby is born. I will take it. My nurse will care for it as it deserves, as fits its station. I will send a carriage for the mother. I will send her where I please. She will be provided for, but far enough away from any place where she can harm my grandchild's future with her shameful ways. And you, all four of you, will leave Vienna. I do not wish it to be known that my heir was born in . . ." She looked around the room, as if searching for the ugliest words, but finally sighed and said, "Spittelberg." She continued, "If you raise a hand to stop me, or if I ever hear of you again in this city, I will have no choice. You will die."

We did not speak, but as the cries from Amalia's room began again, our hearts cried as well. I looked at my friends. Nicolai nodded at me to confirm what I already knew: he would rather die than let this woman have her way. Tasso, too, still standing in the corner, looked ready to bite and scratch her. Even Remus's neck was flushed.

My hands shook at my sides. I prayed my knees would hold. "You cannot take this child from its mother," I said. It was a whisper. "We will not let you."

She stared at me as if she thought me so frail her mere gaze could knock me over. "From men," she finally said, "I expect stupidity. I would have hoped yours had been removed."

Then the door to Amalia's room opened. The *Hebamme* peered out. Her calm expression was gone. Her hair was tousled, and though she hid her hands behind the doorframe, the streak of blood across her brow made it clear why. She took in the crowded room.

"You must get a doctor," she said to no one in particular.

Tasso stood, but Countess Riecher held up her hand. "She will have the best in Vienna." She walked to the window and yelled orders to her coachman below to fetch the Riecher physician.

XXI.

When he arrived, night had come. Remus lit a candle, and gave the *Hebamme* a lamp. The doctor was a small, nervous man, and he entered the room like a startled mouse, his eyes darting about for signs of danger. He held his black bag like a shield. He located Countess Riecher in the dim light—as if spotting a nook in which to hide—and bowed slightly, shuffling to stand beside her, certain that the filth of this room was less likely to collect around her person.

He consulted briefly with the *Hebamme*, and I heard Countess Riecher whisper to him, "Save the child, Doctor. At whatever cost." He was momentarily startled by the grave suggestion, but he nodded firmly and stepped to Amalia's door, raising his hand as if he would knock, then reconsidered and stepped inside. The *Hebamme* followed him and closed the door.

He gives her something to quiet her. Her screams fade, and I wonder if she is screaming within her head just as I did under the surgeon's knife ten years before. "You must hold her down," the physician instructs the *Hebamme*.

Tasso is nestled in the corner, staring at the floor. Nicolai's eyes are closed, but I know he is not asleep. Remus has his elbow in one hand, the other across his face, as if deep in speculation. I am sure we are all thinking, *We have failed.* Countess Riecher has her jeweled hands crossed before her chest. What seems like hours pass and she does not move. She does not stir when Amalia moans.

I will die before they take that child from its mother.

The doctor shouts urgently, and we all look up—even Countess Riecher appears truly alarmed for the first time. We try to see through the wood of that door.

The air is so close it is hard to breathe.

.   .   .

And then—a croaking. The others are not able to differentiate this sound from Amalia's moans and the doctor's orders, but I hear every note. It is the sound of two tiny lungs unfolding. They suck in air and blood and the water of the womb. They hold a first breath, unsure what to do with it, and then, a first wail—the song of life. My three friends look up. The baby!

And I hear now, without doubt, it is a boy. *Our son.*

We stand.

His wail dies out. It ends with three gasps *Ah! Ah! Ah!* Then he cries again. What a cold terror is this world! My ears delight in his every cry even as a gulf opens through the center of our world—*Listen! Listen!*—for there are more sounds I want, and they are absent.

I cannot speak. I cannot move. The world continues on without me. Tasso's shoulders are drawn forward, his elbows out. Every hair on his hairy neck is raised. In Remus's eyes there is anger. Nicolai squints. He blinks. His fists are raised.

The baby cries for its mother.

Make some noise I can hear!

I cannot breathe. I sway. A shadow brushes past me: Remus. He argues with Countess Riecher, and the soldiers grab for their swords. One whistles, and the other two, who have guarded the front door to the coffeehouse, stomp upstairs. They stroke the smooth bludgeons in their hands.

"We are not afraid of you!" Nicolai bellows.

No! I try to say. *No! Can't you all hear? We have failed already!*

The doctor stands at Amalia's door. His hair and face are slicked with sweat. His collar is undone. Blood is spattered on his face, across his chest. It covers his arms up to his elbows, as though he has dipped them in a bleeding river. He is holding that screaming child. The *Hebamme* shines a lamp above the doctor's shoulder. The wet child glistens, crying, then freezes in a silent choke for air, staring at the ceiling. His hands reach out and he startles—and cries again.

"I saved the boy," the doctor says. "But I could not save the mother."

. . .

My ears have already heard this truth, which now crashes into my body. Remus catches me as I totter. I cannot drive the air from my lungs. I drown on air. I cannot move, but the world does not stop with me. Nicolai is shouting, and the soldiers beat him down with their clubs, then kick him with their boots.

The baby is crying! Countess Riecher is opposite me, the child between us, but she turns her face away, disgusted by the blood. The nurse wraps the screaming child in a sheet and presses it to her chest. Then it is over; they are gone.

Tasso kneels next to Nicolai. The giant moans with pain. The *Hebamme* still holds the lamp, like a statue, as Remus walks with me to her bed.

Amalia is covered by a sheet. The upper half of it is white, the lower half glistens red. Remus pulls it back so we can see her face. It is perfect—no blood at all. She could be sleeping, but I hear that she is not, for she does not breathe, and this silence is truly the loudest sound I have ever heard. It shakes every part of me, and I would break into a thousand pieces if Remus did not hold me tightly and hug me like a son.

XXII.

When her mother died, a thousand people filled that perfect church. A full choir sang. The stones of the church rang for her. So many flowers were laid before her tomb it seemed to rest on a bed of roses.

Amalia was buried in the cramped cemetery behind St. Michael's Church in Spittelberg. Weeds grew in place of flowers. Vines smothered the gnarled oaks. Tombstones lay toppled on the graves as if they merely prevented the corpses from escaping to a better place.

On the day we buried her, the cold rain fell so hard that Amalia's simple wooden casket floated in the grave until we threw in dirt to weigh it down. The young priest sped through his blessings and turned to go, and that would have been all, but Nicolai began to chant the Agnus Dei.

It was the first time I had heard him sing in years. His resonant voice rose over the hushed rain. I bowed my head so the drops fell on my neck and flowed in icy rivers down my back. The rain mingled with my tears. Tasso's and Remus's feet slowly sank into the mud, but they did not pull them free until Nicolai had finished the invocation.

The cold rain, mixed with our grief, made me ill. A fever came on, and for ten days I lay in Amalia's deathbed. Remus had cleansed the room of her blood, scrubbing the walls and floors and bedposts tirelessly, but still it remained in the cracks between the floorboards, invading my dreams. Just as blind Ulrich had, Remus cleaned again and again—yet still I heard her breathe. I heard her whisper loving words. When they tried to move me into Nicolai's room instead, I screamed.

They brought me a doctor. He bled me and gave me bitter herbs, but I did not improve. My friends thought they would have to bury me as well. But after several weeks the fever disappeared and the room no longer smelled of blood. Still her sounds were stored deep in my memory, and I held them in my ear like a silver locket with her portrait drawn inside.

One night I was awoken by the screaming of a child. I shot up in bed, dashed into the parlor, past the sleeping Remus and down the stairs. I was in the icy street, barefoot, poorly dressed, before I was fully awake and in my senses. The crying came from a distant house. I saw a window lit, a mother pacing with a bundle to her shoulder. The throbbing chill in my feet was nothing like the aching in my heart.

Many evenings we sat silently in the parlor; frost grew across the panes and blotted out the night. Even Remus did not read a book.

"We must steal him back!" Nicolai shouted suddenly one night in fury. When Remus and I did not reply, he continued, more quietly, "We would have loved him. That is more than she can say."

"Quiet, Nicolai," Remus warned. He looked at me as if he feared such talk would bring on my fever once again.

"I will not be quiet! I will not be quiet until we do what is right. I will raise an army. These people in the streets will help us. A hundred men is all we need."

"Nicolai!"

"Remus!" he shouted back. "Have you no courage?"

"Stop it, please," I told my friend. "I thank you for your courage, Nicolai, but it is in vain. You know I think the same as you, but that house is a fortress; the empress's soldiers would come to their aid. It would be too much risk—for us and for the child."

"But we must try," he insisted.

"No," I said firmly. "We must pray that he will be happy with the destiny that God has chosen for him. Otherwise, we must forget him."

Nicolai respired like an angry bear, but he did not speak.

"You must swear to me you will never speak of this again."

Tears gathered in his eyes. His lip quivered.

He swore my oath.

. . .

My friends and I stumbled through life like forlorn actors bereft of
any playbook. Then, one day, we received two visitors. The men, each
nearly Nicolai's size, climbed up the stairs and pushed their way into
the parlor. I did not get out of bed, but I heard every word. They had
been sent, they told Remus, by their employer, to remind the "Swiss
castrate" of his pledge to leave Vienna. I heard Nicolai's chair creak
as he rose to challenge them, but Remus quickly stepped between
them. He said he would deliver the message. "He has until the New
Year," one of the men said. "Then we will be forced to accompany
him on his travels." After they left, Remus came into my room and
repeated Guadagni's message. "Perhaps it is time we left," Remus
said. "Time to start anew."

"What do you mean?" I asked.

"The coach is ready," he said. "We can leave for Venice any day we
wish."

"Leave for Venice?" I said, shocked. "We made that coach for
her!"

"Moses, she would want us to go."

"I do not care," I said. "She is dead and she is buried here, and I
will not lose her again. I will not leave Vienna."

Another week passed. During the day, Nicolai and I sat in the darkened room. And sometimes, in the early hours of the morning, when
neither of us could sleep, we sat together at the open window, blankets drawn over our shoulders against the early winter cold, and
stared down the empty street toward the city.

My friend tried to lift my spirits by telling me stories. "A monk,"
he said once, "told me that in Norway, people sleep through winter
just like bears. Months at a time." On another morning: "The moon
spins so fast around the earth, that if we stood on it, we would shoot
off and burn up in the sun." Or: "I met a man, right here in this
street, who makes dresses for the empress. Each single gown takes ten
men a year to make, and she wears them only once." Sometimes I

even managed to smile sadly at him, but I rarely spoke. We sat for hours in silence. Just his presence was a comfort.

One early morning, in this silence, Nicolai suddenly spoke. "Moses, today is Christmas." The nights were long at that time of year, and so, though the city was slowly awakening, the sky was still the darkest gray. Frost on windowpanes softened the glow of lamps. Snow had fallen a week before, and for once the Spittelberg air did not reek of urine and decay.

I could not say whether he was right or wrong about the date. There were no signs of celebration in the street. "It used to be my favorite day of the year," he said. "What beautiful Masses we would sing!" He laughed sadly. His eyes grew moist. "Forty-five years, Moses! Forty-five years and I spent every morning in a church. And now, for five whole years, I haven't said a single prayer."

I looked at him, but he shook his head.

"No," he said. "Not a single one."

My friend was covered in blankets. I could not see where they ended and where his bulk began. He shrugged and the whole mass rose and fell.

"I want to pray, I do," he said. "It's not that I've given up on God. I'm no Job, but still, I don't complain. I deserve all of what I've got and more. Of course there are certainly some things I would like to ask God for." Nicolai shrugged again. "But if I want to ask God for anything, there are so many things I need to tell Him first. How to begin? And so every Christmas it's the same. I tell myself it is fine to wait a little longer, and that at Easter I will pray."

"I will go to a church with you today," I whispered, "if you wish."

He looked warmly at me, happy to have heard me speak, happier still that I cared so much for him. But he shook his head. "No, Moses. That's the problem. I don't wish. Perhaps the final reason, among so many, is that when I sit in that confessional and I hear that voice ask me if I have sinned, I fear Staudach's face on the other side."

Hatred stirred in me at this name. It had been a long while since I had thought of the abbot. But I realized in that moment that I did

not fear his power anymore, as Nicolai evidently did. "Perhaps you
are not ready to be forgiven," I suggested.

"Perhaps," Nicolai began. "But if that were true, would I want it
so very much? Remus says—"

But I held up a hand, for I had heard something. A whisper in the
night.

"What is it?" he asked.

"Listen," I said. I leaned forward, and the whisper came again,
fifty times louder. Every ear in the city heard the pealing now.

She had called me to Vienna, and now she was calling me again. That
great bell rang throughout the city and summoned the faithful to
Christmas Mass. Even from such a distance, the sound was immense.
Nicolai covered his ears, though he smiled in pleasure at the vibration passing through him.

That giant bell rang with a million tones, and those overlapped to
ring millions more. Like the rainbow, which is light pried apart into
all the colors of the world, these were all the sounds of the world. I
heard my mother's bells and Amalia's sighs of pleasure, and they shook
me and passed away into the frozen earth, and then they were with me
once again, preserved forever in that pealing. I found myself crying
into my hands. I cried that she was gone, and I cried for the dreams I
had lost, and I cried for that boy who would have been my son.

Surely he heard the pealing, too, in his palace just below the bell.
I wished he could hear them as I did, but most likely this sound was
as frightful to him as thunder. Who was there to comfort him? Who
shielded his ears and clutched him to their breast? Not his father, not
his grandmother; that nurse was all he had. I pictured that small
woman who had cowered behind Countess Riecher here in our parlor. How would she cover her own ears and protect my boy's ears all at
once?

This conjured a vision in my mind: I held him, pressed his one
ear against my chest, protected the other with my palm. I held him
tight and rocked him. I sang softly, and though he could not hear my

voice above the ringing, this calmed his straining limbs. This vision was so real I found myself cupping my arms in the blanket. I felt the warmth of his body. I felt the inflation of his breath.

And then I looked down and saw that my arms were empty. Remorse filled me so keenly that I stood up and looked out the window, toward the black, pealing morning.

I saw what happiness I had lost, and in that instant, I saw how I would gain some part of it back again.

XXIII.

The composer Chevalier Christoph Willibald Gluck was asleep when the ghost slid into his bedroom. It glided to his bedside and coughed. The maestro did not awake. "Hello!" the ghost said. "Wake up!" Still Gluck did not stir, so the ghost shook his arm.

Gluck's eyes shot open. He jerked up in fright. "Who's there?" he asked.

"Light a candle."

Gluck leaned to the table beside his bed and did as instructed. When the ghost's face was illuminated, he gasped.

"Orpheus!" he said.

Orpheus nodded gravely.

"Will you sing again?" he asked. "Will you sing for me again?"

Orpheus seemed to consider this a moment. "I cannot say," he said. "It is not for me to decide."

"Who decides?" Gluck threw back his sheets and climbed out of his bed. "Who decides?" The ghost stepped back as Gluck advanced.

"The . . . the music," said the ghost. "The music decides it."

Gluck nodded. "Yes," he said. "Yes, of course." The composer took Orpheus's hand in both of his. For a moment he pressed it to his brow in supplication. "Orpheus," whispered Gluck, "but why have you come to me tonight?"

"Music," said the ghost, as if reciting a message committed to memory, "has blessed you with Her favor. Now you must do something in return." And then Orpheus told Gluck what he must do, when a ringing bell woke the composer from his dreams.

It took me several days to get everything in order. I told my friends what part they must play, and the danger it entailed. "May the empress cut off our heads," said Nicolai. Tasso turned white at Nicolai's words, and so the giant slapped the little man on the back, knocking him several steps across the floor. We bid Herr Kost goodbye and told him he might seek other tenants. Remus had Nicolai's shattered lenses replaced. I bought a short knife, which the bladesmith said was the sharpest I could hope to find in Vienna, and I wore it on my belt. I purchased a lump of the softest beeswax, some woolen batting, and a yard of muslin, which I cut into strips.

Tasso brought me the small iron stove he used on cold nights beneath the stage. He collected all his possessions in a bundle, then returned for a final evening at the theater—Guadagni was singing *Orfeo* once again.

Late that night, we heard Tasso running up the stairs. He darted into the parlor, grinning wickedly. "Now I never can go back!" He slammed the door behind him. When I asked him what he meant, he scurried first to the fireplace—the stage where I had sung my concert several months before. He crept back and forth like a cat burglar. He peered up at the ceiling. "I watched his feet through the cracks above," he narrated in a crafty whisper, "but I listened, too. I waited until he sang high and loud, and then"—Tasso yanked an invisible line—"I pulled. His song became a scream. He fell!"

"But then," Tasso's face turned pale and grave, "I almost died." He nodded thrice—once at each of us. "You see, Guadagni was expecting this. Must have dreamed about it every night. His scream was just a battle cry! He landed like a cat. He pulled a knife from his shirt, and even before he saw me in the darkness he stabbed the air." Tasso jabbed to his left, his right, murdering half a dozen men. "He would have killed us all!"

Tasso shrugged nonchalantly. "But I was too quick for him. I grabbed a loop, set loose a counterweight, and shot right past his head. Kicked the knife out of his hand. I smiled and waved at him from the chute. 'You won't survive the night,' he snarled, and tried to climb back onto the stage, but he couldn't manage it—flailed there like a drowning rat clutching some scrap of floating wood until two stagehands came and pulled him up. They laughed at him! The whole theater *laughed* at Guadagni!"

We, too, laughed and cheered the hero Tasso, but finally Remus cut us off and pointed out that Guadagni likely meant his threat. "You'd better hide away in the coach until we're ready," Remus advised. "He'll come looking for you here." Tasso's eyes grew wide in terror. He vanished like a mouse.

As Remus had suggested, Tasso spent those last two days preparing our coach and team of mares. He tried to teach me to drive them, but I found this as difficult as juggling. When I finally judged we were ready, we filled our new home with our belongings. Last of all, with Nicolai's help, we lifted Tasso's stove to the coach's roof and then I strapped it down.

It was midnight when we departed our rooms for the final time, on December 30, 1762, one day short of Guadagni's deadline. It took us the better part of an hour to ease the giant coach down the icy, pitted street. Tasso sat on his perch and coaxed the mares slowly, taking utmost care not to crack a wheel. We came to the glacis and beheld a full moon shining silver on the wide expanse of snow. This plate of ice crackled as we passed, as though the earth below were stirring in its sleep. We drove through the palace gate and into the city. The streets were empty, windows dark. The city slept, just as I had planned it.

Tasso steered the carriage to the Riecher Palace, and when we arrived, I leaned out the coach door and whispered exactly where to stop.

I turned back to my friends. "Ready?" They nodded, and we set out.

We walked back toward the Stephansdom, which was a black tower in the sky. Remus and I held Nicolai's arms so he would not fall on the patches of ice. We soon came to the church and slipped inside. We paused in the entrance. The cavernous nave was lit by the glow of candles whose light barely warmed the branched pillars of the ceiling. We saw no one, but I heard the creak of a pew, and a soft footstep on the stone, and I knew we were not alone. Nicolai squinted toward the altar as if something wicked hid behind it.

I whispered to Tasso to follow me. I showed him which door I wished to open. The little man scurried toward it through the shadows. I listened to the clink of metal as he probed the lock. Then I heard the joyful creak of hinges.

We climbed the stairs slowly. Nicolai crawled on all fours in front, and once we knew we were out of hearing of those in the nave, he said between heaving breaths, "I feel the burden . . . of my sins . . . lighten with each stair." I silently hoped he did not tumble down and kill us all.

We finally reached the top, and for several minutes we rested. I lit a candle. Nicolai mopped his brow with the sleeve of his tattered coat. He squinted up at the sixteen bell ropes hanging through the sixteen holes in the ceiling.

"If this bell takes sixteen men to ring it, how are we three to do it? You overestimate my girth if you think I am worth fourteen men."

"No," I said, standing up and walking to one of the ropes. "Sixteen is not necessary. It is simply a matter of timing. Not even sixteen men could lift her, but you three can make her rock. You can make her swing."

I grasped the rope with one hand and pulled hard. The rope could have been hooked to the ceiling for all I felt it budge. But I listened. Those sixteen ropes passed through sixteen holes in the ceiling, and then through sixteen pulleys, and into a single strand, which curled around her wheel. Those pulleys gave the slightest squeak. The Pummerin rocked the slightest hair. Now I listened for a second squeak—the sign that her movement had crested and reversed—and when I heard this, I tugged again. The squeak was louder this time. I repeated this process—then again, again, again—giving sharp, timed tugs to the rope, and gradually I perceived a give.

"They're moving!" Tasso said. He pointed at the ropes.

They were indeed. All sixteen ropes gently bowed their tails upon the floor in perfect coordination.

"It will take a while," I said, "before she swings heavily enough to ring. But that is fine. I have much to do."

Remus laid his hand on a bell rope. When he felt it drop in his hand, he pulled it along. "I can feel it," he said. He ran his thumb

along the frayed fibers as if the rope were some exotic creature he had
never read about in any of his books.

"You keep it going," I said, and let go of my rope.

I took the beeswax, wool, and muslin from the sack, and began
with Nicolai's ears. I filled the cavities with the soft wax, and then
stoppered it with wool. I wrapped muslin around his head several
times to hold the stoppers in place. He soon looked like a maimed
soldier, escaped from a surgery.

"Can you hear?" I asked.

"Has the bell started ringing?" he shouted so loudly that Remus
cringed. I thanked God that we were cloistered in the city's highest
tower; no one would hear us shout.

"Tasso, you're next!" I said. Nicolai climbed to his feet and
grabbed the nearest bell rope. He pulled with all his strength, but
timed it poorly.

"No!" yelled Remus. "Now!"

Soon they were pulling in unison, and the bell ropes were dancing. I finished Tasso's ears and began Remus's.

"And then I will do yours," Remus said.

"It is not necessary," I replied.

"What do you mean?" he asked. "You will go deaf!"

I had no time to explain. "My mother," I said, "she was a bell."
He looked puzzled, but then I plugged his second ear, and we could
talk no more. As Remus took his station, it occurred to me I should
have reviewed my plans with them one last time. But now, the swinging of the bell was enough to pull Tasso off his feet. Remus sat down
with each pull and then stood when the bell reversed and dragged
him back up. Nicolai pulled the rope from above his head to his
waist.

How long before she would ring? And then, how long until someone arrived to stop them? The timing must be perfect. But before I
left, there was one more thing—one more thing I had vowed to do.

I dashed up the stairs, plunging into darkness. I felt my way until
I broke into her belfry. The moon shone through the open sides,

casting sharp shadows along her lips as she swung, and I crept beneath
her. Her still gentle rocking breathed a cold wind across my face. I
judged a mere ten minutes before she would strike.

I took the knife from my belt and cut at the leather wrapping
around the clapper, which they had placed there to dampen the massive ringing. I tore away scraps of leather and clumps of woolen padding. It was slow going, but after several minutes I had set her free.
Tonight she would ring as she was created to.

I hurried down the stairs. "Keep pulling!" I shouted as I rushed past
my friends, each rising up and gently falling down, but they did not
hear me. Round and round I flew down the steps of the tower, and
thankfully I reached the nave before I fainted. I blew out my candle.
I slipped through the church and escaped into the night.

When I was halfway across the square, I heard the faintest hum,
and it filled me with such joy that I stopped. I closed my eyes. A boom
throbbed the night. I let it shake me from head to toe. It washed away
any remaining fear.

"Yes!" I yelled up to my friends. "You are doing it!"

They were! They were ringing the empire's largest, loudest bell,
which tolled like footsteps on the heavens now. *Boom! Boom! Boom!* The
ringing filled even the silence between the strikes, and every ear in
Vienna must have heard it by now. Soldiers shot up in beds, thinking
the Prussian army was closing in. The empress awoke and called for
her minister. Children screamed in every house, startled from their
dreams. Dogs brayed at the sky. The vibrations set ice and snow sliding off roofs. The ringing cracked windows throughout the Innenstadt, as far away as the imperial palace. Everyone knew this sound,
but surely, they thought, she had not rung this loudly in fifty years!

I ran out of the square.

Climbing onto the coach, I unstrapped the stove on top. I struggled to lift it to my shoulder. Several of the windows in the Riecher
Palace glimmered, but the one nearest to the coach was still dark. I

threw a momentary prayer to God. I tottered back, stumbled forward, and heaved the stove through a window.

A thunderous crash. The tumbling stove banged like a bouncing cannonball and shattering glass jingled and tinkled across the darkened room, but I prayed that mine were the only ears that could discern the sounds above the pealing.

. From my perch on the coach's roof, I looked up and down the street, confirmed that the ogre was not peering out of his gate, and then, as if it were a door, I stepped through the window.

As it turned out, the drop to the floor was farther than I had expected, and I soon found myself sprawled in broken glass. But in a moment I was up again—no time to dwell on the cuts and scrapes. I shook off the shards like a dog shakes off water.

I seemed to have landed in some sort of library. I shoved the stove beneath a desk and crept toward the door and listened. But just then, my luck ended. Through the tremendous pealing, I discerned a footstep, then, in horror, I spied the tremble of the turning doorknob. My calculations had been all wrong! I had been heard. I barely had enough time to dash behind the door when it opened and Countess Riecher herself strode in.

She held her hands against her ears, so the sleeves of her silk dressing gown bunched up around her shoulders. I marveled at the sharpness of her elbows. She gazed at the smashed window for a moment. "That damn bell," she murmured, and turned away.

Perhaps she had not heard me after all. She appeared to be searching along a shelf.

I did not move.

She located what she sought and, with a quick movement, released one ear, grabbed something from off the shelf, and plugged it into her skull.

Of course! I realized. She lives just below the bells. She was just the sort to have some means of blocking out the sound. When she turned back toward the door, I still stood there, hoping she would mistake my shadow for some forgotten bust or statue. But, of course, this was not a woman who forgot anything. She peered at me in the dim moonlight, trying to discern my face. She backed away.

I lunged for her. She yelled, but even if her husband had been lying in bed on the other side of the wall, he could not have heard her.

Her eyes grew wide. "You," she said, though I doubt she heard herself above the din.

"You!" I cried back. I spread my long arms and towered above her. She attacked.

She scratched my neck and tried to pry out my eyes with the daggers of her polished nails. I yelped and tried to fend her off, but she was a lioness—all claws and roar.

With each booming of the bell she doubled her attack. Then she had one hand tugging on my hair while the other tried to crush my neck. I could not breathe. She could not hear me wheeze, but I heard her growl in my ear.

I pulled out my knife and swung it at her face. It missed, but she glimpsed it glinting in the moonlight and she recoiled, letting loose my neck. She backed against the wall. I pointed the shaking knife at her chest and heaved for air.

I had bought the knife only for the bell. I did not wish to stain its metal with her evil blood.

There was a chest on the floor that looked as if it had accompanied some noble general on an important campaign. I deemed it suitable to store the countess until the bell quieted and I was gone. I gestured with the knife for her to climb in, which she did, but with her final glance, I felt a chill, for her eyes told me that I would not survive our next encounter. I latched the chest, and continued on my mission.

The palace was alive. Fortunately, everyone needed both hands to protect their ears, so the Riechers and their servants were but clumsy shadows in the dark passages. It seemed as if the pealing had actually increased in volume. I pictured my three friends leaping to the ceiling and being gently lowered down again. My feet tingled as the house shook beneath them.

My ears heard every footstep, every voice cursing the blasted bell—and finally there was the sound for which I had come: a baby's cry. I slipped past human shadows as I ascended the stairs, toward the crying, down the passage that led to Anton's wing. There I almost collided with another shadow, and when he mumbled, "That blasted bell!" I heard that it was Anton Riecher himself.

But he was deaf to his crying son, even though the screams came from a door not ten paces away. He ran past me down the passage toward the stairs, no doubt hunting for his mother. I sprawled along the wall as the footsteps disappeared down the stairs. Then I hurried down the passage and burst into the nursery.

XXIV.

That kind nurse, and the baby: four ears to protect and only two hands that knew how. The sight broke my heart. The woman was lying on the bare wooden floor, contorted as if she'd fallen down a flight of stairs. From the single window, a blade of moonlight cut across them. The baby lay against the nurse's chest, one ear pressed into her bosom. The nurse held her right hand against the child's outer ear—only one hand left for herself. Her head twisted against her left shoulder, her left arm wrapped around her skull to reach her right ear.

This might have worked, but the child writhed in her hold, his body wracked with screams. I dashed toward them and snatched the child, pressing him to my chest. One hand sheltered his exposed ear, and with the other, I drew a glob of beeswax from my pocket. I plugged one ear and then the other as he thrashed in my arms. His face was red and he paused his cry only when he had no air left to scream.

I clutched him to my birdlike chest—which was wrought to sing, not to grasp a child—and held his head with my palm, my long, delicate fingers petting his brow. The bell still shook the city. I began to sing so the child—my son!—felt my voice inside of him. It calmed him just as it had calmed his grandmother in her sickbed, his mother at his birth. Soon his crying stopped, and he looked into my eyes.

I knew this face. His mother's eyes stared up at me. And then, as I sang, those eyes fluttered. He was asleep.

The nurse on the floor was still shaken, still pressing her ears with all her might. She looked up gratefully, trying to make out which of the household servants had come to her aid. When I stepped forward into the moonlight, she seemed no more surprised than Gluck had been to see Orpheus in his room. Perhaps she, too, had dreamed of me.

"I am afraid I will have to lock you in that wardrobe," I said to her, and pointed. She studied my moving lips. "I would not want them to blame you. Tell them you put up a fight." No, she did not understand a word, but she let me lead her to the wardrobe, and stepped inside it as if I were helping her into a waiting carriage. I locked her in. She did not yell for help.

And then I was alone with my son. This lovely sleeping face! An angel in my arms! But as I cocked my head back and forth, I realized that the buzzing sensation was reduced. I listened: each booming crash was softer than the last. There was only one explanation: someone had climbed those stairs and seized my friends. The bell still rang from momentum, which meant I had only several minutes until it subsided into silence, and there was still much to do.

I wrapped the child in some blankets from his cradle and dashed down the passage. The house had calmed somewhat—everyone had found a spot to sit quietly and hold their ears until the pealing stopped. But I heard one person as I reached the bottom of the stairs. Anton was standing in the door to Countess Riecher's study—the door to my escape.

"Mother!" he yelled. He stepped into the room. He regarded the broken window. "Mother!" he yelled again. With his stoppered ears, he must have heard his own voice as if down a long tunnel.

"Mother?" he cried once more, not three paces from the chest, from which occasional thumping sounded. Then he shrugged and closed the door. He turned toward the stairs—if he had looked up he might have glimpsed me peering down at him—but he chose to continue the search for his mother on the story below. He vanished down the stairs.

In a moment, I was in the study, the door closed behind me. I had one foot on the window ledge when I looked down at that chest. In my haste I had shut the clasp, but left the lock ajar. I corrected this mistake and threw the key into the icy street.

It would be hours before they had the woman out.

· · ·

I stepped carefully out onto the carriage and climbed into Tasso's seat, which the little man had suited to himself, not to a musico twice as tall. I clutched my precious bundle with one arm while with the other hand I took the reins. *Careful*, I told myself, *with horses you are a fool.* I turned the beasts as if they were a team of rheumatic grandmothers. "Slow," I told the gentle mares. "No need to rush. We have four hundred miles ahead of us."

We clunked to the door of the Stephansdom. As I stopped the carriage, I heard the Pummerin strike the naked clapper for the final time. Her ringing still hung in the air, but it no longer hurt Vienna's ears. I climbed down, and with the Riecher heir tucked safely against my chest, I went into the church.

It was exactly as I had feared. I hid behind a pillar and peeked around it to see my friends in shackles. Six soldiers guarded them, while another man, the church's *Kirchner*, shouted in their faces. They had undone the wrapping around their heads, though Nicolai's muslin was still wound around his neck like a scarf. All three men picked occasionally at the wax in their ears.

"Do you know what you have done?" the *Kirchner* roared. "That is a holy bell! You have woken every soul in this city. The empress herself! She must think we are besieged!"

Nicolai squinted and tried to make out the man.

"You will be punished!"

"I would do it a thousand times again!" Nicolai said. He held his hands above his head as if he would tear apart his shackles. "No prison will ever hold me!"

Remus told his friend to quiet down. "Now is the time for meekness," he murmured. "I would prefer to keep our time in the empress's detention to a minimum."

"Years!" shouted the *Kirchner*. "That is what you have before you. Look what you have done!" The *Kirchner* pointed at the floor of the church, where tiny shards of the stained-glass windows sparkled like a million rubies.

"They can be fixed," said Nicolai. "Tasso here could fix them in a day."

"Can he fix every window in Vienna?" the *Kirchner* screamed.

"Better than an army of your half-wit—"

"Nicolai!" Remus yelled.

The *Kirchner* instructed the soldiers to take the men away to the most unpleasant of the empress's prisons. Two soldiers pushed Nicolai toward the door, and one took each of the other two. The last two marched behind. I crept around the pillar so they would not arrest me as well.

Hurry! I implored.

And, as an answer to my prayer, just then the church's door burst open and a man hurried through. From under a long, warm coat peeked his white dressing gown. He saw the soldiers and their captives. "Stop!" he yelled. He raised both hands like a conductor calling for attention.

The party obeyed his forceful order. The *Kirchner* peered at him. He gasped. "Chevalier!"

"Release these men!" Gluck bellowed as if speaking to the distant altar. He strode to Nicolai. "Give me the key!" he ordered the nearest soldier. The man obeyed, and Gluck began to unlock the shackles.

"But Chevalier!" the *Kirchner* said. "Did you not hear? It was these men who rang the bell!"

"Of course it was these men!" Gluck exclaimed, still speaking as if to a distant audience. "I ordered it!"

Nicolai was free. He rubbed his wrists and stared in awe at the composer.

"You?" gasped the *Kirchner.*

"Him?" Nicolai muttered.

"I!" Gluck bellowed to the heavens. He set to work on Remus's shackles. While no one was looking, Tasso had slipped his hands through his and laid the shackles silently on the floor. He scurried behind a pillar.

"But why?" asked the *Kirchner.* "Why?"

Gluck paused in his work. To me it seemed as if he held Remus's hands in his—as a lover would. He looked at the *Kirchner*. "Have you no ears? Have you no heart?"

"I . . . I do," stammered the *Kirchner*.

"Then, sir," Gluck said in a reproaching tone, "next time you hear beauty calling in the night, I suggest you listen."

XXV.

Tasso drove us from that city as though all the devils of my past made chase just behind us. Early morning traders jumped out of our path as we raced west and joined the Salzburg Road. But we had gone only as far as Hütteldorf before we were confronted with a problem. The child had begun to scream. Singing did no good this time. Tasso told me to stick my little finger in his mouth, which seemed to work temporarily, but Remus knew better; babies eat more than fingers. He told Tasso to stop the coach. We were in a dismal place. The taverns and shops along the wide, pitted road were fine enough, but the houses up the lanes sagged as if they were soaked through with water. The sun was rising. Soon the Riechers would be after us.

"But we cannot stop!" I insisted.

"This is imperative," Remus said. "Remember, anyone hunting us will be seeking four impoverished men and a child. We must comport ourselves as the wealthy men we are, and hide the child as best we can. His screams, and our haste, will only draw attention to us." Remus reached into Herr Duft's small chest of gold, which was still nearly full. He took out a single coin, descended from the carriage, and disappeared up one of those dismal alleys. Thirty minutes passed, and the child began to mistrust my finger. He screamed until his face turned red. He screamed until his lungs were empty. Tears poured down his cheek. I watched helplessly and feared I had made a dreadful mistake.

Then Tasso pointed out the window. Remus was trudging down the lane. Lumbering just behind him was a slouching figure with long arms hanging almost to its knees. Countess Riecher's ogre? But Remus looked pleased, and when they stepped closer, I saw that this gorilla was a woman—the most peculiar specimen I had ever seen. She was very tall, and round in all the right places, and many of the wrong ones as well, with cheeks that proceeded in rolls of fat down to her bulging bosom, and a belly that fell toward her knees.

Remus opened the door and she poked her square face into the coach. Her chin was much manlier than mine; she had black hairs where I did not. She considered Nicolai, Remus, and me. The baby renewed its screaming, its face purple, but she did not seem to see or hear it. She weighed Herr Duft's gold coin in her hand and studied us again, as if she were trying to decide which was heavier.

"And the same again in three months' time?" she asked Remus over her shoulder.

"The same again. But please hurry. We have no time."

"I must have my things."

"We will purchase whatever you require along the way."

She gave a sly grin at this offer, and the carriage tilted as she squeezed through the door. She towered above me, massive. Her hands were huge and chapped—a butcher's hands.

"Are you the father?" she yelled over the baby's screams.

"It is his late sister's boy," Remus offered.

"But he shall call me Father," I blurted.

"He can call you pope," she said, "as long as you pay me when it's due."

I nodded that I would.

"Give him here." She held out her arms. He kicked and batted his arms as I lifted him gently. She snatched him and held him up for her inspection. He cried into her face.

"Fine-looking boy," she said. "What do you call him?"

In the excitement of our flight, this question had never occurred to me. Now everyone was looking at me. The baby turned and cried toward me as well.

"His name is Nicolai," I said.

The older Nicolai clapped his hands in joy.

"Well, Nicolai," she said into the baby's face, "I suppose you'll be wanting your breakfast."

She shooed Tasso off the seat with a flick of her hand. The carriage's springs groaned as she heaved her body down. Then she shocked us all; a dexterous finger popped two buttons in her chemise, which set free a flap. Suddenly, we were all staring at a swollen breast, a fat nipple as thick as a finger.

"Close your mouths," the wet nurse snapped, pushing little Nicolai's head into that soft mound, but our jaws were too heavy. She shook her head. "Fine, but don't expect me to hide the tools of my trade."

The gorilla's name was Fräulein Schmeck. She quickly took control of our establishment, one hand pressing little Nicolai to her breast, the other rubbing oil into big Nicolai's temples (her huge hand could span his face), all the while shouting orders to Tasso as he steered the carriage, and detailing her demands to Remus and me of what we must buy at the next town. By noon of that first day, we all mused silently to ourselves over whether there was a way to evict her from our coach. But a day later, with a happy baby, Nicolai feeling healthier than he had in years, enough quiet for Remus to read his books, and many miles between us and Vienna, we abandoned all thought of overthrowing our new monarch. She was not a fine lady, but once she realized that our wealth had no apparent limits, she decided she should live as one. She bought creams and perfumes. In Salzburg, she ordered gowns. The baby must have silken and cotton dresses, she insisted, and all manner of wrappings to contend with the various solids and liquids he expunged. She commanded us as though we were the hired help—and we obeyed every order.

In fact, she ruled our home—whether coach or villa—from that New Year's Eve for seven years, until, in 1769, she made me buy her a cottage above the Bay of Naples. I expect that she is still there now, smashing grapes in her massive fists to make their juices into wine.

And so our group was six as we crossed the Alps that winter. We raced through Salzburg and Innsbruck and reached the low Brenner Pass

just in time for an early thaw. And then, by spring, I heard Italian
spoken by toothless farmers and their black-haired daughters with
sparkling eyes. The language I had once thought was made for opera
resounded like the singing of birds as we passed through chestnut
groves. We changed horses again and again, and the sun grew warmer
every day. We sat on the roof of our coach as Tasso drove us down
onto the Venetian Plain. Remus sprawled with a book. Nicolai called
for us to behold the wonders he claimed to perceive through his
lenses: fat grapes already ripe in March, nuggets of gold lying on the
road, birds twice the size of a man flying before the sun.

I sang the arias I had heard Guadagni rehearse in his house, and
farmers paused in their milking to listen as we passed. Children
chased after us in wonder. In the middle of it all, atop that massive
coach, Fräulein Schmeck sat cross-legged, like a goddess of fertility,
one round breast drying in the sun, the other hugged by a fattened
child, who gorged himself on milk.

I remember one day, so many years before that flight over the Alps,
back in Nebelmatt, when I sat on the edge of our belfry and my mother
rang her bells. I was looking down at the windings of the Uri Road far
below, along which a column of soldiers slowly marched. The day was
so still that I could hear the clanging of swords and the shouts of the
wagon drivers. I must have craned my neck and leaned slightly forward, unconscious of the edge, curious to examine these exotic beings
swarming past my home. I don't think I would have fallen, but my
mother, although entranced by her bells, was suddenly alarmed by my
gentle leaning. She dropped her mallets and grabbed both my arms,
drawing me back from the edge. She hugged me tight. Her face looked
so alarmed that I pointed down at the column on the road as if to say,
Mother, I was only looking at the soldiers. She, of course, had heard nothing,
but now she squinted and perceived glinting metal—the dark human
snake sliding down the road. And then her face grew sad. She looked
at the soldiers and then down at me, as if to say, *Oh my son, I am so sorry*.

I had no idea then what she meant.

But years later, sitting on that coach, my friends and my son at my side, Italy opening before us, I finally understood: *I am sorry I have made your world so small*, she had meant to say to me. And so I smiled atop our coach, because I understood she had wished all of this for me.

Nicolai, my son, have I made up for all that I robbed from you? Have I replaced with love your destiny of wealth and privilege? Your double inheritance? Think back through all you know: Our life in London, just the two of us. So much fame that crowds mobbed our carriage. Perhaps you recall that I did have other loves—though in my heart they were all but echoes of that first. Does not the smell of horse's dung bring back for you our travels throughout the Italian lands in our great black coach? By that time, our coach had satin curtains and mattresses of finest down, and gold and silver coins—the fruits of my success—that fell to the floor each time Fräulein Schmeck shook out our blankets.

Certainly you remember something of the years in Naples. You still had three laps to sit upon then, in addition to your father's. You had your nurse, whom you loved as a grandmother. You had tiny Tasso, whom you soon outgrew. You had Remus, whom you called uncle, and whose books you stole and hid beneath your bed.

But the fourth, Nicolai, your namesake, I am sure you have forgotten. We had to leave him behind in Venice. We buried him beneath a paving stone on a narrow street, as is common in the city, with no mark of any kind. He had lived just six months after we arrived in that city he had always dreamed to visit. Remus found him dead one morning, fallen forward in his kneeling prayers the night before.

As to our life in Venice, even if you do not remember much, you know it well, both because we have spoken of it and because it is the stuff of legend. History records the footsteps of its heroes, and in late 1763, on the night of my debut in Teatro San Benedetto, I became a hero. Every record of my voice tells how I stunned the audiences in Venice, and the thicker volumes even tell of you in my arms as beautiful women showered us in rose petals from their balconies. Since that spring, my life has been recorded by so many others it is not mine to tell.

But I have reserved one last secret.

In that spring after we fled Vienna, Tasso drove our coach until, if he had swung his whip once more, we would have plunged into the sea. And then we all climbed down from our perch—small Tasso, giant Nicolai, ugly Remus, the gorilla nurse, the musico, and his baby. No one had thought to mention to me that Venice was an island, which would have been reason enough for me to choose another goal. I quaked and said I would not board the ferry. Nicolai and Fräulein Schmeck held me down while Remus drew a blindfold across my eyes. Still, as I lay on the deck, I wished I had a sack of buckwheat to embrace.

And then we had arrived. We marveled at the palaces sunken in the sea. Remus held Nicolai's elbow so he would not tumble into the fetid water. We strolled the narrow lanes and bought Fräulein Schmeck whatever cloth or perfume or jewelry she desired. At Piazza San Marco you squealed in delight when you saw the ships on the Canale di San Marco. Nicolai stared up at the shadow of the basilica. He nodded once at me and then marched into Basilica San Marco like a soldier ready to face a foe that far outnumbered him. Fräulein Schmeck was swarmed by peddlers. She stroked or smelled or tasted everything they offered her. She spent our gold. Tasso wandered to the water and stared out at the ships at sea. Only Remus remained with us. He smiled at me.

"Will you wait for us right here?" I asked.

"Of course," he replied.

Then you and I were alone. I carried you along narrow lanes the sun never touched, over bridges where we paused so you could stare at the gondolas sliding below us. I asked everyone, *Dov' è il teatro?* They pointed, and I followed their directions, but when you gasped and strained your hand at a shaft of sunlight glinting in the windows of a palace, or at the Grand Canal, we took that direction instead. We lost ourselves again and again, but every passerby helped us on, until finally we came to the theater I sought, Teatro San Benedetto, whose name your mother and I had whispered so often to each other. It was still early in the afternoon, and the small square was empty, though I heard rehearsal from inside the theater. The building had a grand façade with pillars half-sunken into the wall and three double doors of polished oak. I sat on the stairs and placed you on my knee.

"Nicolai," I said. "We are here."

You looked at my mouth and bounced on my knee.

"I wish she were here with us, but she is not. I will do what she told me I should do. I will pound on those doors until they open them and let me sing. They will make us rich, and everyone will know our name. That is what she said would happen, and I am sure she was correct. Nicolai, we can never speak of her again. All that has happened must be a secret. We can let no one connect that poor castrate in Vienna to the musico I will become. No one may know that you are a stolen son. I do not want them to take you from me."

You looked from my lips to my eyes, which were filling with tears. You did not understand a word. But you knew I was sad, and your lower lip began to curl.

So I stood up, and we paced back and forth across the empty square. I put you to my shoulder. I hugged you tight, and I let the world wait ten more minutes for my voice. For, at that moment, my son, I sang for you alone.

Author's Note

Real sounds inspired me first: my wife singing an aria from Gluck's *Orfeo*; a harsh, metallic peal from the belfry of an undersize Alpine church; the chatter of Swiss cowbells; a recording of medieval chants penned at the Abbey of St. Gall. With the research that followed, I set about establishing an accurate historical setting in which to set loose my fictional characters.

The Abbey of St. Gall was dissolved, under Napoleon's influence, in 1805, making Abbot Coelestin Gugger von Staudach (1701–1767) the third to final abbot. Abbot Coelestin oversaw the stunning baroque renovations of his millennium-old abbey, including construction of the Church of St. Gall, now a UNESCO World Heritage Site.

For Vienna's eighteenth-century geography, I relied on Joseph Daniel von Huber's *Vogeschauplan der Wiener Innenstadt* (1785). Spittelberg's decrepit taverns of ill renown were largely demolished in the early nineteenth century, but what I imagined to be Nicolai and Remus's house on the Burggasse still stands to this day, and the ground floor is indeed a charming coffeehouse. The Riecher Palace is based on the Fürst von Cläri's Palace; Guadagni's house, on a more modest structure near the Scottish Gate—neither exists today. Many of Gluck's, Mozart's, and Beethoven's operas were premiered in the Burgtheater before it was demolished in 1888. Details of the theater mechanics and Tasso's substage are based upon the exquisitely restored baroque theater at Çeský Krumlov.

Orfeo ed Euridice premiered on October 5, 1762, and the events leading up to it, including the preview performance on August 6, 1762 (which took place at Calzabigi's house rather than at Guadagni's), are recorded in Count Karl Zinzendorf's meticulously kept diaries. There exist only two, very spare reviews of the premiere, in the two issues of the *Wienerisches Diarium* that were published following the performance, dated October 6 and 13. Neither review even mentions the performers' names. I drew Moses's listing of nobles attending the premiere from the Burgtheater's subscription records.

Gluck himself left Vienna for Paris in 1774, and there he rewrote his *Orfeo*, changing the hero from a castrato mezzo-soprano to a tenor voice. Gaetano Guadagni returned to London in 1769, but there he failed to live up to his reputation and, out of favor, left again two years later. He retired to Padua, where he was known for singing solo puppet performances of Gluck's *Orfeo*. He died penniless in 1792, having given away his fortune to his many students.

The Pummerin was cast in 1705 from 208 Turkish cannons and survived until 1944, when it was destroyed in a fire set by wartime looters. It was melted, recast, and rehung in 1957. It rings every year to celebrate the New Year. Austrians watch the swinging bell on national television.

Sometime around 1750, Count Karl Eugen brought two Italian physicians to Stuttgart for the purpose of castrating young boys, and so the duke's court is the only known location of systematic castration north of the Alps. In Italy, boys continued to be castrated for Europe's opera houses throughout the nineteenth century, though the golden age of the musico passed with romantic opera's rising preference for the tenor voice. The last musico, Alessandro Moreschi, sang in the Papal Choir until 1913.

In a very few places, when my story and history conflicted, the story won out. Most egregious, Staudach's church was finished only in 1766, too late to castrate Moses in time for Gluck's opera. Moving construction back a few years seemed a small crime, well worth the opportunity to pair the beautiful building with Gluck's stunning opera, both of which, more than two hundred years later, are enduring symbols of an age.

Acknowledgments

I am very grateful to Alexandra Mendez-Diez for her many hours of reading and commenting, all done six time zones and an ocean away. I am indebted to Bridget Thomas for her many invaluable improvements to language and style. Thank you to the writers at Thin Raft, Basel, for their years of encouragement.

To Dan Lazar at Writers House, thank you for giving the novel new life, and for making it so much better. Thanks also to Stephen Barr for his great insights. In Sarah Knight, I found a fantastic editor whose limitless enthusiasm kept me going. I am grateful to Shaye Areheart, Kira Walton, Karin Schulze, Linda Kaplan, Annsley Rosner, Sarah Breivogel, Heather Lazare, Patty Berg, Katie Wainwright, Rachel Berkowitz, Jill Flaxman, and Christine Kopprasch for their hard work and support. Thank you to Domenico Sposato and my other colleagues at the Minerva Schulen Basel, and to Franz Gstättner, Ernst Zöchling, and the Dombauhütte St. Stephan.

Mom and Dad, of course I couldn't even have begun without your support and guidance. To Rebecca and Sam, thank you for all your love. And last, of course, an ocean of thanks to Dominique—without you there would be no book.

About the Type

This book was set in Mrs. Eaves, a modern revival of Baskerville that retains the openness and lightness of the original. In 1996, when Zuzano Licko, cofounder of Emigre Foundry, designed the typeface, her aim was to explore possible alternatives for Baskerville, which critics claimed was illegible due to the high contrast in its stems and hairlines. Licko reduced the contrast by widening the proportions of the lowercase letters. Mrs. Eaves was one of the first digital typefaces to be designed on Apple's Macintosh computers. The typeface is named after Sarah Eaves, who was first housekeeper and, later, wife and partner to John Baskerville in his print and type shop.